Dead Land

ALSO BY SARA PARETSKY

Love & Other Crimes

Shell Game

Fallout

Brush Back

Critical Mass

Breakdown

Body Work

Hardball

Bleeding Kansas

Fire Sale

Blacklist

Total Recall

Hard Time

Dead Land

A V.I. Warshawski Novel

Sara Paretsky

HARPER LARGE PRINT

An Imprint of HarperCollinsPublishers

DEAD LAND. Copyright © 2020 by Sara Paretsky. All rights reserved. Printed in the United States of America. No part of this book may be used or reproduced in any manner whatsoever without written permission except in the case of brief quotations embodied in critical articles and reviews. For information, address HarperCollins Publishers, 195 Broadway, New York, NY 10007.

HarperCollins books may be purchased for educational, business, or sales promotional use. For information, please e-mail the Special Markets Department at SPsales@harpercollins.com.

FIRST HARPER LARGE PRINT EDITION

ISBN: 978-0-06-297876-9

Library of Congress Cataloging-in-Publication Data is available upon request.

20 21 22 23 24   LSC   10 9 8 7 6 5 4 3 2 1

For Martha and Vince Baggetto and Marzena Madej,
who helped me through the hardest night of my life.
If English had better words than "Thank You,"
I would use them.

Dead Land

The Dogs of August

August 14

The long buzz on my front doorbell woke me, and then I heard the dogs. I pulled on jeans and staggered to my door, where Donna Lutas was leaning on the bell and screaming, "Will you fucking get out of bed and deal with this?"

I ignored her, stuck my feet into the running shoes I'd left outside the door, and hurried down the stairs, past a gauntlet of angry neighbors—including Mr. Contreras, resplendent in magenta pajamas.

Peppy and Mitch, the two dogs I share with him, were hurling themselves at the lobby entrance in a frenzy. A smart detective does not open her home at four in the morning when an unknown danger on the other side has roused the dogs, but Donna Lutas was yelling threats, the Sung baby was crying, and everyone was babbling incoherent worries—Should we call 911? Should we shoot the dogs?

I opened the front door just wide enough to slither through. A large brown dog with a square face and an anxious expression was tied to a lamppost near the entrance, a paper bag on the walk next to him. He had a white piece of paper wound around his collar. I unfolded it and held it under the lamp to read.

Warshawski—

You seem to know your way around dogs even if you're terrible with people. Look after Bear until I come back for him.

Coop

I jogged down to the street, tripping on my shoelaces, hoping to see what direction Coop was heading. That was a fool's errand: he had tied his dog to the lamppost and slipped into the darkness before Mitch and Peppy started barking.

I turned back. Bear was whining, anxiously licking his lips, when I got to him. I unhooked the leash.

"What's going on, huh, boy?" I said softly.

The dog whined again and started down the sidewalk. I stood on his leash long enough to tie my laces, then let him lead me. We'd gone about five blocks when I realized he was trying to get to the South Side, to wherever Coop lived, not following a trail. However, when I tried to turn Bear around to head to my place, he lay on the sidewalk and refused to budge. I'm strong, but not strong enough to carry a big dog half a mile.

I squatted on the sidewalk next to him, feeling naked despite the hot night. I was wearing a sleepshirt and jeans, no underwear, no socks, no phone, no house keys.

"If Coop left you with me, he's not going to be at home, boy. Best come with me now. We can get some sleep and sort it out in the morning. Let's make the best of a situation neither of us wants."

I don't know if it was my words, my tone, or just his sad realization that his lot was hopeless, but he got up and plodded up the street with me.

"How'd a steady boy like you end up with an explosive device like him, anyway?" I asked the dog.

I barely knew Coop—I didn't even know if that was his first or last name or just a nickname. I didn't know where he lived, where he was from, where he might go if he'd fled Chicago.

We'd met a handful of times, and each time, he'd gone from angry to volcanic in under a minute. Maybe he really had killed Leo Prinz and thought the cops were closing in on him.

"Except, if he was going into hiding, he'd surely take you along, wouldn't he?" I said to the dog. "And why me? He's made it clear he despises me. No insult, but what am I going to do with you?"

We'd reached my building. I picked up the bag Coop had left.

"*Another* dog?" Donna Lutas screamed. She was still standing by the open door to her unit. "You can't bring another dog in here."

"Yes, Vic," Mr. Sung said. "It is too much, all this barking, and then, we never know if someone is breaking in, wanting to shoot you, but maybe hitting one of us by mistake."

Mr. Contreras usually speaks up for me, but not tonight. Mr. Sung was only reiterating what he himself often said, albeit more sympathetically: *Why did I hurl myself into danger? Didn't I care none about the people who cared about me?*

Peppy and Mitch didn't help: when they saw me escorting Bear up to the third floor they began barking and straining to follow. They didn't want some interloper taking attention that belonged to them.

"The fucking last straw!" Lutas cried. "I'm going to the management board in the morning to demand they evict you. Three dogs? When the limit is one?" Lutas represented our building with the board of the company that managed our property.

She was a junior associate at one of the big downtown law firms. She worked ninety-hour weeks, the way all the juniors do. I knew she was sleep deprived. I knew I was not a congenial neighbor: a recent encounter with an assailant had broken one of the stairwell bannisters. I still couldn't rouse any sympathy for her—she'd gloated as she served me with legal papers demanding that I undertake repairs.

She probably would go to the board to try to evict me; maybe she could, especially with the other residents glaring at me.

I opened the paper bag Coop had left and took out a blanket, Bear's food bowls, and a few toys. I set everything up in the kitchen and went back to bed, but I felt like a heavily starched shirt, stiff, unbending, listening to Bear's toenails scratching the floors as he explored the apartment. At the end, he came into my room and sniffed at me for a few minutes, then gave a heavy sigh and plopped to the floor by my bed.

"If only" is a fool's game. But I couldn't help thinking, if only I'd followed my first wish, to spend my birthday hiking with Peter Sansen and the dogs in the country, none of the rest of this would have happened.

1

South Side Sisters

July 27, V.I. Warshawski's Birthday

The girls lined up along the wall, their faces glistening with sweat, still breathing hard.

"We could have won if Lureen had moved her fat ass into place to block—" one girl began, but Bernie silenced her.

"No one who plays for me calls another player a bad name. And there is only one way to lose a competition. What way is that?"

The girl who'd issued the insult turned her head away, but the other seven chanted in unison, "Dishonesty."

"Right!" Bernie said. "If you don't do your best, you are dishonest to yourself and to your team. If you do your best, you've won, even if the other team outscores you. You learn from mistakes, *n'est-ce pas?* Losing a match is only a loss if you don't learn and grow from it."

"Yes, Coach."

"Louder. You *believe* this!"

"Yes, Coach!" they shouted.

The South Side Sisters had lost their match to the Lincoln Park Lions. Bernie—Bernadine Fouchard—had coached them with the ardor she brought to everything in her life. The girls loved her: they'd started sprinkling their conversation with French phrases, they copied her mannerisms—the way she stood with hands on hips; the way she smacked her palm against her forehead and groaned, *Mon dieu.*

Bernie's sport was hockey—like her father, Pierre, like her godfather, my cousin Boom-Boom, both former Chicago Blackhawks stars. Unlike them, even though she was a gifted player, there wasn't any way for her to make a living at the game, so she was doing the next best, majoring in sports management at Northwestern, where she played for their Big Ten hockey team.

This summer she was interning in a Chicago Park District youth camp, coaching soccer. She'd played enough soccer as a child that she knew the basics. She'd jumped into the sport with the energy she brought to everything she did. Even though her kids hadn't had all the private camps and other opportunities that came to girls in affluent communities, Bernie inspired them to play with something close to her own ferocity.

I'd come down to Forty-seventh Street to watch the eleven-year-old Sisters play their final match of a round-robin tournament. The South Lakefront Improvement Council—SLICK—had helped sponsor the Sisters and wanted them to take a bow following the game. SLICK was holding their monthly meeting; the girls were supposed to wait in the hall until someone came out for them.

A woman whose tightly curled hair was dyed a rusty brown opened the common room door and stuck her head into the hall. "Can you girls keep it down—oh! Are these our soccer players?"

"Yes," Bernie said. "We are a wonderful team, but we are not wonderful at waiting in the hall. When do we go in?"

"Very soon." The woman tittered, as if Bernie had made a mildly amusing joke. As she shut the door, we heard a man yelling from inside the room.

"You damned liar! Where'd you come up with this pile of crap? You go to Lying School? Because you sure as hell didn't learn this in any environmental studies program."

The girls put their hands over their mouths to muffle their shocked laughter.

I moved to the door and stuck my head through. The meeting room had served as a community meeting hall back when Prairie Savings and Loan was a Bronzeville landmark. It held a shallow stage and perhaps a hundred fifty folding chairs, arranged today in concentric semicircles. The seats were full, not because the community wanted to attend a meeting on a late summer afternoon, but because family members had been rooting for the Sisters and now wanted to see them get their awards.

Two men and a woman, all in later middle age, were trying to run the meeting, but the shouting from the audience had apparently taken them by surprise. One of the men had a gavel that he kept pounding against a wood block while shouting, "Order, order!" The woman—thin, wiry, wearing a blue T-shirt with the SLICK logo—was bouncing up and down in her chair, trying to scream at the heckler in the audience. The second man didn't look up; he was writing on a white pad in a slow hand.

The protestor was a white man in his forties, his skin tanned like old leather, wearing khaki shorts and a T-shirt with a faded sunflower on it. He might have been handsome, but fury had distorted his expression.

His wrath was apparently directed at a young man on the stage who was awkwardly balancing a computer on a music stand: like much of the South Side, the building where SLICK held its meetings didn't run to amenities like podiums. He'd apparently been making a presentation about filling in part of the lakefront around Forty-seventh Street; a sketch of a sand beach, playground equipment, and a bar and restaurant was projected onto the wall behind the stage.

"But, sir, this is part of the original Burnham plan, or at least, it's how Burnham—"

"Like crap it's the Burnham plan." Although the younger man had a mike, the protestor's shout drowned it out.

The man charged up the aisle to the stage. The youth flinched and dropped his mouse. When he bent to pick it up, his computer hit the floor. The picture on the wall behind the stage disappeared.

Before the protestor reached the steps, several audience members were there, blocking his path. He wrestled with them, still shouting abuse, at both the speaker and the trio running the meeting.

A pair of Chicago cops appeared from a far corner. They pinned the man's arms behind his back and marched him down the aisle and out the door, shoving me to one side. A forest of cell phones rose up, recording the moment.

Much of the audience had cheered the cops, but a few yelled in support of the protestor. "Let him speak!" "Let him breathe." "The whole world's watching."

The man with the gavel continued to slam it against a wood block. In the hall behind me, the girls were watching, openmouthed, as the cops hustled the protestor out of the building. When they'd disappeared, the soccer players began an excited chatter that Bernie didn't try to silence.

"That is Leo he was attacking," she said to me. "Good that the police have arrested him!"

"Leo?" I echoed.

"He is working for this SLICK this summer. He helped me organize today's celebration for my team. He does not need this attack."

She ushered her players into the room, where they clustered behind the last row of chairs.

The woman on the stage was now marching back and forth across the short platform. She slapped a wooden pointer against the open palm of her left hand, as if it were a field marshal's swagger stick.

"Our council is committed to protecting the lake and the lakefront," she screamed. "We scrutinize every action that impacts Lake Michigan. I've been living on the South Side since I was nineteen; I raised three children here. I've dedicated my life to this community and to our lakefront. I resent professional protestors coming in here trying to overturn the applecart."

"Hear, hear!" cried the gaveller. "No professional protestors."

The second man on the stage still didn't look up from the documents he was working on.

"We need a motion to accept the report as Leo presented it." The woman smacked her pointer on the table so hard that the note maker dropped his pen.

"But I haven't finished," Leo objected.

"That's okay, son," the gaveller boomed. "Everyone who wants the details can get them from the SLICK website."

A white-haired woman near the front of the room got to her feet. "I'm not a professional protestor, Mona; I've lived on the South Side longer than you, I've raised children here, although what that has to do with protecting the lakefront I don't know. However, I also have some knowledge of parliamentary procedure. We can't vote on a proposal whose details we don't even know."

"You're not recognized, the chair does not recognize you," the gaveller roared, his cheeks swollen with rage.

Next to me, Bernie was frowning, worried by the way the meeting was devolving. "This isn't right. Why won't they let Leo finish?"

I didn't try to answer. "This would be a good time for your girls to get their awards. Otherwise the meeting will turn into a gong show and your kids will be ignored."

Idea and action go hand in hand with Bernie. She blew a sharp trill on her coach's whistle. The room became silent. She nodded at her team, and they marched to the stage, chanting,

> *"South Side Sisters coming through*
> *We finish any job we start to do.*
> *We played our best*
> *We passed the test*
> *We're the champs*
> *So forget the rest."*

The girls stepped in front of the table. They stomped, twirled, and performed an elaborate choreography with their arms. The audience burst into spontaneous applause, everyone relieved to abandon the fights over plans for the lakefront.

Mona went to the mike where Leo had been speaking, told the girls what a credit they were to the South

Side, to the values of hard work and determination, and presented each with a certificate and a red rosette. Another sponsor, a local pizzeria, handed out coupons for free pizzas, and the girls marched off the stage, yelling their chant again, more loudly than before. Their families followed. In a few minutes, only about a dozen people were left inside. I stopped to ask the white-haired woman what was going on.

She shook her head. "I wish I knew. Everyone is trying to cash in on the economic boom that's supposed to come to the South Side when the Obama Center goes in, but this landfill proposal came out of nowhere. Mona and her gang are pitching it as a goodwill gesture to the community, a new beach like the one they put in at Thirty-first Street. Even so, that isn't something they should build without public hearings, and this is the first we've heard about it."

She stopped and eyed me narrowly. "What's your interest in this?"

"Just a curious bystander. I grew up in South Chicago and I vaguely remember SLICK from when U.S. Steel was closing the South Works plant. SLICK had a plan for repurposing the site, but I don't think they ever got funding for it."

The woman grimaced. "Name of the song for getting the city to invest in the South Side. Big plans and nothing ever comes of them. The same thing may happen to this little beach proposal, but Coop—the guy who got hustled out just now—seems to think it's more than that. Or maybe he resents any change to the lakefront. Some people do."

"Who is Coop?"

"You could say he's a professional protestor, except that would imply someone's paying him. But no one really knows who he is. He showed up a year or so ago with a big dog. He seems to spend his life walking up and down the lakefront with it. He apparently spends a lot of time in the library studying up on the history of the lakefront parks—he knows more about Burnham than I do. Than Mona and her cronies do, for that matter."

"The meeting seemed chaotic," I said. "Is Leo in charge of SLICK's planning? Is that why he was making the presentation?"

She pulled a face. "Oh, no. It's typical chaos where SLICK is concerned. They got some kind of grant to digitize their maps and so on, which Leo did for them. Mona tried making the presentation, but she couldn't figure out how to run PowerPoint or to match her remarks with the slides. It would have been funny if it hadn't been so pathetic, but they had to ask the young man to take over."

I was just as glad I hadn't been in the room for that part of the meeting. I wondered about the woman's interest—she apparently knew a lot about Park District plans.

"I'm just a local resident. Tired of SLICK being a mouthpiece for the Park District without taking the neighborhood wishes into account. The landfill may be a good idea, but it's like everything else in this town—no transparency. Decisions made in private meetings where money changes hands. I've lived here for fifty-three years. I'm tired of it."

She spelled her name for me, Nashita Lyndes. I handed her one of my cards, which identifies me as an investigator.

"An investigator?" She brightened. "Were you here to dig up information on the city's plans?"

"Sorry, Ms. Lyndes: I was here with the soccer players. Anyway, trying to find information on anything this city is planning would require a nuclear-powered shovel. A mere steam-powered machine couldn't handle the job."

2
Savages

Bernie had come back into the room, not looking for me, but to talk to Leo. She seemed to be pleading with him about something; he looked at the SLICK officers and shook his head regretfully.

"Some people are born without spine," she said as she joined me at the back of the room.

"And it's your job to inject a few bone cells to stimulate growth?" I said sardonically.

"If it would work!"

Bernie ran to catch up with her team, which was heading to the parking lot of a large strip mall on Forty-seventh Street. I followed more slowly: she had to make sure her girls were leaving with a responsible adult.

When she'd finished, her mouth and her shoulders

drooped. "These girls, they were my whole life for nine weeks and now, poof! It's over, they're gone, as if it had never happened."

"You start another segment next week, right?" I asked.

"At a West Side park. I begged to stay with these girls, but the Park District has no more money for programs in this neighborhood."

I shared her outrage: the city can come up with funds for landfill and a new beach but not for a group of African-American and Latinx girls.

"Aren't they going out for pizza? Why don't you join them—they adore you, they'd love to have you there."

"It's not organized. Some will go with their families tonight, but others are saving their coupons for later."

"Peter's buying me a birthday drink at Sal's before dinner. Want to join us?"

Peter was Peter Sansen, the archaeologist I'd been going out with for the last few months. Sal's was the Golden Glow, the bar owned by an old friend of mine.

"Your birthday! *Ma foi—je suis crétin*! I forgot. Of course I will come." She grinned roguishly. "And I will be very tactful and let him take you to dinner alone. Anyway, later on, Angela and I are going roller-skating with the rest of our group."

Angela Creedy, one of Northwestern's basketball

stars, was sharing an apartment in a rickety Victorian house with Bernie and two other student athletes.

As we walked to the car, Bernie enthralled me with her shrewd decisions in today's game.

Time was when Forty-seventh Street mostly held bars and tiny shops that catered to Bronzeville, back when the Loop banks gouged African-Americans and the downtown shops barred them from the premises—except, of course, as janitors. Now there were blocks of new housing, big impersonal chain stores, gyms, and a giant liquor outlet, which had hastened the death of the old bars.

Houses and shops ended at the Illinois Central railroad tracks, the eastern boundary of the neighborhood, but the street itself continued east under the tracks, feeding into Lake Shore Drive. Between the Drive and the railway embankment was a narrow strip of land being returned to prairie; the parking lot I'd used lay there.

As we headed under the tracks, we heard the kind of hollow tinkling made by a xylophone, discordant, disturbing.

At six o'clock, runners, cyclists, picnickers were thick on the ground, heading through the viaduct to a footbridge that crossed the Drive. Someone wearing headphones and pushing a runner's baby buggy bumped into me and swore at me. I moved closer to a pillar and finally saw where the music was coming from: a figure shrouded in gray, bent over a red plastic piano, like the one Schroeder plays in *Peanuts*. Like Schroeder, the figure was getting an amazing amount of sound out of the toy.

I hadn't heard her when I walked under the viaduct earlier in the afternoon, but she clearly had set up housekeeping there. If she'd been asleep earlier, I suppose her gray rags had blended into the gray underpass.

I was trying to push Bernie along, but she was listening wide-eyed to an ominous rhythm the pianist was producing in the instrument's lowest octave.

"Do you hear that?" she demanded. "It's 'Savage.'"

I shook my head, uncomprehending.

"How are you not knowing it? It's the greatest song of the last ten years, about this woman Indian chief. Her name was Anacaona, and the Spanish murdered her when she wouldn't be their whore. My whole high school sang it for First Nations Day, but it's so much more than that. Like, for women, when we have a march, to protest rape or the horrible incel bastards, we drum and we sing it. Who is playing this song in this place? Is there a protest? Should we be joining?"

Bernie tried to sing, but she couldn't find her way to

the pitch or the rhythm. All I could make out from her tuneless chanting were the words "savage" and "cruel."

The pianist suddenly brought the tempo down. The music shifted from an Afro-pop beat to a heavy three-two meter. After a few measures, I made out what sounded like the lament from Purcell's *Dido and Aeneas*. I began to sing, "'Remember me, remember me, but forget my fate—'" Bernie cut me off. "No, no, that's not how it goes: it's 'Remember me, and announce my fate.'"

"Sorry," I said meekly. "I was singing Purcell's version. Who wrote the one you know?"

"Lydia Zamir. First she was an ordinary musician, but then she started writing songs about women, you know, like for #MeToo. She was in love with this man, and they traveled around to different rallies, and then they were shot and killed at one of these horrible mass murders. Some *crétin* with too many guns opened fire on them."

Bernie glared at me, as though demanding that I deal with the problem of idiots with too many guns. When I didn't say anything, she said, "It's very strange to hear Zamir's music like this, under a railway track in Chicago."

I walked slowly toward the shrouded figure—I assumed it was a woman, because the body was so slight, but I couldn't tell. I got close enough to see that the instrument was a miniature upright, the pint-size keyboard about eighteen inches from the ground. The red plastic case was chipped and scuffed. When I squatted, hoping to ask about the music, the figure scuttled toward the back of the viaduct, clutching the piano.

Bernie's fingers went to her mouth. "Oh, no—she's scared. I wanted to ask how she knows this music. Maybe she was a friend of Zamir's—that would be totally amazing!"

She moved cautiously, as if she were approaching a squirrel in a forest, but the woman howled, turning her back to us.

A cyclist stopped next to us. "This isn't a zoo where you can stare at the animals. This is a woman who is entitled to her privacy."

"But she is out here, in public," Bernie objected. "I am not treating her like a specimen, but she knows an important song. Why cannot I ask her how she knows it?"

"Because she doesn't want to talk to you. Surely her body language makes that clear." The cyclist positioned herself between the woman and Bernie and me.

"You know her?" I asked. "She seems very vulnerable here. Shouldn't we try to get her help—a doctor, a bed?"

The cyclist curled her lip. "Are you a mobile social worker? She doesn't want to be in an institution."

"Are you a mobile psychic?" I asked. "You channel this person's thoughts and wishes to the larger world?"

Her nostrils flared. "You may think you're being funny, but you don't know what you're talking about. People who know her, know to leave her alone. The fact that you want to bother her means you don't know her."

"What's going on here, Judith?" A man had appeared from the lake side of the viaduct, a dog trotting at his heels. The man was wearing khaki shorts and a T-shirt with a faded sunflower outlined on it. When he stopped to talk to the cyclist, the dog sat, staring up at me with wide sad eyes.

"These are two busybodies." Judith jerked her head at Bernie and me. "Well-meaning, perhaps, but not respectful."

"We are not busybodies," Bernie cried. "We are respecting the piano player, but this Judith, she thinks it is her job to keep all the world from knowing about this music. And as for you, I know you from the meeting just now, when you were attacking Leo. Maybe it is time you yourself minded your own business!"

"Yes," I said. "Didn't the police escort you from the SLICK meeting an hour or so ago?"

He smacked a fist into his palm. The dog watched him, hackles stiff. "Don't tell me you're one of Mona Borsa's stooges. What she do, hire you to follow me—"

"You're not important enough for me to follow. You're barely important enough to talk to," I snapped. "There's a talented musician living here in squalor and your buddy Judith has appointed herself spokeswoman. I want to ask if she wants medical attention—"

"And me, I am wanting to know how she learned the song 'Savage,'" Bernie interrupted.

"And neither of you has any right to disturb her. We look after her!" Coop cried.

"You're doing a heck of a job," I said. "For starters, she needs food, clothes, a bath, and a proper bed. She also deserves access to a proper piano: only a real artist could get sound like that from a dinky plastic job."

"And that's your business because of what? You're some music talent scout?" Coop jeered.

Judith said, "The city seems to be filled with social workers who think they know what's best for people without asking them. Whenever anyone forces this woman into a shelter or a hospital, she runs away."

"Does she have a name?" I asked.

"If she does, that's none of your business. All you need to know is that she's allergic to most people, especially to strangers. She lets Coop bring her food, she trusts Bear. Sometimes she trusts me, as well. You can set your mind at rest and go help people who want your assistance."

Presumably Bear was the dog.

"We are not social workers," Bernie bristled. "Me, I am a hockey player and a soccer coach and Vic, she is a detective. If the police—"

"Detective?" Coop shouted. "Then Mona Borsa *did* cross a big red line! She knew the police couldn't arrest me for speaking up in the meeting, so she hired you to be a provocateur—"

"Enough!" I cried. "You can ask me any question about who I am and what I'm doing here, but don't jump down *my* throat without facts. I'm not that inexperienced kid you attacked in the SLICK meeting, so back off."

Bear, the dog, was looking from Coop to me, not sure whether he needed to intervene. He got to his feet and stood between us. I took a few steps back.

"You weren't arrested?" Bernie said to Coop. "Why not?"

"First Amendment," I said tersely. "He only spoke, even if he was yelling: he didn't touch anyone."

"At least you're a cop who knows the law, but what the fuck were you doing at that meeting, if Mona Borsa didn't hire you to bird-dog me?"

"Guess what? My world doesn't revolve around you. But your anger is disturbing the one person you claim to be protecting."

Although some passersby were keeping well clear of us, we were attracting a crowd. Whether it was Coop's and my argument, or the people staring at her, the pianist had backed as far into the wall as she could, clutching her piano and whimpering.

"Yes, and she knows important music," Bernie said. "Which is the only reason I want to talk to her."

"Don't." The woman Judith had been silent while Coop and I were arguing, but she turned now to Bernie. "She's been badly wounded and she can't tell the difference between a stranger who wants to support her and a stranger who wants to hurt her."

Her tone was still arrogant, but her words made sense; I put my arm across Bernie's shoulders. "It's a good point, *piccola*. Too many people are here, and we're all getting in each other's hair. Let's get up to the Glow."

Bernie let me escort her through the underpass, but her feet dragged. She paused on the far side to look back. Coop and Bear were squatting next to the pianist, who slowly returned to her nest of blankets and crates.

Judith waited on the sidelines while the woman adjusted her piano's legs until it seemed stable. When the woman began to play again, Judith resumed her ride; the rest of the crowd dissolved. Bernie was listening intently to the playing.

"That song I also know!" she finally said. "At least, I think so."

She began singing in her tuneless way,

"The art of loving
is the art of death
Love's opposite isn't hate, not hate
Love's opposite is lonesome
One lone swan."

"That song is beautiful, but so—so *mélancolique*, Vic, is it not?"

"Very," I agreed, but I was listening to the piano: mixed in with the banging in the bottom octave, the pianist was weaving the melody from Grieg's "Swan," one of the lieder my mother used to sing.

3
Trader's Folly

Bernie left me outside the Glow. She'd brooded over the episode all during the drive, not so much over the homeless singer, but over Judith and Coop's high-handedness.

"And you—why didn't you help me get past him to talk to her? She is not his property, *enfin*. Have you become too cautious in your old age to stand up for the right thing to do?"

"Maybe so. Old, covered with barnacles, or maybe mildew, which makes my joints creak too much to move fast. But please remember that I took an afternoon from work to watch you coach your South Side Sisters. I'd like a word of thanks, instead of an attack for not intervening with a woman who howled with pain when I tried to approach her."

"I do thank you, Vic," Bernie said in a wooden tone. "My girls played hard; they were worth watching. Still, I am not much in the mood for sociability with you and your friends. They will all agree with you and then I will become really cross and we will have a big fight, which should not happen on your birthday."

"We elderly don't have enough energy to fight you, Bernie, but go on home. Say hi to Angela."

Bernie kissed me lightly on the cheek to show no lasting ill will and headed toward the L.

Peter Sansen was already standing at the bar, talking to the owner, Sal Barthele, when I came in. His face lit up when he saw me, which took away my grumpiness.

"Happy birthday, beautiful. Sal has created a cocktail just for you."

Sal nodded at Erica, her head bartender. While Sal turned her back to me and poured and stirred from a collection of bottles, Erica went to the sound system. Sal handed me a glass just as Piaf's throaty voice came on singing, "*Je ne regrette rien*."

"Seems like a good way to start a new year, Warshawski: regret nothing."

I leaned across the mahogany bar to kiss her and saw she'd been working with bourbon. I don't usually like it, but the cocktail was a perfect balance of sweet, sour, and bitter.

"Patent it, quickly," I said. "It's mind altering. You don't want one of your enterprising traders to steal the recipe and license it."

The Golden Glow is two blocks from the Board of Trade, and for the hour or two after the closing bell, it's usually packed with traders celebrating victories or drowning sorrows. We'd arrived between that crush, and the smaller crowd that comes in when the theaters close. Peter was drinking another of Sal's signature cocktails, Trader's Folly, which has powered more than one stupid investment decision.

"Bernie acquitted herself well as a coach?" Sal asked.

"Impressively," I said. "Ardor and smarts—an unbeatable combo. The hard part came afterward."

While I was describing the wild community meeting, Murray Ryerson came in. Sal stocks Dark Lord beer just for him; she had a bottle open by the time he reached the bar.

"What happened at the SLICK meeting?" Murray asked. "Something the boy reporter needs to know about?"

"Don't think it will be a blip on Global's radar," I said.

Murray used to be one of the top investigative reporters in the Midwest, writing for the *Herald-Star*, until Global Entertainment bought the *Star*. He still sort of covers Illinois politics, when the editors don't think the story will threaten any of their pals in power, but he mostly does Chicago fluff on Global's cable station.

"The Park District wants to fill in part of the lake at Forty-seventh to create a beach there," I added. "A highly inflamed guy named Coop made the usual tedium interesting, but the part of the day that's stuck with me is this pianist Bernie and I encountered. She was banging on a toy piano as if it were a drum, but she could get it to make music. The unusual part was the way she cut well-known bits of the classical repertoire into an R and B sound. Purcell and Grieg were the two I recognized."

"Come on," Murray scoffed. "You say she did this on a *Peanuts* piano? You were under a viaduct at a busy intersection. You heard what Bernie persuaded you to hear, not what some homeless woman was banging on a piece of plastic."

I flushed. "Don't act ignorant in public, Murray. Yo-Yo Ma could play Bach on a washtub bass on the floor of the Board of Trade and everyone would recognize it. But Bernie knew the words to one of the songs, about a woman murdered by the Spanish in the fifteenth century. She was the head of one of the nations that the Spanish encountered when they arrived. Sad to say, I hadn't heard of her, but her name was something like Ancona."

"Anacaona," Sal said. "From Hispaniola. Where they were so primitive before European arrival that women could be leaders of the nation. My sisters and I grew up on her story. The Spanish wanted her gold and her land. When she fought back and lost, they offered her a choice between being a whore or death. She chose death."

Sal and her sisters had been born in Chicago, but their parents were Haitian émigrés.

"If you go there today, you see hardly any trace of the original inhabitants," she added. "It's hard to imagine them because people are either like me, descended from Africans who didn't exist there in 1492, or from the Europeans. It's disturbing, as though one is always walking on the feet of a ghost."

Murray had been scrolling through his phone while Sal was talking. "Looks like Lydia Zamir wrote the song Bernie recognized today."

He handed his phone to Sal, who took it to her

sound system at the back of the bar. "The Albatross Song" from Patricia Barber's *Higher* was playing. At the end of the cut, Sal stuck Murray's phone into the dock and turned up the volume. The sound of a grand piano filled the bar, ominous chords rumbling from the bottom of the bass clef. From the high treble came darting notes like a hummingbird diving into a flower and quickly pulling back. And then a contralto began the song that Bernie hadn't been able to sing:

> "Anacaona, queen and chief,
> You were a savage
> Yes, a savage.
> You couldn't comprehend
> Why the Spanish took your land
> You were too savage
> For European law and rule.
> To a savage we seem cruel
> We landed on your shore,
> Cried, 'Choose death or be our whore!'
> We killed because
> We are so savage."

At the end of the chorus, the piano segued, just as the woman under the viaduct had done with her plastic upright, to the funereal meter of Purcell. The vocal line took up "Remember me, but announce my fate" for a few measures, and then, while the piano stuck to "Dido's Lament," the singer began wailing the single word "savage" over and over.

The volume and the intensity of the music brought conversations in the room to a halt. A couple of tables signaled for their bills. One woman clicked to the exit on stilettos and said, "I come to a bar for a drink, not for political indoctrination. I won't be back."

Sal swallowed a scowl and nodded to her bartender. Erica began moving among the tables with samples of Trader's Folly on a tray. After a few minutes, people were talking and laughing again.

At the bar, Peter read over my shoulder as I scrolled through the highlights of Lydia Zamir's life. Bernie's passionate summary had skimped on some of the facts. Zamir had grown up in Kansas, where her gifts as a pianist were recognized early. After study at the New England Conservatory of Music, she'd played with some regional symphonies and summer festivals. At a festival in Santa Fe, she met and apparently fell in love with a Chilean-American writer named Hector Palurdo.

Over the course of a few years, Zamir stopped performing the classical repertoire. She taught herself guitar—"Really, a piano with six strings instead of eighty-eight," she said in an interview—and began setting Palurdo's poetry to music, along with that of Mistral and Neruda, two earlier Chilean poets.

Then, four years ago, Zamir and Palurdo were performing at a fund-raiser at an outdoor venue in Kansas when the shooting occurred. Someone opened fire from a hilltop. Seventeen people were killed, including Palurdo. Fifty-two were wounded. Zamir apparently survived. She'd held a concert in Hector's memory, with proceeds going to the families of the dead, and then she'd stopped singing.

"She grew up in Kansas and he was killed there. Jealous lover?" Murray, who'd retrieved his phone from Sal, was hunting the same information. "She's from some map-dot called Eudora and the murders were near Salina, a bigger map-dot. . . . About three hours from her hometown—no distance for an angry lover to cover."

He scrolled further, reading aloud under his breath. "Palurdo grew up in Chicago, but his father was an immigrant from Chile. He came here in the seventies, worked as a welder, died about eighteen months before his son was murdered. Hector wrote poetry, short stories based on folk stories of indigenous people, but he was mostly an essayist, covering human rights in the Americas. North and South."

Murray drained his bottle. "You stumbled on a genuine mystery, Warshawski." He changed his tone to sound like an old-time radio announcer. "Who is this homeless woman and how come she's playing Zamir's music?"

I made a face. "You want me to say she's Lydia Zamir."

Murray grinned wolfishly. "Great story, if she is."

"She could be, I suppose, but—how did she end up here?"

"Her lover's home was Chicago," Peter said.

"I suppose," I agreed. "The music is so idiosyncratic, it's not something that a random street person would—would inhabit, the way this woman under the viaduct seems to. But how could a gifted musician be so lacking in supports that she ended up in a pile of rags on Forty-seventh Street?"

"Hey, Vic, you know how this goes," Sal said. "No one is immune."

Sal and I sit on the board of a shelter for refugees from domestic violence—she's right: family disconnect covers all levels of talent and economics.

Murray rolled the empty bottle of Dark Lord between his fingers. "Falls from the heights always make good stories. Grammy for 'Savage,' shared a stage with Beyoncé, known as the star-crossed lover of a South American revolutionary, ends up on Chicago's streets."

"Was Palurdo a revolutionary?" Peter asked, going through the screens on his own phone. "It sounds as though he covered the same kind of territory as Luis Urrea and Isabel Allende."

"South American writers are always revolutionaries, at least in Hollywood's imagination. I see a winning series here: How do our overachievers tumble from Mount Everest to Death Valley?" Murray sketched something careering down a mountainside in the air.

"Right," I snapped. "Washed-up basketball stars loading UPS trucks, former Pulitzer Prize winners reduced to preening on cable."

I regretted those toads as soon as they hopped out of my mouth. I put a conciliatory hand on Murray's arm. "That was below the belt: sorry."

He gave a perfunctory nod but took off soon after without saying anything else.

"He won a Pulitzer?" Sansen's sandy eyebrows went up.

"Yep. It was an important story and he did a great job with it, about a group of aldermen who owned a shell company that was using school grounds on the West Side as hazmat dumping grounds. The story brought a flurry of federal interest to City Hall for a few short months, but then Global bought the paper, and it was clear Global management wanted to be good old boys together with the perps. The follow-up story was killed."

"It was a hard business," Sal agreed, "but Murray didn't have to sign whatever he signed to agree to kill the follow-up. Could've taken it to an indie outlet and given up that Merc convertible he drives."

The talk shifted. Sansen and I left soon after to go dancing at Colibri, a hot new venue on Lake Street. When we got back to my place, I looked up "Savage," the first track on Zamir's album *Continental Requiem (in D minor)*.

YouTube had a recording of Zamir and Palurdo singing "Savage," not a video, but one of those recordings where still images of the singers flash on the screen: Zamir bent over her guitar, strong fingers on the strings, Zamir looking at Palurdo, love and daring in her face, teeth gleaming white, dark hair falling in waves below her shoulders. Palurdo's teeth were crooked and cigarette stained. In one photo, Palurdo held up a sign, I CAN'T SING, while Zamir held one reading, HE SAYS HE CAN WRITE.

I felt a contraction below my diaphragm. They'd been vibrant, in love. I don't think I'd ever felt that deep joy, not in my youth when those feelings are so intense they pierce you. And then—murder. Carnage. Seeing her lover die with all those others killed and wounded. Small wonder if PTSD had driven her to live below a train track with a toy piano.

Sansen took my hand and held it gently. "Do you think the woman you saw today is Lydia Zamir?"

"You can't tell from these pictures, but it's the sound, the splicing of Grieg with her own rhythms for 'Swan Song.' Same here in 'Savage,' where she's interwoven Purcell with that Haitian *kompa* beat. It would have been fun to see where she would have gone next with her music, but I'm guessing the carnage she witnessed silenced her voice."

Sansen nodded. "I've worked with people in Iraq and Afghanistan who've experienced mass slaughter. It's not something you recover from easily, or really, at all—it's like shrapnel in the heart that can't be extracted. I know the pair you encountered outside her hideout rubbed you the wrong way, but they may well be right—that she's too allergic to people to be in a facility where she could get help."

"The music matters to me, too," I said.

"Of course it does. I was forgetting—" Sansen pulled me to him.

My mother had been a musician, a singer with a great voice, but war, poverty, family responsibilities—me, the only child to survive after a series of miscarriages—derailed her career. She'd wanted me, or at any rate, she'd wanted her child, but her music had suffered.

4

Jailhouse Blues

I had my pain dream that night, where my mother was encased inside a thicket of tubes. I cut the tubes away, trying to reach her, but each time, a new forest of them sprang up. My own cry of her name woke Sansen as well as me.

I was lying in the dark, clutching Peter's hand, willing my heartbeat to slow, when my phone rang.

"Ms. Warshawski? I mean Vic? I—it's Angela. Angela Creedy, and I'm sorry to wake you but Bernie's in trouble."

I sat up, trying to move my mind to the present. "She's been hurt?"

"I don't think so, ma'am. Vic. But we're at a police station. She told me not to tell you, but honestly, I don't know what to do."

My brain had that lurching feeling you get after a mere two hours of sleep. Or from the news that your goddaughter has been arrested. I found a pair of jeans on the back of a chair and started dressing while Angela told me where Bernie was being held—the Second District, Fifty-first Street just off the Ryan. Two miles, more or less, from the homeless piano player.

Peter blinked at me as I sorted through my wallet, checking for the card that proves I'm a member of the Illinois bar.

"What's up?"

"Bernie's in trouble."

"You want me to come with you?" He started to get up.

I bent to kiss him. "You'd be a witness to murder and you wouldn't like that."

"Depends on who you're killing."

"Bernie. She's at a police station near the piano-playing homeless woman."

"You sure you're okay on your own?"

"One of us needs to be alert tomorrow. Later today, I guess. You're meeting donors, but I don't have anything going on until late morning."

I pulled on my soft leather boots and headed into the night. On the side streets, no one was out and I made good time to the expressway, but traffic on the

Ryan was heavy and moving fast, requiring a level of concentration that I had trouble maintaining. It was a relief when I reached the Fifty-first Street exit without hitting anything.

Angela was sitting on a bench inside the entrance, but she jumped up when she saw me. Six-foot-two guard, she made my five-eight feel short when she bent to hug me.

"Oh, ma'am, thank you for getting here so fast! They wouldn't let me go into the back with her; I don't know what they're doing to her." Angela came from Louisiana, with the kind of manners we northerners imagine are commonplace in the South. It was hard for her to use my first name.

We weren't the only people in the station in the middle of the night. Wentworth district is a lively one, lots of aggravated battery and assault, plenty of arson and car theft, the occasional homicide.

A couple about my age, looking as tired as I felt, was vying for attention from the desk sergeant with a pair of patrol officers who'd brought in a man so drunk he couldn't stand on his own. A woman near us was having a very loud argument on her phone with someone who wasn't taking responsibility for whatever Damian had done.

I took Angela to the far end of the room. "What

happened? Did Bernie go to the Forty-seventh Street viaduct?"

Angela nodded miserably. "We went roller-skating with our two other roommates. Everyone was having a good time, Bernie, too, at least mostly, but she kept talking about this lady, the piano player, how even though she was homeless, she knew all of Lydia Zamir's songs, but that you were too chicken to help her. She said this guy had frightened you away."

She bit her lips and looked at me. "I told her that was BS—who ever frightened *you* away from doing what you know is right? But Bernie said, well, never mind what she said."

"She said I was getting old and didn't want to admit it," I said.

Angela's dark face turned a shade deeper with embarrassment. "Something like that. Of course, kids my age, we all know Lydia Zamir, especially 'Savage'— sometimes that's what our team sings in the locker room to build team spirit before a game. Bernie said Lydia Zamir was dead, but Latisha, one of our other roommates, said no, she hadn't been killed. So then Bernie decided this lady was really Lydia Zamir because who else would know her music?

"Finally, about midnight when the other two went back to the house, Bernie said she was going to take the L down and see, was this really Lydia and did she need help. She said this would be the perfect time because the guy wouldn't be around. I tried to talk her out of it, ma'am, honest, but—"

"Not to worry," I said when she broke off. "We all know what Bernie's like when she thinks she's driving a puck to the net."

Angela produced a small smile. "So she hopped on the L and I—it's not the safest ride, you know, not at night, so even though I thought it was a mistake, I went with her. It took forever—it was almost two when we finally got to the viaduct. We walked from the L—we had no idea it was two miles! Anyway, the lady was sleeping in this bundle of smelly old blankets. Bernie went right up to her. I kept telling her not to, but she called her 'Lydia,' and the lady woke up.

"At first it kind of seemed okay. Bernie had downloaded a Lydia Zamir playlist. She put on 'Savage,' and the lady unwrapped her piano and picked out a few notes. But then, Bernie put on 'Swan Song,' which is about how swans mate for life, and the lady practically began screaming, then she started pounding on the piano keys.

"Then this guy showed up with a big dog. Bernie and he, they started going at it. Bernie acted like she was in the middle of some fight on the ice. The guy was super angry and he slugged Bernie, and the woman was screaming."

She wrung her hands. "I know I could have helped her out, but I don't believe in fighting, and besides, you know how it is, if the cops find an African-American in the middle of a street fight! I was begging her to just come away with me, but then the cops did show up. Even though this man hit Bernie, he somehow made it seem like Bernie had attacked the lady. Of course she didn't—but she did punch the guy. As soon as the cop cars appeared, though, the guy stopped fighting and went around to the lady, so it looked like it was just Bernie making a disturbance."

Her voice trailed away.

I gave her a quick hug, told her I'd take it from here, that I'd order a Lyft car for her if she didn't want to wait for me to drive her back. I joined the queue at the desk, waited my turn behind distraught friends and family to ask for Bernadine Fouchard. I wasn't distressed myself—too tired and, frankly, too angry with Bernie.

The officer said, "You the mother?"

"Family friend. And lawyer." I started to pull out my Illinois bar card but the desk officer shook his head.

"I believe you. We're cooling her off in one of the

cells." He spoke into his lapel mike; after a moment a sergeant came through the locked doors at the end of the corridor, a lanky woman with fine mousy hair that had escaped from the hair claws she used.

"Bernadine Fouchard?" the sergeant said. "She's Canadian, so we were going to call the consulate in the morning, let her contemplate her sins until then. She has to learn she can't go around harassing people unless she wants to be on a short list for deportation."

I squinted at her name badge: PIZZELLO. "Is that the charge, Sergeant Pizzello?" I asked. "Harassment?"

Pizzello shook her head. "There was some kind of bust-up over near the lake. People were screaming at each other, the kind of thing that makes someone call the cavalry, but no one involved is pressing charges. Fouchard claims she was attacked by a guy on the scene, but he said he was out walking his dog—"

"At two in the morning?" I interrupted.

"He's a night owl," the sergeant said. "The patrol teams over there say they see him in the park in the middle of the night."

"What does he do? Roam around imagining he's Robin Hood?"

Pizzello suppressed a smile. "No one knows what he does. He's one of those fixtures you find in every community. He's got a few pet obsessions—litter, animals, and apparently this homeless piano player. He's also got a temper, but he hasn't done anything that merited an arrest. So far."

"He have a name?" I asked. "If it's the guy I'm thinking of, the people around him call him 'Coop,' but he must have a last name."

The sergeant spoke into her lapel mike, listened for a moment, but shook her head. "The patrol team only knows him as Coop. They also know his dog, Bear, who apparently is the better-behaved member of the pair. Anyway, Coop told my patrol unit that the homeless woman was screaming for help; he went to protect her.

"Fouchard's not that big and ordinarily I'd take that claim with a grain of salt. Two grains. But one of my guys says she tried to fight with them when they took her to the patrol car, and she landed a pretty good shin kick. She could have been charged with assaulting an officer, but this is an older, more laid-back team. Fouchard had a friend with her; my guys let her ride with them."

The sergeant led me to the holding cells. The station was new; the cells were small but clean. Bernie was sharing space with two other women. One was snoring loudly, the other was snarling curses. Bernie was staring at her shoes, hunched over in a ball of misery.

Despite telling Angela not to involve me, her face lit up when she saw me with the sergeant. "Vic! Vic, I'm so sorry, I thought I was doing the right thing but I should have listened to you and to Angela. Are they going to put me in jail? Will I be thrown out of school? Oh, Mama and Papa will be so angry, so disappointed." She burst into tears.

When she learned she wasn't going to be charged with a crime, she flung her arms around Pizzello and made extravagant promises of good behavior.

The sergeant extricated herself. "Don't go roaring into situations where you don't know the players, Ms. Fouchard. And in particular, stay away from the Forty-seventh Street viaduct, or you'll find yourself facing an order of protection."

5
Story Hour

I didn't remember the drive home, or putting Bernie and Angela into a Lyft car. I went to bed without undressing and woke some five hours later. Peter had taken off, leaving a note in glyph-like letters that read "Happy Day After Birthday." He'd also made an art-work breakfast plate: a croissant with a chunk of robiola, one of my favorite cheeses, surrounded by orange segments. I was seriously thinking of falling in love.

I looked at the city news feed while I ate. Bernie's skirmish with Coop hadn't sounded interesting enough to local journalists of any stripe—print, broadcast, vlog, or blog—to make it from the police blotter to Twitter. That was a relief: it meant that Murray hadn't noticed Bernie's name on any of the data streams he followed, which meant Lydia Zamir—if it was Zamir—might be able to remain at the underpass dealing with her own demons. It also meant that Northwestern wouldn't find out about Bernie's skirmish with the law—which could jeopardize not only her hockey scholarship but her university career.

The person I wondered about most in this story wasn't Zamir, or even Bernie, but Coop. Since he operated on the shortest of tempers, he could easily hurt Bernie if they clashed again. He'd shown up so pat at Zamir's side when Bernie and Angela were there that he might pop up if I appeared.

It was after ten, later than I usually like to swim under a midsummer sun, but I leashed up my two dogs and drove to Forty-seventh Street, leaving the car in the lot where I'd parked yesterday. I took the dogs across the footbridge over Lake Shore Drive to the lake itself.

The shoreline here is rocky and not very inviting, but if you're willing to pick your way down the boulders, you come to some of the best swimming in Chicago. The lake floor is granite, so the water is clear, and unless the city installs the beach described at yesterday's SLICK meeting, the rocks limit the number of people who can deposit Pampers, condoms, and broken bottles. The bike and running paths were full, even in the middle of a workday, but once we climbed down to the lake, the three of us were on our own.

The temperature was in the low nineties, which in Chicago translates as miserably humid, but the water was cold. The dogs and I swam for half an hour, and when I came out, I threw balls for them for another few minutes until my skin was dry enough to get dressed.

Back at the viaduct, I tied them to a bike rack at the eastern edge of the viaduct, where they'd be in the shade but wouldn't be able to get near Zamir, who was sitting in her nest of grimy blankets, the piano showing red against the darkness. She wasn't playing, but as I slowly walked toward her, I could hear her crooning, rocking in time to a rhythm only she could hear.

A crate behind her held polystyrene cartons of uneaten food. My stomach turned, thinking what might be growing in a chicken or shrimp dinner on a hot day. A cardboard box contained a jumble of clothes.

I had written a note on my letterhead, stating simply that if she wanted medical help or someone to talk to, she should call me. I'd enclosed a couple of twenties, and placed it, with a liter of Gatorade, next to the piano.

I retreated to her perimeter but squatted, not saying anything, just being, in case she wanted to talk. She stopped crooning and pulled her piano close to her chest, cradling it, but after three or four minutes when I didn't move or speak, she relaxed enough to push the piano an arm's length away. After another moment, she began picking out notes and crooning again.

I stood slowly, massaging my hamstrings. I backed up another few steps before saying, "I'm Vic. My phone number is on the letter. Call if I can help."

I returned to my dogs just as Coop rounded the corner with Bear. The three dogs seemed happy to meet each other; it was the man who showed hackle.

"What are you doing down here?" he demanded.

"I have a passport," I assured him. "It's all legal."

"Not if you're bothering her, it isn't." He jerked his head toward the piano player.

Mitch, my big black lab mix, didn't like Coop's tone. He wedged himself between us and made an ugly noise in his throat.

"You looking after your person?" Coop bent over Mitch, his voice suddenly soft and cajoling.

His whole affect changed along with his voice: he looked willowy, not sinewy, and Mitch responded by letting Coop scratch his ears. Bear and Peppy, my golden, shoved up against Coop's legs, demanding their share of attention.

"You two are a couple of turncoats, aren't you?" I said severely to my dogs, who grinned.

Coop stood back up. "If you have dogs like these, you can't be all bad. Just don't go interfering in business you don't understand. We don't like outsiders prying into our lives down here. No social workers, no do-gooders."

"Fortunately, I'm neither. On the other hand, I'm someone who doesn't react well to threats, so try dialing it down a decibel or two. Pretend I'm a dog that you want to be on good terms with."

That forced a laugh out of him. "What breed?"

"Half Rottweiler, half pit dog. I'm loyal but fierce. And one of the people in my network of concern is the young woman you let the cops drag off early this morning. How did you happen on the scene so patly? And why didn't you take responsibility for your part in the skirmish?"

"My part was to make sure no one, including your 'network of concern,' distresses her." He jerked his head toward the pianist. "She's had enough disturbance for three lifetimes. When people like you or that kid come around, it pulls the skin off her wounds and starts them bleeding again."

"All the more reason to get her help."

"All the more reason for you to fucking mind your own business." His tone had turned ugly again.

I was getting whiplash trying to follow the switches

between Nice Coop and Nasty Coop. Using a tone of exaggerated meekness, I said, "Tell me how to get in touch with you, Coop, so that I can check in advance whether I'm planning activities that will alarm you."

He studied my face for a moment, then replied with surprising calmness, "I don't know who you are, just what you say you do. I don't know who you're loyal to or who's paying you. If I don't know those things, I can't trust you. When your kid showed up in the middle of the night, that scared the bejesus out of me. It would be typical—"

He bit off the sentence. I tried to ask him "typical" of what or whom, but he shook his head and refused to say anything else.

I took the dogs and drove slowly back to my office. If Lydia was a target of some malign person, she wasn't at all hard to find. The most sense I could make of the situation was that Coop himself straddled some line between delusion and reality, and that Lydia was a bit player in his fantasy world. Which Bernie and I now inhabited as well.

When I was at my desk, I checked with Bernie, to reenforce the police injunction that she stay clear of Lydia Zamir. She was still subdued and in a compliant frame of mind.

"I promise, Vic. Anyway, I have one week to learn

softball. That is my new coaching assignment, can you believe? At least soccer is like hockey, moving up and down the field, but softball—standing around chewing gum. How can you motivate team spirit while you're waiting around like in a doctor's office for something to happen?"

"Get them all singing 'Savage,'" I suggested. "It will pump everyone up while they're waiting."

Right before hanging up, Bernie said in an offhand voice, "Vic, you remember Leo? Leo Prinz?"

"I don't think so," I said.

"He made the speech about the Lake Michigan beach, and the crazy man tried to attack him. You were there."

"So I was," I agreed: the excitement over Zamir, Coop, and Bernie's night in the police station had pushed the SLICK meeting from my mind. "What about him?"

"They want him to finish his talk. Apparently some community person made the SLICK woman realize she couldn't act like a dictator, so he has to make the whole speech. I told him I'd go. I thought you might like to come. You know, in case anyone attacks him again."

"Bring your hockey stick," I suggested. "You're much fiercer than either Leo or me."

"No, please, Vic. Angela has to take her girls to Blue Island that day. I want someone I know."

"You know Leo," I said.

"I'll text you the details," she said, as if I'd agreed.

"Bernie!" I expostulated, but she had hung up.

Five minutes later, I got her text with the details of the SLICK meeting, scheduled a few days from now. I deleted the text, but at dinner that night with Peter, I whined about Bernie's exigency.

"And why someone as forceful as a whirlwind is interested in this young man is beyond me. He's not a very rugged specimen."

Peter laughed. "She's got enough ferocity for two or three. As you do, yourself, Vic. But in you, there's the extra dimension of wanting to heal the world, which means you're constantly trying to look after strays even while you complain about them."

"Is that a compliment or a complaint?" I said.

"It's why I love you," he said quietly. "And why I worry when your compassion drives you into the path of danger."

My throat tightened; I couldn't speak, but leaned across the table to squeeze his fingers.

The next day I had a client meeting in the South Loop, just a ten-minute drive from the viaduct where Zamir camped out. She wasn't playing, and it took a moment or two for me to see her in her nest; her rags blended almost seamlessly into the filthy concrete wall. That was why I'd missed her when I walked past yesterday. I stood looking at her for too long a time—she became aware of me, whimpered, and clutched the piano, which had been buried under a blanket.

Peter's description of me felt too grand—that I was trying to heal the world—but it's true that someone as hurt and needy as this woman made me want to intervene. I couldn't think of anything more to do than I'd already done, but on an impulse, I scribbled my home address and landline on the back of one of my cards and left it on the edge of her blanket.

"Please call me, or come to me, if you ever feel you can trust me to help you."

At least Coop didn't appear on this visit, but two days later he erupted into my life with a vengeance. I returned from an early run with the dogs to find him and Bear in front of my apartment building. As soon as Coop saw me he bounded down the walk, a newspaper crumpled in his hand.

"Did you do this? After I warned you to stay away?"

"Did I do what?" I asked. "Leave a newspaper on your lawn? I don't know where you live, and even if I did, I wouldn't erupt into your life like Mount Etna."

"Damn you, don't play innocent bystander with me."

He was shaking with fury, so much that he dropped the paper as he tried to shove it against my face.

I picked it up and turned my back to him so I could read it. The text box above the fold was outlined in thick black.

In the heavens, dying stars burn with a fierce heat before becoming black holes. What about Chicago's human stars from yesteryear? Did they burn out or simply fade away?

In the *Herald-Star*'s riveting new series, Pulitzer Prize winner Murray Ryerson looks at the lives of people who used to be household names in this city. Some, like Brett Craven, burned like meteor showers and disappeared behind bars, while others, like Lee Swann, disappeared into bars. Some are living out their days peacefully in neighborhoods or small towns across the country. Perhaps the most dramatic and the saddest is Lydia Zamir, whom Murray discovered living under a railway viaduct.

Below the fold were two pictures of Lydia. The first had been shot during a performance at Vancouver's

Queen Elizabeth Theatre. She was wearing a simple white tunic over black trousers. The photographer had caught her with hands on the keys, her eyes half shut, her expression intent as she concentrated on the place inside her where the music lived.

The second picture showed her under the viaduct. Like the concert shot, it had been taken without Zamir's knowledge, with a wide-angle lens that showed her sitting amid her soiled blankets, pounding furiously on the toy piano. As in the concert photo, her eyes were half closed, her attention focused inward. A thread of saliva hung from the corner of her mouth.

My stomach turned. WHAT HAPPENED TO THIS BRILLIANT MUSICIAN? the subhead ran, but before I could read the article, Coop had snatched the paper from me.

"Well?" he demanded. "You going to deny you made this happen?"

"I didn't make it happen," I said. "But it was because—"

"Goddamn you!" He wadded up the paper and flung it on the ground. "When I specifically told you—warned you—"

"I told you the last time I saw you that I don't respond to threats. Mitch! Peppy! Let's go."

I walked past him, but he grabbed my shoulder as

I was unlocking the front door. "No!" I snapped. I ducked under his arm and shoved an elbow into his rib cage.

I turned and braced myself against the door, ready to kick if he came at me again, but the blow to his ribs acted like a cold shower. He put his arms down and backed up a few steps. His color subsided from umber to ordinary tan.

All three dogs had been letting out short urgent barks—*danger!*—but had been unsure whether to intervene: What should they do when two good dog people went to war? They stopped barking when Coop backed away, but they kept circling us, panting anxiously.

The noise had roused Mr. Contreras. He surged from the building in his magenta pajamas, waving a hammer. "What's going on here? Who's this creep? I saw him grab hold of you, Cookie—you need me to knock some sense into him?"

Coop said, "I don't know who you are, but your Cookie here is the creep: she sicced some slimeball on a fragile woman."

"What the heck are you trying to say, young man?" Mr. Contreras demanded.

"Murray," I said before my neighbor moved into a

higher gear. "He wrote a story about a woman who's living under a viaduct. It turns out she used to be an important songwriter. Murray decided that would sell papers, or make the *Star*'s advertisers happy."

Mr. Contreras took a moment to absorb that: he's over ninety, still alert and reasonably fit, but he needs extra time these days. After a pause, he asked me, "You send Ryerson down to bother this woman?"

"No," I said at the same time Coop said, "Yes."

"I ain't talking to you," Mr. Contreras said to Coop. "What happened?"

I told him the part of Lydia's history I knew. "Her music was distinctive, back when she was performing— she mixed the classics with rhythms that she picked up from indigenous people in the Americas. This guy here, Coop, he calls himself—"

"Because it's my goddamn name," Coop growled.

"Watch your language around ladies, young man," Mr. Contreras snapped.

Coop opened and shut his mouth a couple of times but didn't speak—an effect Mr. Contreras often has on younger men.

"Anyway, he's super protective of Lydia, warned Bernie and me off her. I told Peter Sansen and Sal about her on my birthday, and Murray was there. He thought it would be interesting to run a series. I'd forgotten that, because of the excitement over Bernie's arrest—which Coop also instigated."

I glared at him, but he was already back at full boil. "So it was your fault," Coop shouted. "We had TV crews down there this morning. I protect her identity because she doesn't want people bothering her, but thanks to you and your friend Murray, she almost got hit by a train. She ran up the stairs to get away from the cameras and was on the tracks."

"Was she hurt?" I cried. "Did she get medical attention?"

"Commuters pulled her off the track in time."

"Has she seen a doctor?" I demanded. "Where is she?"

"Why would I tell you where to find her? So you can sic another reporter on her? The damned story brought the city in, cops, and Streets and Sanitation. They took everything—*everything*—and dumped it somewhere. I can't find the piano, I don't know where her sleeping bag is—you goddamn bitch!"

"No call to talk like that, young man. You need to learn some manners," Mr. Contreras said.

"I'll talk however I goddamn well please. And you, *Cookie*, you leave Lydia the hell alone." He called Bear to heel and headed back down the walk.

His departure seemed anticlimactic. His rage had propelled him to the North Side, but he hadn't known what he wanted to accomplish when he found me. Maybe just to scream abuse because of a situation he was powerless to control.

6
Murray Signs Up

Mr. Contreras stayed out front for several minutes: he wanted to relive his arrival on the scene with his hammer—"Saved your skin this time, Cookie, didn't I?" he exulted.

I assured him he was right: I could have fought Coop off, but Mr. Contreras had startled the younger man into subsiding without a drop of blood being shed. He had earned some bragging time. I finally reminded him that he was wearing nightclothes in public. He turned a red that matched his pajama shirt and hurried inside.

Upstairs in my own space, I took a shower, pulled an espresso, looked at the box scores, and finally felt calm enough to deal with Murray's story. I started at the end, namely this morning's news feeds from the train station.

A number of crews were there both from cable and the local networks, but they all behaved the same: mikes thrust at Lydia under a barrage of questions. She'd been momentarily frozen and then had grabbed her piano and fled up the stairs.

Global's team had been the most nimble, chasing up to the train platform after her. They'd gotten some dramatic footage of two men and a woman lifting Lydia out of the path of an oncoming train. She apparently hadn't been able to hold on to the piano, since I didn't see it in subsequent frames. There were the requisite interviews with the three commuters who'd saved Lydia, and a shot of the ambulance carrying Lydia to a hospital. I didn't see Coop or Bear in any of the videos.

I finally turned to Murray's story, which filled two inside pages. Besides the front page pictures of Lydia playing, the paper ran her graduation photo from the New England Conservatory, her appearance at fifteen with the Kansas City Youth Orchestra, and one of Murray sitting with Lydia's mother in the Zamir home in Eudora, Kansas; a pitcher and two glasses sat on the table in front of them.

"We never wanted Lydia to go to Boston to school," Debbie Zamir told me. We were talking in the living room of the comfortable frame home she and her husband have lived in for the last forty years.

"We always thought her piano teachers here in Kansas encouraged her to have a swelled head about the size of her talent, but she wouldn't listen to anything her father or I said; she had to go out east to study. She could have gotten a nice job here in Kansas, being a school music teacher, or even a choir director. But she was so sure she was going to be like Judy Garland in that movie and become famous. And then she met that Communist writer and that was the end of everything. She turned into a hippie, playing a guitar at rallies for immigrants. She never held down a real job. And then he was killed."

Lydia did return to her parents' home in the wake of the shooting. Mass murders always leave a residue of trauma for those unfortunate enough to be involved; the Zamirs knew their daughter couldn't be expected to recover overnight, but they were disappointed that she seemed to make no effort to return to normalcy.

I sat with the paper open in my hands. The death of a beloved brings a torrent of grief that comes close to drowning us, but to have that death be from murder, and a murder one witnessed—what can possibly look like normal after that? I finally went back to the story, to Lydia's mother telling Murray,

> "We hoped being back here, maybe she'd find a job that could keep her steady, but she—it was terrible. We couldn't get her to accept counseling, she was up at all hours, playing the piano, playing the guitar, singing horrible songs about blood and death. When she finally left, I hate to say it about my own child, but it was a relief."

Murray had also spoken to Lydia's instructors at the New England Conservatory, who said she arrived with good technique, although a spotty musical education.

One of her instructors, a Professor Szydanski, said, "We are used to helping kids overcome gaps in their training, but the one thing we can't do is figure out in advance who has a special spark, even with all the video auditions kids have to submit these days.

"Piano—all music—is like any art, or maybe it's like a sport. You have a group of kids who all look brilliant when they're fifteen, and then some mysterious alchemy happens over the next few years. A handful find something deeper in themselves that turns them into world-class performers. The rest are good, and we're proud of them, but that mysterious inner piece is missing."

Szydanski said he couldn't possibly comment on why Lydia was living on the streets, if it was Lydia—when he looked at Murray's photos, he didn't recognize her. "She looks eighty, not forty."

The story ended with Lydia's dorm roommate from New England, who "loved, loved, loved" Lydia's protest songs. She'd seemed so ordinary at the conservatory. "It sucked that she wasn't making progress with her auditions for chamber groups or postgrad fellowships, especially since I was getting a ton of callbacks. She tried to be a good friend and not let it show, but it's hard—and then I started hearing her songs on just about every streaming service. 'Savage' was brilliant—so fun! It's a shame she's not doing any new stuff."

When I'd read it through a couple of times, I called Murray. "It's an interesting story, but there seem to be missing pieces," I said. "Although great shot of you drinking—what, margaritas?—with Lydia's mother."

"Iced tea," Murray said sourly. "Kansas isn't dry these days, but you'd be surprised how many of its inhabitants are. What's missing? I'll bite."

"Hector Palurdo, Zamir's lover—he grew up in Chicago, and his mother still lives here. What did she have to say?"

"Don't try to play 'gotcha' with me, Warshawski. Of course I tried to find her, but she wouldn't talk to me, text me, respond to emails."

"And the woman under the viaduct? Did she confirm or deny?"

"Ah, yes. That was an interesting exercise. The first time I went down there, she started pounding her damned piano and screeching."

"Did Coop and Bear show up?" I asked.

"That's the guy with the dog? Oh, yeah, chip on his shoulder the size of the Sears Tower. But then, I took a few days to grow out my beard, slept in my oldest clothes, came back as a street person myself."

He paused, as if waiting for applause.

"Ingenious," I said politely. "Did it make her trust you? I didn't see any quotes in the story."

"Yeah, well, the best I can say, besides getting a rash, is it fooled the guy Coop. He comes around once or twice a day, bringing food or whatever, so he looked me over, told me if I hurt Zamir he'd cut me to pieces and feed me to the dog. The dog looked bored, but maybe the guy has fed him so many human parts over the years he can't stand the taste anymore."

I had to laugh. "But the woman herself? Did you being homeless make her talk to you?"

"Nope. If I mentioned Palurdo or his family, she began shrieking her head off. If I asked her about her music she'd plunk it out on that idiotic excuse for a piano. I told her I'd met her mother and she turned her back on me."

"Do you think she can speak at all?" I asked.

"You want to try?" he jeered.

"Not at the moment. At the moment I'd like to know where she is, and that she's safe."

"What?" Murray was jolted.

"You didn't monitor the feed?" I asked. "Camera crews arrived early this morning; Zamir fled up the stairs and along the tracks to escape them. Someone apparently called an ambulance, but there's no word on where they took her."

For a moment all I heard was Murray breathing heavily on the other end of the phone, the clicking of his keyboard, then a smothered "Oh, shit!" and he hung up.

He rang me back a few hours later, as I was crossing the Loop on my way to a meeting with the one client who I jump through hoops to please. "She's vanished," he said abruptly.

"Your sommelier?" My mind was on the client I'd just left, who was worried about a container of Ligurian wine that had evaporated.

"Damn it, Warshawski, this is serious."

"Murray!" I gathered my wits. "You mean Lydia Zamir?"

"No, Michelle Obama," he snarled. "Of course I mean Zamir. Ambulance crew took her away, supposedly to Provident, only the hospital doesn't have any record of her. She might have been logged as a Jane Doe, but she took a hike before they did more than recommend sending her to the big house for an MRI."

Provident was part of Cook County's health care system. I clicked on a map app; they were the closest facility to the Forty-seventh Street station, but didn't have an imaging unit.

"And you want to find her because . . . ?"

"My editor thinks we need to make sure she has appropriate medical care, housing, the works."

"Gosh, Murray, I'll have to take back a tenth of my nasty thoughts about Global Entertainment's moguls. Big corporation with an even bigger heart. The headline practically writes itself. Can't wait to see tomorrow's edition, but right now I have to get to a meeting."

"Wait a second, Vic."

I was on Wells Street, where it crosses the Chicago River. I watched a crowded Architecture Center tour boat pass below. People were taking selfies with the Merchandise Mart in the background.

"Murray, I really have to get going."

He ignored me. "People up the food chain are apparently afraid of legal exposure."

"Surely your legal team vetted the story before it ran."

"Of course. But that was before Zamir's agent saw her old client being chased by our camera crew all over social media. Not to mention ABC, CBS, and the rest of the alphabet."

"Touching. What's this agent been doing while Zamir's been aphasic on the streets?"

"Doesn't matter. Senior staff needs a head on a block just in case, which means I need to find Lydia and get her into a locked ward."

"Murray, you have a staff. I have me. You have a budget that flies you to Kansas. Did Zamir run back to her parents? Speaking of running, I'm going to have to sprint not to keep Darraugh Graham waiting."

Murray hung up but called again an hour later. "You grovel sufficiently to keep Graham happy? Lydia's parents haven't heard from her. Look, Vic, can you see if Zamir has gone to Elisa Palurdo? Palurdo absolutely won't talk to me. And the guy, Coop—I can't find a last name or an address."

I was on the L. Between the train noise, people shouting into their mouthpieces, and a group of teens sharing a rap download, it wasn't possible to talk. I called him again as I walked up Milwaukee to my office.

Before I spoke, Murray said, "Don't remind me again about all my resources. I want this done privately. Global is a snake pit of rumormongers and backstabbers. I don't want any sharks smelling my blood in the water."

I bit back a snarky comment on the mixed imagery. "Global will pay?" I didn't try to keep the derision out of my tone.

"Of course not. Why do you think I'm calling you? You're the one person I can trust to investigate without word getting to my management."

"No freebies, Ryerson. I have bills to pay, just like you."

"Out of my own pocket."

"This call has been recorded for quality assurance, Murray. It's one-fifty an hour plus expenses. Five hundred up front—check, credit card, or even good old-fashioned Ben Franklins." I typed in the code on my office street door. "I'm about to email you a contract. When you've signed it and sent it back, with a down payment, I'll fit you into my schedule."

He thanked me meekly.

7

A Teaspoon in the Desert

I started my investigative career right after my thir-
tieth birthday. I'd been with the public defender for
five years. I'd done my share of plea bargains, of trying
to save the sorry asses of sorry punks. I'd also seen my
share of people railroaded by cops and prosecutors: the
State of Illinois compensates courts that have high conviction rates, not high clearance rates. I had often been
the one tiny pair of nail scissors cutting at a fitted-up
noose.

It used to make me furious that the macroscum, the
policy-makers, the good old cronies, the brokers and
bankers, almost always got a pass. If you could actually indict one of them, they had a bottomless bucket
of money to pay attorneys and investigators. My clients

had to share my attention with upward of twenty others in the same hearing.

I figured that as a solo op, without a politically needy boss to tell me whom to save and whom to condemn, I could uncover the vermin hiding in the shadows. When I saw my first business cards, I was so excited I handed them out to passersby on Wabash Avenue: Yes! V.I. Warshawski, Private Investigator, would see that justice rolled down like waters!

Every now and then it did, but most days I felt like a child pouring water on a desert with a teaspoon.

I'd help Murray out because we were old friends with a long history. I'd help him out because Lydia Zamir's story was an all-too-common American tragedy: she'd lived past a mass murder, but she'd been hideously damaged by it.

I'd help him regardless of money or outcome, because I had an uncomfortable realization—a lurching in the pit of my stomach—that I shared responsibility for this morning's disaster. It was I who'd told Murray about Zamir. I'd been judgmental, on my high horse, accusing him of selling out. I'd essentially goaded him into writing his big exposé.

I'd do what I could to find her and help her, but I hated knowing that if I was successful, Global's executives would preen as if they'd done something noble, while nothing would change in the big picture. No assault weapons would be taken off the streets, no assurances that Lydia, and the thousands of others damaged by these assaults, would be the last people to see such harrowing violence. At the end of the story, they would still be packets on an assembly line of death.

My lease mate, Tessa Reynolds, came into our office bathroom as I was frowning at myself in the mirror. "Warshawski, if you looked at me like that, I'd confess on the spot."

I tried to smile but told her what had been going through my mind.

Tessa looked at me soberly. "Think about it like this, Vic: maybe you are only a drop in a bucket—or a teaspoon in a desert—but there are some fragile plants that will die if your teaspoon goes away. Go up to La Llorona and get yourself a bowl of tortilla soup and get back to scooping and pouring. Oh, and lock the bathroom door if you want privacy."

At that I did smile. And I did go down the street to La Llorona.

Tessa and I had moved into our warehouse when this stretch of Milwaukee Avenue was still mostly Hispanic and mostly blue-collar. La Llorona was one of the few survivors of the invasion of boutiques, loft apartments, and chic restaurants. It was a comforting place, like the diners of my childhood, where all the regulars knew one another by name. Mrs. Aguilar gave me soup and a glass of her homemade limeade. We talked about our families and mutual friends.

By the time we finished, I wasn't filled with the thrill of the chase, but I was ready to face the world again. I sat on a bench outside the café to call the hospitals on the near South Side. Posing as a worried sister, I asked for Lydia by name, and then for Jane Does. Not even Provident acknowledged they'd received a Jane Doe today. I guess if Lydia had disappeared without treatment that was understandable, but it still troubled me.

The morning shift would be on duty for another hour. I jogged up the street to my car. Traffic was predictably thick, but I still made it to the hospital with twenty-five minutes to spare.

I bypassed the main entrance and went to the ER, which was full on a weekday afternoon, because American medical insurance dictates that if you're poor, you go to an emergency room, not to a doctor.

The woman running the admitting desk was experienced, but weary. So many people had passed through her hands today, and so many were clamoring for attention in the moment—including me—that it was hard for her to cast her mind back to the morning's catastrophes. She called one of the ER techs, who emerged from the back, as harassed as the admitting clerk herself.

I'd downloaded photos from Murray's story and showed those to the technician. He was wary, thought he should call his supervisor.

"Believe me, please, I'm not interested in a lawsuit," I said. "Lydia has been in mental torment for a number of years. We can't get her to get help, but at least if we knew where she was, we could keep an eye on her, make sure she was warm in winter and had access to help if she was ready for it. Now, though—the city has dismantled her nest and we don't know where she is. Please—if she was here, if she left—"

I spread my hands, pleading, distraught.

The technician and the clerk exchanged glances, minute head nods. The technician called up Lydia's chart on his tablet. Jane Doe, brought in by ambulance at 8:03 A.M. They couldn't recognize her from the younger pictures, but the homeless woman under the viaduct was definitely their patient. She didn't speak, didn't answer questions about her name, age, day of the week, but there was no obvious sign of injury or head trauma.

"We wanted to send her to Stroger for an MRI—

we don't have imaging facilities here—and we'd moved her gurney to the hall for transport, but when we came back about an hour later, she was gone."

Stroger was the main hospital for the county system.

"Do you know what she was wearing?" I asked.

"She was in a hospital gown when we last saw her. Her clothes were foul; we threw them out and put a pair of jeans and a T from our donation chest in a bag under her gurney, but I can't tell you what design was on the T. She had lesions on her haunches, bruises up and down her body. One of our LPNs sponged her off and put some ointment on her wounds."

"Do you have any idea who came for her?" I asked. "I thought maybe my brother—but he says not."

The two shook their heads. "One of the patients who was also waiting for transport said your sister got up from the gurney and wandered into the main part of the hospital, but someone would have stopped her. Unless she'd gotten dressed, I suppose. Someone else said a man came in and carried her away in his arms. I'm sorry—but we're so short-staffed and overcrowded—" The clerk gestured at the waiting room.

The shifts were changing; her replacement needed briefing, the angry and scared crowd of patients needed attention. It was time for me to thank them and take off.

Two different stories of how Lydia had left, but my

money was on the man lifting her fragile body from the gurney. Had to have been Coop. He'd come to me, vented his rage, and then raced back to the South Side. He must have a car to get around town with that big dog.

I drove over to the Forty-seventh Street viaduct, wondering if Zamir might have returned. Murray had been right, though—she'd vanished without a trace. Streets and San had made a thorough job of cleaning out her nest: they'd been through with a power hose to wash down the walls and sidewalks. Even the graffiti was gone. The only trace of Lydia's residence was three bouquets laid on the ground where she'd played.

The evening rush hour trains had started. Most raced past, heading to the south suburbs. Whenever one stopped, I'd buttonhole the commuters to see if anyone had witnessed this morning's event. No one who bothered to talk to me had been here for the drama, but everyone had watched it on their devices during the day.

I stayed on the platform for another hour, so I could intercept homebound commuters. Everyone knew Lydia by sight, because they'd passed her for the last year or so. The news coverage gave everyone strong opinions about her flight along the tracks, the city's destruction of her home, and Metra's abysmal attention to passenger safety.

Some people were focused on their screens or on getting home, but most listened to me eagerly when they realized I knew something that hadn't been on the news, namely that Lydia had left the hospital.

A lot of people sort of knew Coop, enough to say hi when they biked or ran the lakefront. No one could tell me his last name, though, or where he lived. He sounded like a genie—when Lydia rubbed her piano, he sprang from the soundboard.

In between trains, I sat in the platform shelter, away from the sun's glare, to answer emails and do a little work on some of my current projects. The walls were covered with the usual graffiti, as well as ads for elder-care, childcare, expert tutoring and tailoring.

There was also a notice from SLICK, announcing their next community meeting on the lakefront land-fill. The type was so small that a suspicious person might think they didn't want the public to know they were going to meet.

Bernie had wanted me to attend to help support Leo. She'd texted the meeting details to me, but I hadn't seen any point in going and had forgotten about it. Fortuitously enough, the meeting was taking place tonight. I'd go—after all, I was already down here. And it was possible Coop would turn up.

I wandered back along Forty-seventh Street toward the bank building. I was hungry again—the tortilla soup hadn't been that substantial. One of the new restaurants on the street, African Fusion, was bright, clean, and full. No better testimonial than that.

8
Dining Out

A harried staff member told me to take a seat anywhere. Only one table was free, and I was lucky
to get it.

After a moment, as I peered at the food the people
around me were eating, I realized that the trio who'd
run the first SLICK meeting I'd attended was in the
corner next to me. Their table was covered with so
many documents that when a waitress arrived with
their food, the woman gestured impatiently for her to
set the dishes down on my table.

"Sorry—I don't think you were planning on buying
me dinner," I said, startling them into looking up. Actually, in a reprise of the meeting, only the man who'd
been banging the gavel and the woman looked at me—
the guy who'd been bent over his notes at the meeting

continued to hunch over a series of maps of the lake-front.

"Mona, isn't it?" I said. "I was at SLICK's last meeting. Do you think tonight will be as exciting?"

The gaveller puffed out his cheeks and growled, "Better not be," but Mona said, "Are you new to the neighborhood? I don't remember seeing you around here before."

"Just someone who enjoys using the lake," I said. "I'm trying to find the man called Coop, actually, which is why I wanted to come tonight. Do you know how to reach him?"

"Are you working with him?" Mona demanded.

"If I were, I'd know how to find him. Do you have his last name or a phone number?"

"What's this about?" the gaveller said.

I took a piece of fried something from one of their bowls, which they'd left in front of me. Normally I don't tell anyone my business, but I wanted help more than hostility.

"The homeless woman under the viaduct, Lydia Zamir. I'm sure you saw the news about her."

The capillaries in Mona's mottled face turned a deeper red. "I complained about her to the alderman and to the Metra authorities for almost a year. There are rats and raccoons in that wildlife corridor next to the embankment. Her sitting out there with open food was like an engraved invitation for them to come eat and have bigger litters. Every time someone got her into a hospital or shelter, though, she'd run back to our neighborhood. Helped by that creep Coop."

The fried something was spicy, which I liked, but gooey, which I didn't. I tried a spoonful of a slaw, which was crunchy with a pleasing peanut under-taste. I was about to cut into a whole grilled fish when the gaveller noticed.

"You're eating our food!"

"It's been on my table getting cold," I said. "I thought you'd decided you didn't want it."

The note-maker finally looked up as his pals grabbed the food and slapped it onto their own table. "Watch out; you're spilling sauce on the map. It's the one Taggett gave me—I haven't had time to make a copy!"

He dabbed anxiously at the document in front of him. Glare from the overhead lights made it hard for me to see, but I could tell it depicted the lakefront. A thick black line showed the current shoreline; dotted lines a few inches to the right, filled in with orange and green, presumably showed the proposed landfill.

Mona saw me looking. "This is private business! Simon, put all those papers away so we can eat.

Taggett's coming tonight—we can go over it with him after the meeting."

Gifford Taggett was superintendent of the Chicago Park District. Like every other office in the city or county, who you knew mattered more than what you knew. Taggett had served as ward committeeman, fronted deals for road construction, roughed up opposition to garbage dumping in the marshes on the far South Side. As a faithful foot soldier for the Cook County Democrats, he'd been handsomely rewarded with the patronage-rich post of park superintendent.

"If the map belongs to the Park District, surely it's public business," I said. "I'm a Cook County taxpayer, so I have an interest in it."

"These are preliminary drawings." Simon rolled up the map after one last anxious dab with his napkin.

"They're not the ones your boy Leo showed at your last meeting?"

"The process is iterative," Simon said stiffly. "After tonight, we'll have a sense of which way public reaction is leaning." Assisted by an impatient Mona, he shuffled the other papers into a haphazard stack and set them next to him on the bench.

The harassed server came to take my order. I pointed at the crunchy slaw and grilled fish my neighbors were eating and she raced off again.

"By the way," I said, "you never did tell me whether you saw what happened this morning with Lydia Zamir."

Simon nodded. "That's all anyone could talk about in the office today. Metra needs to get fencing in place so no one else can get onto those tracks."

"You know she's missing, then?"

"Hadn't heard that," the gaveller huffed.

"I called Streets and San and they came out with a power hose to clean that underpass," Mona said. "If she shows up there again, I'm going to take stronger action."

"Right," I said. "The rats and all. Did you know her name before she made today's news?"

All three shook their heads, but Mona added, "Even if we'd known she was some kind of singer, that didn't make it right for her to camp out under the tracks like that. The noise she made—we're trying to attract tourists and businesses here. A smelly loud homeless person, even if she's a musician, drives people away. She used to sleep on the university campus, but they managed to force her to leave. SLICK doesn't have that kind of power."

"I think we're inured to the homeless in America," I said. "I see them in front of Neiman Marcus when I'm on North Michigan, but that doesn't keep people out of the store. Why do you think Coop cares about her?"

Mona's thin red lips flattened. "To make himself into a nuisance. If we want *x*, he demands *y*, simply to be as obstructive as possible."

"So you don't think he has a genuine interest in her well-being?"

"You mind telling us your name and why you care?" The gaveller's eyes were bright with suspicion.

"V.I. Warshawski." I handed out cards.

"Investigator?" the gaveller growled. "What does that mean?"

"Someone who carries out inquiries into the causes or background of events." I smiled brightly.

"Did Coop hire you to follow us?" Mona demanded.

"Funnily enough, Coop thinks you hired me to follow him. Unfortunately, my trailing skills have gotten soft in the online era. I have no idea where he is. That's what I was hoping you could tell me—his last name, a phone number, an address."

"He's never signed in at any SLICK meeting," the gaveller complained. "He only shows up when he wants to cause trouble."

"Which means he'll probably be there tonight," Simon added.

"He has anger management issues," Mona said.

"People tell me he can't hold down a job because he ends up blowing up at his boss or coworkers if they rub him the wrong way."

She couldn't tell me what people had said this—just people.

The three finished their meal as my food arrived. They paid quickly but had some trouble extricating themselves from the table—they kept dropping spreadsheets and maps, but the gaveller put his substantial bulk between me and their table to keep me from lending a hand.

9

A Super Meeting

E ven though I got to the Prairie Savings and Loan building late, a lot of people were still in the lobby. Community groups—birders, fair housing advocates, community benefits supporters—were handing out flyers. Everyone was eager to talk to me about the need to protect the lake or to make sure local people got jobs if the city undertook a major reconfiguration of the shoreline.

"Taggett's coming. It's our chance to confront him." I heard this a dozen times: no matter what project or political viewpoint, everyone knew that the park superintendent was the first and last court of appeal.

When I'd pushed my way into the meeting room, I looked around for Bernie. She was in the front row, close to the stage where Leo Prinz sat. From the back of the room, I'd seen Simon push Leo away from the table where the SLICK officers were seated. He was laying out charts and maps and apparently told Leo to move his computer—the uproar from the crowd meant I couldn't be sure what anyone was saying. Leo was balancing his computer on his knees, frowning at the machine, which kept sliding off his legs. He looked up once at Bernie, but blushed and turned instantly back to his laptop.

I managed to work my way to the front and tapped Bernie on the shoulder.

She sprang up, oblivious to the people she bumped into. "Oh, Vic! You're here! *Merci mille fois.* Leo is nervous; it does him good to have friends in the audience. He is brilliant, you understand, but shy."

"That's okay, Bernie—you have enough energy for two. Or sixteen, for that matter."

I found a chair near the back, behind the white-haired woman I'd spoken to after the previous meeting. Nashita, that was her name.

From the snatches of talk around me, excitement over Lydia Zamir appeared greater than interest in Gifford Taggett and the lake. Landfill and federal guidelines weren't as gripping as learning that a singer with a tragic history had been camping nearby.

I tried picking out strands of conversation: people were vehement about the quality of Zamir's music—some thought she'd been a talented and fearless artist, others that they were tired of so-called artists hammering their audiences with political messages. Still others were focused on Metra's responsibility for this morning's near-tragedy.

"They should never have let her camp out underneath the tracks to begin with," a white man on Nashita's right harrumphed.

Nashita rolled her eyes. "Marshall, get a grip: the streets are the city's responsibility. They're nothing to do with Metra."

On my own left, an older African-American man said that Hyde Park–Kenwood was an exclusionary community. He wasn't surprised no one helped out Lydia Zamir before they knew she'd been famous. "This neighborhood likes to think they're full of liberals but they're as bigoted and hostile to the homeless as any other place in America."

Mona Borsa couldn't figure out how to get on top of the chaos. She paced up and down, whipping her pointer against her jeans. Not even her teammates were watching her.

Nashita shook her head. "Mona's screaming herself into an early grave. And Curtis is just as bad." She looked at her wrist. "I'm giving them ten more minutes before I take off."

Someone in the lobby had handed me a SLICK flyer, which identified Mona's brother officers. Curtis Murchison was the gaveller. The man with the charts and maps was Simon Lensky. Along with Mona, they were the elected unpaid managers of SLICK. The flyer also thanked Leo Prinz for his stellar work digitizing SLICK's papers this summer.

I read about SLICK's activities: a youth sailing program, group swims at the Sixty-third Street beach, fishing trips from the Thirty-first Street harbor, beach and shoreline cleanup days. The trio rubbed me the wrong way, but I had to respect their commitment to the part of the city I treasure most.

Leo finally grew exasperated enough to move some of Simon's documents away from the table in front of him. The older man glared and ostentatiously picked up the pages one at a time to lay them into a squared-off stack.

I was calculating how much more time to give Coop when crowd attention abruptly shifted to the back of the room: Gifford Taggett had arrived. I'd never seen the park superintendent in person, but his horsey face was prominently displayed in every park building I ever went into. He had thinning reddish hair combed severely back over his ears; that and the horsey face made him look a bit like England's Prince Philip. The superintendent was flanked by a young African-American woman and a Latinx man—more subtle than wearing a T-shirt proclaiming TAGGETT SUPPORTS DIVERSITY.

Mona and Curtis applauded enthusiastically. Audience members joined in, muted, wary, but conversations quieted. Taggett grinned easily at the crowd, shook hands with people on the aisle, stopped to talk to a few who apparently knew the superintendent well enough for him to linger with them, laughing and buffeting their shoulders before moving on.

A couple of older men were also with Taggett. They had the look of money, even though one, who might have been in his seventies, was wearing baggy khakis and a faded T-shirt. The other was about ten years younger and could have posed for the *Wall Street Journal*'s Off Duty section: what the wealthy board member wears to community meetings in the summer—linen jacket over open-necked raw silk shirt.

There were a couple of empty seats in the middle of a row. The Off Duty man tapped Taggett on the arm and gestured at the chairs. Taggett gave a command to his support team, who grimaced at one another but buffeted their way across people's knees to carry the chairs to where the two men directed them—along a wall so they had an easy escape route if they became bored.

Taggett leaned against the wall where the moneymen were sitting, his acolytes still on either side, but standing upright: acolytes cannot slouch in public. Several cops followed Taggett and stationed themselves near the main exit.

Mona got things going, although not quickly: she needed Taggett to know how hard she, Simon, and Curtis were working, and so she detailed the sailing and fishing and cleanup and youth sports SLICK had accomplished recently. Most people, including the moneymen, were focused on their devices, but Taggett, good politician, led the audience in applause.

Finally, Mona turned the meeting over to Leo, to complete the presentation that Coop's arrival had cut short the last time. "Since we're graced with Superintendent Taggett's presence tonight, we thought we should look at the whole picture before we vote on the proposal."

Leo stood but didn't move away from the table—he'd learned that he couldn't hold the computer, push the PowerPoint buttons, and use the handheld mike all at the same time.

Someone dimmed the lights and Leo began flashing images onto the wall at the back of the stage.

He started with a history of the 1930s project that had reshaped the lakefront, when the shoreline was pushed about half a mile to the east. The 1934 World's Fair had been held on the new landfill, South Lake Shore Drive was built on it. Leo had photos and maps, but he was nervous and clicked through them too quickly for us to admire. By the time he put up the slide showing the current plan, I was only half-listening.

Leo flipped through a series of maps and aerial photos—the current lakefront, projected new shore-line, proposed amenities.

The maps included lists. I could read the headers, but the contents were too small to make out, especially since the paint was peeling on the wall being used as a projection screen. Current park use, anticipated use with the new beach, estimated completion time, estimated costs.

Leo was flipping through the slides so fast that Taggett's friend in the rumpled T-shirt said, "Slow down, son—this isn't the Indy Five Hundred."

The audience laughed, but the criticism flustered Leo. He dropped the laser pointer he'd been using. When he stooped to pick it up, he banged his head underneath the table. Some of Simon's papers floated off the table; several landed in the audience, which caused renewed laughter, especially when Simon swore and demanded that the presentation stop until he recovered his papers.

Bernie jumped from her chair and gathered the pages to hand to Leo. When he took them, the top one caught his eye and he stared at it, puzzled. He bent over Simon, holding the document in front of the older man, but we couldn't hear what either man said. Curtis and Mona came over to look at the document.

The mike picked up Leo's voice saying it wasn't in the presentation. Mona started an impatient reply, but Simon cut across her, saying it was a preliminary report. "We've only asked you to show what we know is in the formal plan."

Taggett noticed the audience getting restive over the interruption. "Let's take a breather." He had the kind of booming baritone that silences a room. "Son, you've done a great job. I'm impressed and I'm sure everyone else is, too, but why don't we let the audience get some questions in."

A man near the front stood and demanded to know about environmental impact studies. Curtis slammed down his gavel, but Taggett said, with apparent good humor, "Good question. These are early days, and we all know we have a lot more work to do, including getting the feds on board with us."

The community benefits people wanted guarantees about jobs for local residents; Taggett said he was in active conversations with Fourth and Fifth Ward aldermen. Someone talked about property being flipped along Lake Park north of Forty-seventh Street. The moneymen looked up from their devices at that. Taggett said he'd heard rumors but no one could show him hard data, and the men returned to their screens. I wondered if they might themselves be property flippers.

A lot of people demanded a budget: property taxes had quadrupled in the last decade and taxpayers were fed up.

"I'm glad you raised that point tonight," Taggett said, "because we've been working with some of the top economists in the world on this proposal. They've looked at the potential for new markets in the city and realize, as many of us do, that the South Side is underserved in every way. The fact that these economists are connected to the University of Chicago has not biased them in favor of putting this project in their own backyard."

He paused for laughter, which arrived on cue.

"Larry Nieland's opinions carry just a little weight around the world, or at least the king of Sweden thinks so."

A reference to Nieland's Nobel Prize got another laugh, but also a respectful round of applause.

Taggett finished with another laugh line: "I'm not going to try to use the language of a University of Chicago–trained economist—they talk about elasticity and I think about my twelve-year-old's basketball shorts falling around his ankles. But Larry can answer those questions and more besides. Why don't you come up and field a few?"

Nieland moved to stand in front of the stage. He was the older of the moneymen, the one in the rumpled clothes. Mona rushed over to give him the handheld mike.

"I've been an adviser on a number of projects in places like Santiago and Montevideo where we've had great success putting together public-private partnerships. It doesn't seem right to me, as a Chicagoan, that South America should have all the benefit of that kind of development. I've been glad to offer input to Superintendent Taggett on some of the possibilities for infusing private money into public works."

"Does that mean a new beach will be a private place?" a woman in the middle of the room cried out. "Why are we paying taxes if you're going to turn it over to some private company?"

Nieland said, "Private investors get the benefit of a development that makes the city a more attractive place to live and do business. That brings jobs."

"But a development," someone else called. "That sounds like buildings, not a beach."

Nieland smiled, an easy grandfatherly smile that went with his shock of white curls. "Forgive my academic language. We're helping Superintendent Taggett develop a plan, that's all. Those of you who've read my work know I don't believe that a government knows the best thing to do with its citizens' money; that's why we're asking private investors to step forward."

Taggett clapped enthusiastically. "Let's get back to the things we all came here to discuss, namely a new beach to replace the slippery rocks. No matter how many DANGER signs your Park District puts up—and we are not a remote government, we're out there every day trying to keep your parks safe and clean—people will keep swimming from the rocks. They slip and fall, break hips and heads. We're here to fix that."

Taggett nodded at Mona, who told Leo to put up the map of the proposed new beach.

"Who's the guy with Nieland?" I asked Nashita. "He looks too well-dressed to be another academic."

"I don't know," Nashita said. "But he looks as though he gets rich on private-public partnerships."

10
Democracy in Action

I wasn't getting anything from the meeting, except a crick in my neck from straining to see Leo and Bernie in the front of the room. I texted Bernie that I was heading home. When the lights went down, I threaded my way along the aisle to the exit.

Coop was entering just as I reached the door. The lights were still dimmed; he didn't see me at first.

"Have you come to attack poor young Leo again?" I said. "Shouldn't you pick on targets closer to your own weight class?"

"You?" he hissed. "What are you doing here?"

"I was hoping to see you. Wondering if Lydia was okay, wherever you've stashed her."

He slammed a fist into the palm of his other hand.

"I don't know where she is. If you do, don't play games with me."

"You didn't know she was at Provident?" I whispered.

"Yes, but the place is lousy with cops; I figured until they were ready to discharge her no one could get at her. When I got back there, she'd disappeared."

"They told me a man had taken her from her gurney when they were waiting to transport her to Stroger for an MRI," I said. "That wasn't you?"

"It goddamn wasn't me! Mona Borsa and her team of goons got the city to collect her and put her into a locked ward."

He started toward the stage, but I grabbed his arm. "Use your head, Coop: if that were the case, there'd be a trail showing who'd picked her up and where they'd gone."

"Then this is worse! They sent someone to kidnap her."

He tried to break away from me, but I tightened my grip. "Oh, please! Mona and Curtis can't figure out how to run a community meeting. They couldn't kidnap an eggplant from a shopping cart."

Coop gave a reluctant smile. "But in that case—you don't have her, they don't have her—who took her?"

He'd calmed down enough that I dropped his arm.

"I have no idea, but it's way past time to involve the cops."

"Don't call the fucking cops. They won't help—they're in bed with your pal Mona."

"Coop—what's your last name?"

He curled his lip in a parody of a smile. "Maybe it's Coop."

"Cops want *you* for something you're trying to keep private?"

"I try to stay private, which is easy to do if you don't randomly distribute your personal information."

"If you're trying to stay private, then you should lower your public profile," I said dryly. "What's your connection to Lydia Zamir? Do you know the Palurdo family? Is that why you're so protective of her?"

"Oh, mind your own damned business!"

The last sentence came out as a shout. Everyone in the room turned to look, including Bernie. When she saw me with Coop, she grinned wickedly and mimed the swing of a hockey stick, but Leo reacted in alarm. He called something to Bernie, apparently a plea for support. She climbed onto the stage. After a brief argument—I guessed she was urging Leo to show some spine and confront Coop—she shrugged and let him lead her through a rear exit.

Taggett, who'd watched the minidrama in amusement, said, "This is what happens when you spend too much time on your computer—real people frighten you." People laughed again, and Taggett added, "That's why we need to get our lakefront more usable—entice kids like young Leo there out into the fresh air."

Coop eyed the stage, but when he looked at Taggett, he saw the cops, and dropped back. I left as Mona tried to resume the presentation. However, Leo had taken his computer with him. She tried to get Simon to show his map of the proposed beach project, but the audience was restive. Nieland and his buddy put their devices in their pockets and got to their feet.

When I left the building, I saw the dog Bear tied to a bike rack. He looked at me mournfully as I passed, as if he, too, wanted some peace and quiet.

"Not on this side of Jordan, dog," I said. "We have to stay on our toes, take our lumps, which in this case means ignoring your boy's wishes and going to the police."

Lenora Pizzello, the sergeant I'd met when Bernie was picked up, was on duty when I got to the Wentworth station.

"Ms. Warshawski." She came out of her cubbyhole to greet me when the desk sergeant sent me back. "Please tell me your niece isn't tearing up the South Side again."

I didn't correct her about our relationship, just said, "I hope not. Although this is about the homeless woman at the center of Bernie's fracas. I don't know if you saw the news?"

"Oh, the woman under the viaduct. I hadn't made the connection. There was some commotion this morning, right?" She called up the story on her phone. "Right, got it. Lydia Zamir. She was taken off by ambulance to Provident. Don't tell me she died."

"I can't tell you anything. That's why I'm here—she's disappeared." I gave her a thumbnail of what I'd learned at the hospital. "The guy with the dog—you said your patrols know him—I thought he'd taken her but I just saw him and he says he has no idea where she is."

The sergeant made a phone call, apparently to the 911 response center, asking for any information from Provident.

"What in sweet Jesus's name are they doing at that hospital?" Pizzello demanded into the phone. "Someone snatched in broad daylight from their transport waiting area and no one thought it was worth phoning in?"

Pizzello turned back to me. "Okay, I'm going to turn you over to one of my officers to make a statement—everything you know about the missing woman, and the guy with the dog."

What I knew took about fifteen minutes to report, but getting it all down, repeating it for another officer, double-checking with Provident, questioning my involvement, all that took time. One of the officers was young and knew some of Zamir's songs; he even played "The Swan" for the older cop.

Of course, they wanted to know why I cared—I must have a client; surely I didn't randomly spend my time looking for people without collecting a paycheck?

I thought of Peter's words. "Just trying to heal the world. Me and Wonder Woman. I'm also trying to make sure my goddaughter isn't involved, or that someone doesn't try to make her a fall gal."

"She has an alibi for the time that the Zamir woman was grabbed?"

I silently cursed myself: using Bernie as a cover story for Murray had made her interesting to the cops, who like to go for the simplest answer first. "She's coaching softball with seventeen ten- and eleven-year-olds in Humboldt Park," I said. "Anyway, the hospital people say it was a man who carried Zamir from the gurney; no way would you think Bernie Fouchard was a man."

I showed them a picture of Bernie and me at the start of her summer coaching stint. I have a good four inches on her. The cops agreed she didn't look much like a man, certainly not one big enough to carry an adult woman, even an emaciated one, from a gurney and out of the hospital.

When they finally let me go, I drove by the viaduct one last time, but there wasn't any trace of Lydia. It was close to ten now. Noisy teens were crowding the bridge that led across Lake Shore Drive, drunks were sitting on benches around the parking lot on the east side of the tracks. A few hearty joggers and cyclists threaded their way through the mix.

While I waited at the light to turn onto the Drive, I thought I saw Coop and Bear head up the track into the Wildlife Corridor. The light changed before I could get a good look and I drove on, too tired for more investigating.

Bernie called while I was still on the road, wanting to rehash the events of the night. Leo and she had gone out for a drink, but they'd quarreled over his refusal to confront Coop. Bernie was at her own apartment in Evanston, oscillating between annoyance with Leo and a desire to go beat up Coop on his behalf.

"Why not let things sort themselves out?" I said. "The law of unintended consequences will come into play if you go after Coop yourself. By the way, what was on that paper that you picked up, the one that got the SLICK officers so wound up?"

"Just more drawings of the lakefront. I didn't study

it. We fought over that, also. He was wanting to do something about the foyer, something about the drawing, and that mattered more to him than this Coop. Or even me."

I commiserated with her but changed the subject to the girls in Humboldt Park she was working with for the second half of the season.

She gave me an enthusiastic rundown and signed off just as I reached my exit.

Murray was parked in front of my building. He unfolded himself from his Mercedes and sketched a wave.

"News?" He came up the walk to me, since I didn't bother to wait for him.

"Are you going to be that kind of client, Murray? Bugging your detective for up-to-the-minute reports?"

"Maybe," he said. "I've had seven messages from various members of the Global executive team in the last seven hours, which is seven more than I've had in my life. Thought I'd share the stress."

I stopped with my key in the front-door lock. "Why do they care so much?"

He gave a sardonic laugh. "Twenty-four hours ago, Lydia's 'Savage' was downloaded forty-three times. Today it topped fourteen thousand. Lydia's agent is smelling gold through one nostril and blood through the other. All at once, Lydia's a valuable property again, and visions of Bitcoins are dancing in her agent's head. Spinning Earth is ready to do a deal, but they need a warm body to hold the pen. Everyone thinks I'm hiding Lydia to help with a bidding war, or to get my share of the gate, or whatever."

Spinning Earth was Global's music and streaming subsidiary.

"Since when did you imagine that angst in the executive suite would goad me into action?" I said. "I'm not interested in their woes. I took this case as a favor to you, but if you're going to hound-dog me, I will resign."

"Sorry, Warshawski. I'm not a nervous person as a rule, but the relentlessness of the queries has made me break out in hives."

"There's calamine for that," I said dryly.

Murray pressed his lips together to swallow an angry retort.

I relented. "I can't tell you more than you know yourself: Lydia disappeared from Provident. She was never formally admitted, so there's not a paper trail. She either walked off, wearing nothing but a hospital gown, or a man lifted her from the gurney and carried her away. I lean toward scenario two but I have no proof of anything. I'll keep looking, but you can't rag me—it doesn't help."

"Yeah, I know. It's just that little matter of a pay-check. I like to eat."

"You're wedded to this entertainment behemoth," I said soberly. "I know at our age new jobs aren't that easy to find, but you're a good—make that exceptional—investigative journalist. I hate you wasting your gifts on soft targets."

He looked at me for a long moment. His expression seemed despairing, but it might have been a trick of the single bulb above the outer door.

11
Generation Gap

While Murray and I were talking, the dogs had started to bark. I got the outer door open as quickly as I could, but not before Donna Lutas emerged from her apartment, hands on hips, ready for battle.

"Hey, Donna," I said. "You a Lydia Zamir fan? Does your team at Devlin & Wickham sing 'Savage' to psych yourselves up before you head into court?"

She looked blank for a moment, long enough for me to open Mr. Contreras's door. The dogs jumped on me, squeaking hysterically. Behind me I heard Lutas say something about the condo board, but I figured my best strategy was not to turn around.

My neighbor ushered me inside. "Dogs heard you talking to Ryerson out there. Mitch didn't like it. Peppy neither, but Mitch was worse."

I smiled appreciatively. Mr. Contreras resents almost every man who's ever been part of my life, but for some reason, Murray gets his goat more than most.

"You're going to get me evicted," I said, scratching Mitch behind his ears. He grinned, sure we were all doing the right thing.

"What's Ryerson doing here, anyway?" Mr. Contreras demanded. "You ain't throwing over that digging guy for him, are you?"

"Nope. I'm helping Murray look for Lydia Zamir."

"Oh, the singer gal." Mr. Contreras's paper is the *Sun-Times*, but after Coop's furious visit, he'd read Murray's story in the *Herald-Star*. "They showed it on the nine o'clock news, her being chased by the TV cameras. Could have got her killed. That's Ryerson, not thinking of anything but his own fame and glory."

I didn't argue but switched the subject to my own futile search for Zamir. I focused on the things Mr. Contreras would enjoy most, like the hospital not noticing Zamir was leaving in time to stop her. I told him about Bernie's infatuation with Leo Prinz, and her disappointment that Prinz didn't share her warlike spirit.

Mr. Contreras was sure, sight unseen, that Leo wasn't good enough for Bernie. Of course, not even Prince Harry would have made the grade with him.

When I'd taken the dogs for a last jog around the

block, I logged on to my home computer to do a little research.

I started with Larry Nieland, the Nobel Prize–winning economist. He had a joint academic appointment at Chicago and the Pontificia Universidad Católica de Chile. That seemed odd, but when I fished around for more information, I saw that Chicago had actually helped build the Chilean economics school back in the 1950s. There seemed to be a lot of back-and-forth between the two universities, with Chicago-trained economists forming a big part of the Pinochet government policy advisers in the 1960s and 1970s.

Nieland was doing a postdoc at the Santiago campus when Pinochet came to power. He now owned an apartment in the hills above the Chilean city of Valparaíso, as well as his condo in Chicago.

Like many business and economics professors, Nieland sat on a number of company boards both in the States and in South America. He had his own closely held company, Capital Unleashed, which "offered investment advice and support to a curated list of clients." He could probably have afforded a better shirt than the one he'd worn to the meeting.

Some of his money went into sailing. In Chicago, he kept a ninety-foot yacht that had been built for one of our robber barons in the 1870s. He also had a modern racing yacht, which he'd entered in several ocean races.

My beloved city is hovering near bankruptcy. How much were they spending on Nieland's carefully curated advice for the lakefront? I wished I could get Murray involved, to help ask some of these questions, but I didn't trust his discretion these days.

I turned my mind to Lydia Zamir's disappearance, which was a more urgent worry: I needed to find people who knew her. I looked up her agent, Hermione Smithson, whose office was in Boston, near the New England Conservatory. Most of Smithson's clients appeared to be classically trained. I hadn't heard of any of them, but when I checked their disc and streaming sales, only three had significant numbers.

I suppose Smithson got a commission from concert bookings, but she was not a young woman; she'd turned seventy last year. If Lydia Zamir's career was coming back to life, Smithson would want a piece of that action.

The next morning, Zamir's disappearance had made the national news feed, while the footage of her on the Metra tracks appeared on all social media platforms. Photos of Provident Hospital purported to show how easy it was for a person to be kidnapped without anyone noticing—someone had uploaded a picture of a

Chicago cop in a hospital waiting room, bent over his device. Whether it was Provident or Northwestern, whether it was from yesterday or five years ago, was impossible to tell.

After I'd checked the overnight reports of dead bodies and called the South Side hospitals to see whether a semistarving Jane Doe had come in, I phoned Zamir's parents in Eudora, Kansas. They knew about the dramatic chase along the Metra tracks, thanks to a helpful neighbor.

"That nice reporter called to tell us she'd disappeared from the hospital, but Lydia hasn't tried to reach us."

"That must be stressful," I murmured.

"Oh, you get used to it." She sighed. "Looking back, I don't think we were ever as close as some of my friends are with their daughters. I always hoped she'd move back, start a family, but she wanted to do something big that got her a lot of attention. One of her teachers called her an ardent spirit, but I thought she just acted, well, I hate to say this about my own child, but, well, conceited. And after she got involved with that Mexican, she paid even less attention to her father and me."

"I thought he was American," I said. "With a father from Chile."

Debbie Zamir ignored that. "All he ever talked about were those people trying to cross the border into our country. He never cared about hardworking people who are already here. That doesn't sound American to me. And then Lydia would go on and on about how Hector unleashed a well of creativity in her. His books were the most exciting thing she'd ever read. I tried to read them, I really did, but they seemed like nonsense to me. All about Indians appearing in visions and talking about plastic in the drinking water.

"It was like Hector hypnotized Lydia. She started writing songs about savages, and the lyrics were crude, not like the beautiful pieces she used to play for her recitals. If I tried to comment on them, she'd get angry and say 'you have to face the truth.' Well, she wouldn't face the truth: all that political agitation did was expose her to violence."

I was digging my nails in my palms hard enough to draw blood, trying not to shout at Zamir's mother. "Seeing someone die—anyone—it's terrible. And when you see your lover dead by shooting—unbearable. She needed help."

"We tried to take care of Lydia after the shooting. Our doctor referred her to a very good psychiatrist in Kansas City, who prescribed Haldol and Ativan for her. She threw out the pills; she said they kept her from remembering Hector."

To change the subject, I asked who Lydia's Kansas friends were, but Debbie Zamir couldn't give me any names. Lydia had left for her conservatory training twenty years ago and hadn't stayed in touch with childhood friends.

"Where did she go when she left you after the shooting?" I finally asked.

"She took off for Chicago and moved in with Hector's mother. We couldn't believe it when we saw the news reports that she was living in the streets. I was sure she was with the mother."

I asked Ms. Zamir if Lydia had known Arthur Morton, the killer, before the massacre.

"What do you mean, did she know him?"

"Did she ever mention his name? Did she ever worry about him stalking her?"

"I keep telling you: after she left for the East Coast she never told me her secrets. And certainly not for the few weeks she stayed here after the shootings. She was too strung out to talk about anything. If she'd met the boy who did the shooting, I wouldn't have known."

My head was starting to hurt from the effort of dealing with her mix of truculence, hurt feelings, and anger over her daughter's refusal to conform. "What about a man named Coop? He looked out for your daughter while she was living under the railroad tracks."

"Coop? Like a chicken coop? There weren't any boys with a name like that in her school, at least not that I ever heard of."

"He might have come to the trial," I suggested.

She was silent for a beat. "I didn't go. Maybe I should have, maybe it would have made Lydia less agitated later. I thought that immigrant, that Hector, was a bad influence on my girl, and—and it didn't break my heart that he was dead."

The words were aggressive but there was an undercurrent of remorse that kept me from pouncing on her. There must be something I could ask, something Lydia's mother could tell me, but her hurt feelings and her random accusations made it hard for me to think. I gave her my own phone number and email address and hung up, massaging my sore temples.

After that conversation, I wasn't in the best mood to question more strangers, but it was important to finish the list of people who had known Lydia. I called Hermione Smithson, the agent.

Smithson's receptionist said that "Madame" had no interest in talking to detectives. I explained my mission; after a few minutes on hold, I was put through to Madame.

When I explained that I was looking for Zamir, Smithson demanded to know my interest.

"I was hired to find her."

"By whom?"

"My clients appreciate my discretion, ma'am. You know that she has disappeared, right? I was hoping she'd been in touch with you."

"A reporter called me yesterday asking for her. If you're trying to help the media avoid responsibility for her disappearance, I have no interest in talking to you."

"I'm not trying to help anyone avoid responsibility for anything," I said. "Ms. Zamir's disappearance is a big news story. That's reviving interest in her work, isn't it?"

"She is getting some long overdue attention," Smithson said cautiously.

"Do you think some unscrupulous person might be holding her hostage to drive up her commercial value?" I said.

There was silence at the other end for a long beat before Smithson said, "I'm in discussions with various recording companies. If she's disappeared she's less valuable—a company could get her old releases, but not any new content."

"Have you seen or talked to her lately? She isn't capable of new content."

"Are you a trained psychiatrist and musician as well as a detective?" Smithson mocked. "A few months in a rehabilitation facility with the right medications and the right therapists can make a difference in a hurry. I've seen other musicians come back from farther down."

"You wouldn't be holding her, then, would you, to drive up Spinning Earth or Deutsche Grammophon's bids?"

"How dare you? That's a complete outrage. Whatever your name is, don't bother to call back." She hung up.

Complete outrage? Maybe, but not beyond belief.

I looked up the piano teacher Murray had talked to, a Professor Szydanski, Gershon Szydanski. Of course he had seen the stories about Lydia. He was also fascinated by her success as a singer-songwriter.

Apparently she hadn't shown much interest in composition when she was a student. Szydanski had looked up her record; she'd majored in piano, minored in voice, had taken a few composition courses but hadn't produced any memorable material.

"Most of our students are like Lydia," he added. "They are gifted, they go on to have good careers as performers and teachers, but we don't often see their names in the music press. When they get national or international recognition, we're pretty excited."

He went on in that vein for several minutes; I finally interrupted to ask if he knew where she was, or if he could give me names of New England students she'd been close to who might help out.

"Sorry, Ms. Warshawski, but she graduated at least fifteen years ago. However, even when they're students here, we don't like to be too involved in their private lives."

Before hanging up, I asked if he knew Hermione Smithson. He laughed. "She's a fixture here, as much as we all are, I suppose. She puts down a seine and sees which students she can fish up. I guess that's unkind. Hermione doesn't cross a legal or ethical line, but she grabs rights from naive performers that they'd be better off retaining."

"Lydia's street value went up about three hundred percent after those camera crews chased her along the train tracks. I don't see any way that Smithson could be involved in her disappearance—the logistics are formidable—but she's still benefiting from the drama."

"Oh, my God, I have given you a totally false impression of Hermione if you think that." Szydanski was alarmed. "She's a thorough New Englander: you know, the old-school model of morality and rectitude and so on. She'd never collude in a kidnapping."

We finished on that note.

I'd put off trying to reach Hector Palurdo's mother for as long as I could, but there wasn't anyone else to talk to. I started by looking for background on the family.

The broad details were easy to find from Hector's Wikipedia page: Palurdo's father, Jacobo, had fled to Chicago from Chile in the 1970s, about a year after Pinochet came to power. His mother, Elisa, taught English as a second language at one of the community colleges. Jacobo had taken a class with her. One thing led to another. They'd married. Hector was their only child.

Elisa was still listed as a member of the language faculty at the same college where she'd taught Jacobo, but the departmental secretary said she was on long-term leave. She absolutely would not give me a phone number for Ms. Palurdo. I could send the secretary an email and she would forward it.

I tried to find her through other avenues. After her son's murder, Elisa started a blog called "Death Trail." A year ago, she'd gathered the essays into a book, but she'd also kept up the blog. I skimmed the summary on one of the online book sites.

At first, Elisa had written about mass shootings in the States, tracking the guns where she could, listing the names of the dead, the families left behind. She'd started with her own son's death, and the lives of the other grieving families. After about a year, she'd expanded her coverage to the Americas, and then she started counting dead children in Syria, Yemen, and Sudan.

She'd become a target of the hate fringe that finds exposés of gun violence a visceral threat. I guess that wasn't a surprise, but it was thoroughly depressing.

It also explained why it was hard to dig up her home address or any phone numbers. It took me two hours and a lot of fees to private search engines, but, in the age of Google and Apple, unless you've never used a credit card or had a bank account, you are ultimately traceable. Elisa Palurdo lived on Edgebrook Terrace in the Forest Glen neighborhood on the city's northwest side.

12

Quicksand in the Valley of Regret

Technically, Forest Glen is part of Chicago, but when I drive through the streets that wind between the Chicago River and a forest preserve, I feel as though I've stumbled onto a film set for Norman Rockwell's America: old trees shade well-kept homes. Many are standard Chicago lots with small houses, but just as many are big enough to be called mansions. A lot of the city's power brokers have homes here—it's sometimes called the City Hall annex.

Maybe if Donna Lutas made the condo board evict me, I could move here. The houses are about two hundred thousand above my price point, but perhaps someone in the city, maybe Parks Superintendent Taggett, needed a live-in investigator.

Although Elisa Palurdo lived in a small brick home, she had plenty of security herself. The lot was covered with motion sensors. She had a dog who didn't bark but growled with credible menace when I rang the bell. No one answered. I rang a second time, then noticed the security camera over the door.

"My name is V.I. Warshawski." I spoke to the camera's live red eye. "I am trying to find Lydia Zamir, who disappeared from Provident Hospital yesterday morning. If you'd call my cell phone, I'll explain why I'm looking for her. If you know where she is, I will not betray her confidence. My website lists references."

I stuck my hand into my handbag, slowly, so any watchers could see I wasn't reaching for a weapon, and slowly extracted a business card, which I put through the mail slot, to the dog's increased rage. I felt its breath on my fingers and quickly removed my hand.

"I'll drive a few blocks away to keep people from paying attention to my car or your house. I'll wait half an hour in case you're willing to speak to me."

As I drove away, it seemed as though my sardonic thought about the parks superintendent had conjured him: a block from the Palurdo home, he emerged from one of the great houses and headed toward a black Lexus SUV. I stopped to see what my tax dollars were paying for. The SUV included a chauffeur, who sprang from the driver's seat to open both rear doors. Taggett paused with one hand on the door and another on his device.

In a moment a man whose silver hair matched his summer suit came out of the house and strolled to the car. The chauffeur tucked the two inside and headed out. I hadn't seen the second man's face clearly, but I was pretty sure he was the Off Duty guy who'd been with Larry Nieland last night at the SLICK meeting.

I parked in a grocery store lot, where I read some of Elisa's blog posts from the time of her son's death.

I watched my son die. Not in person. I, his mother, was not there to cradle him in my arms as the Virgin could do for her son. No, I watched him die a thousand times. On television, on the Internet, on my phone. His death was a titillating circus-show for the world.

He and his partner, Lydia, were speaking and singing to raise money for the land and the people who work on it when a man opened fire and murdered him, along with sixteen other mothers' children. Fifty-two others suffered serious wounds.

Thirteen months after his death, I can write of the pain in my heart that won't go away. I can write of the pain of the other families. I can write of those wounded by those bullets. I can write of the damage to the mind and voice of Hector's nightingale, Lydia, who lost her voice. All these things I can write, but instead I will tell you the story of the AR-15 that the murderer used.

She went on to detail a visit to the Orestes factory in Utah where the gun that killed her son was manufactured. She followed it to its first buyer, and then managed to trace it through several online sales: she was a dogged and skillful investigator.

I was engrossed, reading about the day the killer—whom she refused to call by name; *I will not add to his quest for glory*—when my phone rang: blocked caller ID, but it was Elisa Palurdo on the other end.

"Why are you looking for Lydia?" she asked, after we established that I was me and she was Elisa.

"To make sure she's safe. If I can see her and know that she's where she wants to be, and that she's not abused or exploited, I will protect her privacy. If not, I will try to get her to people or a place where she feels safe."

We both knew Elisa wouldn't have called if she

wasn't willing to see me. After a few more perfunctory questions, she told me to meet her at a branch of the public library on Devon Avenue.

Palurdo arrived on foot about five minutes after I pulled into a parking space. She was in her sixties, with gray hair piled onto her head by a wide clip. The early photos I'd found of her had shown a striking woman with humor lines at the corners of her eyes. Those had gone. She looked about warily when I approached her, and gave a perfunctory smile that did nothing to ease the deep lines around her mouth.

"We are reasonably safe here," Palurdo said. "Schools are the most dangerous locations for shootings in America. Then malls and places of work and worship. So far libraries have mostly been exempt. Not completely."

She led me into the building, nodding and exchanging greetings with staff at the main counter. I followed her to an alcove that had a view of the front door. A woman sitting on a bench there was frowning over her phone while a toddler grabbed at her pant leg, whining in a soft miserable voice—the child wasn't expecting attention.

Elisa took two padded chairs and turned them so that we had a semblance of privacy. "Every time I see something like that, I want to shake the mom—or dad—and say, 'Look at your child, you don't know how precious your time with that child is.' I remember all the times I didn't pay attention to Hector when he was little, all those 'Mommy, Mommy, Mommy' moments that drive you mad—and after your child is dead, you think—what would it have cost me to be patient for twenty seconds?"

"I never had children, but I have had plenty of impatient moments. And regrets. My mother died when I was sixteen and I have all those regrets of disappointing her—when she was alive and even now, when I think of her dreams for me. The valley of regrets can pull you down into its quicksand bottom: it's best not to linger there."

Palurdo produced her unhappy smile again. "That could be a good title for an article—'Quicksand in the Valley of Regret.' Lydia—I have worries about her, as well—especially after seeing the news."

I asked the last time Palurdo had seen or spoken to Lydia.

"Maybe eight or nine months ago." Palurdo frowned, thinking back. "She had come completely unraveled. She spent a few months with me—she'd been to her parents and felt they didn't or couldn't grasp the magnitude of the horror she'd been through. She was standing behind him, you know, behind him on the stage, and his blood was all over her.

"When she was here, she was nervous, angry, overwhelmed with grief. All understandable, but it was hard to share the house with her because I myself was barely putting one foot in front of the other. My husband had died eighteen months before Hector's murder and to lose both of them—!"

"You were married a long time?"

She nodded bleakly. "Forty years. He came as an immigrant who spoke no English, and he was always shy, even a bit fearful. When Hector started speaking in public about asylum seekers, and about the disappeared in Chile, Jacobo was angry in case it brought attention to us."

"From the U.S. government?" I asked.

"No, from Chile's, even though by then, Pinochet had been out of power for years."

"Was your husband a political refugee?"

"He was a welder. And never political. But you couldn't live under the regime without developing fear, I guess." She sighed.

I asked how Jacobo had died—wondering if there were some trail of murder that led from Chile to him to his son.

Elisa burst my conspiracy bubble. "Coronary. He was a heavy smoker. I always told him cigarettes were more lethal than the remnants of Pinochet's army." She gave a small smile, the remnant of intimate moments.

"After Jacobo died, Hector wanted to find his Chilean roots. He had studied Chilean history in college but he became obsessed with it. He wanted dual citizenship, which Jacobo had always opposed: my husband came here without papers. He became a U.S. citizen during the Reagan amnesty, but he was still afraid of deportation if Hector came to official notice, either here or in Santiago. After spending time in Chile, he became obsessed with land reform, first there, and then he began raging against land use in the United States as well. Lydia only encouraged it in him, which annoyed me. It's why they were taking part in that event in Kansas."

"I didn't know the Kansas thing was about Chilean émigrés."

"It wasn't. It was about protecting the land but also helping people who work on the land. Hector thought the big agricultural companies were as exploitive and damaging to workers and the environment as the hereditary landowners in Chile." Her eyes pinched shut, holding tears at bay. "And then an ordinary, nonpolitical mass murderer killed him."

"Do you think Hector would have been so passionate about these issues without Lydia?" I asked.

She paused. "I wanted to say, no, never, but the truth is they wound each other up. And then—it was his heritage, after all. It troubled him that we never traveled as a family to Chile, for example. We often took vacations in Mexico, but Jacobo said Chile was filled with unhappy memories. His parents were dead; poor people often die young, and his only sister— he came to Chicago like my own grandparents did—looking for a better life.

"My mother hated me marrying a foreigner and one with no college degree. I suppose that's why I could sympathize with Lydia—her mother saw Hector as a foreigner, a Communist, someone who was leading her daughter astray." Elisa smiled sadly, twisting the wedding ring she still wore. "That's why I put up with Lydia's extreme emotions for a long time. She didn't seem to realize I was in mourning, too. We might have ridden it out, if only she hadn't been called to testify at the killer's trial."

The Kansas state police had caught Arthur Morton fairly quickly. He was hiding in the hills near Ellsworth, Kansas, where he'd built a makeshift cabin and had stored his cache of rifles, guns, ammunition, and bullet-resistant clothing, along with food and water.

"Did you ever think Lydia knew Arthur Morton, or anyone in his family, before the killings?" I ventured.

Palurdo's mouth tightened in anger. "You know this kind of slaughter is meaningless. The FBI, their forensic psychologists want to dig into the killers' motives, but that's always superficial. Such people have weapons, they have anger, they find a target. Anyway, if this creature was targeting Lydia he could have killed her easily—she'd flung her body over my son's."

I didn't say anything, but Palurdo laughed derisively. "Oh, you think maybe he wanted Hector out of the way so he could have Lydia? What drove Lydia to the brink was at the trial he was represented by an expensive law firm. They were able to plead his sentence from the death penalty to life in prison. For me, that was—I don't want to say it was okay—but what good would taking his life do? But Lydia—she was confused. She opposed death, she opposed war and senseless slaughter, but they had to restrain her in the courtroom—she tried to attack the killer right there, at his attorney's table."

Elisa Palurdo stopped to take a bottle of water from her handbag and drink. Her face was covered with beads of sweat.

"She screamed that she wanted to pull the heart from his chest with her own fingernails. I—I wouldn't have thought such cries would affect someone capable of that kind of slaughter, but in fact, a week after the sentencing hearing, the killer did commit suicide."

"What? Was he out on bond?"

"In his cell." Palurdo's lips set in a tight line. "I had zero interest in his fate so I can't tell you the how's or if he'd shown signs. All I can tell you is that his death didn't assuage Lydia's anger: she attacked the lawyers. Not physically, mind you, but with emails and letters. She stood outside the building downtown where they have their offices, holding a big cardboard sign. They got a restraining order on her and she tried to stay with me again, but by then—oh, my God, having her here was awful."

"The law firm was here in Chicago?" I interrupted.

"The main office is here. Who knows where the vermin or his family found money to pay those kind of fees."

I asked for the name of the firm, but Elisa couldn't remember it.

"You think she might be hiding in their building, hoping to kill them? This long after the trial?" Her eyebrows rose in skepticism, but then she shrugged. "Anything is possible when everything that anchors you to the planet is taken from you.

"Lydia even destroyed her music. She gave a concert in Hector's memory, and then she took an axe to her favorite guitar and chopped it to bits. 'An axe for the axe,' she said. She made a bonfire of the guitar and her sheet music and sang the Irish ballad 'The Minstrel Boy.' Over and over. She was—it was as if she was skidding in the atmosphere, cloud-surfing. I couldn't persuade her to get medical help. I couldn't persuade her to respect my own grief. She said the medication fogged her mind and made her forget Hector and she never wanted him far from her mind. It was terrible, terrible."

She covered her face with her hands. I didn't try to touch her, just sat quietly. The woman with the whining child had vanished at some point. Another woman approached our space, felt the level of emotion, moved on.

At length Palurdo drank more water and looked up at me, her eyes bleak. "I rented an apartment for her, but I couldn't be around her. And then I found she had moved out, and was living on the streets. Hector had gone to university there. I guess she felt some kind of closeness to him in that neighborhood—I don't know. I went down to try to talk her into moving back to the apartment, or getting medication. By that time she couldn't speak, at least not to me. And now this—" She waved her arms, encompassing the recent drama around Lydia.

"There's nothing I can do to help you find her," she finally said. "She isn't with me. She doesn't have friends here, at least not as far as I know."

"What about Hector's friends?" I asked. "Would she have gone to them?"

Elisa hunched a shoulder, said snappishly that she couldn't possibly know, but eventually gave me the name of a boyhood friend and a college roommate her son had been close to.

I took out my phone and showed her a picture I'd taken of Coop at last night's meeting. "Does he look familiar? I only know him by one name, but he seems heavily invested in Lydia's welfare."

Palurdo took the phone from me and frowned over it. "He showed up at the house one evening. That made me angry, because Lydia had given him my address: she knew I was getting death threats because of my blog posts. I'd stressed to her the need to keep the house a private place."

"Who is he?"

She shook her head. "I don't know. Someone who'd been at the event where Hector was murdered. He had a strange name, Hawk, Bird, something like that."

"Coop," I said.

"Yes, I think that was it. I never knew who he was. Lydia talked to him, but I wasn't part of the conversation. He took off, with a dog that he'd tied to a streetlamp, I remember that. He came another time, but I'd moved Lydia into her apartment by then. I haven't seen him since."

When I got up to leave, I begged her to let me know if she heard from Lydia. Palurdo nodded perfunctorily. She stayed in her seat, rolling the water bottle between her palms, looking at the floor.

13
The Usual Suspects

Arthur Morton had grown up on a ranch in western Kansas, near a town called Salina. In 2009, as the family's debts mounted in the midst of a prolonged drought, they'd been forced into foreclosure. The loss of land that had been in the family since 1869 was too much for Arthur, Senior: the day after the foreclosure, he shot himself.

At his father's death, Arthur had dropped out of high school, drifting from job to job with the big agricultural combines that dominate the state. He'd blamed the family's woes on the usual suspects—Muslims, Jews, gays, feminists. He'd subscribed to websites that fueled his rage, he'd stockpiled weapons.

I thought of Elisa's comment that Hector had been killed by a nonpolitical mass murderer. She'd been thinking of the government-sponsored death squads of Latin America. I wondered if members of Chilean or Guatemalan death squads were ever as politically passionate as someone like Arthur Morton.

His trial had been held in Salina, Kansas. Sometime between the state police finding him and the start of the trial, his public defender had been replaced by a team from the firm of Devlin & Wickham.

I whistled under my breath: Elisa Palurdo had said they were a big firm, but I hadn't been expecting one of the mammoths. Devlin & Wickham routinely charge a hundred fifty dollars for six minutes of their expert advice. How had an indigent ranch hand managed their fees? His mother had been working at a bakery in Salina since her husband's death—not an income that could cover a six- or seven-figure legal bill.

Despite his high-powered counsel, Morton had been found guilty of most of the charges against him—murder, grievous bodily harm, various weapons violations. Morton had been interviewed by multiple psychiatrists, chosen by both defense and offense, and they agreed that he was not mentally incompetent, but that he had been derailed by his life experiences. Lonely and poor, he had been an easy target of the kind of hate messages posted on the dark web.

The jury had taken all this on board; they'd found

him guilty but had recommended he be spared the death penalty. However, between the verdict and the sentencing hearing, he'd been found dead in his cell. He hadn't hanged himself, as I'd assumed, but had overdosed on nicotine patches. Like most states, Kansas had a tobacco-free policy in its prisons. Morton had apparently been a smoker, someone had given him a bunch of patches. Maybe his mother had bribed a guard. Maybe his lawyers had come through for him.

I looked through the list of Devlin & Wickham's partners. I recognized some of the names but didn't know any of them personally. I actually did know someone who worked at Devlin, but it was Donna Lutas, my ground-floor neighbor who thought I was a menace to the condo. Maybe if I promised to move out by Labor Day, she'd go through the company files to find information on Arthur Morton for me—like, had his lawyers smuggled a whole bag of nicotine patches into his cell? And who had paid his legal fees? And why had anyone cared?

I called one of the managing partners and spoke to his administrative assistant. I explained that I'd been hired to find Lydia Zamir.

The voice on the other end became so frosty that I wished I'd put on my parka. "We have nothing to say to you."

I ignored that. "I know Devlin & Wickham had an order of protection against her. Did she come back to your firm in the last day or two? Did you have to call the police?"

The woman put me on hold, which lasted long enough for me to do my hamstring stretches. When she finally returned to the phone, it was to hand me off to the head of Devlin's security team.

We chatted about who I was and what right I had to involve myself in Devlin's private business. "I'm trying to locate Lydia Zamir," I said. "If you can't tell me whether she returned to your building in the last forty-eight hours, it makes me wonder if you kidnapped her from Provident and are holding her someplace where you don't want her found."

The security chief found my suggestion completely outrageous. He also advised me to be careful about committing libel, since Devlin was a firm with a lot of power.

"Slander," I said. "If Devlin doesn't know the difference between libel and slander, they shouldn't be practicing law."

That somehow annoyed him further. He hung up on me, but I called the managing partner's office again.

"The defense that Devlin conducted for Arthur Morton—you did some amazing work there."

"What's your point, Ms. Warshawski?"

"I've handled murder trials," I said. "They are big time eaters and you bill in six-minute segments."

"Many firms do."

"Arthur Morton was technically indigent and had been assigned a public defender when Devlin & Wickham stepped in. I wonder how he came to be a client?"

"We don't discuss our clients' business, Ms. Warshawski. If you've done death penalty pleadings, then you know enough law to understand confidentiality rights."

"Of course," I agreed. "Someone paid those bills. I was wondering who?"

"You cannot seriously imagine we'd share that information with you."

"Just living hopefully," I said. "My other question has to do with your client's death. If you turn me over to the people who actually represented him, then I can ask them. Basically, I'd like to know if they brought him those nicotine patches themselves, or if they, or even his mother, paid a guard to do it for them. I'm betting it was the former, because Saline County wouldn't be like Cook County, where it's possible to do a quid pro quo, so to speak, with a guard—"

She hung up on me midsentence.

All I knew about death from nicotine patches was

what anyone who's watched *Thank You for Smoking* knows—that it is possible in a movie. I looked it up online and came away with hazy information. Thirty patches would perhaps do it in three hours, but there seemed to be some obstacles.

For one thing, you'd need a prescription. Could Arthur Morton have gotten one filled from the Saline County prison? At least in Cook County, the idea of a prisoner being given nicotine patches to quell his cigarette withdrawal would cause a laff riot among the guards.

For another, it would be hard to get a prescription filled for thirty patches. If Morton could have gotten them, wouldn't someone in a small jail notice he was covered in patches and beginning to suffocate?

I sent an email to Chicago's deputy chief medical examiner, a man named Nick Vishnikov who inhabits that gray area between friend and work acquaintance.

Can someone really commit suicide with nicotine patches? How many would you need?

Before putting the whole Lydia-Hector story to one side, I called the two men whose names Elisa Palurdo had given me, his boyhood friend and his college room-mate. Neither had seen Lydia recently—like Elisa, they had felt unable to respond to her as she became more agitated.

"What was her relationship with Hector like?" I asked.

"Hector was on the road the last few years," Stu Shiffman, the roommate said. "He liked to talk to me when he was in town—you know I teach Latin American studies at Northern Illinois?—he had become deeply interested in Chilean history and politics, and I was one person who knew enough to help him with resources, but we didn't get together socially, so I didn't see him with Lydia very often. Still, I thought Lydia was good for him, or maybe they were good for each other. His best-known book was a collection of short stories based on some of the oldest histories we have of the Americas. Lydia wrote her famous song, 'Savage,' culled from the stories Hector unearthed about the First Nations at the time of Columbus."

We chatted for a few more minutes. Just as we were saying goodbye, he said, "One thing—after his father died, Hector started traveling to Chile more often. He'd gone a couple of times, hoping to find relatives, I think, but after Jacobo's death, he wanted more specific help in tracking down what happened to victims of the Pinochet regime. Between forty and fifty thousand people were tortured or disappeared and the postregime truth and reconciliation efforts were brief and didn't account for most of them."

"Was Hector's father a refugee from Pinochet?"

"I don't think so. I got the idea he was a blue-collar guy who emigrated because he couldn't find work when the Chilean economy started to come apart."

"When was that?" I tried to remember what little I knew about Chile—the destabilization of the economy when the socialist Allende was president, the right-wing Pinochet coup.

"No, after that," Shiffman said. "It's a complicated history and I won't take your time with all the details—who did what to the economy and the infrastructure—but about a decade into the Pinochet regime, inflation and unemployment both began to climb. Pinochet had undercut a lot of the social network, so people who couldn't feed their families or afford health care looked elsewhere.

"Some looked to the north and from what Hector said, his father was one of those. I have a feeling, too, that Jacobo was pretty red—another good reason to leave Chile. Leftists were prime targets of the Pinochet death squads. I know Jacobo Palurdo didn't want Hector at the University of Chicago—Hector told me his father thought it was an elitist institution that would make Hector ashamed of his roots."

It was something to think about, but not a help in finding Lydia. I couldn't think of anything else to do, so I finally put her out of my mind to attend to jobs for other clients.

I worked doggedly for three hours, ignoring a text from Murray, and met Peter Sansen for a late dinner. My phone buzzed as we were having drinks at the bar—Bernie. She rang again five minutes later, and again as the waiter led us to our table. This was followed by a text: You must phone at once. URGENT, URGENT, URGENT.

For Bernie, urgent could mean anything, but her recent arrest made me uneasy. I excused myself and went outside to call.

"Vic, I thought maybe you were in bed with Peter and not answering your phone until morning. I need you, *à l'instant!*"

"What?"

"Leo! He's dead! They found him—found his body—he was in that wild park by the viaduct."

14
Thorough Search

Someone took the phone from Bernie before I could ask where she was, but from the background sounds before the phone went dead, I guessed she was with the police at the crime scene. Peter settled the drinks bill and drove me to Forty-seventh Street.

The Burnham Wildlife Corridor was narrow, but it stretched about two miles, from the parking lot at McCormick Place—Chicago's big convention center—to the Forty-seventh Street viaduct. As we approached the northern edge, we could see bright circles of police flashlights bobbing among the shrubbery. Gapers slowed the exit to a maddening creep. When we finally left the Drive, Peter let me out near the parking lot.

The sidewalk was even thicker with gawkers than the Drive had been, but I'd learned the art of breaking through a crowd on the streets of South Chicago. I quickly made it to the front, not bothering to apologize to anyone cursing me after colliding with my elbows.

The entrance to the parking lot was barricaded. I told the officer on duty that I was Bernie Fouchard's attorney and asked to be taken to her.

The man looked at my credentials with painstaking— and pains-giving—care before grudgingly deciding I was actually an attorney and might be allowed in to see my client. He called someone for permission and pulled the sawhorses apart to let me pass.

All the local TV stations had cameras set up, aimed at the entrance to the lot. The sight of a new body entering the enclosure caused major excitement: three people rushed up with their mikes, wanting my identity. Beth Blacksin, from Global's cable news channel, recognized me and hollered for the name of my client. When I kept on walking, the other reporters converged on Beth, demanding my name.

Once I was in the main part of the lot, the strobes and arc lights from the police blinded me. I squinted through the glare and finally saw a knot of uniforms at the north end, where they'd herded some twelve or fifteen people into a makeshift holding pen.

Most of the detainees were older, worn-out people, mostly men, in threadbare shirts and baggy trousers, some in their winter parkas, since they had no safe place to store them in summertime. A handful of women was segregated from the men onto a couple of benches where they were watched by a trio of women cops. On one bench, wedged between a massive woman in a halter top and long skirt and a younger woman, pencil thin, whose twitches and rolling eyes betrayed an urgent need for medication, I saw Bernie. She was hunched over, her hands clutching the edge of the bench.

I ran to her, calling her name, and she hurled herself into my arms, breaking down into sobs.

One of the women officers put a hand on Bernie's shoulder, as if to pull her back to the bench.

I gave a shark smile. "I'm her attorney. We're going to confer in private."

"I need a lawyer, too!" The large woman next to Bernie surged to her feet, hands on hips. "Why does the white girl get a lawyer and I don't?"

One of the male detainees staggered over. "You can be my lawyer anytime, sugar."

"It's been a long time since I got an acquittal," I said. "Best find someone with a better track record."

"Sweet thing like you can't blind talk a jury?" the man scoffed.

The woman was more belligerent. "Little white girl

gets a lawyer and I don't? What does that say about justice in America?"

"Probably everything," I agreed.

I started to hand out cards when a female officer jogged over. "What's going on—oh. You. And your troublemaking niece."

"Sergeant Pizzello. Yes, it's me. What happened here and what does it have to do with Bernadine Fouchard? Who is my goddaughter, not my niece."

The sergeant frowned at us. "We're still sorting that out. Ernestine," she added, turning to the angry woman. "I know this lawyer. You'd be better off with the public defender, but even if you weren't, you're not facing any charges. We're only getting statements and then you'll be free to go. Unless, of course, someone saw you bending over the victim and removing his wallet or his phone."

Ernestine and the drunk man retreated, both muttering phrases like "bitches with too much power."

"We'll start with your client, *sugar.*" Pizzello flashed her own shark smile. The strobes turned her teeth a ghastly purple-gray. "Or is she your niece?"

"Goddaughter. But she's my client all the same. Are the dead man's wallet and phone missing?"

Pizzello nodded but looked at Bernie. "Bernadine

Fouchard, this is the second time you've been involved in an incident in this park. It had better be the last, because even if your lawyer is the hottest investigator in town—meaning, even if she's better than me, which I doubt—nothing is going to keep your little behind out of my holding cell. So you tell me, and your lawyer-like godmother, what the sweet fuck you were doing here tonight."

Bernie looked at me. "They searched me in a nasty way. Even my breasts."

"You *what?*" I shouted at Pizzello.

She bit her lip but said stolidly, "The victim's phone and wallet were gone. We searched everyone. Plus, girlfriend is covered in blood."

That much was true: Bernie had blood on her T-shirt, and she'd wiped her hands on her jeans. I ignored that to protest Pizzello's strip search. "Out here in the parking lot? Where God and every leering passerby could see you? Even the South Side's sorriest addict has a right to privacy. I'm going to mention this. Not to the Police Review Board, but to the TV reporters who are hovering around the entrance like crows searching for carrion."

She didn't respond, but at least she didn't try to bluster.

I pulled Bernie away. "Talk directly into my ear. She's probably recording you. What were you doing here?"

Her voice trembled, but she had good nerves. Standing on tiptoe, she whispered that Leo wanted her to go with him to the park at night. They were supposed to have dinner at the African Fusion café on Forty-seventh and then walk over together. When an hour passed without him showing or answering her texts, Bernie decided to look for him in the park. When she got there, though, the parking lot was full of the drunks; people were even shooting up.

"It was *dégoû*—disgusting. I went back to the sidewalk. Runners and people with dogs, they were all going back and forth, it felt safer. Then one of the drunks came out of the bushes over there—" She pointed up the track, toward the railway embankment. "He was yelling and I didn't pay attention at first but then all these other people started coming out of the park and the drunks in the lot started yelling, too, about a dead man."

Her fingers dug into my forearm as she tried to steady herself.

"What did you do?"

"I was scared it was Leo," she murmured. "I—I went to look."

I told her she could repeat the story to Pizzello.

"You went and looked at him?" The sergeant was incredulous. "What made you do that? Did you want to make sure he was really dead?"

"I didn't know why Leo stood me up," Bernie said in a small voice. "And then I thought, if he was dead that would explain it."

Pizzello rolled her eyes. "It would, indeed. Really, what made you go look at the body?"

"She told you," I snapped. "Maybe you'd have run as fast as you could to the nearest intersection and hailed an Uber to drive you home, but the Fouchards are made of strong mettle. Steel on ice. They don't shy away from their fears. You know how to reach me, which means if you want to talk to her again you call me."

I put an arm around Bernie's shoulders and steered her past the officers and civilians. Pizzello said to our backs, "The phone, Ms. Steel-on-ice? Do you have his phone?"

"You know I don't. You know it wasn't inside my bra and panties." Bernie's voice trembled, but she held her ground. "You have *my* phone, though, and I want it back."

"Let's have it," I said to Pizzello. "I'm getting her out of here and getting her home."

"We need her clothes, fingerprints, DNA," Pizzello said. "She admits to handling the vic—let's see whose blood—"

"How long has your team been here? And this is just occurring to you? I'm taking her to a doctor. If you want to send a tech along to collect her clothes, go for it."

Pizzello scowled. Neither of us was on very solid legal ground here, but she had the added disadvantage of being in a public setting. She finally summoned a crime scene tech from the area where Leo had been found. Bernie and I went into the CST van.

Bernie gave the guy her blood-stained clothes; I put the knit top I'd been wearing over her. Since I'm four inches taller, it covered her down to her hips. I helped myself to a paper gown from a shelf in the van and wrapped a second one around Bernie. She was shivering, and paper wouldn't keep her warm, but it was the best I could do.

The tech took scrapings from Bernie's fingernails, did a DNA swab, and inspected her head and arms for bruising. I stood over him like the avenging angel, making sure every item was sealed in an evidence bag and properly labeled.

I videoed him as he filled the bags and labeled them,

put all the clips into Dropbox, and mailed them to my own attorney.

"I've been doing this job for five years. I don't need you leaning over me while I work," the man snapped.

"Probably not," I agreed. "I just want to make sure that if the day comes when we're all standing in front of a judge, we agree on the number of bags you tagged and what was in them. And I want Ms. Fouchard's phone. I assume by now you've inspected the SIM card."

"I don't have the phone," the tech said.

I texted Sergeant Pizzello, who called me to say that the phones had been taken to the Edgewater district for analysis.

"How funny," I said, "and not in the side-slapping way. My client doesn't have a receipt. So why don't you make a call over to the station for us and we'll pick up her phone on our way to Evanston."

A few minutes later, a uniformed man appeared in the van with a bag of cell phones. Bernie picked hers out.

The sergeant caught up with us as we walked to the exit.

"I mean it about finding you down here again, Fouchard." It was a face-saver, so I didn't try to fight it, not even when she added a warning to me to make sure that Bernie didn't leave town.

My own phone had been beeping me. I kept one arm around Bernie, but took my phone out to read texts from Peter. He hadn't tried to get past the crowds; he was parked up the street, near the old bank where the SLICK meetings had been held.

It was an ordeal, getting out to the street. When the camera crews saw me at the sawhorses with Bernie, they rushed us. "Come on, Warshawski, who's your client?" Blacksin shouted.

I didn't answer, but the TV crews made us more interesting to the onlookers, who crowded around the sawhorses. The officer on duty studiously looked at the parking lot, ignoring our plight. Bernie was having trouble staying on her feet. Her body was wet with sweat, and she was starting to shake.

"Beth, this young woman is about to faint," I cried. "Get your camera guy to make a hole for us."

"An exclusive in exchange?"

"Do it because you're human!" I screamed. "Just do it."

The cameraman didn't wait for her word; he began stepping backward, paying no attention to what was behind him, camera at his head. I pushed through after him and got Bernie to the curb, texted Peter, put her over my shoulder, and staggered to the intersection where he was waiting for us.

15
Shortest Way from A to B

Peter and I drove Bernie to my place. I wrapped her in blankets. Peter prepared hot tea laced with honey while I sponged Leo's blood from her hands and face. I put her into my T-shirts—several layers, despite the warm evening. By and by the symptoms of shock eased. Peter helped me open the sofa bed and we left her to sleep.

It was getting on for midnight; we were both ravenous—we'd raced out of the restaurant having eaten nothing but a few olives. Before making a snack, though, I called Pierre and Arlette Fouchard to let them know what was going on. It wasn't an easy conversation: they wanted Bernie on the next plane home and couldn't believe, or at least Arlette wouldn't believe, that the police had a right to demand she stay within their jurisdiction until they'd questioned her formally.

We finally agreed that the Fouchards would get in touch with my own lawyer, Freeman Carter, whose rate for six minutes stacks up nicely against any other firm in Chicago.

"She did *not* kill anyone," Arlette said fiercely.

"No, of course not, but she wasn't in any shape to give me details on what happened tonight. She'll call you in the morning," I promised.

Peter opened a bottle of Brunello I'd been saving, while I cooked up *trecce* pasta with mushrooms and Parmesan. We could talk about the night's drama only in short, disjointed bursts.

"Will the police leave Bernie alone now?" Peter asked.

"Hard to say. She was covered in Leo's blood."

"They think a lover's quarrel?"

"They think the shortest way from A to B. On the other hand, she's a young woman whose father is a Chicago sports hero, and it would be quicker and quieter to pin the killing on a homeless person."

Peter put down his glass. "*You* don't think she killed him, do you?"

I was too tired to say what I thought or didn't think. That I didn't know what their relationship had consisted of, or how deep feelings had gone on either side in the short time they'd known each other. Or that Bernie could swing a stick with a well-trained aim and great power, that she had a fierce temper. She was also tenderhearted, though, and I couldn't imagine her killing someone. Unless greatly provoked in the moment.

My thoughts made me dizzy. That and exhaustion. Peter and I stumbled to bed, leaving the dishes where they were, which meant when I got up the next morning, I had a table full of cheese-crusted plates and silver.

Bernie was at the kitchen table, picking pieces of *trecce* out of the pot I'd left in the sink. She was pale; the shirts I'd bundled her into last night hung on her, making her look like a street waif. Peter made espressos for the three of us, but didn't linger: he was getting ready to leave for a dig in Turkey and the preparations were exhaustive and exhausting.

"I'm supposed to be in Humboldt Park this morning," Bernie said when he'd left. "The program starts in an hour."

"If you're up to doing the job, I'll drive you, but it would be better if you took some time off."

She shivered and pulled one of the T-shirts over her hands. "I don't know what to do. Mama wants me to come home, Papa says I should tough it out. Also, he said you told them I am not permitted to leave."

"That's right," I said, "but they are hiring a proper lawyer for you, one who has an active practice and will make sure the police don't act rashly." I told her about Freeman Carter and the notable cases he'd handled.

"I cannot tell the police anything, because I do not know anything." Her dark eyes were troubled, and she spoke without her usual fire. "I guess one of those homeless men must have hit Leo to rob him."

"How well did you know him?" I asked.

"Are you trying to say he had a secret life that got him killed?" Her eyes came to life with anger.

"I'm not saying anything, but unless I know *some-thing* about him I can't begin to start an investigation."

"You will investigate? But this lawyer, this Carter—"

"He'll represent you with the police or in court if, God forbid, it goes that far. My job is to get the facts to make his job easier."

"Oh." She subsided. "Our relationship, it wasn't that long. I told you—I met Leo when we were talking to SLICK about sponsorship for our girls soccer team. We met for coffee now and then.

"When I was arrested—I was very angry about this man, Coop, that he started the fight and then nothing is done to punish him. He attacked Leo in the meeting, and nothing happened. Me, I was taken into a police station, just for talking to Lydia Zamir, but this Coop—

the police take him from the SLICK meeting where he's trying to attack Leo, and they kiss him on both cheeks! I thought Leo and I could trick him, maybe, into doing something where it would be his turn to be punished."

I looked at her uneasily. "What did you imagine doing?"

"Nothing." She looked disgusted. "Leo is not a fighting kind of person. Leo wants—wanted—he said let a sleeping dog lie, and I said a sleeping dog wakes up in two seconds and goes for your throat."

She sat up straighter, remembering the argument—slumped again as Leo's death came back to her.

"Why on earth was Leo going to the park at night?" I couldn't imagine why anyone, especially someone who didn't like fighting, would want to go after dark to a place filled with drunks and addicts.

Bernie's face pinched with worry. "We were supposed to go there together, after dinner. He wanted to see for himself what kind of animals were in the park at night. It is called a wildlife preserve, you know, but no one ever sees any wildlife there."

"He was a zoologist?" I asked. "Besides being a web designer?"

She shook her head. "No. He was doing a degree in urban planning. Yes, he can do web work, but it is—was—his side occupation. He could do things for small, poor places like SLICK, who need something simple, not a big project with hundreds of pages. He is—was—more of an expert with data analysis, which SLICK needs very much for their new project. He wanted to see for himself if animals would be disturbed by building in the park."

"But they weren't going to—the new construction would have been across Lake Shore Drive."

"To animals it is all part of one thing," Bernie said.

"Perhaps," I said. "Data gathering in a wild park in the dark. Did that sound romantic to you?"

Despite her misery, Bernie couldn't hold back a giggle. "Not romantic, no, but Leo said he sometimes has seen Coop in the park with that dog and—and—"

She broke off, looking at me slantwise.

"You hoped you could confront Coop away from the street where it would be less likely the cops could intervene?" I suggested.

"*Oui*," she agreed.

"Okay, step me through it. You waited at African Fusion, Leo didn't show, you walked to the park and retreated from the parking lot to the street?"

She nodded, picking at her cuticles.

I pushed on her: how dark was it—she would have

been there about half an hour after sundown, when the sky was still light. She really made no effort to look for Leo or for Coop?

"Okay, I did go into the park for a little distance. I couldn't understand—he wasn't answering my texts and he hadn't shown up at the restaurant. I thought maybe I was mistaking when we should meet. When I got to the park I saw a path, it goes maybe two hundred meters and then divides in two—I walked to where it divided.

"A man and a woman were sitting on a bench, sharing a bottle. I described Leo, I described Coop, but they were not caring about anything except their bottle; they could say nothing of who else was in the park. They did offer me a swallow from the bottle. Then it started being too dark and a man was coming down the path, shouting angry words, you know how people do when they are drunk or high or—or crazy. I started feeling too alone, so I left and went to the street."

"This is different from what you told the police last night," I said. "When they realize you actually went into the park, not just the parking lot, they'll jump on you, like Boom-Boom and Pierre on a loose puck."

"Who will tell them?" Bernie said.

"Just because those people on the bench were drunk doesn't mean they won't remember you," I said. "If they feel pressured by the cops or the state's attorney, believe me, they'll put you on center ice. If they confront you, it's not a hard problem to fix—you were in shock after seeing your lover—"

"We weren't lovers," Bernie protested. "I mean, yes, maybe we had sex, but it's not as if we were—I don't even know the word. We weren't in love."

"That's not how Sergeant Pizzello will see it. She'll wonder if you had a quarrel, if you picked up a tree branch or a discarded bottle and smashed in the back of his skull."

"Vic, no!"

Her face took on a greenish pallor. I shoved her head down to her knees. When her breathing became less shallow and she'd drunk some water, I said in a softer, more coaxing voice, "I need to know what really happened last night—you went up the path looking for Leo and turned around without seeing him? Or you found him dead and panicked but didn't leave the site?"

"It is what I said last night: this one man comes running out, aghast, a dead man in the bushes. I ran in and saw Leo. I called 911." Bernie clenched her teeth to keep them from chattering. "But when the police arrived, they treated me—they treated everyone in the park—like criminals. They brought us to that space, and then, you know, they grabbed my phone from me when I was talking to you."

"You never saw Coop?"

She shook her head. "I did wonder—I thought I saw his dog on the hillside that leads to the railway track—but everything was so confused. Anyway, maybe it was a coyote. People say there are coyotes in all the parks, although me, I have never seen one."

My questions had worn her out to the point that she agreed to go home to rest instead of trying to get to work. Before I drove Bernie to her and Angela's Evanston apartment, I called Nick Vishnikov in the medical examiner's office. He won't always answer questions about people in his morgue, but today he was willing to tell me that Leo Prinz had been killed by blows to the head.

"Multiple? More than one hand involved?"

"One skillful hand as nearly as I can make out. He was hit four, maybe five times, but the first blow would have sufficed. And if you're helping the police uncover evidence, it's a smooth object you're looking for. Not a tree branch."

"Baseball bat?" I suggested.

"Wounds suggest something smaller in diameter."

"It was after sundown when someone came on his

body," I said. "Any idea how long he would have been dead?"

"Not an exact science, Warshawski. This can't be said in court, but my best guess is maybe an hour before he was found."

"How tall was the assailant?"

"You think this is *NCIS*? Too many variables—like was he sitting or standing."

"Just wondering—hoping, I guess—that the assailant had to be taller than five-foot-four."

"You got a shrimp for a client, do you? Victim was a hair under six feet. A short assailant would have to have stood over him, or found him sitting. By the way, Warshawski, what's this about nicotine patches?"

In the excitement around Leo and Bernie, I'd forgotten emailing him about Arthur Morton's suicide.

"Kansas guy who died in custody, supposedly of a nicotine patch overdose."

"Could be done, I suppose, but you don't usually get access to enough patches, especially not in prison. Did he have the patches on him when he died?"

"I guess—I don't know, but why else would they have given that as the cause of death?"

"It depends on how big he was, his health, his tobacco tolerance."

I didn't know that, either, but I thought Morton had been a biggish guy.

Vishnikov muttered under his breath, doing calculations in his head. "Eight patches would do it in nine or ten hours, I suppose, assuming prescription strength, assuming no one noticed. If the guards were doing their job, they should have seen him covered with sweat, clawing for air. Horrible way to go. Later, Warshawski."

I packed the dogs in the car when I drove Bernie home. She called her boss, the program director for the citywide sports mentoring program, to explain why she'd missed work. The call went through my car speakers so I heard the director's frosty response to Bernie's apology.

"I thought I saw your face on the news. If you're involved in a murder investigation, that isn't the most stable leadership for girls who live in high-risk neighborhoods."

"Seeing Ms. Fouchard rise above that level of trauma will be a great leadership example for the girls," I butted in. "This is V.I. Warshawski; I'm Ms. Fouchard's lawyer and I'll be glad to meet with you to discuss the situation. Just give me your address and I can be there in half an hour."

There was a pause on the other end and then a grudging, oh, very well, as long as Bernie showed up tomorrow.

Bernie made a face as the call shut down. "Really, what she knows is that no one else will go to Humboldt Park for the tiny money this program pays me."

16
Found?

The iron gates in front of the parking lot at Forty-seventh Street were padlocked, with yellow crime scene tape draped lavishly around the entrance. A couple of squad cars sat in the lot, inhabitants chatting with each other through the open windows.

I took side streets and parked west of the train tracks at Forty-first. The streets here rose steeply above the tracks. A crumbling limestone wall was supposed to keep people from tumbling onto the trains below. Standing there, I could see the landscape laid out in strips: first four sets of tracks, then the narrow wildlife park, the wide lanes of Lake Shore Drive, and beyond them the lake, glittering under the sun, begging me to stop detecting and start swimming.

Directly below me, plants had been bulldozed to

create a staging area for construction refuse and equipment. A steam shovel sat in the middle of a gravel and dirt clearing, broken concrete, rebar, and ordinary dirt piled behind it. A freight train was lumbering past, filled with the oil tankers we've been told are banned from heavily populated areas.

It was more fun to watch the lakefront and the beach. From this perspective it looked as though everyone was having a good time, frisking with dogs, with children, with beach balls and volleyballs. On Olympus, you don't hear the quarrels.

I didn't know if the police had searched for a weapon this far north, but they didn't have any presence here. I went back to my car for my day pack, then scrambled down the hillside. I waited as the long line of freight cars rumbled by, waited for a little commuter train to zip north, then picked my way across the rails to the park.

Past the construction area, the park continued north in a halfhearted way until it ran into the giant parking lot that served the McCormick Place Convention center. Near the north end I came on a set of wicker huts and benches. A sign told me this was one of the "gathering places" in the park, where local artists had been invited to create installations. A trio of cyclists had stopped there to repair a wheel.

I looked in the huts but didn't see anything—like Lydia, or Coop, or a murder weapon. I showed the cyclists the photo of Coop on my phone, but they didn't recognize him. As I worked my way south, I checked around the dirt mounds and other rubble in the construction area. There was plenty of rusting metal, but nothing with the highly polished finish the weapon supposedly had.

I didn't really expect to find the weapon, but I hoped for a trace of Coop and his dog Bear. They were so liable to show up around any excitement in the park that I wondered if he might have a campsite hidden in the bushes.

The day was hot. At the north end of the park, little restoration planting had been done and most of the ground cover was the kind of tough scraggly weed that attracts ugly biting insects. I'd brought a water bottle but had worn only a baseball cap, not a hat with a protective brim. Light glinting from the windshields of passing cars on the Drive made my eyes ache.

I found a number of hidey-holes in the shrubbery where people had staked a claim. The hideouts were filled with blankets and old shopping carts, Styrofoam containers holding half-eaten food, shaving supplies, one with five cartons of tampons. Most were empty, the inhabitants off doing their daily routines, whatever those were. I stumbled on a sleeping man with a large shepherd, who growled and flicked his tail when I came too close.

I hadn't brought gloves with me. I didn't want to touch the stashes I came on with my bare hands, but I poked at them cautiously.

At one point, I passed a clutch of birders. They were happy to chat but they didn't recognize the photo of Coop on my phone. The bright sun made it hard to see the screen, but even tenting it under our hats didn't produce oohs of recognition. The birders also hadn't heard about the murder in the park—they'd wondered why the cops had the south end cordoned off, but they hadn't asked, just walked along the shoulder of the Drive and come into the park through the brush.

A quartet of German tourists showed up as I was talking to the birders: they were walking the eight miles from the Loop to the University of Chicago campus and seemed undaunted by the heat, the insects, and the possibility of a killer in the weeds—indeed, they seemed to think that killers were a routine part of Chicago life, almost a tourist attraction.

I left the two groups chatting about crime, restaurants in the area, and the American or German names of the birds flitting through the high grasses.

Farther south, prairie grasses, milkweed, and other

new plantings made the landscape less grim. The park widened. I crisscrossed it from train embankment to road, swatting at flies and mosquitoes, not seeing anything that looked more out of place than the usual array of cigarette butts, empty snack bags and bottles, until I came on a place on the embankment where the grasses and bushes were mashed down and ringed with crime-scene banners.

Flies were sucking greedily at a dark blotch among the leaves and grass stems. The remnants of Leo's blood and brains. Bernie had seen Leo lying here, the terrible sight of blood and splintered bone and brain, just as Lydia had seen Hector. You never put that vision behind you; I hoped, in time, it would stop being the central image in Bernie's mind. I was less optimistic for Lydia.

Broken grasses fanning out from the murder spot showed the search area. I was surprised that the police hadn't stationed an officer to protect the crime scene, but maybe, even though they'd been searching at night, aided only by arc lamps, they'd found everything they needed. Besides, unless Leo's phone showed up, or some other concrete evidence, finding the killer would be almost impossible.

The broken grasses went all the way up the embankment. The techs probably searched the tracks if they'd climbed this far, but they'd been searching at night. I climbed the hillock to the tracks, following the trail left by the scene of crime team.

Every time a chipmunk ran through the undergrowth, the skin on my back prickled: I kept sensing someone behind me swinging a smooth blunt instrument, one that was missing microscopic paint chips. I would twirl around, but never saw anyone behind me.

The limestone wall I'd seen at Forty-first Street continued down here. It wasn't much of a wall anymore—after a hundred and fifty years or so of Chicago winters and no maintenance, large sections had collapsed. When I clambered over the tumbledown stones, I loosed a small avalanche of dirt.

I stayed close to the wall, despite the rough terrain, not trusting my balance if another freight roared along. Scrubby trees grew along both sides of the wall, giving enough shade to keep the worst of the sun at bay. The birds kept up a bright chirping as I moved along. The insects, too, buzzed happily as they helped themselves to my blood.

I kept a hand on the stones to steady myself, but even so, about a hundred yards shy of the platform, I tripped over an exposed root and fell heavily into a hole near the wall.

The landing jolted my tailbone. I moved my arms

and legs cautiously; nothing seemed broken. I sat with my elbows on my knees, my head in my palms, glad to be out of the glare of the August sun.

It wasn't until I'd sat for some minutes that I realized I was hearing human noises underneath the relentless bird trills: short gasps for air, not quite suppressed. I looked up and saw I'd landed in a rudimentary cave created by the fallen rocks. Against the back, chittering in fear, was Lydia Zamir.

17
Cave-In

Zamir was holding her arms tightly behind her back, straining the tendons in her neck. Her hair was so grimed that it looked as though someone had glued clumps of steel shavings to her scalp.

She was wearing jeans and a T-shirt, both so big on her that she appeared to be a stick figure, a caricature of a woman. I supposed this was the outfit the Provident staff had put underneath her gurney. If she'd been able to change out of a hospital gown and make it out of the building without being stopped, she had periods of extraordinary self-possession.

I shifted inside the makeshift shelter, moving my legs so that she had a clear path to the exit. I leaned against the side of the little cave, feeling dirt cling to my sweaty clothes and damp hair.

"You're an impressive woman, Lydia Zamir," I said. "You're strong, you're resourceful, even in the middle of the pain you're feeling you managed to get away from Provident Hospital undetected."

I waited a few minutes. The fear in her face seemed to ease. She brought her arms from behind her back, keeping her eyes fixed on me in case I made any unexpected moves. In case she'd hidden something behind her back, I kept my own eyelids lowered: I didn't want her to think I was spying.

"My name is V.I. Warshawski—you can call me 'Vic.'" My voice came out hoarse from thirst. "I was down here last week to watch a group of girls play soccer, and on my way home, I heard you playing your piano. The young woman who was with me recognized your music. She and her friends are athletes, and your music inspires them to do their best work."

She flinched and made a brushing gesture, as if trying to sweep away talk of her music, but she didn't speak.

"Your friend Coop is very worried about you. He is looking for you, but I won't tell him I've found you unless you want me to."

She seemed to be trying to say something, perhaps Coop's name, but I couldn't be sure. It may have been so long since she had last spoken that she couldn't produce any words.

"I've talked about you to a lot of people in the past few days. Hermione Smithson is eager to sign you to a new recording contract—apparently the news story made hundreds of thousands of people—"

She waved her hands again in agitation and produced a squeaking sound.

"Don't worry: I won't tell Ms. Smithson that I found you. Or your old piano professor at the conservatory. What about your mother? That must have been painful, when Mr. Palurdo was murdered, to have your mother talk about him in such a cold way."

The mention of her mother brought on another bout of hand flapping. When I described my conversation with Elisa Palurdo, Zamir turned her head aside, but she still made sure I knew she didn't want me to tell Hector's mother that I'd found her.

"How about Coop?" I said. "I don't know how to find him. Do you want me to tell him where you are? If so, you'll have to tell me how to find him."

She started rocking herself, eyes half-closed, muttering under her breath. After a time, when I began to think she'd gone completely away, she choked out something, words, maybe, but I couldn't make them out.

I pulled my phone out of my daypack and handed it to her, but she whimpered.

"You don't want a phone?" I asked.

She pointed at my eyes and then my phone.

"You think I can use my phone to spy on you?" I said patiently. "I wouldn't, but it's a reasonable worry. Can you tell me how to reach Coop? No? Then I will go buy some food and water for you. I promise I will tell no one I have seen you."

I held out both hands, palms open. "Can you trust me that far?"

The gesture alarmed her so much that she thrust her own hands behind her back again. I brought my hands back to my lap.

"I'm going now." I swung my legs around so they were sticking outside the enclosure. I scooted out, then turned around to repeat my message. "And should I tell Coop you're here, if I see him?"

After some kind of interior conversation, she gave a half nod.

I pushed myself upright, using the limestone rocks as support. I was desperate for water. I couldn't fathom how Zamir had survived for two days up here without anything to drink.

As I stumbled along the gravel between the tracks and the crumbling wall, I saw amid the garbage a number of partly full water bottles. Zamir had to be a skilled forager to survive on the streets; presumably she knew to look for these.

At Forty-seventh Street, I hoisted myself onto the platform. A young woman was waiting for a train, buds in her ears. She didn't seem to notice me, a dirt-crusted stranger behaving strangely. That's how crooks and people on the margin survive: those on the middle of the page aren't paying attention.

I made my way down the stairs to the street. A strip mall around the corner from the station entrance included a 7-Eleven. I bought the kind of packaged food that wouldn't rot in the heat, along with several quarts of water and the basics for hygiene—soap, toothpaste, toothbrush, tampons just in case.

Before going back to Lydia, I sat in the shade outside the store, slowly drinking a can of ginger ale, along with a pint of water. When I felt about halfway to human again, I went to an electronics outlet and bought a burner phone with six hundred minutes.

A train screeched to a halt as I reached the platform again. The woman with the earbuds climbed on, three people exited. None of them was watching me, but I still waited for them to leave before I slid down from the platform and moved back up the gravel track to Lydia's hideout.

There were a couple of high-rises in the area, and anyone at an upper window could see past the tree foliage to what I was doing, but I doubted they could make out the hideout: I hadn't seen it before falling into it.

Lydia was sitting at her hole's entrance, below the shadow of the rocks, as if to keep me from venturing too close. I handed her the bag of groceries and toiletries and showed her the phone.

"You have to eat, you have to stay hydrated. I've programmed my number into this phone: you call me if you need me. When you're ready for medical help, I know a doctor who will respect your privacy and care for you without charge."

She crossed her arms in front of her face. Despite their sickening thinness, the movement was queenly, a vestige of her concert-playing days, arms lifting like a swan's wings to float over a keyboard. The gesture evoked all the losses she'd endured, her lover, her voice, her music. My stomach twisted in a mirrored pain and I turned my own head away.

In the park below I caught sight of the yellow crime scene tape marking the spot where Leo had died. If Lydia had come out to forage after sundown, she'd have had a perfect view of Leo's murder.

I squatted back in front of her. "You know there was

a killing last night just below you? I know it must have brought back horrific memories, but I still hope you can tell me if you saw the person who committed the murder."

The swan's wings turned back to bony arms. She began beating her own head, giving a high-pitched scream. I tried to take her hands, but she struck out at me. I backed away and sat on a log about five feet from the hole.

The evening rush had started; trains were thundering past every five minutes or so. I think they must have covered the noise of her screams. At any rate, she was far enough from the platform that commuters getting off a train probably hadn't heard her.

I could just make out her shape at the edge of her hideout. She was watching me, waiting, I suppose, for me to leave.

"Lydia, I'm not trying to distress you, but if you saw the murder, please tell me. I wouldn't talk about it, except that your own life could be at risk. If someone thinks you saw them, they could try to find you, to hurt you. I can help find the murderer; I can make you safer than you are now."

She gave a caw of laughter, so raucous that I first thought crows had moved into the trees above us.

When the sound died down, I said, "If you change

your mind, if you want me, or want Dr. Herschel, I programmed both our numbers into your phone."

My words sounded meaningless even to me. A teaspoon of water in the desert? If it was a droplet I'd be surprised.

18
Staying Afloat

Witnessing Lydia's pain had drained my last reservoir of energy. I thought of her agent's blithe statement, that the right meds and the right rehab would bring Lydia back in a hurry. I couldn't imagine a return to anything like normalcy, let alone creativity, after listening to that raw caw of a laugh.

When I'd slip-stepped down the embankment to the Wildlife Corridor, I stopped at the murder site. The wall and trees blocked Lydia's hiding place. Unless she'd been foraging near the wall, she'd probably been invisible. I tried to take what comfort I could from that, but I hated leaving her there alone, prey to all the creatures of the night.

On my way out, I passed a man on a bench, talking loudly to a listener only he could hear. He'd been living rough, judging by the condition of his boots and the puffiness around his eyes. If he had killed Leo, it would have been the work of a momentary rage. If he, or any person in similar straits, had killed Leo, he wouldn't have been looking around for witnesses. I hoped.

The police still had the parking lot barricaded. It was easy to skirt the iron fencing and get to the street— hard to know what they were protecting by closing off the lot.

One of the men in the squad car called out to me, but I kept moving. Instead of plodding north to my car, I crossed the overpass to Lake Michigan, stripped to my skivvies, sank into the water. I floated and paddled and watched the gulls. They may be garbage collectors and predators, but they are graceful in flight—like Lydia's arms, floating above an invisible keyboard. Above the gulls I saw the lines of planes heading into O'Hare, themselves like a stream of giant birds. They appeared from the eastern horizon in a seemingly unending line. Inside the windows passengers craning at landmarks wouldn't notice me, a tiny speck in the water below.

A two-masted sailboat floated at anchor in the near distance. Maybe it was Larry Nieland's yacht. It was called the *Abundance,* I'd read on his website—named by the robber baron who'd originally owned it, still fitting for a twenty-first-century man running a firm called Capital Unleashed.

Why had Leo gone early to the park, instead of meeting Bernie for dinner as they'd planned? And why hadn't he let Bernie know? Had his phone been stolen before he could text her?

I shut my eyes and let the waves carry me about. The water here was so clear and clean, I hated to think of a big sand beach with its concomitant soiled diapers, used condoms, broken liquor bottles—all the things that make Chicago's lakefront unpleasant in the summer. Maybe I'd join Coop in attacking anyone who wanted to put landfill here.

Yes, Coop. The rage that bubbled up in him like lava. If he'd seen Leo would he have gotten into a furious fight?

Leo wasn't part of SLICK—he was a summer hire. Did Coop understand that? He had seemed to hold Leo responsible for SLICK's actions. And SLICK itself had no power, no decision-making authority. They couldn't control Park District decisions, even if they wanted to; raging against Mona and her cronies was useless.

All these thoughts of anger—my own, Coop's, hypothetical homeless people—destroyed my peaceful mood. I turned over and did the crawl back to shore.

When I emerged, a family had arrived, a baby in a stroller, six older children, five adults, including a grandmother. They'd brought in a giant cooler attached to luggage wheels. While my skin and bra dried, I watched the family dynamics, all of them being loving with one another, even when disagreements arose. They were speaking Polish, the language of my Warshawski grandparents, but I'd never learned more than "hello" and "thank you."

I had spent a lot of time in my thirties debating whether to have a child. It hadn't seemed right, with the kind of life I lead, the work I do, my unsettled love life, but every now and then, when I see a family like this, I feel a twinge of melancholy. Tonight, I longed for the warmth of a family to return home to.

The grandmother saw me watching and offered me an ear of grilled corn, which I gratefully ate. I finally pulled on my filthy clothes and walked north, sticking this time to the easy paved path on the lake side of the Drive. I had started up the iron steps to the rusted overpass at Forty-first Street when I saw Coop and Bear approaching from farther north.

The dog greeted me happily, snuffling around my jeans legs to smell the leaf mold. Perhaps Bear smelled Lydia Zamir as well. Coop was less enthusiastic. I interrupted his surly greeting to tell him I'd found Lydia.

"Who have you told?" he demanded.

"As opposed to 'where is she, how is she doing?' Does that mean you already know where she is?"

He was taken aback. "No. No, I don't. Where is she? Is she all right?"

"She is not well, but you know that. She's worse because she depleted herself running from Provident Hospital. She's worse because of Leo Prinz's murder: even if she didn't witness the actual killing, she must have noticed all the cop activity. She showed extraordinary fortitude in getting away from Provident unseen, but that has taxed her health to its limit."

He started his litany about her current situation being my fault, but I cut him short. "Even if that's true, it's irrelevant. She needs help this minute. You are the one person she responds to, but you seem more interested in feeling outraged than in helping her get the care she needs."

"You know jackshit about her or me," he shouted, tendons on his neck sticking out.

"What is your connection to her? You're not a brother. Were you a lover before she met Hector Palurdo?"

"I was never Zamir's lover," he said through stiff lips.

"Did you know her in Kansas, before she met Pal-urdo?"

"Even if I did, it's irrelevant." He mimicked me savagely. "Tell me where she is."

"Where were you last night when Leo Prinz was murdered?" I asked instead.

"You think *I* killed him?" He gasped.

"Did you?" I asked. "I saw you go for him twice at those SLICK meetings. Anger Mismanagement could be the name on your personnel file."

"Have you been digging into my life?" he said so ferociously that his dog moved against his legs, either protecting him or slowing him down, hard to tell. "How—"

"I don't know your last name, or where you live. Mona Borsa from SLICK mentioned you get fired from jobs for not controlling your temper, but she didn't know your surname, or at least she wouldn't tell me."

"People think they can be anonymous in a big city, but everyone always has their nose stuck in your business," he grumbled. "Anyway, I didn't kill Leo Prinz. I shouldn't have jumped him in the SLICK meetings; Prinz was just a mouthpiece for the people with money. That's who needs to be whacked, not some poor clueless kid."

"Who are the money people?"

"They're always the same. The ones who think they own land and sea, even though they've done nothing to create the land or care for it."

"The money people in this particular case," I said impatiently. "Should the guy Taggett deferred to at the SLICK meeting—Larry Nieland, the economist—should he be whacked?"

Coop looked at me strangely, then said, "If I had my way, all economists would be whacked. Now tell me how to find Lydia."

My shoulders sagged and I leaned against the rusty stairwell railing. "I'm telling you because I don't see other options. I hope it's not a mistake."

I described how to find her hideout. "If you really care about her, get her to a place where she can receive proper medical attention. I left a phone for her with my number programmed into it, along with the number for the best doctor in Chicago, or really, anywhere. Charlotte Herschel is a Holocaust survivor; she's worked with victims of torture. She can help Lydia and she would protect her privacy."

I took one of my own business cards from my day pack and wrote Lotty's details on the back.

"It would be a big help if you gave me your own

name and phone number. That way I wouldn't have to rely on blind luck to see you when your friend needs you. I brought her food and water, but she must have a bed and a bath and real nourishment if she's going to survive."

"You don't need my phone number, or any name for me except 'Coop.' I'll look after Lydia."

All my old street fighting anger rose in me, but what good would it serve to break his nose—even if I had the energy to do it right now? I hoisted myself up the rusty steps of the old iron street crossing and made my way to my car.

At home, I washed my hair and put my filthy clothes into the laundry. The trip down four flights of stairs to the basement washing machines and back felt like the final ascent on Everest, so weary were my muscles.

I lay on my living room floor to straighten my spine and undo the kinks in my neck. I phoned Bernie while I lay there, to make sure she was managing to keep her own fragmented spirits together. To my relief, Arlette had flown in from Quebec to care for her daughter.

"Victoire, how much danger is there for Bernadine?" Arlette demanded. "They will arrest her?"

"I don't think so," I said. "I have to think that one of the homeless people who sleep in the park killed

Leo. Maybe to rob him, maybe because they thought he was infringing on their space. The police are dogging Bernie because of the previous altercation she was involved in."

Arlette said she had spoken with my criminal defense lawyer, Freeman Carter, who'd agreed to represent Bernie if she were arrested. "All of this is a shock, *naturellement*. Mr. Carter, he has suggested a counselor, a psychiatrist, but for someone like Bernadine, the best cure is movement. She will go back to her coaching job tomorrow and run around in the hot sun with her little athletes. That will restore her spirit."

"There's one thing I need to discuss with her," I said. "Bernie says she went to the park to look for Leo because she thought she might have misunderstood where they were meeting. And I gather he wasn't answering her texts—his phone had likely already been stolen. Still, I have a feeling there's something she isn't saying?" I prudently didn't accuse her of lying, not to Arlette. "Bernie isn't the kind of person to wait around for a dilatory lover."

"*Di-la-torie? Quoi?*"

"Someone who keeps you waiting."

"Ah, yes. I will ask her these things and believe me, she will tell me the truth, no fear over that. And I will stay for a few days. These girls, they live out of packages, as if there were no such thing in Chicago as real cheese."

That made me laugh, but when we hung up, my own spirits were still oppressed. Running around in the hot sun was not a good cure for me, certainly not the running around I'd been doing today.

19

Unending Grief

I phoned Lotty to let her know I'd given her clinic number to both Coop and Lydia Zamir. When I described the condition in which I'd found Lydia this afternoon, Lotty insisted on talking face-to-face. We met for a late supper at a café near her condo building.

Lotty hadn't paid attention to Leo Prinz's murder—she refuses to follow news about any violent deaths. "I would have no time for surgery if all I did was read about the day's shootings and stabbings. There is a limit, anyway, to how much misery the mind can absorb before it buckles under the weight."

That meant I had to tell her the story from the beginning, from stumbling on Zamir after Bernie's soccer match, through Bernie's near-arrest, Murray's article, the disastrous aftermath on the train platform, and then the suspicious way Coop kept popping up.

Lotty asked questions, and discussed the answers with her usual intelligent sympathy. The conversation helped wash some of my own misery from my bones.

"Do you believe this Coop killed the young man?"

I grimaced. "I would feel confident it was a homeless person camping in the park if it weren't for the fact that Leo went there when he was supposed to be joining Bernie. I guess it's possible he spent the afternoon in the Wildlife Corridor, but it seems more likely that someone arranged a meeting. He'd seen something on one of the maps at the SLICK meeting that bugged him—maybe someone assured him they could explain the map if he came to the park."

"This man Coop doesn't sound as though he thinks ahead like that," Lotty said shrewdly.

"True enough," I agreed. "He explodes on provocation, but only he knows what the provocation will be. Maybe not even he knows. I wish I could get him to bring Lydia to you. Or hospitalize her."

Lotty shook her head. "Look what happened when the police took her to Provident—this woman who is malnourished and exhausted found the strength to flee, probably on foot, a distance of what?"

"About two miles," I said. "You're repeating what others around her have been saying, that she's allergic to care."

"There's a lot of debate these days about involuntary treatment," Lotty said. "It's not my field, of course, but I do encounter families who are dealing with this issue. Even for someone who is deeply delusional, there is still a need for some autonomy, some decision-making. Only Ms. Zamir can decide if she's ready for care. Right now, the idea frightens her."

Lotty laid a hand over mine. "*Liebchen,* forgive me if I step on your toes, but—I'm wondering if you are overly involved with Ms. Zamir's situation because she is a musician. A musician in trouble is perhaps a reminder of your mother, whom you couldn't save."

She was echoing what Peter had said earlier. I smiled painfully. After a moment she moved the conversation to less stressful topics: she and Max were planning a music lover's vacation, from the Marlboro Festival in Vermont to England for the York Early Music Festival.

I myself was planning a hiking trip in Quebec's Laurentian Mountains: before his murder, my cousin Boom-Boom had built a cabin there next to Pierre Fouchard's. I'd inherited the cabin, and usually rented it through the agency the Fouchards used, but I had claimed it for a week later in the summer. I couldn't join Peter in Turkey for his dig, but I didn't want to spend the whole hot summer in Chicago.

Talk of music and hiking moved Lydia's mental state and Leo's death from the middle of my head to a small side room. Arlette Fouchard moved it closer to the middle again: she called as I was unlocking my front door to tell me she'd interrogated Bernadine about why she'd waited around for Leo when he stood her up.

"She said she was angry. She was wanting to give this Leo a piece of her mind. And then, when she saw his dead body, it was an enormous shock, she felt guilty, only she is ashamed to say about her anger. I believe her, Victoire. Me, I know when my child is lying to me."

I, too, believed Arlette had dug the truth out of her daughter: I used to witness her interrogation methods with her husband and my cousin Boom-Boom, when the two men were playing for the Blackhawks. Arlette was thorough, merciless, and effective: *You say there was a flat tire, but I see the spare is still in the trunk? Ah, you stopped for beer. Yes, that I believe.*

Bernie's reported answer felt authentic, too. She would have been pacing the sidewalk, building up a head of steam so that when Leo appeared she would be ready to lay into him with a highly polished—no. Not possible, don't let your mind go there, Victoria.

I sat at the piano, moodily playing scales with one finger. Lotty might be right, that Lydia's condition affected me more because she made me think of my mother. Her other point, that Lydia deserved to make her own decisions about her care, hit two contradictory impulses in me.

I myself hate being told what to do, especially unsolicited advice about what is good for me, so I had definite empathy for letting Zamir decide what she wanted for herself. At the same time, though, I can't bear to leave wounded people by the side of the road.

I realized that I was picking out the vocal line to Grieg's "The Swan," one of the songs that Lydia had taken apart for her own work, and one of my mother's favorite short lieder.

I turned away from the piano to call Murray. "I'm retiring from your case, Murray: it's work I can't do."

"Warshawski—no! I need—"

"I'll return your retainer, and there's no charge for the time I spent on the search."

"What the hell?" He was angry. "Did someone offer you more money to leave her hidden?"

"That is an insult I won't respond to," I said coldly. "Leo Prinz's murder in the Burnham Wildlife Corridor last night—you know about that, right? That was around the corner from where Zamir had been camping out. The police are all over those streets, looking for a weapon and a killer. If Zamir is there, the cops will find her."

"They would have found her by now if she were hiding out near where the Prinz kid was killed. She could have moved to a different part of town, or someone took her in."

"In which case it would be beyond my resources to find her," I said. "I've talked to her agent, to people she went to school with, to her mother, and Palurdo's mother. None of them knows where she is. Maybe she was snatched from Provident, as one person who was in the hospital waiting area claims. Finding that person would take the cops or the FBI, not a solo op with other clients."

Murray was sidetracked briefly by the mention of Hector Palurdo's mother. He demanded a detailed report of the conversation; I gave him the highlights, since Elisa Palurdo hadn't said anything he couldn't have learned from other people.

"I've never known you to walk away from an investigation," he said. "Someone got to you, didn't they?"

"What is going on in your head, Ryerson? First you think someone outbid you, now you think someone warned me off? It's my turn: What's your real agenda here? It isn't just that your boss threatened your career, is it?"

"I'm paying you out of my pocket because I don't want the company to know I hired a detective," he insisted.

"I can't make sense of this, Murray. Actually, come to think of it, I don't believe your initial rationale for hiring me. Since when does Global Entertainment stake their reputation on looking after a mentally ill person's health care?"

"I said it's because the Smithson woman was threatening a suit."

"Global has so many lawyers that if they stood hand to hand they'd circle the equator with a few spares to reach the North Pole. A music agent whose glory days are behind her would make them laugh. Tell me a different story." I wished I could sic Arlette Fouchard on him—she'd shake the truth loose.

"Give me one more day, Vic," he pleaded.

"I've resigned. I'm returning your money. That's final."

My last call of the day was to Peter Sansen, to tell him how I'd been spending my time and why I needed to go to bed early, and alone. Still, five minutes on the phone with him helped calm some of the turbulence in my mind.

Despite my troubled state, I slept deeply. I was stiff when I woke up—the mildew on my aging joints, I suppose—but my mind felt clearer. I did a long and thorough workout, ending with a four-mile run with the dogs to the lake and back.

Before heading to my office, I used an encrypted service to leave a message for Elisa Palurdo: she deserved to know that I'd found Lydia, but that I was respecting her desire to be left alone. Palurdo phoned half an hour later. She wanted to know where Lydia was, and what shape she was in.

"She's not well. She needs proper food and a proper bed and significant medical care. But what she needs and what she's willing to receive—"

Palurdo interrupted me, distressed. "You should have called me yesterday. You should call an ambulance! Tell me where she is!"

"I can tell you how to find her, but she doesn't want to see you."

Palurdo didn't respond for a long beat, then said quietly, "That's probably because she feels my rejection. But—because of Hector—maybe she will listen to me now and get whatever help I can bring her to accept."

"Getting to her means you'd expose yourself to public view," I warned. "You'd have to be cautious and you still might make both her and yourself vulnerable to the kind of haters who are stalking you."

"I'll be careful," Palurdo said in the same small voice.

I gave her a detailed description of how to locate Lydia's hideout.

"Oh, how could I know the burdens Hector would bring me?" Palurdo burst out. "All the—"

She cut herself off; after a moment, she said in a quieter tone, "I don't mean it like that. Being Hector's mother was a joy. But when you hold your baby and imagine his future, it doesn't include his murder, his lover's disintegration, your own unending grief."

20
My Name in Lights

All the good health I'd felt after my long run evaporated with Elisa Palurdo's phone call. I imagined packing a bag and leaving for Turkey with Peter. While he was absorbed in his excavation, I would slip off and disappear into an Anatolian cave and let Chicago go. Let Mr. Contreras figure out what to do with the dogs, let Elisa figure out what to do with Coop and Lydia, let my paying clients fend for themselves. I was tired of organizing events, patching the leaks in other people's plumbing.

A homeless man I sort of know was selling *Street-Wise* near my office. Like Lydia, Elton was too allergic to other people to go into a shelter, but at least, when he'd had pneumonia last winter, he'd let me take him to County for treatment.

When I bought a paper from him, he gave me a few fragmented sentences, dancing uneasily from foot to foot, and finally backing down the sidewalk. When he was at a safe distance, he called, "Dude wants you."

He jerked his head at a bullet-colored Land Rover across the street. "Came out and rang your bell and got back in."

Before I could thank him, Elton had darted to the Polonia Triangle, a minute park created by the intersection of three streets not far from my office. He somehow made it across six lanes of traffic unscathed. Perhaps the traffic island made him feel safe, like Lydia in her hole.

As I typed in the door code to my building, I stood in profile so that I could keep an eye on the Land Rover. No one emerged, but about five seconds after I'd turned on the lights inside my office, the outer doorbell rang. I switched my computer screen to read the security camera that surveys the street and saw Murray Ryerson. Someone was behind him, but Murray's a big man; all I could see of his pal was a shoulder in a tan jacket.

My immediate, overwhelming feeling was fury. I'd told him no, and he'd come to wheedle me into yes.

"Busy day here in the detecting mines, Ryerson," I

called through the intercom. "You're not on my calendar."

"I'm here with Norm Bolton, Warshawski. We only need five minutes."

Norm Bolton? I asked my device, which told me a Norman Bolton headed Global Entertainment's Spinning Earth division. Music, TV, streaming, the company's big moneymakers. I scrolled through the rest of the Spinning Earth subdivisions. The *Herald-Star* was in Bolton's fief, but such a small contributor to Global's profit centers that it was lumped with "miscellaneous" media.

I waited for them in the doorway of my office suite.

"Lucky for both of us I don't carry," I said to Murray. "Otherwise I'd be spending a lot of years in Logan while your friends and family grieved over your grave. How can I persuade you that 'no' means 'no'?"

Murray didn't answer. He kept his eyes on his feet as I escorted him and Bolton into what my architect called "the client zone" when she tried to bring the high ceilings and cement walls into human proportions.

The client zone has a couch and a couple of faux Barcelona chairs. Also side tables with lamps and boxes of tissues—asking for a detective's help can be very emotional. I figured that wouldn't be the case today, or at least, the emotions weren't likely to run to distress.

Bolton was short for a man, not quite my own height. Perhaps that's why he crunched my fingers together when we shook hands. I twisted my wrist around his so that he was forced to let go. We both pretended this hadn't happened.

While they settled themselves—Bolton on the couch, spreading his arms across the top of the cushions, Murray in one of the side chairs—I went around the partition corner to get my bankbook from a filing cabinet. I wrote out a check to Murray for the amount of the retainer he'd paid and handed it to him before rolling my desk chair around to face the couch.

Murray laid the check on the side table. "Vic, wait—"

I ignored him. "Okay, gentlemen: I can give you five minutes. The clock has started."

"Is that your usual approach to clients, Ms. Warshawski?" Bolton looked amused. "Tell your story in five minutes or get out?"

I made a pretense of scrolling through my phone. "Someone accused me the other day of slowing down with age, so I wondered if I'd forgotten your hiring me, but I don't see you in my client log."

Bolton thought that was funny enough to deserve

a loud crack of laughter. "I do want to hire you, Ms. Warshawski. Ryerson speaks highly of you as an investigator, which is more or less what I have in mind. I understand you and he have worked on a number of high-profile situations together over the years."

I looked thoughtful. "High-profile situations . . . that would be corp-speak for major crimes. Is there such a crime you'd like me to tackle?"

Bolton abandoned his space-grabbing posture to lean forward, hands on knees: he was in earnest. "It's Lydia Zamir, Ms. Warshawski. I understand you've become a part of her life."

"Then you understand more than I do, Mr. Bolton." I looked at him steadily, but he didn't show any discomfort.

"Wasn't your goddaughter arrested for trying to intervene in Zamir's life?"

"She wasn't arrested," I said. "I'm sure Murray didn't tell you she had been—he's too good a reporter to fiddle with facts."

"Anything involving Fouchard or Boom-Boom is news in this town, Vic, you know that as well as I do," Murray put in. "Some guy in the Second District made the connection to Boom-Boom when your kid was brought in. It didn't take Picasso to connect the dots to Zamir."

"I think you mean Seurat." When he looked blank, I added, "Dot painter. Bernadine Fouchard was never arrested. And no matter what Fouchard did or who knows her or my cousin's names, I still am not part of Lydia Zamir's life. So if you were hoping for an exclusive interview, with me or with Bernadine, I have to disappoint you. Two minutes left."

"Your life would make a great TV series," Bolton said. "Your work has all the drama we look for in our short series—the chases, the high-profile situations, and then you're a female, and that's hot right now."

"Yep. Every thirty or forty years, being female is hot, and then the men in charge get bored with us and revert back to filming the creatures they know best: the faces they see in the mirror every morning."

The corners of Norm's mouth twitched as he fought back a frown.

"Warshawski, PI?" Murray said. "I thought this was about—"

"Seeing the dynamic duo in action," Bolton cut across him. "I told you: the two of you have a reputation in this town. We want to see how you go about an actual investigation, and the Zamir story is perfect— it's got everything, from murder to sex. I went to the Golden Glow last night, and your gal Sal is phenomenal. And she gives us diversity."

"Right. Glamorous African-American lesbian, a twofer."

"Exactly." Bolton smiled as if we were buddies. "You can even bring in the old guy you live with."

"Old is hot, as well? Thank you, but I have an active real detective practice."

"A hundred thousand an episode," Bolton said, "with a guarantee of a minimum of six episodes, even if the series never airs. We'd start with Lydia Zamir— follow you as you try to trace her. And, you know, people love being on camera—if we put out a call saying that anyone who's seen Zamir gets a cameo on the show, we'd get the public involved in the investigation."

"Wow," I said. "As Lieutenant Kojak used to say, a hundred—no, six hundred thousand—is sure a lot of balloons. And having a whole lot of strangers underfoot while I tried to track down a lead—that makes it irresistible. And yet, I will persist in resisting." I permitted myself a small tight smile, self-congratulation at my witty riposte.

Murray kept his eyes on the floor, but Bolton said, "One-twenty an episode."

"Don't you have a legal team that handles these kinds of negotiations?"

"I'm on the Global executive committee," Bolton

said. "We have fluid lines of command. Believe me, the board, including Oscar Taney, is behind this project."

I didn't need Siri to tell me that Taney was the majority owner and chair of Global Enterprises.

"We want to find Lydia Zamir," Bolton said. "We owe her a good outcome to her story after our TV crew frightened her into running off—even though it was totally unintentional and certainly within the bounds of modern journalism."

"Always good to check the liability box," I agreed gravely. "Have modern journalism's bounds expanded to include chasing people into the path of danger?"

This time Bolton did frown, but he decided to overlook the comment. "You find her, we get her medical care, it's win-win—especially for you, since you walk away with close to three quarters of a million."

He pulled some papers out of his breast pocket and laid them on the glass tabletop in front of him. "The details are in here. In fact, we'll make it one-twenty-five."

He took out an elegant little fountain pen, found the relevant page, and wrote in the new amount. When he put the pen back inside his jacket, I longed to see it leak all over the tan linen weave.

I looked at my watch. "Gentlemen, you were so beguiling I let you have nine minutes. Now I have real-life clients, who don't want their business on cable for the world to watch. *Fino al prossimo.*"

Bolton got to his feet. "Offer's good for twenty-four hours, Warshawski—you'd be smart to take it."

I walked him down to the outer door, basically wanting to be sure he actually left the building. Murray stayed behind. When I got back to my office, he was standing at my desk, playing with a letter opener that a knife-making client had created for me.

"Explain to me what in Conan Doyle's name was going on just now. No way does Global think they want me in a docudrama. There wasn't even the pretense of a screen test, for one thing, and for another, that's not how people at Bolton's level operate. He'd send a flunky down, and it wouldn't be for this kind of money. Either the company is so desperate to get hold of Lydia that they'll go through this ridiculous charade, or they're dangling all these balloons in front of me to keep my attention from something that they don't want me to see. Am I working on a project that touches Global's interests?"

Murray shifted uncomfortably. The letter opener started to fall and he grabbed at it, slicing his fingers.

"Go bleed over that ludicrous contract while I get a wet cloth," I said. "Real blood on the paper will make it seem like an authentic docudrama."

While Murray tended to his cuts, I scrolled through my list of open projects. I didn't think any of them connected to Global's interests, but Global has a thousand tentacles—any of them could be attached to one of my clients without my knowing.

"Okay, I'll bite," I said. "What made you be a party to this repellent idea?"

"Bolton pitched it differently when he called me this morning." Murray kept his attention on his fingers, drying them one at a time before taping over the cuts. "He said everyone at Global knows how much I want to get back to significant journalism—and you know that's true. He said there's a lot of talk around town about work we did together—they even teach the Humboldt Chemical investigation at Medill."

Medill, Northwestern's journalism school, wrestles with a few other universities for top national billing.

I sat on the corner of my desk. "You get a royalty for the case study?"

"No." He flushed but kept fiddling with the Band-Aids, not looking up. "Just saying, you and I have a reputation. Bolton said if we both wore a wire while we hunted for Zamir it would be a ratings bonanza and would open the door to other reporting assignments."

"And you bought it? How could you be so totally naive? Wearing a wire while talking to witnesses? Protecting the source—that's what you do when you're digging deep. And there's no deep digging here, anyway. Just titillation. Did Bolton know you'd asked me to find Zamir?"

"No. He's been pounding on me from the moment Zamir disappeared from Provident, although at first it seemed to be coming down the pipe to me through the *Star*'s editorial team. When you showed up on different news feeds because of the Fouchard kid being connected to Prinz, they thought they could work out a deal with you—of course they know we have a history."

I digested that. "Murray, turn on your J-dar. Guy is flattering you and trying to buy me off. There's something he doesn't want us to know, or maybe he wants to be there doing damage control if we find it out. I can't believe Zamir is important to them."

He finally looked up. "Yeah, but I don't know what it could be. I read everything I could find on Zamir after they started bird-dogging me. It's a big story, but big like an opera—not big like a cover-up. Global is mad about gun control, I mean mad against it, and the Zamir story starts with that mass murder in Kansas. But that was four years ago. It's been superseded by Parkland and El Paso and way too many others."

"Elisa Palurdo is living with death threats from

mass slaughter deniers," I said, "but even that will only be news if one of the freaks actually kills her. As for Zamir, she's afraid, or she wouldn't have fled the hospital, but I can't believe she's afraid of a living, breathing threat, or she wouldn't have been living openly on the streets before your story ran."

"Tell me the truth, Warshawski. Did you find Lydia Zamir? Do you know where she is?"

I smiled sardonically. "You know what Mencken said—the smallest atom of truth comes from the agony of someone who dug it up. You don't throw it about like loose change."

21
Combing Through Trash

Time was when I would have trusted Murray with the information about Lydia's hideout. Not now. He might imagine he was being loyal to me, to the story, to the source, but his first allegiance would be to the person he thought could advance his career.

I felt a painful mix of grief and anger when I escorted him out the front door. His red hair was streaked with gray, and he had deep grooves around his mouth. He was like a man in a rowboat, desperately trying to catch up with a departing ship, and I hated it. Our work had made us closer than lovers at times. I hated thinking I could not trust him.

As I skimmed through the contract that Bolton had left, I wondered if it was standard in any way. It spelled out what Warshawski would do for the consideration of money, which basically amounted to an open-ended agreement for Global to record my every move. My first impulse was to put it through my shredder, but on second thought I sent it to Freeman Carter, my lawyer, asking him to check for any hidden bombs—like whether just touching it made me Global's indentured servant.

I put in an hour for my paying clients, but another aspect of Lydia Zamir's unraveling nagged at me. Her rage at the lawyers from Devlin & Wickham, who'd undertaken the defense of her lover's killer. Elisa Palurdo said Lydia had jumped Arthur Morton in the courtroom and had to be pulled away from him. She'd then gone after the lawyers. It wasn't surprising, but I wondered how extreme her behavior had been, both in court and here in Chicago at the firm.

The Wichita *Eagle* had covered the trial, which of course wasn't solely for Hector Palurdo's murder: sixteen other people had been killed in Horsethief Canyon, which seemed to be part of a state park in central Kansas. The *Eagle* had a paragraph for each of the victims; they'd ranged in age from seventy-five to a baby whose mother was also killed—two bullets went through the baby's tiny chest and into the mother's heart. The photos and descriptions made for sickening reading, but I pushed through it, entering all the names into my Bernie-Zamir case file and searching to see if any of the victims had cropped up in the news in other ways.

Two of the dead were organizers of the event where Palurdo and Zamir were performing. It had originally been an annual music festival called "Tallgrass Sings," which raised money for organizations that protected the remaining prairie lands in Kansas. They'd changed the name to Tallgrass Meet-Up some years earlier and for some time it had collected money for a number of people or groups that used the land or worked on the land. After a number of immigrants who worked on the area's big ranches were detained and deported, the organizers decided to use part of the money they raised for immigrant aid.

Despite Kansas's reputation for extreme conservatism, there'd been a lot of local support for the fundraiser. Ranchers depended on the Mexican cattle hands. Feedlots depended on the Somalis who were willing to work in the slaughterhouses. A number of big-ag companies made sizable contributions—Sea-2-Sea kicked in fifteen thousand with a lot of fanfare, but feedlots and other big-ag companies gave as well.

According to the *Eagle,* this wide-spectrum support only fueled the rage along the dark web fringe. I found some of the posts the news report mentioned. I learned: Jews control big agricultural companies, Muslims want to impose Islamic law on Kansans, Mexican immigrants were all criminals who want to murder women and rape cattle.

At Arthur Morton's trial, the Devlin attorneys painted a picture of a youth unbalanced emotionally by the unfair loss of the family farm. Morton had been susceptible to the messages hammered into him day and night by the dark web—as if the websites had jumped off the screen and entered into his room in the middle of the night against his volition.

Morton's defense resonated with those jurors who spoke to the *Eagle* after the trial. Some had families who'd farmed in Kansas for over a century. They knew the struggles to keep a family farm going when all the government did was offer handouts to criminals, not help to American farmers.

In fact, the support Sea-2-Sea and other agricultural behemoths had given the festival made some of the jurors support opinions on the websites Morton had cruised before the murders. The jurors agreed that evidence proved Morton had acted alone, that he'd killed seventeen and wounded many others, but they saw him as a victim, too, and undeserving of a death sentence. I also found some astonishing defenses of Morton in leftwing blogs, who claimed him as a victim of late-stage capitalism.

Reading the reports left me feeling dirty. Everyone was doing the same dance, over and over, throwing filth, acting outraged, and nothing changed, except hatreds became more entrenched and more people felt entitled to commit mass murder. Even so, I was going to have to swim in the cesspool until I figured out why Global Entertainment was trying to oversee my inquiries around Lydia Zamir.

I created a database that included the names of all the victims and wounded from the massacre. I also included the names from all my current open investigations. While my search engines crawled around the web to find any connections among them, I phoned Bernie, to see how she was holding up.

Despite her mother's claim that running around coaching soccer was the best therapy for her, Bernie sounded despondent. "In my head I keep asking what was Leo doing, going into the park instead of meeting me for supper. Why did he not even text me?"

"Was that typical of him, to be focused so intently on something he would forget what was going on around him?" I asked.

"Typical? I can't say typical; I knew him such a

short time." She paused, thinking, then added, "I told you how after the meeting, the one where he ran away from Coop, he needed to do something about the foyer. I couldn't understand, since he went straight to his computer. So yes, I was annoyed then, but maybe that was typical. And I am the same, after all."

"Is that what drew you together?" I asked. "You're both intense?"

"Oh, he wasn't intense, just focused when it was a problem to solve. Why I liked him—he listened to me. He was not interested in sports, but he started to study hockey after he met me. He learned about Pierre and Boom-Boom, and started asking me how I play, how I keep my teeth from being broken, and even the rules of hockey. No boy ever truly listened to me before."

I let a respectful silence pass before going back to my questions. "He'd been upset about some paper that the SLICK people hadn't told him about. Did he talk about that? Is that what he was trying to look up?"

"He was upset that they did something without telling him—something about the plan for the new beach, that's all I know. And I guess he wanted to check on it. Maybe he wanted to know if it was legal? Or even if it was possible as an engineering project? I don't know. I told you this—he wanted to see what wildlife lived in the Wildlife Corridor."

"Do you know if he fought—argued—with Simon— the documents guy—after the meeting?" I asked.

"I keep telling you! Leo was not a fighter, even though I told him that is the only way with bullies, but he was like, like one of those willow trees that bend down under the wind."

"At least they're still alive after a tornado goes through," I said dryly.

"No, Vic, you are wrong. He is not still alive. Maybe if he fought, he would be."

I apologized—I'd spoken thoughtlessly. "I'm very sorry he died, very sorry you had to see his dead body."

"*Merci, Vic*," she said in the same small voice. "I hope you will find that *canaille* who murdered him."

"I'll do my best, sweetheart."

After we'd hung up, I wondered, though. Leo wasn't a fighter, but he was a data analyst. If Simon Lensky had been fudging data, Leo could have pressed him in a way that made Simon defensive, angry. I tried to imagine Simon luring Leo into the Wildlife Corridor and hitting him on the head to stop him questioning Simon's authority.

I couldn't picture it. The SLICK triumvirate didn't seem organized or capable enough to commit murder— as I'd told Coop earlier, they could barely run a meet- ing. Of course, angry incompetent people can still commit murder. I probably should check on what the SLICK trio knew of Leo's movements after the meeting.

All the SLICK officers were volunteers, so they must have paying jobs doing something else. Simon Lensky worked in the billing department at one of the big downtown hospitals. It wouldn't be easy or even sensible to confront him at work. Curtis Murchison, the angry gaveller, was a security guard at a West Side branch of the Chicago Public Library.

Mona Borsa was retired, after thirty-seven years teaching first grade, and so might be the easiest to confront in the middle of the day. I would never have guessed she'd been a primary school teacher. I imagined her in a classroom, striding back and forth, whacking her palm with a pointer every time an unfortunate child stumbled over a new word.

I called, said I was looking into Leo Prinz's death and wanted to talk to her about background. Mona surprised me by being genial and happy to meet. She was helping plant trees in one of the South Side parks, but she said if I wanted to bring a sandwich she'd talk to me during her lunch break.

I didn't have time to stop for food, just headed straight for Rainbow Beach Park at Seventy-seventh Street. Mona was sitting with a small group at a picnic table on the grassy sward west of the beach. They had finished eating; Mona was collecting everyone's trash in a paper bag.

When I came to the table, her surprising geniality continued, as if our confrontation before the SLICK meeting hadn't happened. She introduced me to the other volunteers and told me I could talk to her while she worked. The volunteers separated, each pulling a wagon that held a sapling and digging tools.

"What did you say you want to talk about?" Mona asked when we got to her spot.

"Leo Prinz," I said. "You know I'm an investigator, right? And I'm looking into his murder."

"The police are handling that," she said, her voice sharper.

"I have an interest: my goddaughter was dating Leo. She and her parents have asked me to get involved."

Borsa eyed me narrowly, the way she must have looked at her first-graders to see who really had stolen the other kids' lunch money. She grunted something that might have been an invitation to go ahead.

"Leo Prinz was studying urban planning. Is that why you hired him?"

"We didn't need an urban planner. We needed someone who could put our presentations together for the Park District and for community meetings. He knew how to do that kind of design, and he was asking less money than more experienced designers."

She took a plastic bag from her wagon and handed it to me. "You can start cleaning up the area while I get the hole dug."

I squatted, but my hamstrings were still stressed from yesterday's hard slog. I sat cross-legged and reached in a circle around me for the wretched refuse of Chicago's park users.

"At one point in Leo's presentation, he got flustered and knocked a bunch of Simon's papers off the table. When he picked them up, one of the documents took him by surprise and he wanted to know why it wasn't in the presentation."

"So?" Mona paused in her digging to wipe her face with the kerchief she'd tied around her throat.

"So—what was in the document that it got Leo's attention?"

"What difference does it make? It doesn't have anything to do with his death. You've missed a bunch of cigarette butts."

"So I have," I agreed. "It's possible that someone asked Leo to meet him—or her—or them—in the Wildlife Corridor. I'd like to make sure it wasn't Simon, or you, for that matter, worried by what Leo had seen in that document."

Mona dropped her shovel. "You're crazy. You think one of us—"

"I don't think anything. I'm trying to get information. What was it that took Leo so much by surprise that he couldn't make it through the rest of his presentation?"

Mona snorted. "Nothing. Simon keeps every document that ever passes through his hands. Then he gets confused about which are current and which are old. Leo saw one of the old ones, but that wasn't what made him leave—that was because of Coop, who's completely out of control. Coop started for the stage and Leo headed for the exit. Coop had already jumped him once. I thought a homeless man in the park must have killed Leo, but now I'm betting it was Coop."

"Tell me about Coop, then." I picked up three empty chip bags and a Seagram's pint.

"He's got a terrible temper."

"What's his last name? Where's he from?"

She'd picked up her shovel and was digging a hole at high speed. "No one knows. A couple of the local stores took him on part-time, but he couldn't keep his temper when customers said something against his code, and they had to fire him. He acts like he's the only person who cares about the environment, so he started disrupting SLICK meetings, as if God had put him in charge of the park."

"But no one knows his name?" I was incredulous. "To get hired, he'd have to give a name, a Social Security number."

She looked at me sideways. "Small businesses use cash a lot of times."

I nodded. Of course they did.

"I tried to find out." Mona stopped digging to glare at me. "That homeless woman, Lydia, she was a public nuisance, but when I went to court to get her admitted, Coop had already got himself appointed her legal guardian. Leo dug up a copy of the guardianship agreement for us. It gave Coop's name as Coop with his legal address in Humboldt Park. Simon and Curtis and I drove over one night, and the address was a vacant lot!"

She thrust her shovel into the ground with such force that she couldn't get it out. I had to help her pull it out of the ground. She didn't thank me. When I said I needed to be going, she had another spurt of her own anger.

"There's a lot of trash you haven't gotten to." She pointed at a well-used Pamper. "And you still haven't picked up those butts."

"There's a lot of trash everywhere, Ms. Borsa," I said sadly. "I can't keep up with it."

22
Missing in Action

I sat on a ledge overlooking the lake, eating a black-eyed pea taco I'd found at a vegan restaurant near the beach. Sailboats were out on the water, runners and bikers were passing on the path below my ledge. Was I the only person in Chicago who had to work in the summer?

Coop had a short fuse, but then, so did Mona, and so did the third member of the SLICK troika, Curtis the gaveller. Mona's pointer that she waved around didn't seem substantial enough to do the damage Leo's skull had received. Curtis's gavel, though—if Leo had roused his wrath, that would pack a nice wallop.

I should have pressed Mona harder on Simon's document. Mona claimed that Leo had reacted to an old paper that Simon had mixed in with current pages. At

the meeting, though, Simon had said it was a preliminary report. Mona didn't seem like a subtle person,
but she'd managed to push my attention away from the
document onto Coop. Maybe I was putting too much
emphasis on the episode—after all, Mona was right—it
was seeing Coop that made Leo flee the room.

I finished my taco and lay down on the ledge. Hu-
midity was low, the sky was a clear blue with a few
wispy clouds. A perfect day for hooky. I drowsed for
some minutes until I felt a sharp nip on my fingers. I
sat up with a squawk: a sparrow, emboldened by my
immobility, had tried pecking at the crumbs on my
fingers—a signal that there is no rest for the detective.

On my way north I stopped at the Second District.
Sergeant Pizzello was not overcome with joy when she
saw me. And she definitely wasn't impressed with my
suggestions about exploring the SLICK trio.

"That organization does a lot of good on the South
Side, especially with getting kids out on the water. A
kid who's trying to keep a sailboard upright isn't going
to be hanging with a gang and holding people up at
gunpoint. I have no interest in finding out what papers
Simon Whatsis dropped at the last meeting, so, no, I
won't try to get a search warrant for SLICK's storage
cupboard at the old bank. I have no interest in going

at cross-purposes with Parks Super Taggett, for that matter."

"Chief of detectives golfs with him?" I said.

Pizzello gave me a dirty look, but muttered, "Boats. They're on the same Mackinac crew."

Hence the Second District's enthusiasm for water sports. "What about the gavel?" I asked. "Highly polished object—could it be the murder weapon?"

Pizzello was about to utter a blistering no, but she pulled herself up. "It's possible, I suppose. But then how did it get into that bit of park?"

"If Leo had arranged to meet Curtis—"

"No. Get over it, Warshawski. Must be nice to be a private eye, spend your life making up ridiculous theories for the police to investigate, but I have real work to do."

I forbore saying that investigating Leo's murder was real work. I don't know why I'd stopped to talk to her in the first place. Maybe because I was feeling whipsawed and was hoping for a case discussion with someone I could trust. And odd as it sounds, I did trust Pizzello, despite her judgment lapse in strip-searching Bernie in the park after Leo's death.

Leo wanted to do something about a foyer, Bernie said. But he went to his computer, not to a building.

Of course, he might have been looking at architectural plans online, but—

"Foyer," I said out loud.

As soon as I got to my office, I called Bernie. "You said Leo wanted to do something with a foyer. Could he have said FOIA?"

"Yes, that is what he said, what I told you, foyer."

To her Quebec ear, the two apparently sounded indistinguishable.

"There's a law that lets citizens demand documents from the government. It's an acronym: Freedom of Information Act, *F-O-I-A*. Was this about the document he saw at the meeting? Did he say if he was submitting a FOIA? Or was he looking at a document Simon got in response to a FOIA of his own?" Either way, no wonder the SLICK leadership was worried about an outsider seeing it.

"I barely understand one word you are saying," Bernie cried. "I cannot tell you what he knew, what he did not know, or where he was wanting this foyer to go. I only know that when we reached his apartment, he is going straight to his computer and writing an email before he is even kissing me!"

Sergeant Pizzello had made me feel a bit stupid for thinking that the SLICK documents had anything to do with Leo's being in the Burnham Wildlife Corridor when he was killed. But if he saw something really out of line—if the Park District, or Simon himself, were fiddling with maps or money and knew Leo suspected it—that might be an ample motive for murder.

"I want to look at Leo's computer," I said. "What was his address?"

"Me, I don't have a key," Bernie said. "We were not together so very long, you know."

"I'll worry about that—just give me the address."

Leo's apartment was on South Ingleside, walking distance from the University of Chicago campus as well as the old bank building on Forty-seventh Street where SLICK met. The building was one of those ramshackle warrens where students could afford rent—a six-flat cut into pieces to turn it into a twelve-flat.

For an old-school solo op like me, it was a good apartment: the front door had a feeble lock that responded to my picks, not something modern like an iris scanner. As it turned out, it could have required voice recognition and the name of the person's great-grandmother, because the door opened when I turned the knob.

I tensed, but at first I didn't think there was anything out of the ordinary, just the typical chaos of a student apartment: papers on the floor, on the chairs, books open facedown and faceup.

I put on some latex gloves to lift the books, looking for a laptop. That was when I became worried. There was no sign of the computer, a flash drive, a backup drive. A printer lay on the floor under the table. The cartridge had come free; I saw it lying next to the wall. Someone had hurled the printer onto the floor hard enough to shatter the plastic case.

Did this chaos predate Leo's death? Someone had come specifically for the computer, Leo had interrupted them, and then had been lured to the park. No, that didn't make sense. But—what, then?

I texted Bernie: Did Leo have roommates.

He lived alone. Why?

I sent her a photo of the disarray and the broken printer. I wondered if Leo had done this himself.

Not Leo! He is always neat, everything put away. Someone broke in. I am on my way.

We had a few more exchanges, all having to do with Bernie thinking she needed to get to Leo's apartment immediately to get on the trail of whoever had broken in. I finally hung up on her.

I went on to explore the rest of the apartment. Nothing in the kitchen, nothing in the bathroom, nothing in the bedroom. A sky-blue backpack turned inside out, the pockets slit.

I debated the matter, but called Sergeant Pizzello.

"We serve and protect, Warshawski. What kind of service do you need now? Or is it protection?"

"I'm at Leo Prinz's apartment. Did your tech crew come through?"

"Why on earth would they? We're swamped, Warshawski. We don't act like *CSI* or *NCIS* on every random mugging in the park."

"I wondered if you'd collected his electronics, so you could see what he'd been up to."

"You're trying to tell me they're missing. And you think something fancy happened to them, such as Mona Borsa sneaking in to filch them. I run into her from time to time when we're policing boating events. She's well-meaning, even if she's bossy, but she is not mentally organized enough to put together some super plot. You PIs are all alike—you want some big drama that will get you headlines, but crime isn't like that, especially not crime in Chicago."

As she'd intended, her remarks made me feel foolish. She asked for Leo's address—not with the intention of stopping by, but to reenforce her message.

"South Side of Chicago, Warshawski, not the North Shore. Prinz was killed by a drunk in the park. His crib was burgled by a stoner on the street who realized the joint had been unoccupied for a few days. End of story."

"You've made an arrest?" I said. "Found blood, phone, whatnot?"

"Not yet, Warshawski, but we will."

"That means Bernadine Fouchard's parents can take her back to Quebec, then."

Pizzello was silent for a beat or two. "Jealous girl-friend with a strong forehand is always a good number two. Keep her in Chicago until we make an arrest. If you want to keep digging, Warshawski, be my guest. I think it's a big time-waste, but that at least will keep you from bugging me."

Simply because Pizzello had wrong-footed me, I sorted through the books and papers on the floor. Leo had been studying urban planning, but that apparently covered a lot of ground: he had printouts of econometric articles, articles on his special interest—how planners need to be aware of the way human spaces change wildlife habitats. The articles I glanced at said that planners need to keep in mind that coyotes are common in all U.S. cities. Bobcats, raccoons, even bears are starting to share urban spaces.

When I saw these essays, I understood why Leo had wanted to explore wildlife in the Burnham Corridor the night he was killed. If the Park District was going to remake that habitat, someone needed a census on what was living in the park. Unfortunately, understanding Leo's research didn't explain why he'd stood up Bernie.

I called the hospital where Simon worked. I wanted to ask him point-blank about the printout he and Leo had argued over at the meeting. I got his supervisor in the billing department, who told me that staff couldn't take personal calls during work hours.

"It's not personal," I said. "I'm a detective; I want to—"

"Has something happened to him?" she said sharply.

"Why? Didn't he come in today?"

"No, he didn't. I tried phoning him and left a voice-mail. He's the one person who understands the Hand-Clasp software; he should leave word where to reach him. Where is he? What's happened to him?"

"We're trying to find him ourselves," I said. "He's the one person who understands a set of documents we're trying to get access to."

I asked if Simon were prone to taking off without a word, but the supervisor said it was completely out of character. "He doesn't have a family, except for the one son who has to be in a care facility. Other than the child, his life revolves around that park group he volunteers for. He loves that work—you should try them. I don't have any names or phone numbers but I'm sure the police could find them."

We hung up on mutual promises to call if either of us got word of him. I called Mona, to see if she'd heard from Simon.

"He was mugged on his way home from the SLICK meeting. He said he wasn't hurt, but he was bruised. He's probably taking a few days off."

"Mugged? Did he—where?"

"Outside his apartment, he told me, when he was getting out of his car. If he forgot to call his boss, it's really not your business."

I agreed. "Even so, I'd like to check in on him."

She was contemptuous but finally divulged his home address.

Simon lived in a well-kept building in South Shore, a stone's throw from the lake. The super let me in when I explained the worry over his disappearance. Like the building, Simon's apartment was tidy and well furnished. The super stood over me while I made sure Simon wasn't in any of the five rooms or the closets. I gave him a twenty for his pains, but he still wouldn't let me explore the place on my own. He ushered me out without giving me a chance to hunt for Simon's stash of maps and architectural drawings.

23

Local Excavation

Simon might have fled town to avoid the police investigation. He might have gotten fed up with his job and gone out of town to gamble on a riverboat. While I crawled home along Lake Shore Drive I considered another half dozen ideas, including the possibility that Curtis or Mona or even Parks Super Taggett had assaulted him.

When I finally reached home, I made myself give up on it: not only did I have no data, but I also had no income stream to support an investigation into Simon's disappearance. It was late afternoon on a long day—I didn't have energy left to start a new project. Instead, I rode my bike to the lake, carrying one of the many important novels I never get around to reading. It had been so long since I'd looked at the book that I started again at the beginning, back on the sugar plantation. I thought I was focusing until my phone startled me awake.

I barely croaked out "Hello" before the voice on the other end cried, "I can't find her."

"This is V.I. Warshawski." I got to my feet, rubbing sleep out of my eyes. "Is that who you're trying to reach?"

"It's Elisa Palurdo, Ms. Warshawski," my caller said. "I followed your directions exactly, but Lydia wasn't there."

I tried to push my brain to work. Lydia gone— she'd fled because of my finding her, or she'd been picked up by cops, or by Coop or—other disturbing possibilities.

"You found a hole sheltered by fallen stones?" I asked. "Up on the train embankment, about three hundred yards north of Forty-seventh Street?"

"Yes, I did find it. The thought that anyone—that Lydia—could be living there! Squirrels jumped out when I shone my flashlight into it. I saw empty food cartons and a dirty blanket, but I couldn't bear to climb down into it myself."

I had a kink in my shoulders from sleeping against a rock. I tried to stretch it out while we spoke.

"What will you do?" Palurdo prodded me.

"There's nothing I can do. She's moved on, whether on her own or with someone else, and I have zero ways to locate her."

"How about the man Coop?" she said.

"It's possible, but I don't know how to reach him, either. I can't hang out along the lakefront, waiting for him to materialize."

"No, of course not," she muttered. "I don't know why I'm upbraiding you, when I myself backed away from Lydia months ago. It's just—I guess I was play-ing a pretend movie, where she would want to come home with me, get proper support, return to being the woman my son fell in love with."

"Do you want to call the police about this?" I asked.

"No, oh, no! I can't bear to talk to the police. And what would I tell them? How would I explain why I was looking for her there?"

"Tell them the truth—you heard it from me. It won't be the first time I've pissed off Chicago cops."

"Can't you come down here?" Palurdo begged. "I'm still on Forty-seventh Street, at a drugstore in a mall there."

I looked at my watch. Just after six. The thought of one more trip to the South Side in Chicago's traf-fic made me want to scream. On the other hand, no way was I going to call the police a third time today.

It would be ugly, anyway, since I'd have to admit I'd found Zamir yesterday.

Warning Palurdo that I couldn't get there quickly, I biked home to collect heavier shoes, work gloves, wind pants, and a windbreaker to put on if I went into Lydia's hole. I also collected the dogs—I'd take them to the lake after I finished with Palurdo.

I made better time than I'd expected. The police barriers were gone from the lot south of the Burnham Wildlife Corridor. Leaning against the side of the car, I pulled on my protective gear, sticking my work flashlight into my day pack with the gloves and hard hat.

When we got to the embankment, I didn't see Palurdo, but she emerged from the box of a waiting room on the platform in response to my text.

Palurdo followed me in silence as I led the way to Lydia's hideout. When we got there, I lay flat, shining my work flash around the hole, but couldn't see anything other than the detritus Palurdo had described.

I gave her the dogs' leashes to hold while I climbed down. Lydia might have lived there only a few days, but there was an unpleasant fetid smell. Holding my breath, I used my work gloves to lift the old blanket. I'd feared I might see Lydia's emaciated body underneath, but no one was there. The only life I saw was some beetles, working industriously on what was left of the food I'd brought. I crouched and shone my flash around the hole.

You couldn't stand in there. My legs were cramping again from squatting, but before I backed out, some impulse made me look up at the rocks overhead. I almost missed the piece of polished wood, so covered in dirt had it become.

I sat down hard. Had it been here yesterday, when I came on Lydia? Lydia had been holding her hands behind her back, as if protecting something. Could have been the gavel. She could have stuffed it up into the ceiling of her cubbyhole for safekeeping.

Lydia couldn't have killed Leo—she was barely strong enough to lift a bottle of water. But—if Coop had killed Leo? Lydia might have hidden the gavel to protect Coop. But that didn't make sense—it would have meant Coop already knew where she was before he saw me yesterday. It was possible, I suppose, if he was really a cunning psychopath, instead of the angry, impulsive man he seemed to be on the surface. If he'd filched the gavel, lured Leo to the park, and bashed in his head, this was not just a calculated move, but the calculations of a terrifyingly insane person. If, if, if. And where was Lydia now?

I didn't touch the wood handle, didn't even try to blow away the dirt, just knelt to photograph it. I was betting it belonged to Curtis Murchison, betting it would have Leo Prinz's blood and skin fragments on it.

"Are you—is there a problem?" Palurdo called down to me.

"Sorry. Just trying to figure out what to do next." I backed out of the hole and hoisted myself onto the rim. I stripped off the windbreaker and pants; sweat had soaked my T-shirt and bra clear through. I took out my water bottle and drank deeply, then poured some of it over my head.

"You don't think she's dead, do you?" Palurdo asked, so nervous that she loosened her grip on the leashes.

The dogs knocked me over in their enthusiasm, then tore off into the underbrush. Palurdo apologized anxiously for not holding on. She offered to help me corral the dogs, but I told her they would come back when their enthusiasm had worn off.

"You go on home. I've had a long day; I'm going to sit and let them come to me."

Palurdo hurried to the train platform, looking anxiously around her, as if fearing her stalkers might lie in wait for her here.

A couple of express trains thundered past. I couldn't sit like a stump with the dogs so near danger. I got to my feet and started thrashing through the under-growth.

Mitch and Peppy must have heard me: in a moment, they bounded up, eyes bright with the pleasure of getting covered in burrs and the stench of something rotten.

"It wasn't Lydia Zamir, was it?" I grabbed their leashes. "Please tell me she isn't dead. Please tell me if she is, you didn't disrespect her body by rolling in it."

We explored the underbrush for half an hour, but the only other humans I saw were some evening birders and the same man who'd been talking to spectral forces yesterday. I found a decaying rabbit and a malodorous raccoon—either could have perfumed the dogs.

I also tripped over some sticks with red flags on them. Surveyors had been at work in here. Maybe Giff Taggett and his pals had decided to jump the gun and start work on their expanded beach project. So often that was how construction got going in Chicago—the destruction of an airstrip near McCormick Place, the reconstruction of Soldier Field, both done in the dead of night, before any public planning process had taken place.

I thought of Larry Nieland and his expensively dressed friend at the SLICK meeting. If money was to be made along the lakefront, it wouldn't be by the community members who'd shown up for the SLICK meeting. More likely, it would be one of the companies on whose board Nieland sat.

The sun was setting when I took the dogs across Lake Shore Drive. The three of us swam for half an hour. The two-master I'd seen yesterday had disappeared, but other, smaller craft dotted the water. By the time we left the lake, the sun was below the horizon, bathing the western sky red-gold. My favorite time of year, these long light evenings with dusk folding us in a soft embrace.

Mr. Contreras bustled out when we got home. While he helped pull burrs from the dogs I told him what we'd been doing, including finding the gavel. I asked if he'd be willing to call the cops to tell them where it was hidden.

"I don't want to answer questions from Sergeant Pizzello about why I was exploring that part of the park. If she gets an anonymous tip from a man, she may guess I'm behind it, but she won't be able to prove a connection to me. I'll give you one of my burner phones so that they can't trace the call to you."

He was delighted to become part of the investigation. He called Pizzello's cell, reported the gavel. "Think you cops are looking for the weapon that killed young Prinz, ain't' cha? You didn't look very hard or far, did you?" He gave them directions to the hole and hung up.

He felt justifiably pleased with himself, so much so he wanted to grill a steak for us to share for dinner. I'd promised to meet Peter, but it was one of his attractions that he enjoyed spending time with my neighbor. We sat in the back garden, having a jolly time—enhanced on my part by Donna Lutas glowering at us from her kitchen door. Once a South Side street fighter, always a street fighter.

24

Something Is Happening, but You Don't Know What It Is, Do You, Ms. Jones?

Pizzello called just after six the next morning. "Warshawski? Did I wake you?"

"Sergeant, you phoned the lazy detective—any hour of the day or night you'd be waking me up."

"Tell me about the gavel," Pizzello said.

I sat up to read from the dictionary app on my phone. "'The gavel is a small mallet with which someone in charge of a meeting or auction—'"

Pizzello said, "I'm not in the mood. I'm sure you know I mean the gavel dumped in some rocks near the expressway."

That was a cheap trick, giving false information in

the hopes of startling me into revealing the truth. I almost fell for it.

"I can't tell you anything about that gavel. When did you find it? Does it belong to SLICK?"

Peter rolled over and put an arm around me, pulled me back down next to him.

"We haven't had time for a forensic analysis yet. But someone left a message on my cell phone last night, telling me where to look for it."

"And you think that 'someone' was me?" I said. "Just a minute while I look at my call log. I might have been sleep-talking—it's how we lazy detectives get through our workload."

"That stung, did it? No, it wasn't you, but I figure you have friends who'd do it for you. Someone had been camping in the hole by the expressway where we found the gavel. Was that Lydia Zamir?"

"Sergeant, I'm guessing you called at the dawn's early light in the hopes of knocking me off-balance, but I can't help you with gophers digging holes by—what, the Ryan? The Ike?"

She skipped a beat, then said, "I read my patrol unit's notes wrong. Wasn't the Ryan, but the Metra tracks down near where the Zamir woman used to camp out."

"Still can't help you," I said.

"What about the man Coop?"

"What about him, indeed?" I said. "I asked you for a last name and an address. Do you have those? If Coop lured Prinz into that wilderness to beat his brains in, he needs to be under lock and key ASAP."

"For a lazy woman, you work too hard," Peter said. He was nibbling on my left ear. "Stop the drudgery and get back under the sheets with me."

I rolled over into his arms. "A hardworking detective would already be out with her bloodhounds following a trail of creosote, not lolling around with an archaeologist."

We could hear Pizzello's squawk from my phone but I didn't bother to turn it off—she shouldn't have tried sucker-punching me.

We finally got up an hour later. Mr. Contreras had kept the dogs with him last night, but when I walked Peter down to his car, they were ready to run.

Peter scratched Mitch's ears. "Could you follow a creosote trail?" he said to the dog.

"He and Peppy have saved my life more than once. I don't know if they smell my fear across the miles, but I wouldn't trade them for fifty Sherlock Holmes bloodhounds."

"That's good." Peter was suddenly serious. "I'm leaving for Turkey in three days. I don't like you chasing after someone who bludgeons people's heads into pulp, even if you do have Mitch and Peppy on your side."

I didn't like the idea, either, which meant I needed to find out who it was as fast as possible. I drove the dogs up to Evanston to check on Bernie. She was getting ready to leave for her day's coaching job, but Arlette was coming with her.

"*Maman!* This is not take-your-mother-to-work day," Bernie protested.

"I think it's a great idea," I said.

"Me, too," Angela agreed. "I wish my mother could come up here to see me coach."

It didn't take much coaxing to persuade Bernie we were right. She was still nervy; she wanted the comfort of her mother's presence, just didn't want to admit it. I drove them to the West Side park where Bernie was working, ran the dogs around, let them jump into the lagoon, and got to my office by nine.

I called the hospital where Simon Lensky worked, but they still hadn't heard from him. Neither had Mona or Curtis.

"But we only meet when we have SLICK issues to discuss," Mona said. "Sometimes weeks go by when we don't talk to each other. If his son had a bad turn, he's probably staying at the care facility."

She gave me the name, but when I called, they also

hadn't seen Simon. He'd been mugged after the SLICK meeting. Leo had been killed. The two events had to be connected through the document the two had argued over, but I couldn't figure out how to find a link.

Over my first cortado of the day, I went back to Larry Nieland's web page, the one where he listed the boards he sat on. The surveyors' sticks I'd found in the Burnham Wildlife Corridor had left me curious about whether a private company was already giving money to the Park District.

I was hoping one of Nieland's companies might be connected to the elegantly dressed man who'd sat next to him in the SLICK meeting, but four of the six were closely held, which meant they didn't have to list their board or their officers for any public documents. One of the U.S. companies was a hedge fund, which meant Nieland definitely could afford a better wardrobe. One was a Fortune 100 company that did everything from building nuclear reactors to trading in dried seaweed.

The South American companies included one called Minas y Puentes—Mines and Bridges—which might be anything. Another seemed to deal mostly with exporting raw materials, although I might have deciphered the Spanish wrong.

When I'd first looked at Nieland's profile, I'd dug up his cell phone number. On an impulse, I called him.

"I don't talk on or off the record with reporters unless the interview has been set up by my public relations manager."

"Very wise, Mr. Nieland. I'm not a reporter, but an investigator, curious about your involvement in the Park District plans to redesign the Forty-seventh Street lakefront."

He paused a beat too long before saying, "I'm not involved in that."

"Then it was an exceptionally generous pro bono act to come to the community meeting last week and pinch-hit for Superintendent Taggett."

"Oh, that. Giff Taggett and I are old sailing competitors and therefore old friends. He's trying to put together a public-private partnership and I agreed to run some numbers for him." Nieland had recovered his geniality.

"And the man with you?" I asked politely.

"Another old friend. What did you say your name was?"

When I repeated it, he cared enough about the call to make sure he had the spelling correct. A man in his position definitely needed to be careful about the person he spoke to, but I didn't think there was any doubt that he had some kind of stake in the proposed development.

I didn't even try to call Taggett. The park super was appointed by the mayor, which meant money that came to him wouldn't be disguised as a campaign contribution, it would be a straight-out bribe. So if Taggett was getting rich from his public-private partnership, I'd have to find his bank accounts, his offshore holdings, all those things that are really hard to track down.

I resolutely turned to my paying clients' needs. These fortunately were fairly easy to sort out. A few background checks on potential new hires, double-billing from a subsidiary that was easy to spot. I was just finishing my reports when Norm Bolton called from Global to see if I was ready to sign his contract. Something about him or the contract made me uneasy enough that I didn't tell him I wouldn't sign, just said I'd sent it to my lawyer for review, that I'd get back to him as soon as Freeman had gone through it.

"You'd do well to act quickly, Warshawski," Bolton said. "Ryerson's ready to move, and we can find another investigator to work with him."

"That might be your best bet then," I said.

"We'll give you another twenty-four hours to think it over," Bolton said after a pause.

When he'd hung up, I added his name and his series offer to my Zamir file. Maybe Murray was raring to go, maybe not, but there was no reason for this project except to keep an eye on what I was doing.

While I had the file open, I read through all my entries. One thing I hadn't followed up on was Zamir's rage at the law firm that had taken over defending her lover's murderer. Zamir had tried to attack the Devlin attorneys in court, but Elisa Palurdo said the firm had taken out an order of protection against her. She'd been picketing the firm, which shouldn't be illegal, unless she was threatening to harm them.

I burrowed into Cook County legal records until I found the order, which was dated about six months after Arthur Morton had taken his life. It barred Lydia Zamir from being within fifty feet of any of Devlin & Wickham's partners. It also barred her from calling or approaching a woman named Jane Cardozo.

Cardozo was listed in the administrative tab of Devlin's website; she wasn't a lawyer but headed their transcription department. All the lawyers in the firm's far-flung empire dictated their thoughts and briefs to a twenty-four-hour central hub in Chicago, where people with nimble fingers and acute hearing turned them into documents. Like all the big firms, Devlin had clients from around the world; they boasted that they could take dictation in fifteen languages, including Arabic, Mandarin, and Thai.

I could understand why Lydia might have gone after the Devlin lawyers, but not what she might have against the transcription team. Maybe in her fragmented state she held the person who produced the briefs as culpable as the partners.

The bigger question was who got the firm interested in Arthur Morton's fate and who paid the fees. Even if they were acting pro bono, what that meant is that Morton wouldn't be charged for his lawyers' time. However, he'd still have to pay the other expenses—travel, photocopying, taking depositions, the fees charged by expert witnesses, and all the other add-ons. In a big case those add-ons can run to the high six figures. If he'd also been responsible for the lawyers' fees, those probably hit the million mark by the end of the first day in court.

Arthur Morton had been the semiemployed son of a bankrupt farmer. Who in his orbit had that kind of cash?

I went back to the trial record to see what witnesses had been called to speak for Morton. His pastor, his high school football coach, two of his buddies who'd joined the marines out of high school. All four men said essentially the same thing: Morton had been an ordinary boy until his father's suicide. He'd become morose, withdrawn, barely managed to graduate from high school. His buddies tried to talk him into joining the marines with them, but he didn't want to leave his mother on her own, or at least he'd been coached into saying as much at the trial—his lawyers trying to make him look like a loving son, not a maniacal murderer.

As the newspaper had reported, Morton's counsel took the position that Morton had come under the influence of extremist websites and that he wasn't responsible for his actions. The trial report listed the websites. Some came from the survivalist movement, but others promoted maximum lethal force against all non-white, non-Christian people. Morton had also bookmarked an Aryan matchmaker's site: keep the race pure by marrying women with guaranteed northern European pedigrees.

The home page for TakeBackOurLand.com showed a trio with caricatured Semitic features, wearing yarmulkes and grinning wolfishly as they stood in front of a grain silo, each with a foot on top of a blond woman in a torn and bloody dress. A giant shell casing, engraved with NOT ON OUR WATCH, HYMIE, was heading for their evil faces. The inside pages had tips on how to protect yourself from the Jews, Mexicans, and Muslims who wanted to take over America's farms.

Farms in western Kansas used to belong to Americans. No longer. They've been taken over by the globalist agricultural companies who are sucking the lifeblood out of Americans. We all know where our wheat and soybeans are going, but you have to bore deep into the manure to find out what's happening to the profits.

"Farms in western Kansas" was such a specific reference. Why not Nebraska or Iowa? Maybe it was one of those sites that knows where you live when you log on and tailors the message to the address. But in that case, they should have given me a message about Illinois farms.

I entered the URLs into my Zamir case file, but the content was so foul that I couldn't bring myself to read any more deeply. Instead I treated myself to an actual sit-down meal at a café up the street. I was a civilized person who knew how to use a knife and fork. I didn't live in a world of hatred.

My own lawyer, Freeman Carter, phoned as I was walking back to my office. He'd asked an intellectual property lawyer to look at the contract Global's Spinning Earth division had offered me.

"He says it's not out of line with contracts for reality

TV shows. It gives Global ownership of everything you uncover while you are under contract to them. They want to include six investigations, starting with Lydia Zamir, and then five that you will mutually agree on. If you're thinking about signing, we'll rework the contract."

I assured him I wasn't thinking about signing. "I just wanted to make sure they weren't preemptively staking out a legal claim to my work."

"It's a very strange offer, Warshawski," Freeman said dryly. "I'll give—what's his name? Bolton—a call. It won't hurt for Spinning Earth to know you have serious counsel watching your back."

When he hung up, I called Murray, to tell him I was definitely not signing with Global.

"Not a surprise, Warshawski, just a disappointment. We could make beautiful music together."

"Nothing to stop us without deeding our souls to Global," I said.

"So you will work with me on Zamir?"

"There's nothing to work on, except the ongoing tragedy of gun violence survivors, and Elisa Palurdo has that ground well covered."

"Tell me the truth, Warshawski. Do you know where Lydia Zamir is?" he persisted.

"I have absolutely no idea. Do you?"

"I've been trying to find the guy Coop," he said. "I'm betting he's the key."

"Any luck?"

"Shaking the cop tree at the Second," he said.

The patrol officers, especially the men, were the kind of source Murray knew how to work. If someone in the district knew Coop's full name and where he lived, Murray would get it out of them.

"When I get it, how about a trade—an interview with Palurdo for Coop's name and address?" Murray said, or wheedled.

"Why do you and Bolton keep thinking I own access to people? I can't get you to Palurdo. Or Lydia. And I will try to keep you from Bernie Fouchard."

Murray cut the connection.

25
Legal Standing

I unlocked the door to my office in a sober mood. If Global wanted to keep track of what I uncovered, they must have some vested interest in Palurdo's shooter, or Lydia, or Hector Palurdo himself.

I tried to see if any of Global's senior staff were related to Arthur Morton. The closest connector I found was a Global board member who also served on the board of Sea-2-Sea, the big agricultural firm. However, he lived in Los Angeles. It was hard to believe he paid attention to the woes of small farmers like the Morton family. Still, just to be prudent, I added his name to the Zamir case file.

I looked up Morton's mother's and grandmothers' birth names. They didn't match any current Global

264 • SARA PARETSKY

executives. I ran their names against my own current client list and didn't turn up anything.

My initial approach to the Devlin law firm hadn't been very skillful. I'd see if a personal approach got me further. Specifically, I'd see whether Jane Cardozo, head of Devlin's transcription center, would tell me why she'd needed a restraining order against Lydia Zamir.

I'd found a photo of Jane Cardozo on a social media site and uploaded it to my phone. She was a woman of about fifty, with dark hair cut short and a humorous look about her eyes. She'd have to have a strong personality to force the partners of a big firm to treat her with respect. Perhaps she'd see me as a kindred spirit, not an invading force. That was my hope, anyway.

I printed a message to Cardozo. Just the basics—I was an investigator who'd been hired to find Lydia Zamir. I was worried that Zamir might have tried confronting Cardozo or one of the partners and been arrested. I was waiting in the lobby—could Cardozo give me five minutes?

I walked down to the Polonia Triangle to pick up the L into the Loop. Elton was leaning against the fountain, drinking something from a paper bag. I waved, but he turned away. I hoped that wasn't an omen.

Devlin & Wickham leased eight floors in the Ft.

Dearborn Bank Building on South LaSalle. It's one of those buildings that make you feel exalted for worshipping Mammon—gold leaf and marble pillars in the lobby, inlaid stone on the floors, and a guard behind a barrier made of the kind of material you think St. Peter probably chose for the Pearly Gates.

When I told him I had a message for someone at Devlin, it felt sacrilegious to speak above a whisper. The guard proffered a metal basket; I placed my offering inside; the guard phoned up to the firm.

I settled down on one of the lobby benches to wait. People came and went at the guard stand. They had appointments and showed IDs, they dropped off packets, they came from inner sancta and picked up packets. Finally a woman took my letter and retreated to the elevators.

I checked in with Bernie. She'd had a good day with her kids and was going out with Angela and her other roommates; Arlette was staying on for a few days, but she was astute enough to leave the young women on their own. I'd brought my laptop and tried to do some work, but I couldn't focus. Five, then five-thirty, came and went.

Donna Lutas, the young woman from my building who constantly complained about me and the dogs, emerged. She didn't seem to notice me as she passed:

she had her phone in one hand and was taking off her ID with the other. She stuck her badge in a pocket of her briefcase. I was tempted to lift it and use it to get in, but I'd save that for an emergency.

I had just decided I was wasting time I could have spent running, swimming, or eating when Cardozo finally appeared. She was with a man who looked vaguely familiar. I packed up my laptop and followed them from the building. They stood talking at the corner of Jackson and Clark for several minutes before the man got into a black car. I was afraid Cardozo might be waiting for a Lyft or Uber, but she started walking west along Jackson. I caught up with her at the next traffic light.

"Ms. Cardozo?"

She turned in surprise, the humorous look not at all visible in her eyes.

"I'm V.I. Warshawski. Sorry to bother you on your way home, but I'm most anxious to discuss Lydia Zamir with you."

"Yes. I saw your message. You know we have a restraining order against Zamir; in the morning we'll go to the judge and add your name to the order, since you are her agent."

"Whoa, there!" I said. "Lawyers, and their agents, cannot afford to jump to conclusions like kangaroos. I am trying to find Ms. Zamir. As my note said, she's disappeared. Her family is anxious to find her. Since she has a hostile history with you and some of the partners, I wanted to make sure she hadn't shown up at Devlin's offices and caused an uproar."

Cardozo's mouth bunched—not anger, indecision. "Oh, very well. But I will record the conversation."

West Jackson near the river doesn't offer a lot of cozy places to talk. We went into a doughnut shop and sat with overboiled coffee at a table as far from the windows as possible. Cardozo didn't say so, but she probably didn't want any coworkers to spot her talking to me.

We both had our phones on the table, ostentatiously recording ourselves.

"No one can tell me why Zamir targeted you after the trial," I said.

"She blamed the firm for the court's sentence; you must know that."

"But surely you didn't play a role in that," I said. "Or am I misunderstanding your position in the firm? Are you one of the partners?"

"Nope. Not a lawyer. Just a legal secretary with a head for operations management."

I lobbed her a few softballs on her career—from setting up the transcription unit while she was PA to old

Mr. Devlin—"One of the greatest litigators in the city, but a true gentleman"—to running the unit after he retired.

"Were you still working for Mr. Devlin at the time of the Morton trial?"

"He had retired long before Hector Palurdo was shot. And was dead by the time of the trial. Zamir was trying to get me to give her access to internal confidential emails. She got quite ugly in her accusations."

"She wanted to know who in the firm decided to take on Morton's defense? I'm curious about that myself."

"It was an internal decision by the partners. Not my business, not Lydia Zamir's, and certainly not yours," Cardozo said frostily.

"It was Zamir's business," I objected. "Her lover had been murdered. Everything about Arthur Morton was her business, including the trial."

"She had an emotional interest," Cardozo snapped, "not a legal one."

"Is that why she targeted you?" I asked, tone all-innocence. "She thought as a woman you might empathize with her emotional distress?"

"Nothing to do with that," Cardozo said. "She claimed Palurdo had written us a few days before the concert or whatever it was and she wanted to know what he'd written."

"And?"

"And nothing. If Palurdo had communicated with the firm, it wasn't handled through my center. And even if I knew anything about it, that's confidential information. She wasn't married to him. She didn't have any legal standing to get access to confidential emails."

I drank some coffee, forgetting how bitter it was, and choked. "Arthur Morton's suicide must have come as a shock."

She nodded. "I don't think anyone was remembering how desperate he was. His father was dead, the farm was gone and his big gesture had done nothing to solve his problems. Maybe we made a mistake trying to keep him from the death penalty—he could have been looking down a tunnel of a lot of lonely years."

It was an unexpectedly poetic image, but it made a certain sense. "Had his lawyers brought him those nicotine patches?"

Her face froze, brief goodwill gone. "Is there some reason that's your business?"

"Sorry. Random curiosity is the besetting sin of a detective." I tried an apologetic smile. "One thing that seems extraordinary is how many of the details you remember. A firm like Devlin handles so much litigation, I'd think it would all blur in your head. I know it would in mine."

Cardozo was still stiff. "Word's been rattling around the firm that you've been asking questions—you called last week, right? We all looked at the case files to see if there were any loose ends."

"What did you find?"

"There are always loose ends," Cardozo said. "But we dotted every *i* in the trial proceedings. There's no reason for you or anyone else to raise questions about Devlin's conduct of the case."

"I wasn't." I tried to make my face look as innocent as a golden retriever's. "My only questions were about Lydia Zamir's history with the firm. Why you needed an order of protection, or at least, felt you needed one. And whether she'd appeared on your doorstep after she vanished."

"She's only been missing, what, less than a week?"

"Ms. Cardozo, we both know you're a savvy woman, smart as well. Law firms like Devlin are brutal places for women, and you've thrived. So please don't spin me lines about studying the Morton file to make sure the firm didn't leave loose ends. Tell me instead about the loose end that you're afraid this current crisis in Zamir's life will expose."

She squeezed the paper cup so hard that coffee sloshed on the table and onto her clothes. She dabbed her blazer with the paper napkins on the table, but they left pilling on her lapels.

"That's my exit cue—get this to the cleaners before the coffee stains set." She got up briskly, the transcription center chief in charge, but as she scuttled to the door, the look she gave me bordered on alarm.

When I got home, I looked up the partners at Devlin. Their photos were on the firm's website. I found the man Cardozo had been talking to as she left work, a Clarence Gorbeck, one of the senior partners. I studied his face, narrow, with dark eyes; a wide, thin mouth that looked ready to snap off heads of opposing witnesses.

When I got home from running the dogs, I called Murray, to tell him the police had found a gavel that might be the weapon that killed Leo Prinz. He had a barrage of questions, which I told him should be directed at Sergeant Pizzello; all I could say was what she'd told me—that the gavel had been found somewhere near the Forty-seventh Street Metra platform.

It was at four the next morning that Coop dropped Bear off, rousing the whole building.

26

A Vampire in a Cave

The doorbell rang around nine. It didn't rouse me, but the noise troubled Bear, who pawed at me, whining anxiously.

As I forced myself from sleep to semiconsciousness, I heard the bell, held down with an insistent finger. "You think it's your boy come back for you? I hope and pray."

I stumbled to my front door and called down through the speaker. It was Sergeant Pizzello, a sharp disappointment to both me and Bear.

"With you in a few," I growled through the speaker.

I took my time about it, turning on the espresso machine, brushing my teeth, showering. When I got out of the shower, Pizzello was leaning on the doorbell right outside my apartment: someone had let her into the building. The sergeant was also calling my cell phone. A glance through my spyhole showed she'd brought a uniformed man: a formal visit. Or perhaps backup in case I turned on my superpowers.

"I don't know how much law you know," I said to Bear, "but it's prudent not to let the cops into your place. They can search, you see, even if they don't have a warrant, if you've invited them in."

I took him out through the kitchen, let him relieve himself in the yard, and then circled around to the front of my building. Before climbing the three flights to my home, I pushed the buzzer at Donna Lutas's apartment.

She came to the door, an eager look replaced by dismay when she saw it was me, not the police.

"It's getting on for ten A.M., Lutas," I said. "Don't Devlin & Wickham expect junior staff to show up at seven and stay until midnight? I'd hate to think you were oversleeping and missing your chance for promotion."

"Thanks to *you* I hardly got any sleep last night and neither did anyone else in the building. I'm working from home this morning. One of the partners is helping me prepare a formal complaint against you to take to the condo board." She slammed the door. Just when I was trying to be neighborly, too, and look after her career.

Behind Mr. Contreras's door, Mitch and Peppy were raising furious demands to join me. My neighbor let them out and they pelted up the stairs. Bear, scared and abandoned, stayed close to me, whining, while my duo kept trying to nose him out of the way, barking fierce commands. (*She's our property. Go back to your own person.*) I clung to the stairwell railing to keep them from knocking me down.

Sergeant Pizzello met us at the top landing.

"You knew I was waiting to talk to you, and you left me out here for twenty—" She looked at her watch. "Make that thirty-one minutes. I don't know how you make a living working these kind of hours, but I'd have you on probation after two days."

"Sergeant, if I'd had any idea you couldn't let a day pass without seeing me, I'd have set my alarm. I was roused in the middle of the night by the arrival of this fellow." I scratched Bear behind the ears. His skin was tight and his mouth was pulled into a rictus of anxiety.

"People tell me you're a cop's daughter. You should know better than to play games with me. If this wasn't urgent, I'd have sent you a text."

"Is it Lydia Zamir?" I demanded, belatedly alarmed: visions of Lydia's emaciated body under a bush in the Wildlife Corridor danced in my head.

"It's the man Coop," Pizzello said through thin lips. "I understand he showed up here last night. Early this morning."

"Right. What I just said—he dropped off his dog. How could you know? I didn't report it."

Pizzello bared her teeth in a parody of a smile. "Information received in our morning reports. The police may not be as clever as a PI, but gathering evidence piece by piece usually gets us where we need to be."

I thought it over. "Oh. My neighbor Donna Lutas did her civic duty and phoned the Town Hall District, who are sick of her reports on my dogs, and didn't send anyone over. However, when you read the city-wide reports, something in the wording made you think of Coop and Zamir."

Pizzello nodded slowly. "We put word out through some of our confidential informants that we had a lead on the gavel and would be following up today. My patrol units all know Coop or at least the dog Bear, and so we staked out the hole with the gavel in it, figuring when Coop got the word he'd hustle over to collect it. He never showed, but when I saw the report of a dog arriving in the middle of the night and rousing the residents at what I knew to be your address, I figured it had to be Coop. And now, I want to go inside to talk to him."

"He's not there, Sergeant." I eyed her steadily. "However, if you have a warrant?"

She scowled. "How about you doing *your* civic duty for five minutes, Warshawski? Why are you protecting him?"

"I'm not. I don't know where he is. He rang my bell. I came down to find his dog tied up out front with a note asking me to look after him. By the time I'd read it, Coop had vanished."

I drummed my fingers on the railing, debating. "My lawyer will flay me when he hears me say this, but here's the deal: you swear you will not touch any document, electronic device, not so much as my coffee-maker, no piece of furniture, and I will let you look in closets and under my bed to see if you can find a trace of Coop."

I recorded her while she agreed to my terms, with the proviso that she could have Coop's note. I let her inside but kept her henchperson in the hall with all three dogs. None of the four appreciated that.

Pizzello walked through my four rooms, checked the bathroom, the tub behind the shower curtain, the walk-in closet in the front hall, my bedroom closet with the safe where I keep my gun. I even opened that for her. She asked to see my license. I showed it. She looked in all the kitchen cabinets, and then checked the back stairs.

"Of course you could have smuggled him out. I was a fool not to post someone back here."

"Sergeant, he was never in my apartment. I don't want responsibility for his dog. I want him, I want to know what he did with Lydia Zamir, who I believe is close to death from malnutrition and neglect."

"How do you know he has Zamir?"

"I don't. Hoping, I guess, hoping that she's still alive, still salvageable. Coop is reportedly the only person she allowed near her the last few months. If you haven't found her in the Burnham Wildlife Corridor, then I hope Coop plucked her from the ground and gave her a bed and a bath and a meal."

I felt weary, beyond the physical fatigue of my short night, and slumped on the piano bench. I can't be near the piano without thinking of my mother, my ardent, musical mother, who very nearly didn't survive a war and then died behind a maze of tubes. She should have been at home, with my father and me, dying in our arms. Why did we let the great medical maw swallow her last days?

I picked out notes on the keyboard, spoke without looking at the sergeant. "We talk so much these days about resilience and whatever its opposite is. Crumbling, maybe. As if resilience could be taught or learned. Almost like another way of shaming people who crumble. Every time we have a mass slaughter in this country, we move in a team of trauma experts, who surely themselves become traumatized by absorbing so much unbearable anguish. Long after Parkland, long after Newtown, survivors take their own lives. Lydia Zamir was creating something like performance art out of anguish."

Pizzello stared at me. "I don't know what you're trying to say. That her incoherence was an act?"

I realized I was playing "Dido's Lament": *Remember me, remember me.* "No, that it was the only way she could make a public expression of a nightmare that isn't expressible. Anyway, I can't speak for her. Just trying to imagine the hell inside her head."

I went to the kitchen to make coffee. I pulled espresso shots and handed a cup to Pizzello, who opened my refrigerator.

"Coop isn't in there," I said.

"I was looking for milk," she said.

"The closest I come is kefir," I said. "It's emblematic of your approach, isn't it? The surprise gesture in the hopes of taking me off guard, when all you have to do is ask. And speaking of asking, has that guy from SLICK, the gavel banger, been able to produce the mallet he uses? He's a security guard at one of the library branches. Bet he could come and go in his uniform and nobody would notice him."

"Good point. We've asked forensics to make the gavel a priority, but you know what it's like in an underfunded department. Can't tell you if it has fingerprints on the handle or traces of Leo Prinz embedded in the head."

"That wasn't my question," I said.

"That's my answer." She put down her espresso, undrunk. "Stuff is foul without milk."

"What makes you sure that Coop is the killer?" I asked.

"My patrol team reported his anger with the Prinz kid at the SLICK meeting. It was out of proportion to what Prinz was saying or doing."

"He wasn't the only person in the room who was acting out," I said. "The guy at SLICK who keeps their records, Simon Lensky, was upset with Leo. From where I sat, it looked as though Leo had seen something they didn't want revealed; Leo and Simon seemed to be arguing about it. And then Taggett intervened, smooth as old Scotch, and diverted attention from the stage. By the way, did you know Simon was mugged after that meeting? And now he's disappeared. His boss has no idea where he is."

Pizzello said, "If you think the parks super is involved in killing Leo Prinz, then you are crazier than Lydia Zamir."

"Could be," I agreed. "I'm simply pointing out that there was a lot of friction in the meeting room that night surrounding Leo, or what Leo was saying. Not all of it came from Coop. I want to know why he's the only one you're interested in."

Her mouth set in a stubborn line. "He fled. As soon as someone alerted him that we were onto him, he fled. Everyone else is where we can talk to them anytime we want."

I smiled blandly. "Great. That means even if you don't want to question Mona Borsa or Curtis Murchison, I can."

She started to utter a grand threat to me about questioning witnesses but realized in time she would only look foolish.

"By the way," I said as I walked her to my front door, "have you found where Coop lives? I can't believe you had to stake out the Metra tracks in the hopes of catching him."

"You'd think," she agreed bitterly. "People see him

all the time but no one knows where he lives. The homeless guys under the Darrow bridge in Jackson Park say he's in the park in the middle of the night sometimes. You found him on the lakefront. Other people see him around grocery stores in Hyde Park. No one knows whether Coop is his first or last name. However, there are only four or five thousand people named Coop in Illinois. My tech wizards tell me none of them is likely to be our guy. He might as well be a vampire living in a cave somewhere. Except the patrol guys tell me he doesn't look homeless."

"A vampire in a cave?" I echoed, derisively. "And you think I'm crazy?"

27
Lease Is Up

I took Bear to my office with me. Every aspect of my life was making me feel helpless: I couldn't find Lydia, I didn't know who Coop was, and I certainly couldn't manage three dogs, especially not in my building. What would I do if Donna Lutas succeeded in getting the board to evict me? I couldn't abandon Mr. Contreras, but I didn't want to share a house, let alone an apartment, with him.

Tessa Reynolds, my lease mate, was arriving as I did. She looked at Bear. "Cute. Did he eat your other two?"

"Don't you need a guard dog?" I asked. "Someone to protect all that valuable metal you work with?"

"I have me." She flexed an arm, displaying impressive -ceps, both bi- and tri-. "Does he have a name?"

"Bear. But he doesn't bark or bite and so far he hasn't eaten. You'd hardly know he was there."

"Especially after he died from hunger." Tessa scratched Bear behind the ears but moved briskly to her studio before either of us got the idea she liked him.

I went into my own space. I put out food and water for Bear and folded a blanket for him next to my desk. He made a slow tour of the room and finally lay down on the blanket with a mournful grunt.

I was going through emails when my office phone rang.

"Bolton," the voice on the other end pronounced.

"Hello, Bolton," I said. Norm Bolton, head of Global Entertainment's media division.

"Where are we, Warshawski?"

"We are still regretfully declining the chance to entertain Global's global viewers," I said.

"You're making a mistake." The sentence came out more as threat than comment.

"What is it about the Zamir story that is so important to Global, Mr. Bolton?"

"Not the Zamir story specifically," he said. "This is a reality show about how investigators work."

"These days it's ninety-five percent desk work, in front of a computer. How about for ten thousand dollars I send you all the URLs I consult and your viewers can create their own investigations?"

"I hope your work doesn't depend on financial negotiations," he said. "That's a ludicrous offer. Trust me: you will be happier in the long run if you sign that contract. After all, we can follow you without paying you."

He hung up.

I called Murray. "Your boy Bolton just phoned; he's not happy that I'm turning down the chance to run around town with a camera attached to my head. He may well have a tap in place on my phone, although my encryption is pretty good—I'm telling you in case you were tempted to call him a repellent worm who crawled out of the dung to run your media division."

There was a long silence at Murray's end before he said, "It's probably the smart decision, but I still wish you'd rethink it. It would mean, well, a lot to me."

What was 'a lot'? His career? His self-esteem? His life? I didn't want to dig in that ground.

As a diversion, I told him about Coop arriving with Bear. Murray liked that—dog stories always draw an audience. I feigned reluctance but finally agreed to let him send a camera crew to film Bear and me, in the hopes that someone somewhere would view the footage and recognize Coop's dog and let us know where Coop was.

While I waited for Murray, I got caught up on emails and did some digging for the truckload of Ligurian wine I'd agreed to find.

Murray arrived with a cameraman who knew something about filming dogs: he brought a carton of meatballs, which coaxed Bear to his feet. Despite the food, his face looked old and mournful, as though Coop's disappearance was merely the latest in a string of human barbarisms he'd witnessed.

TV crews work fast. Twenty minutes after arriving, they were ready to go south with Murray to look for the place where the police had found the gavel. I'd told him about the gavel the day before, but this was his first chance to film the hole where I'd found it.

Murray tried to talk me into going with him and his crew. That made me wonder if he wanted my company, or if Bolton had told him to try to pull me into a joint investigation without calling it that.

To stop his pleading, I told him about Curtis, the SLICK gaveller. "I don't know that he had anything against Prinz, but he does own a gavel. I don't know if the cops are checking on it. I also don't know if they're checking on an argument Prinz had with Simon Lensky, SLICK's documents maestro, but in another development, which doesn't interest the cops, Lensky has disappeared."

That brought a gleam to his reporter's eye, and we parted more or less as pals. He had a couple of good nuggets to put on-air, and I had someone who might confirm that the gavel in Lydia's hideout had come from SLICK.

Back at my desk, I tried to organize my thoughts. Arthur Morton, mass slaughterer, I wrote on one of my big sketch pads. Hector Palurdo, immigrant rights activist and murder victim. Devlin & Wickham, law firm who magically popped up to defend Morton. Lydia Zamir, Hector's lover and creative partner who tried to attack the Devlin lawyers. Global Entertainment, worried about what I might turn up.

Presumably, Global's cable news division had covered the aftermath of the massacre, as had every other cable outlet in the country. Blood, disaster, the inalienable right to own weapons of mass destruction, continue to grab headlines despite the wearying number of times they come together.

When I first started looking at Devlin & Wickham's involvement, I'd wondered if someone at the firm was connected to Arthur Morton, but maybe I'd been asking the wrong question.

What would the right question be? It couldn't be about Sea-2-Sea's decision to take part in the Tallgrass fund-raiser for immigrants and refugees—all the other ag companies had supported it. They wanted to protect the cheap labor, the people who do the disgusting parts of bringing meat to the table. People like my father's parents, immigrants from Poland, who worked on the killing floors of the Chicago stockyards for eleven dollars a week during the Depression.

My grandmother Warshawski scrubbed blood from the slaughterhouse floors; my grandfather hit steers in the forehead with a giant mallet. A kind of outsize gavel. Leo Prinz's head battered like a steer—the image made my gorge rise. I put down my pen and walked around the room. Bear followed me, but on my second circuit he decided I wasn't about to abandon him; he went back to the blanket and lay down.

If Lydia had been stronger, both physically and mentally, I might have thought she'd sought refuge with one of the migrant families she'd met through the Tallgrass Meet-Up. She'd made it from Provident Hospital to the Metra tracks on her own, but the work it would take to get from Chicago to Kansas—I couldn't see it. Of course, Coop could have taken her there. But where?

I went back to the files about the fund-raiser itself. The online photos showed how easy it would be to hide a horse, maybe a whole herd of them, along with a few thieves, inside Horsethief Canyon. I dug up the names of the organizers. Two who'd survived the massacre were so far in retreat from public life that I couldn't find them, but I sent an email to the remaining man, to see if he had heard from Lydia.

With Bear nearly glued to my pant leg, I took one of my burner phones up the street to a coffee shop I never use: if you think someone's tracking you, break your routine. The coffee shop wouldn't let Bear inside, even when I explained that I was his emotional support human.

I took one of their bitter, undrinkable espressos outside and squatted on the curb to call Elisa Palurdo. She hadn't heard from Lydia, she said in a tired voice.

"I was calling about the apartment you said you rented for her. Is there any chance she could be there?"

"Do you know, it never occurred to me," she said in an arrested tone. "I renewed the lease nearly a year ago, hoping I might persuade her to move back in."

"The lease must be up about now," I said.

"End of next month. I guess it's time to let it go. If she isn't there now, I suppose I need to clean it out and hand back the keys."

She'd kept an extra set; she agreed to meet me at the apartment and let me in.

28

No Place Like Home

The apartment was on the south fringe of the University of Chicago campus: Lydia had wanted to live there, Elisa said, because it made her feel connected to Hector.

I bundled Bear into the back of the Mustang and drove again to the South Side. I parked in a covered lot near the university theater. I didn't know how seriously to take Bolton's threat of keeping track of my investigation, but I left my iPhone in the car, happily alerting anyone to the Mustang's location, but not to mine. Bear and I crossed the quads, disguised as a woman with a dog.

Lydia's apartment was almost a mile to the south, beyond the Midway Plaisance boulevard, where the 1893 White City had been built. Once we crossed the

Midway, Bear picked up his pace. He'd been sticking to my left leg as if chained there, but now he surged ahead, trotting down Kimbark Avenue to a three-flat halfway between Sixty-second and Sixty-third Streets. He stood at the locked gate, wagging his stub of a tail.

The gate lock would have been easy to undo, but I waited for Elisa. I didn't know if Norm Bolton or Sergeant Pizzello were keeping an eye on me, but I had that prickly feeling along my scalp that you get when the neighbors are peering from behind their curtains. They would know who came and went, and I was definitely not a regular, although Bear clearly was.

Elisa didn't keep us waiting long.

"That dog!" she cried. "Isn't that the dog that belongs to the man you asked about, the one with the weird name?"

"Yep. This is Bear, Coop's dog, and he knows this building."

She fumbled with her key ring, finally found the one that undid the gate and the one for the front door. Once we were inside the hall, Bear ran up the stairs, his toenails clattering and skittering on the uncarpeted floor. He trotted down the second-floor hallway and stopped in front of a door at the end, his doggy face stretched into a wide grin. We'd clearly found where Coop had been living.

He was barking and whimpering while Elisa fiddled with the lock. She kept dropping the keys, tension stretching her skin so tautly that her cheekbones jutted out in almost skeletal relief.

As soon as she turned the knob, Bear pushed the door open and rushed into the apartment. He disappeared into the back and began to bark, the sharp urgent sounds of warning.

"Must he make that racket?" Elisa cried.

I didn't answer. My lesser nose had picked up the sickly sweet odor the dog had been tracking. I followed on dragging feet. Bear was standing in front of a closed door, scratching at it, hurling his shoulder against it. Just as I reached it, he managed to force it open. We were in the bathroom. A man was in the tub, head slumped at a steep angle. The sight was shocking, so shocking the details registered only slowly: the blood covering his head, congealing in the hair, covering the arms of his suit jacket. The suit—he'd been fully clothed when he was attacked. The tub was dry—he'd thought he could hide in here but he'd been cornered. He'd tried to protect himself from the blows that had battered his head—his crossed arms had fallen onto his knees.

Behind me, Elisa made a strangled sound. She was choking, vomiting, and I turned to try to get her head over the toilet but ended up with the remains of her breakfast on my arm and jeans leg.

I led her to the kitchen, where I took off my shirt and pants and rinsed them in the sink. It was unpleasant to put the clammy clothes back on, but less unpleasant than wearing her vomit. When I'd bathed Elisa's face under the tap, I took her into the hallway.

"I'm calling the police. You stay out here."

"Who—was it the man Coop?" she whispered. "What was he doing in Lydia's apartment?"

"It wasn't Coop. I'm pretty sure it's a man named Simon Lensky."

"Who is he? Why was he in the bathtub?" Palurdo was struggling to regain control.

"I know almost nothing about him, but Leo Prinz worked with him on a presentation. Now they're both dead." I didn't try to answer her other question—why was Simon in the bathtub, why was he even in the apartment—because I could only guess. Whoever killed him hadn't beaten him with the gavel: Simon had been missing only a day or two, and the gavel had turned up before that.

I called Pizzello, instead of 911.

"You know, Warshawski, there are judges who'd agree you're stalking me."

"Sergeant, I'm looking at what's left of Simon

Lensky. His battered body is in a bathtub on South Kimbark. Do you want the details, or should I hang up and call 911?"

She took the address. "And don't touch anything. That includes anything. I'll be there straightaway."

Straightaway from Fifty-first and the Ryan would give me about fifteen minutes to scope the place. I wouldn't have a second chance to look before the cops went through, tagging and bagging.

Bear had left the bathroom while I was on the phone. He'd gone through the rooms, looking for Coop, and now was slumped in the open doorway to the hall.

When I looked through the apartment's three rooms, I saw they'd already been searched, but by pros. Things weren't tossed around as they are when an addict is looking for valuables.

The unit was sparsely furnished, making it quick to examine: a chest of drawers, a bed, and a straight-backed chair in the bedroom; a few chairs, a table, and some bookshelves in the main room. A handful of pans, a few bowls and cups in the kitchenette. The food was minimal as well: dried beans, molding cheese in the refrigerator, a half-eaten bag of tortilla chips. The only concession to taste, a pottery teapot and a collection of loose teas. All these had been spread on the kitchen counter.

Bear's excitement when we reached the building made me certain that this was where Coop had been living, but he'd left precious little sign of it.

The sheets had been stripped from the twin bed, so I couldn't tell if Coop might have left telltale hairs in the linens. The mattress and box springs had been slit in multiple places, along with the curtain hems and pillows. Whatever the killers were seeking was small.

A fifty-pound bag of dry dog food in the mop cupboard showed that at least a dog had been here. The killer must have gone through the dog food, but it hadn't been emptied, the way the teas were, so I stuck my hand inside, probing for something small, like a flash drive, but didn't feel anything.

The closet and the drawers in the bedroom dresser were half open. They were almost empty, except for a few pieces Lydia had left behind, but one drawer held a navy sweater, big enough for a man. Elisa had come into the room behind me; she seized it from me.

"I made that for Hector, after Jacobo died, when Hector began trying to explore his father's roots. You can see it here, the white star of the Chilean flag." The star was on the chest, where it would have covered Hector's heart. Elisa buried her face in the wool, rocking on her heels.

I had trouble looking in the bathroom, with Simon

Lensky's battered eye sockets staring at me. Using a kitchen towel to keep from overlaying fingerprints, I made myself open the medicine cabinet. No toiletries. A tube of organic toothpaste, Lydia's prescriptions for Ativan and Haldol, the bottles still almost full.

There was no sign of a computer or charger—no trace of current electronics. Coop used a cell phone, but he'd probably taken the charger with him when he bolted.

An old sound system stood in a corner, not plugged in. It included a DVD player, but no television. If thieves had come in and taken the computer and a television, they would have taken the sound system, too—so either Coop never had electronics or the killer had taken them.

A guitar case was propped against the wall next to the stereo. I opened and gave an inadvertent gasp. The guitar had been smashed into pieces, the strings dangling like the useless veins of a decapitated body.

Elisa said Lydia had destroyed her best guitar. Had Lydia herself destroyed the instrument? No guitars, no reminders of the music she'd made from her lover's words, returning to the piano but only to a joke piano, as if ridiculing her youthful attachment to music.

The makeshift bookshelf held a few dozen books and some stacks of papers, including maps and pamphlets about Horsethief Canyon, the park where Hector had been murdered. I put those in my daypack, but didn't see any personal documents, no notes saying, "Meet me in the Burnham Wildlife Corridor at midnight," no letters or bills showing Coop's full name. In fact, no documents in anyone's name.

The books were a dry selection of economics and political history. *Capitalism and Freedom: Utopia or Possibility*, by Larry Nieland; *Government and Economics: Peaceful Coexistence*, by Ottavio Misombra. Hector Palurdo's *Once Upon a Time: Ancient Fables for Modern Readers*. His poetry in Spanish and in English.

"Was Lydia interested in economics?" I asked Elisa.

She stared at me dumbly, then squatted to inspect the titles. "These may have been Hector's. I don't know. Lydia might have clung to them out of sentiment. The way I keep all of Jacobo's old protective gear."

She started to flip through the pages of *Once Upon a Time*. Bear gave a warning bark: a moment later we heard the thunder of a police army's shoes on the stairs. Beneath that layer of sound I heard a startled gasp from Elisa. A second before Pizzello came into the room, I saw her slide a paper into her handbag.

29

Brothers and
Comrades Forever

"You have a lot of explaining to do, Warshawski. That was an awfully big coincidence, you stumbling on Lensky's body so patly."

We were back in the Second District, in one of the interrogation rooms. While we'd been at the apartment on Kimbark, Pizzello had double-checked that Elisa Palurdo was the renter and entitled to enter and leave. She was almost disappointed by the confirmation—she was pining to arrest me for something.

Pizzello sent Elisa home, but my stumbling on Lensky's body bugged her. I was guessing her real annoyance was with herself, for not taking my information about Lensky's disappearance seriously. She was too good a boss to offload on her team, too egotistical to blame herself. I was handy.

"Perhaps," I said.

"Perhaps nothing." Pizzello bit off her words, just like an old-school male cop. "You tell me Lensky is missing, and then, when I don't jump to attention, you present me with his body. How did you know he was in that apartment?"

A dozen hot answers sprang to mind, but I bit off my own words before they left my mouth: when you're with the cops, keep responses to a minimum. Any long explanation can be sliced and spliced to use against you in court.

"I'm calling my lawyer," I said. "I have nothing else to say until he is with me."

I'd been searched for weapons, but they'd let me keep my phone—I wasn't under arrest, just being held for questioning. I have Freeman Carter on speed dial. When his secretary answered, I named myself and said quickly, "I am being held at the Second District because I reported finding a dead body. Can you have Freeman or one of his associates—"

Pizzello snatched the phone from me. "She doesn't need a lawyer; she can leave whenever she feels like it. I simply want her to tell me how she happened on the dead man."

I grabbed the phone back. "Helen, I need an attorney present before I answer that question—too hostile an environment here."

Pizzello scowled at me but went to confer with her team. She took my phone with her. She left the door open—I guess to keep an eye on me without using an officer to watch me through the window.

Bear was with me: Elisa wouldn't take him when we left the apartment and I dug my heels over leaving him in a car on a muggy day for however long she might want to detain me.

"Dogs having heatstroke while the police detain their guardians is a good way to add to public annoyance with the CPD," I said. "You're lucky I'm talking to you—don't push it over the dog."

While we waited for my lawyer, I squatted next to Bear and stroked him. This kept both of us calm, while I listened in on the conversation in the hallway.

Simon Lensky's body had been transferred to the morgue. In big cities, autopsies don't happen as quickly as they do on *CSI*, but the preliminary read was that Lensky had died about twelve hours ago, from blows administered ten to twenty hours before that. It hadn't been a fast or pleasant death. It was even possible that if Elisa and I had gone to the apartment a day earlier, we could have saved his life.

My abdominal muscles contracted at that thought. A good detective must not indulge in "should haves," but it's sometimes hard to keep them at bay.

When Stacey Kawasaki arrived from Freeman's office, I gave her a quick précis of the background and the players. As soon as we finished, Pizzello joined us in the interrogation room.

"We want to know what prompted Warshawski to go to that apartment this afternoon," Pizzello said. "Did you have a tip that Simon Lensky was there?"

I conferred with Kawasaki, who agreed I should say I was hoping Lydia might have returned to the apartment Elisa Palurdo rented for her. Pizzello tried to push on that—did I really think someone as ill as Lydia could navigate the streets?

"She made it from Provident to Forty-seventh Street, Sergeant."

Pizzello scowled and switched to whether I was really looking for Coop or had inside knowledge about Lensky's fate—but I let the lawyer handle those.

"Why was Lensky there at all?" Pizzello burst out. "We know there was ill will between Coop and the SLICK officers. What would make him meet with Coop? Or was the Zamir woman there?"

"Your forensics team can doubtless tell you whether Lydia Zamir had been in the apartment recently. Until you find this man, Coop, it's all speculation," Kawasaki said. "We're done here."

"I guess." Pizzello rubbed her eyes. Her fine mousy hair was coming loose from her clip, making her look young and vulnerable. I wondered if she knew that— if it was an interrogation trick to make people like me feel sorry for her.

I murmured to Kawasaki, who repeated to Pizzello, "The timeline on the injuries makes it clear that Bernadine Fouchard had nothing to do with them."

"We'll talk to her and determine that," Pizzello said.

I grinned. "Her mother's been with her nonstop for the past forty-eight hours. I want to be there when you interrogate Arlette Fouchard. In fact, I'll sell tickets."

"Oh, go away," Pizzello cried. "And take that wretched animal with you."

"My phone?" I held out a palm. Pizzello smacked my iPhone into it with more force than was strictly necessary.

The long-suffering Bear followed me to Kawasaki's car, a late-model BMW. I thanked her for coming down to the station, but really, fees from people like me allow her to drive a car like hers, so she should have been thanking me.

After Kawasaki dropped me and Bear at my car in the university's garage, I drove up to Elisa's home on the Northwest Side. She didn't answer my ring, but her dog growled convincingly behind the door.

I smiled winsomely and spoke to the security camera. "I'd like to talk to you about my conversation with Sergeant Pizzello."

When there was no response, I wondered if she was out. I texted: I didn't mention the document you took from the apartment, but I'd like to know what it was. I'm taking Bear to the forest preserve; we can meet you at the library or back here at your house.

She still didn't answer. I drove to the nearby forest preserve. Mosquitoes whined around my ears; planes on the final approach to O'Hare roared overhead, but the setting itself was lush with midsummer foliage. Jogging along the Des Plaines River path was like being in the country—except for the planes. And the traffic on the Kennedy, hidden by the dense woods but still loud. Mitch and Peppy would have been in the underbrush, flushing smaller animals, but Bear stuck close to my left side.

Palurdo still hadn't answered when I got back to my car. I drove to her house, worried about what might have happened to her. I left Bear in the car with the windows open and a pan of water, but as I went up the walk, a man came out, closing the door behind him. He was heavy-set, middle-aged, his gut straining the waistband of his jeans. His face was so deeply creased it wasn't possible to read his expression.

"I'm Jesse. Friend of Elisa and Jacobo."

"I'm V.I. Warshawski."

He asked for ID, I gave it, he opened the door. Palurdo's dog appeared. It was an Akita, famed for their fierce loyalty. This one seemed to be measuring my fat content for roasting. Jesse gave the dog a command in Spanish, and it curled its lip at me.

"For Elisa to see that murdered man, it brought back the horror of seeing her son's dead body. She will talk to you, but I will be there."

He led me down a short hall to a small room that overlooked the backyard. Elisa was sitting there in a chaise longue, wearing a man's flannel shirt over sweatpants: shock had left her cold, and her face still had a waxy pallor. Her hands were wrapped around a mug of hot liquid.

"Do you ever stop?" she said to me. "Do you ever stop running, asking questions, prying at people's lives? Do you take time to think about the damage you do?"

"Did I damage your life by asking you to let me look at Lydia's apartment?" I said. "I didn't plant Simon Lensky's body there. I didn't kill him. It distressed me to see him, too."

"But if you've never seen the dead body of someone you love—"

"The cousin who was the companion of my childhood was murdered," I cut her off. "His body was torn up by the screw of a Great Lakes freighter. I was distraught, so I did what I do when I'm distressed: I ran around asking questions until I found his killer, and the people who betrayed him into his killer's hands. What else would you like to know about me?"

It was unfair, I guess, to play the dead Boom-Boom card. Elisa was suffering, acutely, and really, what business did I have asking questions of her?

The silence built, like a scene from a spaghetti western—camera on Jesse, looking anxiously at Elisa; camera on Elisa, eyes on the mug she was holding; camera on me, eyes on Elisa's small garden, avoiding a look at more misery.

I was turning to leave when Elisa said, "Grief is a selfish bitch. She wants you to shut out the rest of the world, including other people's suffering. Sit. I'll tell you about the photograph."

Jesse perched on the arm of a couch next to Elisa. I pulled up a hassock.

Elisa nodded at Jesse, who went to a side table and returned with an old black-and-white picture of two youths, perhaps sixteen years old, both in cutoff jeans and T-shirts. Both were handsome, one dark, with a chipped front tooth, the other fairer. Their arms were linked across their shoulders, and they were grinning for the camera, as if happy to be alive and together.

"Jesse was with us—with Hector and me—when we found this," Elisa said. "The man on the left is Jacobo. I don't know who the other man is. Jacobo never spoke of him, but the inscription on the back—"

I turned the photo over to see an inscription in a sprawling adolescent hand, *Hermanos y compañeros por siempre.*

"Brothers and companions forever?" I ventured.

"Brothers and comrades is probably more accurate," Elisa said.

"This was on its own? No envelope, no name?"

"It was in a manila envelope," Jesse said, "but not labeled."

"Jacobo had hidden this in his toolbox," Elisa explained. "After his death, Hector and I wanted Jesse to choose among Jacobo's tools. When we emptied the box, a kind of false bottom came out. The photo was underneath. Jesse knew Jacobo longer than anyone—they started at the company at almost the same time, but even he had never seen this before."

I looked at Jesse, who nodded solemnly.

"Anyway, Hector became obsessed with the picture,"

306 • SARA PARETSKY

Elisa said. "He took it away with him, he took it with him to Chile—he wanted to learn his father's history and he thought perhaps someone would recognize the photo, although it must be from the late sixties or early seventies—Jacobo was born in 1953. I don't know who would recognize two barrio boys forty years or more after the fact. If the friend is even still alive, he would look different—life in the mines changed everyone. That much Jacobo said, the rare times he talked about his life in Tocopilla."

"How did you cope with so much secrecy?" I blurted out. "Didn't you ask him about his life, why he left Chile?"

Her waxen skin turned faintly pink. "Of course I asked. I wanted to know for myself, but more important, I thought our son deserved to know his father's background. Jacobo would say only that the past was too painful for him to discuss. All he ever told me was that he was an orphan and his only sister had been murdered. It was after her death that he came to America."

"Did he talk about the murder?" I asked. "How it happened, whether the murderer was caught and tried?"

Elisa said, "The country was in chaos then—the

Pinochet years—so many deaths and disappearances, Jacobo said one individual death couldn't rouse police interest.

"Hector went to Chile, to Tocopilla, where Jacobo was born: he'd told us that much. It's a small mining town on the coast. But the church where his parents were married and where he and Filomena—his sister—were baptized had collapsed in an earthquake. All the records had been destroyed.

"Jacobo always said the Palurdos were an insignificant family, and I guess that was true. His father worked in the mine, his mother cleaned houses for the wealthy in the town. Hector couldn't find anyone who remembered them. He couldn't find anyone with our surname, but when he came home, he was furious. He wanted to know what Jacobo had told me about the mines, the conditions, the lives of the workers. And I could tell him nothing. He had already started seeing Lydia, but he and she became a tighter couple and seemed to feel a missionary fervor for uncovering the history of injustices in the Americas. It was exhausting to be with them."

She drank from her mug. "So many deaths, so many murders. I was on the sideline of history—American girl, ignorant about the bigger world, thought I could

308 · SARA PARETSKY

change people's lives by teaching them English. Instead my life got changed. I didn't even know Spanish when I met Jacobo."

"Yes." Jesse smiled. "You learned the Spanish that Jacobo spoke. We used to tease him on the job, spouting that high-class grammar."

The bitter lines around Elisa's mouth relaxed. "He said he learned his Spanish from one of the wealthy ladies his mother cleaned for. She brought him with her—there was no one to mind him at home—and to the lady he was like a little pet monkey she could feed and carry about. She made him speak the language of the upper classes. His mother encouraged it—she thought educated speech would help him get a better job. When he was here in the States, he kept trying to alter his Spanish accent, because it set him apart from his coworkers."

Jesse said, "We called him 'the Professor' because of his vocabulary, but he was a good welder, a hard worker, always the first to volunteer if someone needed to change a shift. We miss him still, even after these five years."

I waited a respectful moment before asking if there had been anything else in the bottom of Jacobo's toolbox.

"No, and the only family picture he brought with

him—at least, the only one I ever saw—was of him with Filomena, dressed up for their first communion. The clothes were so beautiful—he said his mother had worked for months sewing them. And the two children were beautiful, too. Other than that, no, nothing. Hector also took that photo with him to Chile, but again, he said no one remembered them. The priest who presided over their first communion was dead by then, anyway, it was so long ago. I hoped that Lydia would also have kept that photograph, but I don't think it was in the apartment."

Her smile turned bitter again. "One death after another—that's what I learned from Jacobo, in addition to Spanish, that you must learn to endure one death after another."

30

There Is an *i* in "Quit"

On my way home, I again passed the park super-intendent's home. No one was in the front yard, but as I reached the main road, a black SUV turned off and headed toward his mansion. I stayed at the stop sign, watching in my rearview mirror. Sure enough, it turned into Taggett's driveway.

On an impulse, I made a U-turn back to the house. Taggett was in his front doorway, greeting a child, as I walked up the drive. The chauffeur jumped out of the SUV, gun in hand. It was an ugly thing, probably a Sig.

"Whoa." I held up my own hands, palms spread wide, but Taggett had already flung the child inside and slammed the door.

"Sorry to alarm you," I said, keeping my voice steady, not looking at the gun barrel, treating it like a wild dog that might bite if I made eye contact. "I saw the superintendent arrive home just now and wanted to ask him about the two murders of SLICK personnel."

Taggett stepped down from the shallow porch. "Are you a reporter?"

"Nope. I was at the SLICK meeting you attended last week. I'm sure you know the young man making the presentation was murdered in the Burnham Wildlife preserve a few days later. My goddaughter was dating him."

"A hell of a thing," Taggett said. "But why did you come up here to ask me about it? I have an office, I have a staff. Make an appointment."

"Sure," I said. "I was visiting a friend around the corner when I saw your car pull into the drive. You heard about Simon Lensky, right?"

"What friend?"

"I have friends all over the city," I tried to infuse the words with sinister meaning, as if I were deeply connected. "You don't think SLICK's remaining staff are at risk, do you? Lensky and Prinz didn't seem to have much in common except their work on your plan to redo the lakefront at Forty-seventh."

For a split second, Taggett's face froze, like a halibut on a trawler, and he darted a glance at the gunman. The expression was so fleeting that when he pulled his mouth down in a mime of sorrow I almost doubted I'd seen it.

"God, I hope not. That would be a hell of a way to greet a wonderful improvement to the South Side lakefront. Do you live down there, Ms.—?"

"Warshawski," I supplied. "I grew up near Ninetieth and Exchange."

"Give your goddaughter my condolences. I need to assure my family that they're not under siege." He turned back to the door.

I burst out laughing. "You're watching too many *Game of Thrones* reruns if a middle-aged woman on your sidewalk makes you feel under siege. You're the one whose muscle is pointing a weapon at me. I hope you and Bowser have a permit for that thing."

Taggett scowled, but nodded his head at his bodyguard. The gunman put his arm down, but he was still holding the Sig. It was big enough that a single shot could take out both my heart and my stomach. The skin on the back of my neck tingled as I walked back to the street. I could hear Bowser's steps behind me but I willed myself to keep my pace steady, not to look around, to whistle a lighthearted tune from *Snow White*. After all, Lensky and Leo had been bludgeoned to death, not shot, so Bowser probably hadn't killed them. Possibly hadn't killed them.

When I got into the Mustang, a police car pulled up behind me and followed me until I made the turn onto Lehigh, the main north-south street leading to the expressway.

I drove back to the forest preserve and reclined the seat, waiting for my legs and arms to stop trembling, breathing in deep breaths, getting my whole system to calm down.

Of course Taggett had the police on call—all city department heads get protection as a perk. In fact, it should have surprised me that the cops weren't there the first time I passed the house.

I tried to decode the encounter. That fleeting expression on Taggett's face when I mentioned the lakefront project—someone in the city government would make money from any new development, big or small. If Taggett was getting a cut from whoever wanted to build a new beach and playground, he wouldn't kill to keep the news a secret. In Chicago, that is so much part of the business plan that we pay no attention to the amount of money the city collects from developers eager to do business here. I'm so inured to the corruption that I took for granted that money was changing hands over Taggett's lakefront proposal.

In my mind, Leo's and Simon's murders were linked to that proposal. I suppose Sergeant Pizzello could be right—that they were random muggings. Although why was Simon in Lydia's apartment? And what were the killers looking for when they took both Leo and Lydia's apartments apart?

The cops said the ME's preliminary report put Lensky's death at about two this morning. Coop lured Lensky to the apartment. He cornered Lensky in the bathtub and beat him horribly. He realized his victim was not likely to recover and panicked. He packed up his belongings, left Bear on my front walk, fled to— someplace.

"Bear, what happened in that apartment? Where did Coop say he was going?" I cried out loud to the animal, but he wisely said nothing I could slice and splice into evidence.

I couldn't shut down the churning in my brain. The photo of Jacobo Palurdo, for instance—that was a strange story. His past had been so painful he couldn't talk about it, even with his wife and son. Living through a torturing regime, as my mother also had, creates wells of silence. In time, Gabriella had shared a number of those deeply hidden memories with my father and me, but probably not all, so Jacobo Palurdo's refusal to share memories with his wife didn't surprise me.

I didn't think the photo was what the killers were

looking for when they slit open cushions and the mattress. Maybe Hector had hidden it from his mother, or used it as a page marker, but whoever killed Lensky was looking for something you could hide in a curtain hem or a box of tea leaves.

Being paraded around like a pet monkey by his mother's rich boss must have left its own traumatic memories. I wondered if this patron had also given him dental care—Jacobo's teeth gleamed white and straight in the picture, but his friend's were uneven and one incisor had broken.

Where Coop entered the story didn't seem connected to Hector, but to the park and to Lydia. Coop was furious over the proposal to change the lakefront. The bludgeoning deaths were the work of someone who was enraged, and Coop's anger spilled out like lava from Popocatépetl.

My mind felt like a horrible stew, with beans and overcooked okra turning over and over, not tasty and not improved by continued boiling. I tried to sing under my breath to keep from thinking.

The rush hour was still clogging the expressways. I drove home on side streets, watched ordinary people have ordinary after-work reunions. Men ruffled their children's hair, women squatted to talk face-to-face with toddlers. People were mowing lawns and playing catch in the streets. I felt like an outsider, the Little Match Girl watching happy families through a window.

It was six when I reached home, a mere fourteen hours since Coop left Bear here, but it felt like an event from my distant past, so much had gone on during the day. I let Bear out and stood for a moment, doing push-ups against the side of the car to stretch out my hamstrings and my traps.

I needed to walk Mitch and Peppy, and be prepared for another attack from Donna Lutas and the rest of the tenants. The thought made me put my arms on the car roof and lay my head on them.

"There is no *i* in 'team,' but there is one in 'quit,'" I chivvied myself—one of my old basketball coach's bromides. Of course, there's also an *i* in "win." "I will win," I said, without much conviction.

Mitch and Peppy were not happy that I'd spent the day with a foreign dog. I left Bear with Mr. Contreras, while I leashed up my pair and jogged to the lake, but they behaved abominably. At the lake, they ran away, wouldn't come when they were called, rolled in dead fish, and generally pushed me beyond the brink.

When I finally brought them home, Donna Lutas was coming down the stairs from the upper floors. The dogs lunged for her and it took every ounce of my remaining strength to keep them from rubbing dead fish onto her.

"Can we talk?" Lutas said.

I sighed. "Sure. You want to come to the basement while I wash these two?"

She followed me down to the laundry room. I tied the dogs to a pole near a drain in the middle of the floor and attached a hose to one of the sinks. When Lutas saw what the splash radius was likely to be, she decided to wait upstairs.

I scrubbed slowly, not to be meticulous, but to delay the confrontation. My mother would have condemned me sharply: *Swallow the bad-tasting medicine quickly, get done with it. The anticipation is worse than the taste.*

"Got it: stop complaining," I said, out loud. I turned off the water, towel-dried the dogs, and clomped back up the stairs.

Lutas was standing in the doorway of her own apartment, scrolling through her phone. She was aware that I'd arrived, especially since Mitch gave a sharp bark outside Mr. Contreras's door, but she didn't look up.

"Let me know when you want to talk," I said. "I need to shower and then I'm going out." Peter and I were grabbing what time together we could before he flew out—the only bright spot in a hideous day.

"No, no, let's do it now." She was breathy, nervous, which made me feel less powerless.

I sat on the bottom step, holding the dog leashes in a light hand, but didn't say anything.

"I—uh, I may have been, uh, I may have lost my temper this morning."

"That's possible," I agreed.

"There was significant provocation, you must admit," Lutas said, her voice rising. "The noise, the risk you bring into the building—gunfights in the stairwell are a threat to all of us, not just you!"

When I didn't respond, she demanded that I say something.

"You're doing a good job on your own." I took a last burr from Mitch's left earflap. "I don't see what I can add."

"Don't you think I have a right to be angry?"

"Can you tell me what we're talking about?" I asked. "Are you hoping to push me into losing my temper on tape, or agreeing to something you can use in court?"

"I—no." She gave a titter of fake laughter. "Just—I know I lost my temper, but I'd like you to admit I had a good reason to."

"Ms. Lutas, I don't admit anything. I know you're a lawyer at Devlin & Wickham, but I'm not sure you know I'm also a lawyer. I earned my stripes at Twenty-sixth and California, where the hardest part of the job was to get my clients to shut up in court." I got to my feet and started up the stairs, the dogs following.

"Wait," she said. "I meant to say, I didn't take the time to ask why you brought that other dog in. Salvatore Contreras told me he's connected to a missing person you're looking for, that singer. To be honest, I hadn't ever heard of her when you asked about her last week, but two of the women in my group, they love Lydia Zamir's work. They want to meet you, and they said maybe they could help look for her."

I stopped at the first landing, my jaw agape. "You do know that there are orders of protection against Zamir at your firm, right?"

"Yes, Mr. Gorbeck—my boss—told me, but he talked to the other partners and they agree that the sooner we can find the Zamir woman the easier everyone can sleep at night. He—they—are eager to help you find her."

"Gosh, Ms. Lutas, that's extremely generous—another example of Devlin's pro bono work, like their defense of the man who murdered Zamir's lover."

Her thin face flooded with color. "So you'll do it?"

I smiled. "I'll have to talk it over with my own lawyer. I'll get back to you."

While I showered, I tried to figure out what was going on with Lutas. No, with her firm. What was going on that made Devlin & Wickham want to be privy to my investigation? Perhaps Global Entertainment was a client.

I lay down, wanting to rest for half an hour before going out to meet Peter, but my brain wouldn't shut off. I finally called Murray.

"Crap, Warshawski, don't you look at your messages? Someone at the Second told me you'd been in interrogation all afternoon about Simon Lensky's murder. You know I'm following the Coop-Zamir story. Why the fuck didn't you let me know?"

"Because I was in interrogation at the Second all afternoon. I just got home."

"Well?" he demanded.

"Well, nothing," I said. "Simon Lensky was killed. Sergeant Pizzello wanted to know if I had murdered him. I didn't."

Murray pushed on me. When I'd filled in as many blanks as I was willing to share—leaving Elisa Palurdo and her husband's photo out of the story—I asked him if Global was a client of Devlin & Wickham.

"Who knows? They have both local and imported lawyers on tap. Why do you care?"

"Devlin & Wickham has an order of protection against Lydia Zamir. One of their juniors lives in my building. She does not like me, my dogs, nor the riff-raff I attract. At ten this morning, she told me she was drafting a legal notice to my condo board, seeking approval for evicting me. At six this evening, she was backpedaling: her managing partner wants her and her pals to help look for Lydia Zamir."

Murray chewed that over. "You think, because you wouldn't wear a wire for Bolton, he got his lawyer to open a back door into your investigation."

"The boy reporter has not lost his keen edge," I said dryly.

"If I ask around, jeopardizing my relationship with Bolton, what do I get?"

"How about: I sent you to Zamir's hideout on the Metra tracks. I let you photograph me with Bear. I told you about finding Lensky. You finding a lawyer's name is a tiny payment on your accounts due."

He grumbled for a minute before agreeing, but added, "You know, Warshawski, if I was stupid enough to move into your building, I'd demand combat pay from you. Your neighbor has facts and right on her side."

31
Everyone Joins the Chase

Over dinner, I told Peter about finding Simon Lensky's body, talking some of the horror of the murder out of my system. I told him, too, about the photo Elisa Palurdo had taken from Lydia's apartment.

"And then there's this bizarre business of Donna Lutas—you know, my downstairs neighbor—being ordered to help me look for Lydia Zamir."

Peter listened empathically, but couldn't make more sense of it than I did. "I can only offer you the archaeologist's mantra: keep digging, because you don't know how deep some bones are buried."

Peter and I said our goodbyes in the morning: he was leaving for Ankara tonight and we both hate airport farewells.

"Don't let anyone near you with a gavel," he murmured into my hair. "I like your head the way it is. I sometimes think you would be safer working in Sudan or Syria than in Chicago."

I tried to say something insouciant, but it sounded flat even to my ears. I hoped I wasn't getting old, fearing risk, needing comfort in a lover's arms, but it was hard to let go and say goodbye.

When he'd gone, I took the dogs for a long walk, all three of them, trying to dispel the sinking in the stomach that Peter's departure left behind. Bear was also suffering from melancholy. He plodded along but refused to engage with Mitch, who was nipping at his ankles.

When we got home, I called a dog-walking service to organize care for Mitch and Peppy. Fitting their exercise and Bear's into my schedule had me at my tipping point—namely, the point at which I tip over and can't get back on my feet.

With the dog walkers in place, I drove to my office, taking Bear with me, not just to spare Mr. Contreras the struggle of keeping Mitch from bullying him, but if I found a trail to Coop, I wanted to offload his dog as soon as possible.

When we'd settled in, one with a cortado, the other under a desk with a bully stick, I called SLICK's Mona Borsa. I didn't recognize her voice when she answered, it was so changed by the shock of her co-worker's death.

She and Simon Lensky had known each other for thirty years, she said, in her tremulous new voice. They'd met over shared community issues, gone to the same church, and then had run SLICK, along with Curtis Murchison, for the last eleven years.

I listened to her memories and her grief for some time. When she seemed ready to talk about Lensky's death, I asked if she knew why he'd gone to Coop's apartment.

"The police don't know," I explained.

"I can't understand it." She wept. "Coop—we all were tired of Coop. He was always disrupting our meetings. We have regular cleanup days in the parks, as you saw. We plant trees, we try to keep glass and used diapers off the beaches, but whatever we did, Coop knew it was wrong.

"He attacked one of our volunteers for using Roundup on the running paths. I mean attacked with his fists. He said we were trying to kill dogs and chipmunks, probably even rats, who chew on the plants. If it had been Coop found dead in that bathtub, it would have made sense, he upset so many people.

"But Simon? He wasn't that kind of person, not the kind of person to go around picking fights. After he lost his wife, that was eight—no, it's been nine years now—he buried himself in Chicago history. He cared about his collection of old history books, he cared about the lakefront. He was writing a history of the lake, from La Salle to Lightfoot. What possible reason could that maniac Coop have to kill him, except that he is a maniac?"

"Do you know if Coop invited Simon over to the apartment?"

"Yes." Mona sniffled. "He got a text message from Coop, saying he had something to show Simon about the beach plan."

That didn't make sense: Coop wanted to be off the grid. He didn't use devices that made him easy to trace; if he used a phone, it wasn't a smartphone. He might carry a burner, but an old-fashioned flip phone seemed more his style.

"Are you sure the message came from Coop?" I asked.

"It was signed with his name. Simon forwarded it to me; I saw it myself."

I persuaded her to send it to me, but she sent only the words, not the identifying phone number: You're being used as a fall guy over the beach plan. Meet me at my place at seven tonight and I'll show you the real plans. Coop.

The message ended with the address for Lydia's apartment on Ingleside.

"Why did he go alone, when he knew Coop could jump the rails at a moment's notice?" I asked.

"I know. I told him not to, but he thought, he said, that time of evening, it's still light, there'd be plenty of people around." Her voice trailed away into a fresh bout of tears.

"Tell me more about the lakefront development plan," I said when she'd regained some composure. "Leo Prinz was working on that, too. Leo went through the maps and documents Mr. Lensky was preparing. Was there some controversy over the plan?"

"There's always controversy over any change. Some people hate change—Coop was one of them, and that Nashita Lyndes who's always picking apart our proposals is another. That place where they're planning a new beach, you can't use it unless you don't mind climbing over rocks and gravel. This would be such a gift to the South Side. We never get the city to pay any attention to what we need down here and those two were trying to shut the project down before it got off the ground."

"That last SLICK meeting where Leo Prinz was speaking, he and Mr. Lensky had a disagreement about one of the maps or diagrams," I said.

"That was nothing," she said. "I asked Simon after

the meeting, because Leo was making a song and dance about it. Simon said it was an old map from the thirties that he was using for his book, only he'd got it mixed into the beach proposal. It happened all the time with him, he was such a—not a pack rat—but papers, he hoarded every document he ever saw."

"I'd like to look at Simon's stack of papers. When could I stop by the SLICK office?"

"Oh, you can't," she cried. "He never left them with us, or anywhere except his own apartment. And then, he was mugged after the last meeting. Someone grabbed his case—it was one of those big cases architects use. It held all his old maps of that part of the lakefront and the new ones that Mr. Taggett had given us. That was why he wanted to meet with Coop. He thought he could talk Coop who mugged him to get the plans. Simon could talk him into giving them back. He'd never copied them all—Leo was going to help him do that, but they'd never started work on the project."

She spoke for a few more minutes on how irreplaceable Simon was. The maps and drawings of the proposed new beach had all been given to them by the Park District, but Simon's analysis, his cost estimates, those were things they'd have to do over from scratch.

"And without Leo to help—I don't know how we'll manage."

"Look out for your own safety, Mona," I said. "Leo and Simon both murdered, that doesn't sound like a coincidence to me. You and your friend Curtis need to be careful."

"Sergeant Pizzello told me they are stepping up patrols around our buildings, but it all depends on how quickly they can catch Coop," she said. "That dog of his would probably kill on his command, so I'm wearing a neck brace when I go out at night."

When she'd hung up, I looked at Bear. "Coop might go for someone's throat, but you strike me as the moderating influence in your relationship."

He looked somberly at me—the responsibility of keeping Coop under control weighed heavily on him.

I leaned back in my desk chair and stared at the ceiling. Two of the acoustic tiles had come loose, and the others were covered with grime or cobwebs or both. Climbing up to clean and repair them was number 713 on my to-do list.

I shut my eyes. If it weren't for coincidences, we wouldn't have any novels by Dickens, so I know they exist. But Leo and Simon both dead, Simon mugged and his papers stolen, Leo's computer missing—that was too much coincidence even for *Bleak House.*

Mona took for granted that Coop was the killer. Leo had been killed with SLICK's gavel, which meant Coop would have to have filched it, enticed Leo to the park, and killed him. I didn't know what weapon had been used on Simon, but it was similarly a planned murder.

Coop's anger could certainly ride him to the point where he'd attack physically—as he had the person putting Roundup in the park—but would he sit down and plot out a death? He didn't seem to be someone who thought ahead, but his leaving his dog with me and disappearing—he clearly was fleeing someone, or at least fleeing somewhere.

"Where did he go? Why did he go?" I said to Bear. "Something to do with Lydia? And where is she?"

If she'd died in the park, surely someone would have found her body by now. I was hoping Coop was the person who'd found her. I was hoping he'd moved her somewhere safe.

Coop, Lydia. Coop, Elisa Palurdo. Coop, Leo Prinz and Simon Lensky. Was he really the fulcrum that moved all the activity around these people?

I looked up Debbie Zamir, Lydia's mother, in my database and called her.

"I'm not talking to reporters."

"I'm not a reporter, ma'am. I'm a detective. We spoke a few days ago, but I'm calling again because I found your daughter close to death in a Chicago park four days ago. She disappeared again and I'm hoping and praying she's someplace where she can recover her strength."

Zamir was briefly silent. When she spoke again, her voice was softer. "Do you think she's dead? I've had calls from half a dozen reporters today, including someone from New York, but none of them said that."

"I don't know how much longer she can live without food or proper medical care. Or a place where she can sleep through the night undisturbed. Her friend Coop has also vanished. I need some thread of an idea about where they might have gone."

"I don't know." She was worried, finally, about her daughter; the belligerence was gone from her voice. "It's been so long since we've spoken. I don't have threads."

"Coop is a man in his forties with a big tawny dog. You never saw him?"

She hesitated a second too long. "A lot of people came around after the shootings. Lydia wasn't popular in high school, but her music attracted all kinds of attention. Plus the notoriety of a big shooting—all kinds of weird men came around. They brought flowers, and incense burners, like this was some graveyard. Young women came, too, dressed in Indian costumes, singing that one song of hers that everyone liked so much. We had to get the sheriff to chase them off the land, and then they just camped on the other side of the river with their candles. Some of them had dogs, but I didn't keep track of them."

"When people came, which ones did Lydia respond to?"

"She didn't respond to any of them," Zamir said.

"She never went to the window to watch the young women singing 'Savage'?"

"I was her mother, not her jailor. I don't know what she did in her bedroom." She spoke sharply

"Do you have an email address? If I sent you a picture of the dog, it might spark a memory. I'm desperate to find your daughter, and Coop, the man with the dog, he's my only lead."

"You don't think I'm desperate? My only child? But she went so far away from me so long ago, how do you think you can bring her back?"

She was quiet, waiting for me to come up with the right response, but I couldn't figure out what that would be. She finally hung up.

I studied my dirty ceiling for another long minute before once again calling Murray Ryerson. "You have competition on the Zamir story, Murray: multiple reporters have been bugging Debbie Zamir. Lydia's story even roused someone east of the Hudson. Did you go down to Kansas in person?"

"Not that it's your business, but I'm at the Kansas City airport right now, Warshawski. I couldn't get past the Zamirs' front door this time, which told me someone had beaten me to the punch. She tell you who paid her the most for her story?"

"You were down there offering her money?" I was almost screaming in outrage. "Debbie Zamir is scared for her daughter's life and you wanted to pay her to talk about it?"

He started to justify himself, but I hung up and texted Donna Lutas at Devlin & Wickham: I'm grateful to your coworkers for wanting to help search for Lydia Zamir. Can we start tomorrow?

32

Digging Up the Deep State

Yesterday had been so exhausting that in the morning I couldn't galvanize myself to work. I sat in the garden with the dogs, drinking coffee and watching the birds in the bushes along the back fence. It had rained again in the night, but it hadn't cleared the air: the sky was low and gray, the air thick.

The storm had battered my neighbor's tomato plants. When Mr. Contreras came out to mourn them, I helped him tie them up, pluck off any blackening leaves, and put fresh straw around them to keep blight at bay.

It was noon by the time I'd finally pulled myself together to exercise the dogs and shower. At my office I took care of some outstanding client searches, but in the back of my mind, I was turning over Peter's advice to keep digging.

My subscription search engines mostly harvest data about Americans and Canadians. Given that our own government can't distinguish between hardened criminals and terrified mothers, it's not surprising that it's difficult to get good information from south of the border.

I did the best I could, looking for people named "Palurdo" up and down both Americas. There were none.

I looked for earthquake damage in Tocopilla, where Jacobo Palurdo's childhood church had been destroyed. Tocopilla suffered constantly from earthquakes. There'd even been two this past spring, and there'd been a biggish one in 2007. That made it plausible that all traces of the Palurdo family had been destroyed when their parish church was ripped apart.

Elisa's story bothered me. Not that she was lying—although maybe she was. It just seemed strange that when Hector went to Tocopilla, not one person remembered a family named Palurdo. It wasn't a big town, only 24,000, and if he'd explored the barrios and the city government records, some other person with that name, or someone remembering the family, would pop up. Hector's grandmother had cleaned houses for the wealthy; she'd done exquisite needlework. She'd made something for a rich person's child that would stick in the memory. Maybe Hector had seemed like an out-sider and people were afraid to tell him what they knew.

I hunted for records of those who'd been disappeared and murdered under the Pinochet regime. Those were patchy, but I didn't find Filomena's name. Finally I made a big sweep: *Filomena and Chile*. That gave me a St. Filomena, from the nineteenth century, some hotels named for her, and dozens of hits for a Filomena Quin-tana.

Quintana was very much alive. Her bio, in Spanish, was hard for me to read, but she was sixty-two, so a contemporary of Jacobo Palurdo. She hadn't grown up in Tocopilla, but in Valparaíso, which was apparently an important city both economically and politically. She'd attended university at the Pontificia Universidad Católica de Chile, where she'd studied political econ-omy, had worked for the Aguilar Mining Company and made the transition to television in the 1990s.

Despite her age and television's insistence on youth, she had a large following on a Chilean cable show. I clicked on some of her YouTube clips. She was a strik-ing woman, who carried herself with confidence. Her shoulder-length blond hair was streaked with silver. Her eyes were an unusual green with brown flecks—not one's stereotype of the dark South American.

As an Italian speaker, I could sort of follow her talks,

but it was a strain to keep up. In one, she startled me by holding up a copy of *Atlas Shrugged* in Spanish— *La Rebelión de Atlas.* She seemed to be exhorting her viewers to read it for an understanding of how a human being should live a fulfilling life.

I scrolled through the web hits until I found an English-language entry: she'd been interviewed by Global Media, on one of their political talk shows, *Digging Up the Deep State.* I've watched it occasionally, fascinated by their carefully balanced presenters—one an anorectic blond woman, Stevie something, the other a very dark African-American man, Horace something else.

Quintana appeared with Larry Nieland, the Chicago Nobel Laureate who'd spoken at the SLICK meeting where poor Leo got into an argument with the equally unfortunate Simon.

Quintana laid a fleeting hand on Nieland's arm, saying to Stevie and Horace, "Larry was my professor, my mentor. He brought me to Chicago for a memorable year of study. Such an education. Yes, we discussed monetary theory, but mostly I had to learn baseball, which is not popular in Chile as it is in Venezuela or Colombia. And then I must learn to hate Cubs and love White Sox."

Everyone laughed, Stevie opening her mouth so

wide her cheekbones pushed her eyes half-shut. Compared with their usual conspiracy theory-laden interviews, this was fluff for Horace and Stevie. They bring up everything from how climate Nazis are spreading fear in order to bankrupt the American oil industry, to allegations of cover-ups of the secret work liberals do to promote mass shootings because "they want to take away your guns," as Stevie would solemnly tell Horace. "That's right, Stevie," Horace would respond, equally solemn. "They actually create these shootings and blame them on gun owners. Or they stage shootings with actors so they can make people frightened of guns."

That thought made me dig into the Deep State archive for Horace and Stevie's coverage of the massacre at Horsethief Canyon. Global's Wichita, Kansas, affiliate had had a camera at the Meet-Up. I watched some of the footage; they'd had a camera going when the gunfire opened, but it was so sickening that I couldn't keep watching.

I turned to something even more upsetting: *Deep State*'s coverage of Arthur Morton's trial. Horace and Stevie were in full throttle, showing Morton's childhood home, the farm with dust rising from the ground, barns, and other outbuildings exhibiting signs of neglect six years after Sea-2-Sea had bought the land.

"This is what happens when we let people with a globalist agenda set our foreign policy," Horace said. "Good decent people like the Morton family get swallowed alive."

They had a cute graphic for that segment, of a python squeezing its tail around a mock-up of the Morton farm, then swallowing the outbuildings and the people.

Stevie and Horace questioned whether radicals like Lydia and Hector really belonged in a family place like Horsethief Canyon. Families got together for picnics and music. They didn't want someone pushing politics down their throats.

"Really," Horace said, "you could make a case that the kind of speeches people like Hector made goaded the Morton boy into pulling the trigger."

It's not enough that we're awash in weapons as a country, but TV personalities actually find excuses for mass killers. I left the site, wishing I could make a more forceful exit. I miss the days when you could slam down a phone to end an annoying conversation.

I packed up my office, but before going home, I drove downtown to the Park District headquarters: Lydia's disappearance wasn't the only worrying business I was trying to sort out; there were also the murders of Leo Prinz and Simon Lensky.

The Park District planned to relocate into an actual

park on the Southwest Side, but until that building was finished they were housed in the old Time-Life Building, within spitting distance of the city's most expensive shopping. Chicago's power elite like their creature comforts—really, who doesn't? How would Taggett and his buddies adjust to neighborhood diners instead of Gold Coast bistros?

In the Park District office, I told a woman at the information counter what I was looking for. She slowly wrote it down and handed it to another clerk, who disappeared with it into the bank. Patronage-rich fiefdoms like the Park District build support by employing two people per task.

After a few minutes, the phone on the information counter rang. The clerk grunted a few times, then told me that none of the Forty-seventh Street drawings were available for public viewing. "Until a plan has been put together, the public can't view them."

"I don't understand," I said. "I was in the meeting where SLICK presented them to the public only last week."

The clerk shook her head. "You probably saw some community group's ideas on the subject, but that development is definitely only in the idea stage."

"Taggett was there," I persisted. "He took questions on the proposal."

She gave a thin smile. "*Superintendent* Taggett would never have presented a preliminary idea as a completed proposal. I suggest you talk to your community group and find out what the superintendent said to them when he came to their meeting. They may have exaggerated the state of the proposal in an effort to push him into quicker action than he's able to provide."

I thought about demanding to speak to her boss, but if the official line was to stonewall inquiries, all I would do is waste more of my own time without any result except to increase my frustration. Just to stir the pot, though, or maybe because I hate admitting defeat, I left a note for the superintendent:

Dear Mr. Taggett,

You said if I wanted to talk to you, to come to your office. Here I am.

I understand that the proposals for changes to the Burnham Wildlife Corridor are preliminary only and not available for public viewing. Has your team let you know that Mr. Prinz's computer has disappeared, as have Mr. Lensky's maps and drawings of the park during that well-timed mugging? Thieves could well get those maps out on the Internet, but ordinary citizens don't have access to the maps and drawings Mr. Prinz showed at the most recent SLICK meeting. Can you please tell your highly protective staff to let me look at such drawings as are available?

I signed it with my office phone and email. Taggett might never receive it, of course, but I felt the dubious satisfaction of having the last word.

When I looked at my phone back in my car, I saw a message from Donna Lutas at Devlin & Wickham: I could come into the office tomorrow at eleven, and she and one of her coworkers would help me figure out a way to search for Lydia.

33

A Little Help from
My Friends (?)

Before going down to the Devlin offices in the morning, I called Mona Borsa to tell her about my futile visit to the Park District the previous day.

"They say all the plans are preliminary, and that none of the drawings are available for public viewing, so what were you showing in those public meetings?"

"They gave us drawings, we showed the drawings." Her voice was tired. Simon's death had turned her apathetic.

"Then why is Taggett withholding them now?"

"I don't know. Maybe because all Simon's copies got lost when his briefcase was stolen. They need to make sure they're using the same material they gave us, so they have to double-check their records. I guess. Why do you care?"

"I'm trying to figure out whether the drawings played a role in his and Leo's murders. Leo was arguing with him about one of the maps, remember?"

"No." Her voice sharpened. "That's *your* memory, not mine. I don't remember them arguing about anything at all." She hung up.

I was lucky again this morning with street parking near the old Ft. Dearborn Bank building. Donna Lutas was apparently eager to see me—the guard sent me straight up to the tenth floor. Lutas met me by the elevators, accompanied by another young woman, both in the uniform of striving young professionals—blazers, man-tailored white shirts, pencil skirts. Lutas started to hustle us into the Devlin offices, but I turned to her companion, hand held out, and introduced myself.

"Rikki Samundar, from our Mumbai office." She flashed a smile, teeth very white against dark skin. "Let's see what our three brains can do to find this unfortunate singer."

She swiped a key card against a pair of heavy wood doors and held one open for me, admitting me to the Devlin & Wickham main lobby. The heavy furniture and drapes gave it an atmosphere more of a funeral parlor than a modern law firm, but a six-foot bronze of a bucking horse demonstrated the partners' commitment to fine art.

"The Mumbai office?" I said to Samundar. "How did Lydia Zamir end up on Mumbai's radar?"

Samundar flashed another smile, not shared by Lutas, who was holding her shoulders so stiffly I could have broken pieces from them.

"I trained for the bar under British and Indian law, but all Devlin attorneys need a working knowledge of American legal systems, no matter where we're placed. I'm one of the fortunate ones who gets to intern here at the U.S. headquarters. And I was one of the young research team when the firm undertook Arthur Morton's defense."

She stopped to tell a receptionist we would be in conference room L and that her and Lutas's phone calls should be routed through to there for the next hour. Conference room L held a cart with coffee and soft drinks, a speakerphone, a wall monitor, notepads, and a view of the pillars of the Federal Reserve Bank across the street.

"I've been curious about that," I said. "How did a firm like Devlin hear of a Kansas farm boy?"

Samundar laughed, softly. "Everyone in the world briefly knew about that Kansas farm boy, Ms. Warshawski. However, we have clients among the big ranchers in the west of the state. Specifically, Sea-2-Sea had acquired Arthur Morton's family farm when his father had to abandon it. Local people harbored ill will, thinking Sea-2-Sea had driven the farm boy to desperation and so to murder. By taking on the case, pro bono, with Sea-2-Sea covering the administrative costs, we were able to smooth over some of those feelings."

"That sounds most noble," I said dryly.

"In a big farm state like Kansas, there are vast spaces with many cattle and few humans." Samundar spread her arms, indicating the size of the western lands. "Sea-2-Sea found poison in one of their wells, cattle stolen from other holdings. It was important that they regain the trust of their neighbors."

Lutas was watching me closely, as if to monitor how much of this story I bought. I smiled amiably: yes, I'm on board with your version of events.

"Of course, Lydia Zamir was deeply disturbed by her lover's murder," I said. "She wasn't placated by Sea-2-Sea's goodwill gesture."

"Personally, I was devastated by her deterioration after the trial. All my friends at home loved her *Continental Requiem* album, especially 'Savage.'"

"But professionally, you agreed with the orders of protection."

Samundar held out her hands, palms up, the gesture

of helplessness. "What could we do? She actually tried to attack Clarence Gorbeck—our lead attorney at the trial—physically, not just in court, but also here, on LaSalle Street."

"So how do you think you can help find her?" I asked.

"Her boyfriend was from Chile." Donna Lutas spoke for the first time.

"Hector Palurdo was American," I said sharply. "He was born in Chicago to two American citizens."

Lutas waved an impatient hand. "His father was from Chile, which amounts to the same thing. We've contacted our Santiago offices to be on the lookout for Zamir. It seems Hector Palurdo had an aunt who worked there a long time ago. The Zamir woman might have gone there, looking for his family."

"Filomena Palurdo worked for Devlin in Chile?" I was so startled I ignored her ignorant statement about Jacobo's Chilean birth meaning Hector was essentially Chilean.

Jacobo had told his wife that his sister had been murdered. Or at least, Elisa told me that was what Jacobo had said. I had no idea whose version of events I could trust in this story.

"When did his aunt work for you?" I demanded.

"A long time back. It wasn't Devlin back then," Lutas said, "but a firm we acquired in 2013. And her name—"

"Was spelled many different ways." Samundar cut her off seamlessly.

"Hector Palurdo went to Chile looking for his family and couldn't find any trace of them. How did you learn about his aunt?"

"He was one person, searching by himself; we have a lot more resources." That was Samundar again, the smooth half of the duo.

"Did you leak the news of Palurdo's aunt to Lydia Zamir?" I asked. "She's so frail, mentally and physically, that the only way she'd get to Santiago would be if someone strapped her to a stretcher and carried her."

"That's so sad," Samundar said. "We will definitely tell our Santiago team to check local hospitals on the chance that she did make it down there."

I pressed my fingertips into my forehead, trying to think. I was being spun an elaborate line about Jacobo Palurdo's sister, but why?

"Is Hector's aunt still alive?" I asked. "If you let Lydia know you'd found her lover's South American family, I'm sure she would seek them out if she had the strength."

"Sadly not," Samundar said.

She added "a car accident" at the same moment Lutas said "breast cancer."

"Perhaps she had breast cancer but died in a car crash?" I suggested with a limpid smile.

"I may have been mistaken," Samundar said. "Traffic in Mumbai is so hideous, I'm always imagining that premature deaths come from road incidents."

"You're sure it was cancer and a road accident, not murder," I said.

"You think she was political?" Samundar said. "What do you know about her?"

"I have no idea if she was political. I know only what her sister-in-law told me—that her murder is what made Jacobo Palurdo leave Chile for the States, which means she died more than forty years ago."

Samundar briefly lost her poise, biting her lips. "I'm working with sketchy information, coming in from investigators in Chile. We're relying on the translation services we have here at Devlin, and of course our Spanish speakers have native fluency, but it's not the same as being able to hear the report yourself firsthand. But we are sure that Filomena is dead."

Lutas nodded solemnly, as befit the mention of death.

I changed the subject back to Lydia. "What about your Kansas offices? Are they also looking for Zamir?"

"We don't have offices in Kansas, but we did ask the state police to monitor the passenger lists at the airport, and there's no sign that she arrived," Lutas said.

"Also the trains. Of course, if she arrived by bus or car—" Samundar again held out her palms—impossible to track car traffic. "But the state police will be watching, just in case. And obviously, once again, we'll tell them to check hospitals."

"And morgues," I said, but I couldn't figure out what else to say. Like, How do you persuade local LEOs to grant you access to passenger manifests? Or, How much of these fables do you think I'll believe? Or, Am I supposed to fly to Santiago while you do who knows what here at home?

"There is the man, Coop, who I gather has also disappeared?" Samundar said.

"Yes. As Ms. Lutas here will have told you, at great length, he left his dog at our building three nights ago."

Lutas produced what was supposed to be a smile. "What does he say about when he'll be back for the dog?"

"If I knew where he was, Ms. Lutas, believe me, I would get his dog to him at the speed of light. I hope my not knowing doesn't make you want to resume your eviction efforts with the condo board."

Lutas gave another imitation smile, but her eyes

were not full of love. "Of course not. I know now you didn't want the dog dumped on you. But we're in the middle of a big case, which means we don't get much sleep, and so I don't always keep my cool. I'm sure you remember from your own law experience."

I had to agree—sleeplessness is my overriding memory of my years at Twenty-sixth and California. That and the smell of too many unbathed bodies packed into the tiny conference room where public defenders met with a roster of clients too big for one person to handle. It certainly wasn't like conference room L, whose meeting table was smooth, unmarred by gang symbols and death threats.

"What is Coop's full name?" Samundar asked.

"I was hoping you could tell me," I said. "Not even the beat cops who occasionally had to keep him from disturbing the peace seem to know. You have the resources to track down Jacobo Palurdo's sister's cancer, unless it was her car crash. Surely you can find an American who's been in this city for some time."

"Someone who is that determined not to be found can be hard to trace," Samundar said. "But no one can be off the grid forever. Please let us know as soon as you hear from him."

That was meant as an exit line—both women were getting to their feet—but I stayed in my chair.

"Before we wrap up, Ms. Samundar, you were the junior attorney at Arthur Morton's trial?"

She nodded cautiously.

"So you were likely the person whom Mr. Gorbeck told to bring nicotine patches to Arthur Morton in the jail, right?"

"That will always haunt me," she said. "If I had known I was giving him the means of taking his life—!"

"Did you buy them yourself?"

She gave her practiced smile. "I almost feel as though you are cross-examining me, Ms. Warshawski."

"I almost feel as though I am, as well. Did Mr. Gorbeck give the patches to you? Or did he ask you to buy them yourself?"

"If it were just me you wanted to ask, I would gladly answer, but I can't speak for Mr. Gorbeck. Now, we have other matters to attend to, but do let Donna know as soon as you hear from Coop."

"I will bring Bear to kiss her goodbye in person," I promised.

34

City Services

I'd left Bear in my office while I was at Devlin. When I got back he greeted me with his usual somber expression: I have weighed and found you wanting.

I took him to nearby Wicker Park for a walk, trying to digest what I'd learned from my meeting with Samundar and Lutas.

The real reason they wanted to talk to me had been to find Coop, not Lydia. Either they knew Lydia was dead, or they knew where she was. They'd been clumsy, trying to stir my interest in Chile by suggesting a woman as mentally and physically frail as Lydia could have organized an expedition to Santiago. Did that mean they were trying to get me out of Chicago, or—what? Deflect my search? Imagine that their focus was more on Zamir than on Coop?

Still, Hector had gone to Chile, trying to trace his family. Everything came through Devlin—the search for Lydia and Coop, representing Arthur Morton at his trial, and the strange information about Filomena Palurdo, whose name, Samundar said, was spelled in many different ways. Did that mean she actually had a different name? Or was Samundar trying to send me on a wild chase for a nonexistent person?

When I got back to my office, I called Hector Palurdo's old roommate, the Latin American specialist Stu Shiffman. He asked if I'd found Lydia.

"I'm having trouble getting any kind of lead on her," I said. "One thing that has cropped up in the last few days has to do with Hector's father's sister."

I told him about Filomena and the different versions of her death I'd been given.

Shiffman whistled softly. "The lawyers contradict each other, and they contradict what Hector learned from his father. That's a strange business all on its own. But Hector knew his aunt was dead all the way back when we were in college together. He made his first trip to Chile—I won't remember exactly when, but probably when we were third-year students.

"Hector came home frustrated because there was no information of any kind, her birth, her death, his grandparents' lives. The thing is, if she was killed during the Pinochet years—which is when Hector's father emigrated—my best guess is, hers was a political murder, not a crime of passion or some such."

"Why?"

"Judicial murders for people violating national defense laws were much more common than what you might call ordinary garden-variety homicide. And despite thirty years of hearings, reports, roundtables, and so on, many of those *desaparecidos*—the disappeared— have never been found. Then, too, Hector's father came from a poor family in a poor mining town—the odds are good that his sister would have been a leftist, and they were heavily targeted by the regime."

"These other two versions—cancer or car accident— it's almost as though the Devlin attorneys were trying to protect the regime—but that makes no sense at all, since that ended, what—thirty years ago?"

We thrashed it around for some minutes without getting anywhere. Before hanging up, I remembered to ask him about the photograph I'd seen two days ago.

"I'd forgotten that," Shiffman said. "Hector hoped I could help him ID the man with his father. I sent him to some databases I knew that try to find the *desaparecidos,* but never heard back from him, so I don't know if they were useful or not."

"When I was hunting for anyone named Filomena, I

stumbled on a TV personality named Filomena Quintana," I said. "She was clutching a Spanish edition of *Atlas Shrugged*, by Ayn Rand, which took me by surprise."

Shiffman laughed. "Yes, Rand is very popular in a lot of neo-nationalist, neo-liberal circles in the Americas these days. Go figure."

He couldn't tell me anything else, and while everything he'd said had been interesting, it didn't move my search forward. I did ask whether he'd ever met Coop, but neither the name nor my description of him rang any bells.

I wrote up the details of the conversation in my case file before turning my attention to a problem I was investigating for one of my regular clients. It was past five when I finished. I swapped my backup drives from the fireproof safe in the back, locked everything up, and opened the street door, Bear at my ankle.

Two men climbed out of a Cadillac Escalade that was blocking the entrance to my building's parking area. They started toward me, moving with a kind of swagger that you have to practice in front of a dance school mirror to get right. They had on jackets, which meant they were carrying. Bear snarled and crouched, prepared to launch himself.

"Steady, boys." I spoke to all three of them, but held

a hand near Bear's muzzle. He wasn't on a leash, and I didn't want him shot.

The men retreated to the Escalade. The front-passenger door opened, and Gifford Taggett climbed out. When he started up the walk, his swaggerers followed, eyes on Bear, hands inside their jackets.

"Hello, Superintendent," I said. "If your muscle shoot my dog I will retaliate. And if they shoot me, the dog will go for them."

"Don't get your undies in a bundle, Warshawski." Taggett stopped about ten feet from me. "You've been to see me uninvited and unannounced, I'm returning the favor."

Bear's haunches were quivering from the strain of holding himself in check. I didn't know what commands Coop used with him. I tried "At Ease," "Free," and "Sit," but he kept himself combat-ready.

"Your staff gave you the message I left?" I was surprised.

"Oh, yes." He smiled, a big rictus that showed off big horsey teeth. "It's important to know what hot spots are developing around the city parks, fix 'em before they grow too big to repair. You definitely seem to be a hot . . . spot."

Word and tone were charged with innuendo. He was goading me into reacting—so he could have his punks kill Bear? Or me? Or just knock me off mental balance.

"Sorry, Super, I'm just a simple taxpayer wondering what you're up to in the Burnham Wildlife Corridor." My own voice steady, bored.

"After I read your note, I talked to some people about you. You're a solo op who acts like your dog there, thinking you're big enough to take on people fifty or a hundred times your size. I can assure you—you're not."

"That's good to know," I said. "Do you think you're fifty or a hundred times as big as me?"

"Easily. I have friends in every department in this city, from Streets and San to the police and everything in between. Cops can start checking whether your dogs have their rabies shots up to date and whether your car has any repair issues. Your water might get turned off. Streets and San can forget to pick up your trash. I understand your neighbors in your condo aren't too happy with you. If they learn you're the one letting the trash build in the alley, that would be the last straw. You'd be looking for a new home in a month."

"That could happen even without your help," I said, "but it does amaze me how many places Devlin & Wickham pop up. Of course, they are one of America's biggest law firms, so I suppose it's not surprising that they have you on their books. But I hope they don't represent the Park District. Sixteen hundred dollars an hour for legal advice when every park in the city needs its paths rebuilt?"

The muscles around his mouth tightened and twitched. He hated that I knew something that was supposed to be secret. Of course, it was a guess, but who else was going to tell him about a feud between tenants in an unimportant building? Clarence Gorbeck may have told my neighbor to play nice with me, but something I was doing was bothering Devlin, or at least one of their clients, so much that he'd told Taggett about me.

Don't taunt the viper, my mother used to warn me. *When she is threatened she strikes quickly.*

Taggett took a step toward me. Bear growled softly. What a good dog.

Taggett said, "Why do you care about that park improvement, Warshawski? It's way out of your neighborhood."

"Is that what this is about?" I said. "Northsiders can't go south? We can't have a sense of community and care about the whole city? Really, though, I'm helping investigate Leo Prinz's and Simon Lensky's murders."

"We have a police force," Taggett said. "It would be a good thing—a healthy thing—for you to let them solve these murders and for you to fix your own problems."

That was supposed to scare me. Actually, it did, but I said, "Chicago police only clear seventeen percent of our homicides each year. They need help, and as a trained investigator that's something I can do for my city. About the maps, Superintendent?"

"There's nothing about the maps. Lensky was working with a preliminary plan that we scrapped because it was getting too much pushback from the community. Mona Borsa, who is the kind of hardworking volunteer this city depends on, told me Lensky lost all his documents in a mugging after the last SLICK meeting. It's a shame, because if we had his papers I'd be able to show you that he was looking at a very old plan.

"The cops have a suspect for his killing. They just have to find him. Unless you're hiding him, they don't need your help. Save your Girl Scout badge for something you know about. Which, believe me, is not the city's parks. Leave them to the experts."

He turned back to the Escalade. His triggermen exchanged regretful looks with Bear: both had hoped their principals would unleash them into a fight.

The SUV pulled away from my parking lot with a great squealing of rubber. A squad car trailed them. I'd been so focused on Taggett and his goons that I hadn't noticed he had his usual police escort.

I squatted on the pavement next to Bear and put my arms around his neck. "If you'd gone for their throats, the cops would have testified they killed you and me in self-defense. Don't do it, boy. Let's survive to find Coop."

35

Found in the Shuffle

I drove home slowly, rattled by the encounter. Chicagoans know that politics ain't beanbag, as Mr. Dooley put it all those years ago, but Taggett's threats were out of proportion to my asking about the maps for the Forty-seventh Street beach project. Some people like to use muscle just to show they have it. Taggett had some of that impulse, but he was a savvy player. His threats to me implied I was threatening a deal he'd done over the Burnham Wildlife Corridor.

Money was already changing hands, the woman from the community had said bitterly. Money people had come to the SLICK meeting. Larry Nieland had significant resources, but it was the Off Duty guy who'd been there and at Taggett's home who looked like the real money tree. He wouldn't have been at a small community meeting if he didn't see the lakefront sprouting rich greens that he could harvest.

"I can imagine that putting in a new beach is a serious engineering challenge," I commented to Bear, "but it wouldn't bring global investors to a South Side meeting."

At home, I wrote down the names of everyone I'd talked to over the last month, from Lydia Zamir and her mother, through the SLICK managers, Coop, Norman Bolton at Global Entertainment, Donna Lutas, her coworker Rikki Samundar. Leo, Bernie, Taggett. Murray. Elisa Palurdo. Her husband's friend Jesse.

I was looking at two murders, Lensky and Prinz, whose deaths had nothing to do with Lydia Zamir's disappearance, whose only connection was Coop: he was the cop's main suspect in the murders. And he had vanished with Zamir.

I sketched a tree with all the different names on branches to see which ones connected to one another. Coop's, SLICK's, and Zamir's branches were knotted together. Norm Bolton was linked to Murray through Global, of course, but that didn't explain why he'd wanted to film my search for Lydia.

It was the lawyers who seemed to run through the tangled collection of stories, like the trunk of a real tree that all the branches sprouted from. I'd never gotten word back from Murray on whether Global Entertainment was a Devlin & Wickham client, but Devlin had represented the mass murderer who killed Zamir's lover; they had taken out an order of protection against Lydia, and if my deduction was correct, they had given information about my domestic fracas with Donna Lutas to Park Super Taggett—who was, of course, tied to SLICK.

Rikki Samundar said Devlin & Wickham had gotten involved to protect Sea-2-Sea's water from poisoning, but pro bono work on a capital case to protect a client sounded thin to me. Global Entertainment was involved, too, I reminded myself. My tree's branches were getting too tangled to keep straight.

I hadn't dug into Global shareholders to see if one of them might be the reason Norm Bolton had wanted to film me chasing Lydia Zamir all over Chicago. I took the time now to see who held big enough stakes in Global and in Sea-2-Sea to cross the SEC's minimum threshold for reporting holdings. Nobody on my tree drawing appeared in those lists, but a firm called Minas y Puentes held a biggish stake in Global.

I'd seen their name on Larry Nieland's site—this was one of the Chilean firms where he was a board member. It was a closely held Chilean company, and so didn't have to report its shareholders to U.S. authorities; it was only because Nieland put it on his own web page that I'd heard of it. When I looked it up, I found it was a firm started by the Aguilar family, which owned Chilean copper mines.

Jacobo Palurdo's father had worked in the Chilean copper mines in Tocopilla. This had to be significant—but of what?

I drew roots on my tree. Some were in Kansas, some in Chicago, some in Chile. Flying to Chile wouldn't be useful: I don't speak Spanish, and an investigator who knows neither the language nor the local customs is someone who will be easily duped. Maybe Rikki Samundar and Donna Lutas were hoping I'd fall into that trap—that could explain why they'd spun me a line about Hector's aunt working for Devlin in Santiago.

The dogs had been nipping at each other for some minutes while I created my tree. I took the three to the lake and let them swim, although Bear stayed close to shore.

On the way home, my phone rang, the dramatic chords I use for my private contact list. I fished the phone from my back pocket while trying to hold all three leashes in my left hand.

Arlette Fouchard spoke before I could say "hello."

"It is terrible, Victoire. Someone broke into the apartment. They hit Angela, knocked her out. We are at the 'ospital, the room for *urgence*. I cannot let Bernadine stay in Chicago, not one more night."

I tied the leashes to a bicycle rack so I could focus on the call.

"Was Bernie hurt?"

"No, no, we are coming home from Bernadine's coaching day, we are finding Angela, and the girls' apartment, *ma foi*, it is a disaster. I am staying with Angela until her own mother can be here and then, poof, we are in Quebec."

"You called the police, right?"

"*Naturellement*. And they are saying, girls living off campus in a 'ouse that is falling down, of course someone breaks in. The other two girls, they 'ave moved back into their sorority, but Bernadine, she will return to Canada. That is final."

Her tone bristled with challenge, but I thought she was right. I ran home with the dogs and explained the situation to Mr. Contreras. He was eager to go to the hospital with me, mostly to make sure Bernie really was all right. When I explained that Arlette was with her, and that Bernie was unharmed, he reluctantly agreed to stay home. I promised to let him know if she had been hurt and left him pacing anxiously in the living room, Mitch at his heels.

By the time I reached the hospital, Angela had been

moved from the emergency room to a regular room. When I found her, Bernie was sitting by the bed, her vivid face stretched tight over the cheekbones.

"Vic!" She flung herself against my chest. "This is—this is too horrible. What is happening? Why did they attack Angela?"

"Because I was there." Angela's eyes fluttered open. "I was taking a nap and then I heard them break open the kitchen door. There were two. I tried running out the front door but one of them caught me. He knocked me out, not long—I've been hit like that once before in a hard game. When I woke I heard them still in the apartment, so I lay still until they left. I tried to get to my phone to call 911 but they had stolen it."

It was Arlette who brought her to the hospital. She'd seen too much brain damage in her years as a hockey spouse to take a head blow lightly.

"They have done the scan," Arlette said. "There is not internal 'emorrhage, but she must stay the night here. Her mama will be here, but until then, we take care of her."

"My uncle is driving her," Angela murmured thickly. "Morning, early morning, maybe. Shreveport a long way 'way."

Angela's monitors had been beeping at the nursing

station and one of the nurses came in to clear us out of the room.

"Arlette, I'll drive Bernie to the apartment to pack some things for you both. You go ahead and book your flight. As soon as we come back you can go to O'Hare; I'll wait with Angela until her mother gets here."

An old Victorian house a block from the university had been turned into apartments; Angela and Bernie were renting the second floor with the two young women who'd moved back into their sorority. When we got there, I went up the back stairs to look at the door the intruders had broken down. They'd skipped the first and third floors: this had been a targeted attack.

"Vic—" Bernie's voice trembled. "They were coming for me, weren't they?"

"Baby, they think you know something or saw something or have something that is connected to Leo. You said he wanted to write some FOIA's after the meeting. Did he say anything else? Show you anything?"

She shook her head.

"What about the FOIAs—what did he say about them?"

"I wasn't really listening," she said. "I told you this, that we were arguing against each other over how he should fight this Coop. The foyer thing, he wanted to know about the map he saw, that's all I know."

"Did he say what was on the map?"

"No. He said Simon took the paper from him so quickly he could see only a small piece of it."

"It wasn't the map of the proposed beach, then," I thought aloud. "That wouldn't have startled him, because he knew about that. The drawing was big, eighteen by twenty-four or even twenty-four by thirty-six. That's not something that would be tucked into the corner of a backpack."

"What are you saying? That Leo stole something?" A ghost of Bernie's spirit flared up.

"No, baby, just trying to figure out what the goons are looking for. Get me your mother's suitcase; I'll pack her things. You take care of yourself."

Arlette had been sleeping on a daybed in the living room. Her toiletries—including an array of skin care products with names like "Luminescence Recovery"— were neatly organized in a travel bag. She'd hung her clothes in the hall closet. I folded everything I could find into her case, with the toiletries on top so she could get at them in the airport.

When I finished, Bernie was still standing in the room she shared with Angela, unable to focus. A canvas holdall and her backpack were open on the floor, and she'd put some T-shirts and her hockey stick into the holdall, but she couldn't seem to figure out what to do next.

The backpack was sky-blue, with the Canadiens logo in the bottom right corner. I frowned at it—I'd seen its twin—where?

"Bernie—did you give Leo a Canadiens backpack?"

"What? No, we exchanged no presents. Why?"

"I thought I saw one in his apartment."

"It was the same color, but not our logo. I—I offered to get him the appliqué, but he said he couldn't wear a badge for a team he had no interest in." Her smile wobbled. "Now it is impossible to imagine why I thought he was special."

She started stuffing underwear and jeans into the holdall.

"Did you have the backpack with you today?"

"But of course, Vic, it is how I carry what I need, my records on the students, the laptop, the water bottle. *Tous!*"

She stared, openmouthed, as I picked it up from the floor and emptied it onto the bed. Her laptop, a notebook, hairbrush, sunscreen, a paperback (*Ayesha at Last*), a bicycle lock, a hockey puck with Canada's

National Women's Team logo. Wedged into a crease on the bottom, in between some tampons, an energy bar, and a scrunchy, was a flash drive.

"Is this yours?"

She hunched a shoulder, still openmouthed. "I don't remember it, but it must be, no?"

"Let's look at it, shall we?"

I felt as though I were walking on eggshells, but Bernie opened her laptop and inserted the stick.

Leo had taken five photos of the document, very fast, with his phone. It must have been while he and Simon were arguing over the page. The resolution was poor. The best I could tell was that the document showed the Chicago lakefront around Forty-seventh Street, with the proposed new beach laid out in a dotted line. More dotted lines indicated where new landfill would create a promontory that jutted a good quarter mile into the lake.

Laying the photos side by side on the screen, I saw that each had a few different details—17TH HOLE, THE MONEY SHOT was marked on the promontory. So the Park District wanted to put a golf course along the lake. That would take some ingenuity—there wasn't a lot of land there. Except that as I looked at the pictures, I realized that Lake Shore Drive was missing. They wanted to take up Lake Shore Drive and put in a golf course? That made no sense at all.

DEAD LAND · 371

Bernie shook my shoulder. "I have to go, Vic. Mama is texting me, worried that we've been attacked. We must get back to the hospital."

"Sorry, babe. These pictures—they are dynamite of a kind. I'm going to make sure the Park District knows I have them and then you should be safe. But you go back to Quebec. I'll talk to your program head tomorrow and get your job sorted out."

36
Long Night's
Journey into Day

I spent a long night in the hospital, dozing next to Angela's bed. On my way back there with Bernie, I'd detoured to my building so that Mr. Contreras could say goodbye to her in person.

"Don't you stay away permanent, young Bernie," he said. "Vic and me, we'll get this sorted out, okay?"

Bernie gave him a convulsive hug, spent a few minutes with Mitch and Peppy, but was anxious to return to her mother. The next commercial flight to Quebec wasn't until six-thirty the next morning, but Pierre Fouchard had persuaded the Canadiens owner to send the team jet down to collect his wife and daughter. It was already in Chicago airspace when I bundled the two women into a taxi.

Arlette texted me at midnight to let me know they had landed in Quebec City. Pierre was driving them to their summer home in the Laurentians, where he had good security, including neighbors he trusted. Even though it was a major relief to know Bernie was safe, I had so many other dragons to fend off that I couldn't relax. Hospitals, with their PA systems, their frequent interruptions to check on vital signs, aren't conducive to rest, anyway.

Angela's mother and her mother's brother Jamison arrived a little before six, haggard from their all-night drive. I waited with them while they talked to the doctor, the nurses, the social worker. I drove ahead of them to the Victorian house, stayed while they packed up Angela's things. Hugged Angela, shook hands with her mother and uncle, promised to stay on top of problems here.

Angela gave me keys to the apartment, in case she or Bernie needed me to find items they might have left behind. She also asked if I could take charge of her old Subaru: she didn't have a garage space and, "I know it's a lot to ask, Vic, but, like when they do street cleaning, can you see that it gets moved?"

I took the keys with a murmur of "Of course, no problem," although figuring out how and where to store a second car wasn't a responsibility that raised my spirits. Still, she'd been injured for the sole crime of sharing an apartment with Bernie. I owed her special attention.

After I'd waved them goodbye, I called Freeman Carter, my defense attorney, to let him know what had happened. His firm was standing by to help Bernie; he needed to know about the break-in and that she'd gone back to Canada.

I met with the sports management program director to explain why Angela and Bernie would not be completing their summer work stints. That involved a certain amount of arguing over whether the two could return to campus in the fall. I won, mostly because both young women were significant players on their respective teams.

I dealt with the landlady, who wanted the young women to pay for a new door. When I told her the families were thinking of suing her for not having better security on the premises she backed down, but two fights before 10:00 A.M. was an exhausting way to start the day.

All the time I was talking to these people, the flash drive was burning a hole in my jeans pocket. As soon as

I finished with the landlady, I drove to the Cheviot labs in the northwest suburbs. They're a private forensic engineering company with more sophisticated equipment than I can afford; they might be able to refine and enhance the pictures.

When I explained to my account manager that this little stick might be behind two unsolved Chicago murders, he took it in stride. They've worked with me for years, and their security, both cyber and physical, is always being tested and upgraded. He agreed to email me an encrypted copy of the contents, but to guard the original against all but the most precisely worded subpoena.

Back home, I made sure Mr. Contreras had time to vent his own agitated feelings over the attack on Angela, and on Bernie's safety. He wasn't totally convinced that Pierre Fouchard and the entire Canadiens team could look after her. I agreed that he would be a significant help in looking after her, but in the end he turned down my offer of a plane ticket to Quebec.

I slept heavily for some hours, but returned to consciousness through my worry dreams, where I was facing a wall of fire, my mother and Lotty on the far side, beyond my ability to rescue.

I took an espresso to the tiny deck outside my kitchen door and sat with the dogs, running my hands through their fur, trying to think. To take the pressure off Bernie, I needed to make sure Taggett knew I had the pictures. Not just Taggett, but his private-public partners, whoever they were. Also the Devlin & Wickham lawyers, and Norm Bolton at Global. I wanted them all to know that I wasn't the only person who'd seen Leo's photos. Otherwise, I'd be next in line for the person who liked treating human heads like soft-boiled eggs.

I called Murray, who was angry with me.

"Whatever you're selling, Warshawski, I'm not buying. I am fucking sick to the fucking gills with your holier-than-thou Olympian approach to the world. And to my place in it."

"I can imagine that it's very annoying," I said. "I'm not selling anything, just pondering the Chicago lakefront. Wondering how realistic the plan is to put an eighteen-hole golf course around Forty-seventh Street. The picture I saw showed Lake Shore Drive covered in grass, which had those little holes people hit balls into."

"What the hell are you talking about?"

"We all have fantasies, Murray. One of mine is of Leo Prinz requesting copies of conversations within the Park District or maybe City Hall about these pictures. I imagine someone on LaSalle Street, or maybe Fairbanks Court, reading the FOIA request, and skittering into, oh, maybe Giff Taggett's office. And then I imagine Taggett saying something like, 'Will no one rid me of this meddlesome Prinz,' and another person taking that frustrated outcry as a command and battering poor Prinz's skull in with a gavel. Have a good day."

I hung up. Murray called right back. "Did you really see these pictures? And how did you find them?"

"A flash drive stuck in the bottom of a sky-blue backpack. The people who tore Leo's apartment to shreds can't really be blamed for missing it—it blended so perfectly into a crease in the fabric."

Murray digested this, then demanded copies of the photographs. I demurred, on the grounds that he might interpret my involving him as an example of my holier-than-thou-ness, but finally forwarded the Dropbox document to him.

"I still think you're a pain in the ass, Warshawski."

"That's not a unique opinion," I said, thinking of the worried look the Sung family gave me whenever I saw them on the stairwell or in the garden. And the venomous stares I still got from Donna Lutas, despite her firm's insistence that she cooperate with me in looking for Lydia.

That thought reminded me of Norm Bolton's desire to turn me into a series character. "Did Bolton ever explain to you why he was so insistent on filming a search for Lydia Zamir?"

"We've had this conversation too many times already," Murray said stiffly.

"By the way," I said, before hanging up, "when I was scouring the Wildlife Corridor looking for Leo's phone or any clue of any kind, I found a bunch of surveyor's boundary markers near the railway embankment."

"Is that the real reason you called?" Murray said. "You want me to do your dirty work looking up surveys of the lakefront?"

"No. I wanted to share those pictures with you, which I have done. The survey is gravy."

When we'd hung up, I continued to stare at the garden. Lydia Zamir had come from Kansas. Perhaps, like Bernie and Angela, she'd tried once again to turn to her mother. Coop might even have driven her down to the town, Eudora. Perhaps her mother would be more responsive to me in person than on the phone. Then I could drive to Salina to visit Arthur Morton's mother. Maybe she'd tell me why Devlin & Wickham had taken over her son's legal defense—definitely not a conversation to have by phone.

And if I let Taggett know that I was going away for a few days, he could believe he'd frightened me into withdrawing from my investigation. I'd take Bear with me, partly to keep the dog count within the condo's charter, but mostly so that I could give him back to Coop if I got lucky and actually found him and Lydia. Mr. Contreras and the rest of my building would be safe. Mr. Contreras wasn't happy with the plan, but he was never happy when I left town.

"You can get Donna Lutas on your side while I'm gone. Make her French toast for breakfast—yours is so delicious it would charm someone crankier than her."

"Don't try to butter me up, Victoria Warshawski. I been watching you slather it over other people for years, and I don't like you doing it to me."

He uses my name only when he's distressed.

I apologized, but said, "If you see Lutas, let her know I've gone to Kansas. If she pushes on you for more information, act coy, but let her know that I'm checking into Arthur Morton's background, and the trial."

He cheered up at the thought of helping with the investigation.

37

Trouble in the Fields

B ear and I reached Lawrence, Kansas, a little before three in the afternoon, after nine hours of
hard driving. All along my route I'd seen water standing in the fields, worse in Iowa, but heavy again around
Kansas City, where two rivers joined. In the spring I'd
read about the rains that were keeping farmers from
planting, but seeing the waterlogged fields made me realize how serious the problem was. The U.S. president
had announced a gift to farmers to cover their losses
in his tariff wars, but looking at the fields, I couldn't
imagine how anything could grow in that swamplike
land.

We drove past Eudora, where Lydia Zamir had
grown up, on our way into Lawrence, but I wanted
lunch, a good espresso, and a nap before trying to talk

to Zamir's mother. All those things were easier to find in Lawrence—including the nap, where the bigger town would be more likely to have a motel that accepted big dogs.

When we climbed out of the car in Lawrence, hot winds whipped my face. Two hundred miles south of Chicago, with no alleviating lake winds, the weather was hotter and muggier than it had been at home. I took Bear down to the Kaw River to cool off, but the water was high and running fast; I kept a long rope attached to his collar and didn't let him stay in long.

I found a room in one of the big-chain motels on the west end of town and fell deeply asleep—the drive and the stress of the last few days had taken a toll. It was past six when I woke up, stiff and groggy. I wanted to have a leisurely evening, stretching my muscles in a long run, enjoying dinner with a glass of wine, but I couldn't defer my conversation with Lydia's mother. I was sure she knew something, either about Coop, or where Lydia might be.

On my way to Eudora, I swung by the Decadent Hippo, hoping a couple of double espressos would make me feel less doltish. I took them outside with Bear, stretching my tight traps and hamstrings in between swallows, trying to persuade my body that caffeine and five minutes of movement could offset a long day in a car. I'd missed lunch but was feeling tense about the time. I picked up a bowl of soup at one of the student joints on the main street and ate it messily at stoplights.

When we followed the old highway east out of town, it was an hour from sunset. Storm clouds were building in the western sky, turning the trees and stunted corn plants a menacing blackish-green.

The Zamirs lived at the end of a cul-de-sac near the river and train tracks that created Eudora's western edge. Theirs was the biggest house on the street, an old Victorian with turrets and a screened porch that faced the river. This was where Murray had sat drinking iced tea with Debbie Zamir.

Over the chirping of birds getting ready for the night, I could hear frogs or maybe toads calling from the river bottom. Crickets sawed away. The house had settled into the landscape; the whole setting seemed peaceful, a place where people were at ease in their lives, no loud arguments, no bristling anger. It was hard to place the anger I'd heard in Debbie Zamir's voice in that comfortable house.

When I parked on the shoulder, Bear growled. Low, soft, deep in the throat: he knew this house and he didn't think it was a place of peace. At first he refused to leave the car altogether. I finally persuaded him to get out but no amount of coaxing or his favorite treats could bring him to the house. He stayed behind me in the middle of the sidewalk, on his feet, hackles raised.

Lights were on in the room behind the porch, in what I guessed to be the kitchen, but I saw the flash from a TV screen at the other end of the house, the side that faced the neighbors. I opened a screen door to use a knocker, a piece of tarnished brass that made a satisfying clang as it struck the plate behind it.

After a moment, a man opened the door. "If you're another reporter, we're done talking to the media."

He was thin, and stoop-shouldered, the weight of his daughter's illness bending him over. His mop of curly graying hair and his narrow face made him look eerily like Lydia as I'd last seen her.

I held the screen door open. "I'm not a reporter, Mr. Zamir, but a detective. I'm from Chicago, trying to find some trace of what happened to your daughter. You know she's disappeared, and her health is precarious." I handed him one of my cards.

In the background Debbie Zamir called out, wanting to know who it was, wanting to make sure her husband knew better than to talk to the media. He shouted back that I was some kind of detective from Chicago.

Lydia's mother hove into view. She was holding up better than her husband, at least superficially. Her hair was neatly dressed and her jeans and blouse had

384 · SARA PARETSKY

been ironed. She had on sandals that showed off gold-painted toenails.

"Ms. Zamir, I'm V.I. Warshawski. We've spoken on the phone a few times. I need you to tell me what you know about Coop."

She sucked in air. "Nothing." Her voice wobbled; she took another breath to steady herself. "I don't know anyone with such a strange name, I told you that before."

When he heard her voice, Bear let out a short warning bark. I backed up to grab his leash. He didn't try to jump her, nor to run away, but I could feel his legs trembling as he stood his ground. I knelt to put a reassuring hand on his neck.

"The dog says otherwise," I called from the middle of the path. "He knows you; he knows you did something that hurt Coop."

"What are you talking about?" Lydia's father stayed prudently inside the doorway.

"Were you here when a man named Coop came around to see your daughter, Mr. Zamir?"

"A lot of people came to see Lydia," Zamir said. "But most of the time I was at work. At work, like there was some reason to keep to a schedule. What's this BS about the dog knowing my wife?"

"Your wife was here when you were working. She's

seen the dog, and she's seen his owner. A man named Coop."

"That right?" He turned to his wife, puzzled, not angry.

"Of course not, Tyler." Debbie Zamir was aiming for a soothing tone, but her voice shook.

"Time to stop lying, Ms. Zamir. Nothing you did with Coop in the past could be as dreadful as refusing to act while your daughter is dying."

I was shouting from the middle of the walk. A window opened across the street and a woman asked if everyone was okay.

Debbie Zamir called back—"No problem, just a driver who got lost." To me she said, "Do you have a hold of that dog?"

"Yes." I tightened my grip on the leash.

"If you put him back in your car, I'll come out and talk to you."

"Debbie! You don't know this lady and you don't know this dog. Don't go talking to strangers. You saw what happened when you talked to that Chicago reporter last month. Everything got blown out of proportion and Lydia almost was run over by a train up in Chicago."

"No, Ty, I'll talk to her. She's right: I saw more of the people who came around after the shooting than you did. I'll tell her what I know. You go watch the game; I'll only be five minutes."

Ty looked uncertainly from his wife to me, but defeat had become a way of being for him. He turned back to the living room and the flashing light of the TV.

Debbie Zamir stood in the doorway while I escorted Bear into the Mustang. I had the windows down, and his great head leaned out, staring at us. Debbie skirted the house, clutching the siding, her eyes on the car until she'd moved out of sight. When I followed, I found her standing behind a bench, clutching the back tightly, staring toward the river but not seeing anything.

I stood near her, not crowding her, not looking at her. "Tell me about Coop and his dog."

She seemed to be choking on her thoughts, not able to put them into speech.

"He was a friend of your daughter," I stated.

"No. Yes. I don't know."

"He's probably ten years older than she is, so they didn't meet in high school. Was he at the conservatory?"

"Conservatory? You mean music? No. He wasn't a friend. I don't know where they met. The stupid Tallgrass event, I guess. Maybe he'd been stalking her before. After the shooting, after the funeral and all the media hype, when Lydia came home, he came around."

"You think he was stalking her?" I asked.

"He came around a lot, more than any of the others."

"What others?" I held tight to my patience. If I gave way to anger, she'd clam up completely.

"She had fans all over the world. People loved that *Savage* album. Not what she called it, but that was what it was, full of savages. None of her real work ever got that kind of response. She had beautiful recordings of playing Chopin and Schumann that no one paid any attention to, and then she came under the influence of that Mexican man and she started writing songs that were offensive and dirty. And that's what people liked!"

Her hands were clenching and unclenching the back of the iron bench, so hard that the finials were digging into her palms. "Girls showed up here at all hours, singing that horrible song, dressed—or hardly dressed, trying to make themselves look like they were Indians from 1492. It was ludicrous and horrible. The sheriff came and made them keep off our property, but then they acted even worse: they went down to the railway and set up a sound system. You could hear them all over the county."

She gestured at a barrier of trees about a quarter mile from the house. They grew on top of a low cliff above the railway tracks that lay between her home and the Wakarusa River.

"And Coop joined them?"

"No." She bit the word off. "The men—God, it was sickening, they were even worse than the crazy girls. There were men who thought someone who'd survived a mass murder was sexy. They came around wanting to—who knows what they wanted. Lydia—she was out of her mind. She didn't pay attention to the women, but one afternoon she came to her bedroom window. Naked. Yelled down, this what you want? I was in the yard, trying to make them leave, and so I looked up—I saw—"

Her shoulders began to shake. She mastered her voice with a terrible effort. "Touching herself. Flaunting, but remote, like she was taking some drug and sailing over them, over me, over the world."

The language was strangely, exotically poetic— Lydia's offensive, dirty images had a heritage.

"Coop was there?" I asked.

"He showed up that afternoon. He had flowers, prairie flowers. He'd come five or six times before, always with these flowers he picked from the edges of the fields, and always with that dog. Lydia came down to talk to him, two or three times. She wouldn't talk to me or her father or the doctor, but this crazy man, he was fine to talk to. And he had the nerve to lecture me on what Lydia needed, like her own mother didn't know as much as some stranger off the wheat fields.

"This time he showed up when Lydia was—doing what she was doing. He blew up at the men, he hit one hard enough that there was blood all over his face. The other men left and this Coop charged into the house, even though I was yelling at him to stop, that he was trespassing! Of course, I went in after. Ty, Mr. Zamir, he was at work."

When she stopped again, I said gently, "Was he assaulting Lydia?"

"She was in his arms, he was patting her hair, but she was in his arms naked, and that horrible dog was with him."

She paused, then added defiantly, "I went to get our gun. I shot him."

"You did?" My voice came out in a startled squeak. "How badly did you hurt him?"

"I missed, but the bullet grazed the dog, its shoulder, and then Lydia was screaming at me that I was a monster, how could she live with a monster, she wanted Coop's help. She wouldn't go to a doctor, but she wanted this crazy man who broke someone's nose and came into her room when she was—was—"

She stopped, spittle covering the sides of her mouth. She was panting in little bursts. No wonder the dog had shown hackle at the sound of her voice.

"She left a few days later."

"With Coop?"

"No. He came around, wanting to see her, and she was gone. She hadn't told him. I didn't tell him. He said he wanted me to pay his damned dog's veterinary bill. I told him he had a hell of a nerve, trying to rape my daughter and wanting me to pay his bills."

The clouds had thickened, and the wind was rising, bending the line of trees in front of us.

"What's his name, besides Coop?" I asked.

"I never heard," she muttered.

"Do you know *anything* about him?" I couldn't keep a despairing keening out of my voice. "Anything that would help me find him?"

"He was an environmental fanatic. When he found out Ty—Mr. Zamir—worked for Sea-2-Sea he almost hit him."

"Where does he come from?"

She stood for a long time, kneading the back of the bench, trying to regain her self-control. She finally said, in a quiet voice, "He went to K-State, I think. At least, he wore a Wildcats cap and T-shirt. There's a big rivalry between K-State and the Lawrence campus, the Jayhawks—you wouldn't wear Wildcats gear around here unless you liked getting people stirred up."

38
Yanking Each Other's Chains

The storm broke when we got on the highway, great sheets of water that bubbled across the road like a creek. I had the air-conditioning on and the wipers running full bore, but Bear was whimpering in fear. I opened a window for him and let the wave of water flood the passenger seat, splashing onto me.

Lightning streaked all around the horizon, making me feel that I was in a glass paperweight shaken by a giant hand. A siren sounded, tornado warning. I know you're supposed to stop, get out of your car, lie flat in a ditch, but I wanted to get as far from Debbie Zamir as I could.

By the time we crept into town and made it to our motel, the sirens had stopped. The rain was still falling, but the wind had eased and the lightning had ended.

Bear and I were two sodden lumps as we climbed to our second-floor room. There were two towels, one for each of us.

I sat on the floor next to him, and he laid his heavy head on my knees. "She shot you, huh?" I ran my fingers through his shoulders, but the wound was three years old. I couldn't feel the scar. "She is a scary person, isn't she? A good match for your boy, Coop—rockets that shoot off in random directions at unpredictable times. Poor Tyler, Poor Lydia. Poor Bear."

I was hungry, but too weary to hunt for food. I gave Bear a double ration of his dinner, but settled for a bag of peanuts from a vending machine for myself.

In the morning, I took some extra towels from the housekeeper and tried to dry out the Mustang, but the rain had soaked into the floor mats and the upholstery. The car would need a decontamination cleaning when I got back to Chicago. For now, I'd drive with the windows open unless it started to rain again—in which case, Bear would have to tough it out.

I picked up fruit, kefir, and a goat cheese sandwich at the local co-op grocery, stopped again at the Decadent Hippo for espresso, and headed west. Just like a pioneer, at least, just like a pioneer with an eight-cylinder, 460-horsepower engine on a paved four-lane highway.

The Kansas State campus was about two hours west

of Lawrence. If Coop had been a student there, as Lydia's mother guessed, it would have been twenty or thirty years ago. Student records from that era probably hadn't been digitized, but someone might still be working there who remembered him. He was the kind of person people keep talking about, even years after they've gone.

Superficial research on the Kansas State curriculum showed they were the state's land-grant school, with significant programs in conservation, ecology, and land stewardship. Just the place for someone who attacked anyone using carcinogenic pesticides.

The drive on a weekday morning was easy; we pulled into Manhattan, Kansas, home of the K-State Wildcats—as a million or two signs announced—midmorning. I found a parking space not too far from the campus and set out with Bear. Last night's storm had left muggy clinging weather in its wake; I couldn't leave him in the car.

I spent several hours hiking the campus, talking to people in administration and to departmental secretaries. I finally encountered an older woman in the Conservation Rangers program who remembered him.

"It had to be twenty, twenty-five years ago, so I don't remember the details that clearly. He wasn't a full-time student—I think he registered for some courses, or maybe he audited, but the department chair at the time made him leave because he disrupted the lab sessions. He had a chip on his shoulder the size of an old-growth oak."

She called two of her friends who worked in the ecology and environmental programs; Coop's temper was legendary, and all three women had stories to tell.

Unfortunately, none of them knew his last name, or where he'd come from. The first woman thought he'd been local. "He knew a lot about land and farming, even when he was eighteen years old, so I assumed he grew up in the country."

"But don't you think his family couldn't afford to own land?" one of her friends said. "I always thought the chip on his shoulder came from feeling the other kids looked down on him."

"He volunteered at the Tallgrass Prairie," the third woman said. "Back then, I mean. I don't think he's been there for years."

They explained that the Tallgrass Prairie was a protected nature preserve, a small remnant of the prairie that used to cover the entire Midwest.

"Yes," the second woman chimed in. "They had to ask him to leave—he was always arguing over how they wanted to do things, as if he knew more than anyone else how a prairie should be managed. I think he was arrested for protesting that new Sea-2-Sea feedlot—remember that, about six, seven years ago?"

"Are you sure? That was way out by Montezuma," my informant from Conservation said.

She showed me a map of the state. Montezuma, a town of 150 or so, was off toward the southwest corner of the state. We looked up the Montezuma protest. It had been seven years ago. The Wichita paper had a small graph on it—the protestors had thrown green dye on the first cattle herd as it was released into the lot. I used the computer in the office to log in to LexisNexis, but it didn't show any arrests for the relevant time period.

"Is it possible he lives out there?" I asked. Looking at the map I felt overwhelmed. The landscape was huge—if Coop's family farmed, or he lived on a farm, finding them in that vastness would make plucking needles from haystacks look simple.

"It's possible," the second woman said, her voice dubious. "But it's ranching country, not planting country. Not enough rain there."

The third woman said, "You know what you might do is go talk to Franklin Alsop. He was one of the Tall-grass Meet-Up organizers. If it's like you say, that this Coop was hanging around Lydia Zamir when she went back home, then chances are he was hanging out at the concert, too."

I agreed it was a good suggestion, but said I hadn't been able to track down any of the organizers.

"That's why you came to us." The Conservation secretary smiled. She went to the computer and tapped a few keys. "Yes, Franklin is out by Black Wolf. That shooting, that did him a lot of damage. He lost his trust in people, even his wife. She left him at the end of the second year. If you can get him to talk to you, it could be a help for him. If he thinks he can save Lydia, it may make him less—oh, maybe despairing is the word I'm looking for."

They showed me Black Wolf on the wall map, about a hundred miles to the west, on beyond the town of Salina. Salina was near the farm where mass murderer Arthur Morton had grown up, and where his mother still lived. I could stop to see if she could explain how Devlin & Wickham came to be her son's lawyers and then move on to Black Wolf.

I thanked the three women, who were cheery in their assurances that they'd been glad to help. Bear and I retrieved the Mustang and headed for the open road. Driving in Kansas was liberating after a lifetime of Chicago traffic. I don't often get to push my muscle car to her limits, but we sailed along the Interstate at ninety and reached the Salina town limit in under an hour.

I drove around for a bit, orienting myself. I found

the Saline County Courthouse, where Arthur Morton had been tried, and the jail where he'd died in agony from an overdose of nicotine patches.

After letting Bear stretch his legs, I went to the police station. In Chicago, I can afford to cajole, fight, or ignore Sergeant Pizzello and her clan: the police are stretched too thin to bother about PIs on the fringe of their turf. In small towns, though, the law would be on me like flies on a dead fish if I talked to locals without official knowledge.

Whether you're in Chicago or Salina, there's a sameness to stations and protocol. The Salina building was new, the veneered wood counter still unscratched, but the notices on the walls, the bustle of the officers passing in the hallway, and the woman behind the counter all seemed the same—including the woman's smile, which was both welcoming and assessing.

I explained myself—investigator from Chicago, here to find and talk to Kelly Kay Morton. The desk officer took my credential into the back. After a few moments she returned to escort me to the chief's office.

That was an extreme departure from Chicago protocol, where I dealt with detectives and watch commanders but never division heads, let alone the chief super.

Elroy Corbitt was a big man, with a gut that showed

even in the boonies the cops don't get enough exercise. "What does a big-city investigator think she needs to do in Salina that we can't do ourselves?"

"Not a thing, chief," I said, my voice amiable. "This is a courtesy call to let you know I'm here hoping to talk to Arthur Morton's mother."

"She's been through a hell of a lot, Chicago. Not sure talking to her is a great idea."

"Other people went through a hell of a lot, too, chief."

"And that's water over the dam. Boy's dead, let him rest in peace."

I damped down the spurt of anger that pious wish often raises in me. "You know that big law firm that came in to represent him all of a sudden?"

"From Chicago, weren't they?" The chief spoke slowly. "They send you down here to try to collect from his ma? Blood from a turnip, that would be. She works at Origins bakery, hell of a pie maker, but it don't leave much over when she's paid the rent and whatnot."

"Oh, whoever hired them to represent Arthur Morton paid their bills. They tell me someone from Sea-2-Sea's board had pity on the widow and orphan." I couldn't quite keep the sarcasm out of my voice, and Corbitt's expression hardened.

I added quickly, before he threw me out, "I want to talk to Ms. Morton about her son's death. People in Chicago are starting to raise questions about whether it was really suicide." Okay, one person in Chicago, me. "I want to ask about her son's state of mind, those kinds of things."

"Murder, suicide, accident, hard to prove any of it after all this time, but if that's how you want to waste your time, I don't have any objection." He leaned across the desk to hand me back my ID.

As I headed to the office door, he tossed a squib at me. "When Vesna told me a Chicago investigator was here, I was sure you'd come looking for Lydia Zamir."

I turned and smiled. "I am looking for her, chief, but I'm having trouble getting traction for my search. Are you trying to tell me she's here?"

"Nope. But we had a bunch of reporters show up the last couple of days, thinking her boyfriend had come here to kill Kelly Kay. We've been keeping up extra patrols outside her home, just so you know."

"Lydia Zamir's boyfriend was murdered four years ago," I said. "Unless Ms. Morton thinks she's haunted by a spectral presence, I'd say she was safe from him."

"I don't mean the dead one. I mean the current one, the guy with the violent temper. We got a BOLO on him from your very own Chicago police force. Vesna!" he shouted.

The woman from the front counter came trotting. "Yes, chief?"

"This Chicago lady is leaving, but on her way out, pull up that BOLO we got about the Zamir gal's violent boyfriend, will you?"

"Does he have a name, this violent boy?" I asked.

The chief eyed me narrowly. "I thought you would know it, since the fuss started out up there, and you've been involved in this business from the get-go."

It took a strong effort to keep my expression neutral, but I felt dizzy, the way you do when the air is knocked out of you. The chief had known who I was when I walked in the door, and he waited until the last minute to sucker-punch me. I hadn't told anyone I was coming down here, except Bernie and Mr. Contreras. Mr. Contreras might have talked about it with the neighbors, but he wouldn't think to call the Salina police.

I suddenly remembered urging him to tell Donna Lutas what I was doing. That was how the word spread: she ferried it to her boss, and he'd let Salina's officers of the law know pretty darned fast.

"I like the hayseed act," I said. "Does it get the big-city lawyers to drop their guard around you?"

I waited a beat, then added, "Did Clarence Gorbeck phone personally? Or was it one of the women on his staff—Lutas or Samundar?"

Corbitt nodded slightly, as if to concede a point, but he didn't answer my question, just repeated his command about the BOLO to Vesna.

"You go to Origins, try the blueberry pie. Kelly Kay puts something in it that makes it sing. She's won the Saline County pie contest three years running with it."

"That's quite an endorsement; thanks for your thoughtfulness, chief."

I followed Vesna to the front desk and read the BOLO on Coop, which basically said he was on the run from two Chicago murders and while not known to be armed was certainly dangerous. They listed him only as Coop, so no one had yet come up with his full name.

"They don't include a last name," I commented. "Is he someone people around here know?"

Vesna shook her head. "I don't think so; none of the guys on patrol heard of him."

"Zamir's mother thinks he was stalking her daughter—which makes him a predator, not a lover."

Quoting Debbie Zamir made my mouth feel like chalk. Actually, all the people who'd come around the Zamirs in the wake of the shooting had sounded sickening. Compared with the women donning Indian costumes and singing "Savage" next to the railway tracks, Coop looked like the prince of stability.

I didn't volunteer my personal knowledge of Coop. I felt on fragile ground here, not knowing what Devlin & Wickham might have told the local law about me, or Lydia, or the investigation.

A couple of patrol officers who'd been getting something from a vending machine in the corner came over to look at the monitor with us.

"We wondered if he might be holing up on the old Morton place. It's out near Salemsborg, you know." He tapped on a large-scale map of the county, a spot south of Salina. "No one's taken down any of the buildings—don't know if Sea-2-Sea think they can convert the barn or house to bunks for a crew—but it didn't look like anyone had been in there for quite a while."

I stared at the map. Chief Corbitt spoke behind me. "About ten miles straight down Burma Road, case you were thinking of checking it out. You know this guy Coop the BOLO's asking for?"

"I've seen him two or three times, but I don't know if Coop is his first name or his last. It could be short for Cooperstown. His high school voted him most likely to make the majors."

"He's a ballplayer?" the second patrol officer asked.

"She's yanking your chain, Gerber," the chief said. "To repay me for pulling on hers."

I smiled and thanked them all for their help and left the station, making sure to keep my head up, hips loose, stride easy: I don't care what people say about me.

39
Bye, Bye, Ms. American Pie

I collected Bear and walked into the heart of the town. My phone directed me to the bakery on Sixth Street, near Walnut. One window showcased a traditional four-tier wedding cake, nestled in gold bunting, the other held trays of cookies and miniature cakes and pies. Beyond those I could see a lunchtime crowd of fifteen or twenty—besides Kelly Kay Morton's award-winning pies, the bakery also sold sandwiches and soup. It was almost one now, and this was where a lot of Salina apparently came for lunch.

I was hungry myself. I left Bear in the shade of a nearby awning and went inside to order lunch: cheddar on Origins-baked rye, lemonade, a cup of water for the dog, and a slice of blueberry pie.

There weren't any chairs or benches outside, so I

squatted under the awning next to Bear, feeding him bits of sandwich and pie. I'm not much of a dessert eater, but if I was going to talk to Kelly Morton, I'd have to compliment her baking.

Passersby commented on me and the dog, some thinking we were cute squatting there together, others telling me, sharply, that loitering was against the law in Salina.

"Officer Gerber's on patrol this afternoon," I said to one of the critics. "Call 911 and tell them to send him over."

A choking sound and the woman moved on, muttering under her breath. I try to spread sunshine wherever I go.

When the crowd inside the bakery thinned out, I went back in and introduced myself to the woman at the counter. I praised the meal I'd just eaten and asked if I could speak to Kelly Kay Morton.

"I can pass on a message," the woman said. "She isn't talking to reporters."

"Journalism is a noble profession," I said, "but it isn't mine. Chief Corbitt probably told her, or maybe you, if you're the owner here, to expect me: V.I. Warshawski, a detective from Chicago."

I was tired from travel, from being with strangers, from not knowing what was going on around me, and so I didn't have a polished pitch, but the mention of the chief's name did the trick: the woman went into the back. After a few minutes she returned with a second woman, younger than I'd been expecting, perhaps in her forties, brown hair pulled away from her face in a ponytail. She was sturdily built, skin freckled from the sun, biceps straining the sleeves of the lime-green Origins T-shirt all the staff wore.

"This here is the detective from Chicago. You want me with you when you talk to her, hon?"

Morton's round shoulders slumped forward—fatigue and depression. "I'll be okay, Nancy. Nothing anyone can do to me worse than has already happened."

Out on the sidewalk, we talked first about where to talk—not in her home, not in the nearby Starbucks, where her coworkers might see her. We finally settled on the public library, about a ten-minute walk away.

Bear came to heel as we set out. I hoped Morton might exclaim, *I know that dog,* but the two didn't pay any attention to each other. I worried that the library staff might make me tie the dog up outside, but they let me bring him indoors, as long as we stayed in the entry area, away from other patrons.

The building was new, modern, and filled with children on some kind of field trip. Morton and I settled into chairs in a corner of the foyer, but people still kept looking at us, or maybe at Bear: he's a big dog and his tawny fur stood out in the modernist entryway.

"Sheriff and them say you're trying to dig up dirt about my boy."

I sidestepped the criticism. "I'm curious about the lawyers. Clarence Gorbeck and Rikki Samundar. Have they stayed in touch with you since your son died?"

"You want help finding them?" She was derisive. "You're in Chicago, they're in Chicago."

"They're easy to find in Chicago," I agreed. "Not so easy if you're in Salina. But I hear they came to you, not you to them."

Her eyes filled with tears, as unexpected to her as to me, and she worked fiercely at her fingers, digging flour from beneath the nails. "We had a public lawyer, a nice boy, he was working hard for Artie, but those Chicago lawyers said, they thought—they had all this experience that the public lawyer didn't and they said they could do a better job. They said the company that bought our farm, they would take care of the bills.

"I was desperate for someone to listen to Artie's side of the story, so I said to go ahead. But in the end, all they did was get a jury to say Artie was guilty. They said they'd keep him from the death penalty, but then he was killed anyway."

"The Wichita paper said he died from too many nicotine patches?" I said.

"That's right, but I don't know where he got those patches. The doctor said there was eight of them, up and down his back. How he even put them on, the guard at the jail couldn't say. Wouldn't say." She was concentrating on her left thumb, gouging so hard that a trickle of blood spilled onto her jeans leg.

"Did anyone ever tell you who wrote a prescription for the patches?" I asked.

"The doctor said it was just as well to—I can't think of how he put it, like forget about the past, but he made it sound like a church hat with a little veil on it, the way my mother and her friends used to wear."

"To draw a veil over the past?" I ventured.

She looked up at me, startled. "Were you there? Did the doctor talk to you?"

"No, ma'am," I said. "I've never met the doctor or the guards or any of those people. It's an expression that I've heard people use in similar situations."

She continued to eye me suspiciously. "The big lawyers from Chicago didn't let Artie tell his side of the story. They said it would be a mistake to let him testify, that it always went badly in a murder trial."

"What was Artie's side of the story?" I asked.

"That these other people told him to do it. They sent

him messages on the Internet, on these web pages he looked at, telling him to go to this thing at Horsethief Canyon. He never even heard of the event, Tallgrass Meet-Up, what kind of thing is that for grown people to be doing? Songs about Mexicans and Indians, protesting their treatment, when people like me and Artie's dad lose everything and no one even bats an eyelash?"

I looked at her rough hands and pain-filled face and felt my heart twist with pity. "Did you see the messages from these other people?"

"Artie told me about them, but of course the government came and took his computer and when I came here to look at the web page on their computers"—she gestured toward the interior of the library—"all his messages had disappeared. The librarian did her best and she knows a lot about computers, but not even she could find them."

I tried to digest that. It was such a strange claim, akin to someone claiming he'd heard voices that goaded him to violence. I found it hard to believe.

"Did anyone ever try to talk to you about the messages? I mean, besides the police and the lawyers?"

Her lips curled in disgust. "Are you serious? People called from all over the world. First it was the FBI and the state cops and then it was reporters and then it was people snooping. They wanted to talk about how

Artie—like, they took for granted that Artie commit-ted all those murders—and they wanted to know, how did he do it, did he practice first, did he stake out the area? People wanted souvenirs. They wanted his guns or his clothes, someone even wanted the clothes he was wearing when—when he passed."

She was panting, overwhelmed by the memories. "They treated him—they treated me—like we were some kind of sideshow at a carnival. I—we'd been liv-ing in a trailer park outside town, but people started showing up, even some crazy girls on motorcycles who wrote love letters to Artie, like he wasn't fighting for his life! I had to move out. Until the trial was over they put me up in a room over to Manhattan."

I thought of the people who showed up at the Zamir house, wanting a piece of Lydia. It's not something you think of when you imagine the fallout from a mass shooting, the ghouls who pick through the bones of the lives of those involved.

"It sounds unbearable," I said. "In the midst of all that chaos, I can't imagine you noticed if anyone paid particular attention to what Artie saw on his computer."

She lapsed into a silence that went on so long I thought she'd decided the interview was over. I was wrapping Bear's leash around my hand, ready to get to my feet, when she said, "There was one man came around one night wanting the computer and all. He must have been someone important from the government—he didn't talk himself, he had another man with him, like a bodyguard, like Secret Service, you know. I told him how the government already had all of Artie's things, his computer, even his old high school papers—he didn't write much, but the government, they wanted a journal."

She gave a wry smile. "Getting him to write his homework, that was almost as much work as cooking and cleaning. The idea that he'd write a journal! Anyway, this high-up man, he paid me fifty dollars to look through Artie's things, but of course there wasn't anything there."

I tried getting more details on this strange man from the government—what he looked like, what kind of car, did he speak at all? Of course it had been four years ago and it sounded as though the entire Aryan nation had shown up at her trailer. It wasn't surprising that she only remembered him because of the bodyguard.

Yes, she said impatiently when I asked, she was sure it was a bodyguard. "He was like someone in a movie. You could see the gun under his jacket when he moved his arm. The man himself, he dressed the same as everyone around here—shirt, jeans, but you don't buy shirts like his in Salina. I sew, I used to make our clothes, mine and Big Artie. I never saw fabric like that. It made me want to touch it."

Her words made me think of the men who had come to the SLICK meeting with Larry Nieland. It was ludicrous to imagine a connection between Chicago's parks and a Kansas killer, but I still pulled up Nieland's website on my phone and showed his picture to Morton.

She looked at it apathetically. "It wasn't him. Anyway, I had other things on my mind than paying attention to one more strange-acting man in a world that's full up of them."

She made it clear she'd come to the end of any time she wanted to spend with me. As I got to my feet, I asked if she'd gotten the computer back after her son's death.

Kelly Kay curled her lip. "What would I do with his old computer—stare at it all day like it was a field I was waiting to sprout and grow? They wanted to give me the clothes he was wearing when he died and I thought, you are as disgusting as the biker girls, thinking I'd want them. Guess I could have sold them to the biker girls, but what use do I have for money, anyway? The farm is gone. Artie's gone. His daddy's gone. What I make baking pies, that pays the rent. That's about all I need."

40

The Invisible Hand

I walked Bear back to the car and drove him to the Smoky Hill River east of town so he could cool off in the shallows.

I sat on the riverbank, dangling my feet in the brown water, while I called Gabe Ramirez, the public defender whom Devlin & Wickham had shoved off the case. Ramirez was polite but cautious when I told him who I was and that I was calling with questions about Arthur Morton's history. I'd planned on asking for a face-to-face meeting, but Ramirez said he'd been transferred to Wichita, some hundred miles to the south.

"I'm not here to second-guess you or anyone else." I explained my history with Lydia Zamir and the in-explicable intervention by Devlin & Wickham into my inquiries. Ramirez thawed a bit when I mentioned my own stint as a Cook County public defender. Like PDs everywhere, he had too many cases and too little time to give any of them the attention they ought to have, but of course he remembered Arthur Morton.

"I'm hoping you can tell me about the transfer of Morton's defense from your office to Devlin & Wickham's lawyers."

"At first, I was happy," he admitted. "Preparing defense for a crime like that, you need paralegals and an unlimited budget for research. And the murders were so horrific—seventeen dead, including that baby! The psychological toll on the community was devastating. It was hard to get my mind in the game, so to speak."

"There was no doubt about Morton's guilt?" I asked.

"State police found him with the weapons stockpile, and there's no doubt he had the AR-15 that fired the bullets. He hadn't even cleaned it."

I told him about my conversation with Arthur Morton's mother. "Did you ever see the emails she talked about?"

"They weren't emails." Ramirez spoke slowly, trying to recall evidence he'd last seen four years ago. "At least, I don't remember emails ordering him to shoot anyone. What I saw were messages embedded in the website. They didn't call out Morton by name, but they said something along the lines of 'These are the people who stole farms from good Americans. Someone should strike a blow to protect other farmers.'

"What bothered me, why it sticks in my mind, aside from the rhetoric, of course, was they gave specific details: they said the Tallgrass Meet-Up, which would be full of foreigners, Jews, and 'mud people,' would be a perfect place to make a stand on behalf of white farmers. And the messages described the caves that overlook the area where the Meet-Up was being held."

I paused while the details sank in. "Someone engineered those deaths."

Ramirez grunted agreement. "I was going to plead diminished responsibility because of that, but the big-shot lawyers had a different strategy. They said it would be impossible to prove that Morton was acting under someone else's direction. The state had to share Morton's computer files, of course, and I gave the guy—Gorbeck, yeah, that was his name: Clarence Gorbeck—everything I had from Morton, with markers to the website messages, but they claimed Morton made them up. Gorbeck's assistant said that I'd been too lazy to check for them myself, which I should have done because they didn't exist."

"Someone erased them? Or Gorbeck pretended not to see them?"

"I was angry; I made them let me come in to look.

The messages had vanished. They were never visible on a public machine, anyway, only on Arthur's: whoever sent them targeted him. They had skills way outside my department's forensic abilities."

I realized I was digging my fingers into the soft mud, as if getting a purchase in the ground would show me how to anchor myself in this hall of mirrors. A very sophisticated third party had been at work, preying on Arthur Morton's troubled mind, hoping to goad him to murder, and then erasing evidence of their actions.

"But what changed as a result of the deaths?" I blurted. "If someone else was pushing Morton—or maybe other unstable local people—into homicide, they must have felt they'd gain from it. Did land change hands as a result of the deaths? What effect did they have, besides the ruin of lives?"

"I never thought of that question," Ramirez said after a pause. "I don't know if Sea-2-Sea or any of the other corporate landholders took over more land, but even if they did—that was going on all the time, without a shot being fired. All the big-ag companies out here chipped in to support the Tallgrass Meet-Up. Even if local farmers had a grudge against Sea-2-Sea and the rest of them, slaughtering people at the event would only stop festivals, not the corporate buyout of farms."

"Did you attend the trial?" I asked.

"Of course: I wanted to see what kind of law you got for sixteen hundred dollars an hour, which I learned was the lead guy's going rate." Ramirez grunted. "I was underimpressed."

"I met Morton's mother earlier today. She mentioned some person who showed up at her home late one night, wanting to see her son's computer. Do you know about that? No?" I repeated what Kelly Kay Morton had told me.

"He might have come to the trial," Ramirez said. "The day the jury brought the verdict in, there were journalists from all over, New York, even someone from Australia. And this older guy—I wondered if he was head of the FBI—he looked important, and his clothes, he had on a suit that you somehow could tell he'd paid a lot of money for."

I pushed him as best I could, but again, of course, a lot of time had passed, a lot of trials, he couldn't remember if the man had been white or a light-skinned person of color. Not fat, that was the best he could do, and rich enough to buy a beautiful suit.

"What about Morton's suicide? Did that raise any red flags?"

"That didn't surprise me, at least not the suicide. You're a city person, maybe you don't know the passionate attachment people in a place like this have for their land. Morton's brain was tied into knots by his father's suicide and what he saw as his failure to get revenge on the people who'd caused them to lose their farm."

I digested that. "But the method—that's a horrific method, eight prescription-strength patches."

"Jail should have had a suicide watch, no doubt about it."

"His mother says the patches were on his back."

"He could have persuaded a guard to put them on." Ramirez's tone was indifferent. "The guards had a lot of sympathy for him, believe it or not."

"What, was he some kind of local hero?" I couldn't keep the outrage out of my voice.

"No-o, but—hard to explain. They knew he'd done the murders, but they thought he was a victim, too. In the end, I think the mother made a mistake, letting the Chicago lawyers take over—the jury were local people who reacted badly to a big-city firm. Even I, Mexican-American that I am, was preferable because I grew up around there. If that's it—?"

I was thanking him for his time, when he said, "I just remembered one other thing. Morton said he thought someone was lurking nearby when he was in the cave. He told me he kept thinking he was hearing footsteps overhead. If he was, probably a coyote or a bobcat. There are a lot of wild animals in the canyon. Thing is, he claimed there was another shot when he stopped firing. But those AR-15s, they make a hell of a noise. I doubt he was wearing ear protection.

"I told the Chicago team—even though I didn't believe him, it still was a good distraction. Or *I* thought. They didn't agree. Maybe they were right. You can't ever figure out what a jury will or won't believe, not a hundred percent."

"What made Morton stop firing when he did?" I asked.

"Oh, that—he was a sitting duck himself—he could see the security people had pinpointed his location and were heading his way. He had a mountain bike at the ready and took off, leaving most of his weapons behind."

He hung up. I wiped my fingers on the marsh grasses to get the mud from them, over and over until my fingers were raw from the spiky edges of the plants. All the grasses of Kansas . . .

Bear came to me, muddy himself, but giving me a softer look than I'd seen on him before. It reminded me that I'd forgotten to ask Ramirez whether he knew Coop. I caught him as he was leaving for court—an emergency hearing in the late afternoon. Ramirez didn't know Coop but he remembered a man outside the courthouse with a big dog, buttonholing people for news of the trial.

I looked Bear square in the face. "Were you up on that hillside overlooking the canyon? Is there any way to find out what Coop knew or did?"

If only someone had been photographing the cave—I stopped midthought. Of course people had been photographing. Crowd sourcing. Facebook, Instagram.

I'd brought my laptop, but it would be easier to search on one of the big monitors at the library. The library was open until nine. I logged on to Facebook, which reminded me that it had been six years and forty-three days since I'd last posted anything. I joined the Tallgrass Meet-Up group as well as Friends of Kanopolis State Park, the park where Horsethief Canyon was located. I began combing through their back posts until I got to the festival.

There were hundreds of pictures, mostly of the crowd, and of the performers onstage. There was a seemingly endless number of Lydia Zamir in a flowing green dress, some of her with Hector Palurdo, some by herself. She shook hands with fans, posed for selfies, posed with her guitar. Her smile was genuine and warm and made my gut twist when I compared her face from four years back with what she looked like today.

There were pictures taken from hills and ridges above the concert venue, showing me what it had looked like as the crowd gathered. It wasn't a formal outdoor theater as I had imagined, but a portable stage placed on a largish flat space in the middle of the canyon. One post included a report that the park service estimated the crowd at fifty-five hundred—a big gathering for a venue that was a half-day's drive from the nearest airport.

People had taken shots of the roadies setting up the stage and sound system, they'd photographed the organizers, the crowd, the banners advertising the sponsors, and, horrifically enough, the dead and wounded, lying in pools of blood. Finally, I came on pictures of the higher cliffs.

The yellow sandstone was filled with caves and it was frustrating trying to sort out which one Arthur Morton might have holed up in. I finally realized the stage was facing east, with the setting sun behind it. I pulled all the photos of cave openings into a file and went through them, looking for the sunlit facades that would show a west-facing opening. My shoulders began to ache and my eyes dried up, but I found seventeen images that I was pretty sure belonged to Morton: sunlight flashed off metal or glass inside the cave face, but if someone was lying inside holding a weapon, they weren't visible.

People had photographed the cave because an eagle had landed above it. There were some pictures of the eagle soaring against the setting sun, and three of her (him?) glaring at the crowd below. So that was the person Arthur Morton had heard.

I stared at the bird, in a futile "if only" reverie. Why couldn't the bird have flown into the cave, used those claws and wings to blind Arthur Morton. Lydia, all the families of victims and survivors, including, really, Kelly Kay Morton, would have been saved from the quicksand of blood, horror, grief, that was sucking them down.

I blinked a few times to clear my eyes. When I looked at the eagle again, I saw another telltale glint of sunlight on glass behind it. I enlarged the picture, fiddled with the focus. I was pretty sure I was looking at the scope for a sniper rifle.

41

Swimming in Liquid Lead

I sat frozen, staring at the picture. It had been a two-legged beast above Arthur Morton's cave, one who wanted to make sure at least one particular person had been killed.

How had they set this up? Trawling the Net, looking for someone angry and easy to manipulate? Why had they gone through such an elaborate charade? It's so easy to get a weapon in America, so easy to shoot someone. Unless someone very high profile was after a target and wanted to eliminate all possibility of being traced? And yet a method like this seemed full of pitfalls.

I'd been wondering who of the seventeen dead was the intended victim, but maybe the perpetrator was a sociopath who wanted to see what they could get away with. Maybe they'd manipulated Arthur Morton into mass murder for the heinous pleasure of seeing it happen. That was so extremely disturbing that I found myself shrinking from the people around me— was it you? or you? What psychosis had been bred in the wide-open prairie? Was that the person on top of Arthur Morton's cave?

This investigation had always been big for a solo op, but now it felt beyond my control. No wonder Gabe Ramirez had been glad to hand the trial off to a big firm. I tried to focus on what I could do on my own. And one urgent task was to share my knowledge.

The universe of people who knew about another body on top of the cave where Arthur Morton had been shooting was small. I didn't want to be the one person outside that universe who knew. I downloaded the cave photos to my own drive. I emailed them to my lawyer, with a note explaining where they had been taken and on whose social media pages I'd found them.

I also sent them to the Cheviot labs. I didn't think I was imagining things, but I'd been staring at photos for two hours and I hadn't even seen the scope—if it was a scope—until I'd been looking at the image for a time. In my message to Cheviot and my lawyer I added,

"This is a species of Rorschach: describe what you see. And make sure you save this file."

Just to be safe, I sent the file to the printer and paid the library five dollars for five copies. After all, Gabriel Ramirez had seen the messages directed to Arthur on the dark web sites Morton had looked at. And then an electronic pickpocket had slipped into the machine and removed the messages. The hand able to do that could easily stick a finger into my phone and remove my text messages, and then hike around Facebook and Instagram to manipulate their files.

I packed up, left a ten-dollar bill in their SUPPORT THE LIBRARY box, and went to retrieve poor Bear. I'd had to leave him in the car, and even though I'd parked in the shade and left him with water and the windows open, it wasn't a good option.

It was still light out, sunset a good hour away in midsummer. I drove back to the river. Families were having picnics, teens were racing around on Jet Skis, other kids were playing soccer or baseball. I found a quiet spot in the shallows, away from the boaters, where the dog could splash around and I could try to digest what I'd been discovering since arriving in Kansas.

I've dealt with a lot of ugly people over the years, almost all of them filled with a sense of sublime entitlement that made them feel more special than anyone else on the planet. But pushing a distressed, unstable man into committing murder by proxy put this killer in the Mengele class.

Bear came out of the river, plastered with mud, which he shook off so that it covered my jeans and T-shirt. Compared with the humans I was thinking about, a muddy dog seemed mighty wholesome. I wrapped my arm around his thick neck and hugged him to me.

The more I thought about the altruistic Sea-2-Sea board member stepping forward to pay Devlin & Wickham to run the defense, the less I liked the story. It was so flimsy the wicked wolf could have blown it over with one huff—he wouldn't even have needed a puff. And I'd bought into it.

But a firm like Devlin depends on their reputation. They wouldn't risk it by being part of a conspiracy to commit murder. Surely?

I thought again of the nicotine patches on Arthur Morton's back. Rikki Samundar had more or less indicated that she'd brought them to the prison. It was very helpful of him to kill himself and remove the possibility of an appeal where Gabe Ramirez could renew the suggestion of a second shooter, overlooked by the state.

Another worrying thought came to me. Devlin &

Wickham continued to be interested in the Morton case. They wanted to know what progress I was making in looking for Lydia, badly enough to halt Donna Lutas's efforts to force me out of my home. I assumed it was the law firm that told the Salina police I was coming to town.

It occurred to me that if Chief Corbitt was willing to do Devlin's bidding, he knew what car I was driving; I was an easy target if they wanted to catch me on a violation. I didn't know why they would, but I was feeling nervous about lingering any longer in the town.

I wanted to talk to the warden at the county jail about Arthur Morton's suicide. I wanted to find Franklin Alsop, the Tallgrass Meet-Up organizer whose name the women at K-State had given me. Black Wolf, the unincorporated collection of houses and a gas station, was only six miles outside Salina. Although Salina had a dozen or more motels and hotels, I would feel less like a target if I found a place to stay remote from Corbitt's jurisdiction.

Another map-dot, about thirty miles beyond Black Wolf, advertised an old railway hotel. I'd go there and backtrack east in the morning.

I bundled Bear back into the car. At least the smell of wet dirty dog covered up the moldy smell from last night's flooding of the upholstery. I stopped at a FedEx shop to send the prints I'd made of the cave photos to my lawyer.

On my way out of town I passed a big-box store. Just to be prudent, I bought a couple of burn phones and a few groceries so I wouldn't end up fasting again tonight. A sheriff's car was in the lot when I got back into my car. I turned off my smartphone, hoping that would keep it from broadcasting my whereabouts. When I left the parking lot, the sheriff was behind me. It looked as though the Salina police chief had shared his anti–Chicago PI feelings with the county sheriff.

I signaled every turn I made, had my headlights on, came to a complete stop at stop signs and on yellow lights. I joined the interstate at a modest fifty miles an hour. The sheriff stayed with me until I crossed the county line. I counted three exits, and then slid off the highway to side roads. I made a number of turns, onto gravel roads, back to a paved two-lane highway, and decided I was clear—clear enough to check in with Arlette and Mr. Contreras. I pulled onto a gravel shoulder that abutted a gate leading to a field.

Pierre had given me the number of a friend in Quebec City so that I wouldn't call the mountain retreat to ask for news. I had to take my smartphone out of its safety pouch to look up the number, but I called on the burn phone. Pierre's friend assured me that all was well, that

Pierre had good security in place, but that Bernie was going stir crazy—did I know how long the Fouchards would have to stay at the retreat? I wished I could give a timetable, but I didn't know what I was trying to find out at this point, let alone when I'd find it.

My worries deepened when I hung up: I knew Bernie wouldn't stay put forever, or even for very long. Think, focus, take action, I commanded myself, but I felt as though I were swimming in liquid lead, trying to reach an unreachable shore.

In lieu of other action, I called Mr. Contreras, who grumbled about the dog walkers. This was a pair I'd worked with for many years. My neighbor always grumbled about them, partly because he hates having to admit he's not fit enough to walk the dogs himself, partly because he thinks I'll come back sooner if I believe the dogs aren't well cared for.

"Did Donna Lutas come around asking about me?" I asked when there was a break in the flow.

"Yeah, she did. I asked, was she wanting to slap some eviction notice on you and she said, no, she was just wondering because her firm was giving you help on some old trial. Is that right, doll?"

"Sort of," I said. "They wanted to talk to me about a mass murderer trial, the one I've come down to Kansas to look into."

"Can't believe a sourpuss like her would be willing to help you on anything, but it just goes to show."

It showed that Lutas would curb her killer instinct until Devlin & Wickham found out what they wanted. I didn't say that to my neighbor—he's uncomfortable when I'm cynical. Instead, I promised to call again the next day.

I was getting ready to pull back onto the road when Murray called. I'd forgotten to turn off my smartphone.

"Where are you, Warshawski? I've been trying to reach you all day."

I looked at my message box. Three from Murray, a dozen from various clients. And one from Peter, letting me know he was in Turkey. My spirits sank—it hurt that I'd missed hearing his voice.

"I was in a library," I said to Murray. "You know—turn off your phones, don't disturb the other patrons."

"You're a walking disturbance whether your phone is on or not," Murray grumbled.

"I love being insulted as much as the next person, but I'm short on time now, so if that's why you're calling, put it in writing."

"It's the pictures you sent. If they're genuine, they're a political hydrogen bomb. I got our photo department to enhance them, and it looks like a plan to put in a luxury development along the lakefront—the mile stretch between Forty-seventh and Thirty-ninth. Town houses, condos, shops, private harbor, and a PGA golf course. I want to go public with it, but my editors are being super cautious. They want the pedigree for the information. And we both want to know if it's a real plan or someone's daydream."

"When I looked at the photos, I thought they were getting rid of Lake Shore Drive."

"Rerouting it, meaning tearing up homes and whatnot on the west side of the Metra tracks. I need the pedigree."

"I don't have one," I said. "I think these were diagrams put out by the Park District, but I can't trace them. And I don't know if it's a wish list or a genuine plan. I actually stopped at their offices to ask Taggett about the plans, before I'd seen the pictures, and the next day he sent some gorillas around to scare me. Can't you submit some FOIAs?"

"I don't have any details," he snapped. "I need conversations or emails or some damned thing between a commissioner or Taggett or the mayor with a developer. A mechanical engineer did the drawings. We can't get a good resolution on the name of the mechanical engineer, but it looks like a woman, something like

Mina, middle initial Y, Punter. I can't find a mechanical engineer or a firm with that name. How did you get hold of these?"

"I told you: a flash drive left lying in an abandoned backpack." Maybe I should have explained about it being Leo's—probably being Leo's—but that would have involved Bernie. Murray pushed on me for a few more minutes but finally snarled, "Don't keep me in mind when you're handing out favors," and hung up.

As I eased back onto the road, I thought of the surveyor's stakes I'd seen in the Burnham Wildlife Corridor. Someone was ready to privatize a square mile of lakefront. The parks superintendent was on board with the deal; they'd already started marking territory. No wonder his goons had come around threatening me. The night air was thick, but I was cold.

42

Dots on the Map

The sleepy man who checked me in to the old railway hotel had disappeared when I went back to
my car for my bag. I brought Bear in with me then—
better to ask forgiveness, and so on.

The bed was comfortable, the room quiet. It wasn't
their fault that my dreams were tormented with images
of Lydia Zamir, repeatedly collapsing onto her plastic
piano, the case turning red as blood poured from her
nose and mouth. *Remember me and announce my fate*,
she sang as she expired. When I peered at her dead
body, it was plastered with nicotine patches, shreds of
tobacco sticking out from underneath them.

When morning finally came, I stood under a cold
shower to try to clear my head. I took Bear out for a run

in a field near the hotel, but put him in the car when I went back in for breakfast.

The waitress was a chatty woman, perhaps in her sixties. A pin on her shoulder named her as Clara; she told me she was the hotel's co-owner with her husband.

"He's over to Ellsworth looking at some chickens," she said when she brought me my short stack. "We might put a coop out back. People like the feeling that we're connected to the Old West. How about you, hon? You driving cross-country?"

"Actually, I'm trying to find someone around here."

"Your ex run out on you?"

I produced a halfhearted smile. "A man named Coop. He left his dog with me a week ago and vanished."

Clara put the coffeepot down with a snap. "What makes you think he's here?"

"I thought he might be in the area, not right here on the premises. Is he?"

"Pancakes are on the house. Time you were on your way." Her jaw was set in an uncompromising line. Her eyes looked as hard and cold as river stones.

"How about if I tell you as much as I know, and then you decide whether to send me on my way. If we can do it outside so that I don't have to leave Bear—Coop's dog—in the car—this is a long story."

Her expression didn't soften, but after a pause, she said I could bring the dog in—we'd talk in the lounge. This was a small alcove to the right of the front desk, where she could keep an eye on the outside door, the elevator, and the stairwell.

Bear didn't seem to know her; he greeted her with the polite indifference he showed most people, so I didn't think Coop had been part of the hotel's life. I gave Clara one of my cards, gave her some names to call to check out my credentials.

"This is a tangled mess of a story," I said. "I don't know a clean and easy way to tell it, but it starts with the murders at the Tallgrass Meet-Up four years ago. One of the victims was Hector Palurdo, the partner of the singer-songwriter Lydia Zamir."

"You don't need to tell me about that day. We had friends who were at the concert. I'd had a mind to go over, hand out flyers about the hotel. I'm glad I didn't but—that boy Arthur Morton left a lot of damage behind him."

"Yes, I've been involved in some of the fallout." I told Clara about finding Lydia living under the viaduct, about Coop constituting himself her protector, about the distress caused by the piece that Murray wrote for the *Herald-Star.*

"Oh, we know all about that," she said. "We all saw the story online, how Lydia disappeared."

I told her about the two murders that the police thought Coop had committed. "It's why he ran. I think he took Lydia with him, not as a hostage, but to help her—she was living quite literally in a hole in the ground. I hope she's with him. I hope he's getting her the medical care she needs."

"You get paid for taking Coop back to Chicago for the police to have a whack at? We know about your methods down here. This may be a spot on the map to a lady from Chicago but we're not bone ignorant."

"My father was a Chicago cop and one of the best, most moral people I've ever known," I said. "Chicago and our police are like any other place or occupation—some are bad, some are good, most are in the middle zone. But, no, I don't want to take Coop back to Chicago. And I'm not a bounty hunter. No one is paying me to look for Coop.

"I'd like to give Bear back to him—he's a great dog, but I have two of my own and if I take on Bear I'll be evicted from my apartment. Anyway, anyway, this story keeps sprouting new tentacles, like an octopus with an infinite number of legs. Since I've been down here talking to people about Arthur Morton, I realized—there's no doubt he killed all those people, but a lot of questions about the trial, about his lawyers, about his suicide, could use some probing."

She thought over what I'd said. "What makes you think Coop is around here?"

"The women I spoke to at Kansas State's Conservation department remembered him and thought he might have come from somewhere in the Salina area. Coop is a passionate environmentalist—he showed that in Chicago, although maybe not in the smartest way. I was going to backtrack to Black Wolf this morning to look for a man named Franklin Alsop. He helped run the Meet-Up, he's a conservationist, according to the K-State women. I'm hoping he might know Coop, or at least know about him."

"Franklin? If you get Franklin to talk to you, you're better than anyone around him. Ever since the shooting, he hasn't spoken to a soul beyond 'hi' and 'thank you' when he goes to pick up his groceries or his mail."

"I looked at a map this morning. Black Wolf isn't a town, is it? Can you tell me how to find him?"

She drummed her fingers on a piecrust table next to her chair, then got abruptly to her feet. She went behind the front desk, where she spoke on her phone—possibly to her husband, interrupting his chicken inspection. The conversation went on for a good ten minutes.

She came back with a map, but she sat with it folded in her lap. "I know Coop, sort of know Coop. He's a drifter, ranch hand sometimes, road work, whatever needs doing that is short-term. I can't tell you where he's from.

"Jack and I used to farm. We had three hundred acres not too far from here, and Coop showed up one day in the middle of a thunderstorm. He'd been walking, you could tell that. He had a different dog, not Bear here—this was maybe twenty-five years ago. I had a baby and another on the way and the work was more than Jack and I could do on our own, but we couldn't afford full-time help. Out here you trade with the neighbors, but to keep the place going, with planting and so on, keeping the machinery working, it's not a one-and-a-half-person job.

"Coop said he'd help get the winter wheat in and look after the soybeans if we'd put him up. He might have been twenty-one, twenty-two at the time. We did wonder if he was on the run—he had a temper on him, but he was strong and a hard worker so we didn't want to look too deep. But then he and Jack had a knockdown fight over the pesticides Jack used on the soybeans. Jack started to worry about him being in the house with little Jack and the baby. And then Coop got into a big fight with a neighbor over how they were cultivating. We had to ask him to leave.

"After that, I heard about him from time to time. He wasn't a bad person, just unsettled. I guess he'd been thrown out of college before he came to us, if the ladies over there at K-State remember their dates right."

"Did you learn his full name?"

She shook her head. "He always said if one name was good enough for Prince or Madonna, it was good enough for him."

"What happened to your farm?" I asked. "Sea-2-Sea?"

Clara produced a sour smile. "They don't own all of Kansas, not yet, anyway. We lease the land. Got so we didn't feel like working it, and then we saw a chance to buy this hotel and run it. It's hard work, but fun bringing it back to life."

She opened the map. "Old Highway Forty runs through town. You take that down to Eighth Road."

Her callused finger traced the route. "And in between Avenues I and J, there's going to be a dirt track, east side of the road. That fancy Mustang you're driving, it's going to get caught in the mud there. All the rain we've had this year, we might as well be growing rice and sidestepping alligators, we're that close to being in a swamp. Worst winter wheat crop in twenty years. Anyway, it's a mile, mile and a half up that track, and you'll be on Alsop's land. He calls it the Nicodemus Prairie."

She handed me the map, seemed to be about to add something, but changed her mind.

Clara's comment about walking through a swamp made me stop at a general store on the outskirts of town for some insect repellent for me and a flea and tick treatment for Bear.

I'd filled my water bottles in the hotel but I bought a banana, a couple of apples, and a bag of mixed nuts. Be prepared.

I followed Clara's directions and pulled off the road when I came to the dirt track. I hoped there was only one—the air was unpleasantly thick and warm, and mosquitoes and flies were blitzing both the dog and me, despite our chemical protection. I'd hate to hike a mile in this weather only to find I was on the wrong road.

The track led past tilled fields. Even to my urban eye, the crops looked small and droopy, not the bright green and upright stalks of healthy plants.

We'd been going for about half an hour, my weather-resistant shoes squelching deep enough in the mud that it spilled into my socks, when the cropscape changed.

The neatly squared-off rows—identical horizontally, diagonally, vertically—ended, marked by a barbed-wire fence. On the other side a wilderness appeared: no two plants seemed to be alike. Some were tall, spiky, some short and scrubby. Dotted among them were wildflowers of all colors.

I stopped to watch butterflies and grasshoppers flitting among the flowers. Under the heavy sky, with land stretching to an infinite horizon, it was hard to imagine my city, its buildings and people crammed cheek by jowl. How could both worlds exist simultaneously?

The proposed development on the drawings I'd sent to Murray, about a square mile of luxury shops, homes, golf course, private beach—you could fit all that into this land and not even notice it was there.

Who in Chicago wanted it? Who had that kind of money and why would they spend it there? Uprooting a mile of lakefront, including an eight-lane road, sounded both absurd and obscene, but the city had rerouted Lake Shore Drive around the Field Museum twenty years or so ago—if the money and the will were there, it would happen.

Murray had said it looked as though the mechanical engineers were with a firm called Punter. I'd looked them up before leaving the hotel this morning but hadn't found a company with that name. Maybe this was a phantom project that Leo had taken seriously—but then, why had he and Simon been murdered? Over some other project? Over something completely unrelated that I didn't know about?

Bear dropped to the ground, panting heavily. I poured water over his head and into a collapsible bowl for him before drinking myself.

We'd been alone in the fields all morning, and so when a man spoke behind me, I spun around, so startled I dropped my water bottle.

"Who are you and what do you want?"

43

Tales of a Traveler

My unconscious stereotypes had tripped me up: it hadn't occurred to me that a preserver of prairie and an organizer of the Tallgrass Meet-Up might be African-American. That was the remark Clara had held back from making as I left.

Bear growled softly. I put a hand on his collar and squatted to pick up my water bottle. "My name is V.I. Warshawski. Are you Franklin Alsop?"

"And if I am?"

"If you are, I hope you can direct me to Coop—this is Bear, his dog. Coop left Bear with me, but I'd like to give him back."

"Whoever he is, you don't belong on my land." His voice was like gravel, the words almost giving off sparks as they struck the air.

Sweat was running down my neck and soaking my armpits, but Alsop looked not just dry but cool. The pressure of sky on me, the vastness of the space, his coolness, my drenchedness, I wanted to lie down on the track next to Bear and give up.

"You're my only lead, Mr. Alsop. Coop seems to be a nomad who traveled to Chicago when Lydia Zamir moved there. People tell me Coop was a presence at the Meet-Up. People tell me he likely came from around here, although no one knows his full name or where he grew up. Coop is passionate about land preservation. If he's in the area, they thought you would know. Anyway, aside from giving him back his dog, I'm not trying to find Coop as much as I'm looking for Lydia Zamir."

Alsop's expression shifted, became more alert. "What do you want her for?"

"I found her living in a hole in the ground ten days ago. She wouldn't let me get her help. A few hours later, I ran into Coop. Since he seemed to be the one person she responded to, I told him where she was and begged him to get her proper medical help. When I went back to her hideout, she'd vanished. Coop also disappeared, leaving Bear tied up outside my building. If Coop doesn't have Lydia, then she's either dead or in the hands of some ugly people in Chicago and I should redouble my efforts to find her there."

"Ugly people." Alsop gave a soft laugh, but it, too, had an ugly sound. "Yes, I know ugly people. If Coop is hiding from them, then I'm not going to help anyone find him."

"Not even to save Lydia Zamir's life?"

"To save Lydia's life? Now we're in a melodrama. Who do you work for, that you're investing this kind of effort, traveling here from Chicago to hunt for two people whom I know only as names from a four-year-old catastrophe?"

For the second time that day, I told the story of my involvement with Lydia and Coop. I kept the details to a minimum, but it still took ten minutes. As I spoke, the wind rose, clearing some of the sultriness out of the air, but lightning began to play along the horizon, making me aware of how exposed I was.

When I finished, Alsop stared at me steadily. "You could write a book of fables. You said you should return to Chicago, and that is an excellent idea."

He turned and walked through the field to my right, following a scarcely visible footpath. He knew where Coop was, I was sure. Perhaps Lydia as well. I could yell at him to stop, to listen, but I couldn't think of anything to say that would get past his decision to shut me down.

I'm not usually indecisive, but I didn't know what to do next. You can't tail someone in the open air, especially when that person knows hidden paths and crevices that allow the earth to swallow him up—one moment I was watching Alsop head northeast through his land, a second later, he'd vanished.

I started the trek back to the county road, Bear plodding next to me. The storm broke when we were still about ten minutes from the car. I broke into a jog, a shuffle, really, given the mud weighing down my shoes. I had my head hunched into my shirt and wasn't looking around, but as I pushed the UNLOCK button on the remote, Bear grabbed my jeans leg and pulled me into the mud.

A second later, the back window of the car shattered. Thunder in the sky, thunder on the ground, the two rolled together. I slid into the ditch. The driver's window shattered in another thunderclap.

If I stayed here any longer, the car would be undrivable and the dog and I would be easy targets for the shooter.

"We're going," I said to Bear. "Now."

I jumped from the ditch, opened the passenger door, and started the car while sliding into the driver's seat. Bear hung back for a second but as another bullet slammed into the driver's door he jumped into the passenger seat. I tore down the road, the passenger door swinging wildly. I skidded around a curve, one hand dug into Bear's fur, one on the wheel. When the car straightened out, I slowed enough to slam Bear's door shut.

The gravel road was slick and the Mustang skittered between the ditches. Five miles from Ellsworth, the nearest town, a pickup hauling a powerboat slowed us to forty. They were taking up most of the road, making it impossible to see oncoming traffic, making it impossible to pass. A line of cars built behind us. Maybe we were safer in a convoy if the shooter was following us.

Now that I was driving more slowly I felt the rain pelting in through the broken driver's window. The wipers had been knocked askew by the force of the shots and the steering was getting stiffer. I'd hoped to get east of Salina before I stopped for help, but that meant going another hundred miles or so, and the car wasn't going to make it that far.

Our convoy trundled into Ellsworth. ANOTHER WICKED COWTOWN a sign on the outskirts announced, population 3,120. Ellsworth wasn't that far from Salina, which made me worry that the Salina LEOs would have passed on an alert about me and my searches to their Ellsworth colleagues.

I asked my phone to find me a place to stay. There was a motel nearby, named with surprising whimsy, Tales of a Traveler. A body shop was only a few blocks beyond that, and restaurants and a grocery store were in walking distance. As long as no one shot at me, it was a perfect place to regroup.

I left the engine running while I checked in at the motel, just in case whatever was ailing the car meant it wouldn't start again. The desk clerk pointed out that I had blood on my hands.

I hadn't noticed it, but now, in the motel lobby, I saw that glass shards were embedded in my wet clothes. I had cuts on my hands and one on my neck.

"Someone ran me off the road out by Black Wolf," I said. "I want to get my car into the body shop and stay here while they work on it."

The woman behind the desk clucked sympathetically. "Those kids, thinking they can take their bikes up to a hundred on the gravel roads, they've caused more accidents! I'll call Eddie—he has a body shop, he can come tow your car. No, it's no trouble, and if you have all that glass and so on, better not drive it anymore. But, hon, if you could get some of that glass off you out in the lot—there's a bin there—I don't want it indoors."

While she talked to Eddie, I let Bear out of the car and took him and my big carryall to a secluded spot behind the building, where I solved my glass problem by throwing out my damaged clothes and putting on clean ones. I inspected my fingers and palms. I had one shard embedded in a finger—I'd have to buy some tweezers. I kept the finger elevated while I felt Bear for damage. He had a couple of pieces in his paws, from when he'd leapt in, and several in his haunches, but I was able to work those free without an instrument.

When I returned to the car to get the rest of my belongings, the shattered windows made me think of the bullets. They were likely still in the car; I'd just as soon gossip not start spreading around the town about a shot-up Mustang. Whoever fired at me might well be looking for me; I didn't want to make the hunt too easy.

I put socks over my hands and sorted through the glass, trying to protect the finger with the shard stuck in it. The cartridges were large and easy to find, one under the driver's seat, one where Bear had been sitting. I stuck them into my jeans pocket and went back to the trunk.

I hadn't secured the dog food bag well and it had spilled out in the trunk. Eddie arrived with a tow truck as I was trying to scoop it back into the bag. I lifted out my carryall and my boots, took them with Bear's blanket and bowls into the hotel lobby.

"Jenna told me you'd been run off the road," Eddie said. "Looks like you could use a look-see by a doctor. There's a clinic not half a mile from here. I'll drive you, it's hardly out of the way."

I assured him it would be better for me to walk—the dog needed exercise—the rain had stopped and air would calm me down. Eddie assured me if I changed my mind, he'd be glad to send one of the boys out with the truck to drive me. Meanwhile, he looked the Mustang over, sadly clicking his tongue over the damage.

"Might take a few days to get the windows in. Not much call for Mustangs out here—it's more SUV and ATV country."

I gave him a credit card and my phone number and finally was free to go inside. The motel had one of those alcoves where you could buy junk food, phone chargers, and basic toiletries. I paid ten dollars for a kit with tweezers and another for Band-Aids and disinfectant. When we were settled into the room, I pulled the glass out of my finger with more haste than skill—it tore the hole wider and blood gushed onto the bathroom floor. I wrapped my hand in an ice-filled plastic bag and lay down. Just before losing consciousness, I promised Bear the biggest steak I could find in Ellsworth: "You saved my life," I told him.

44
Honesty Is the Best Policy

I woke in the muzzy way one does from sleeping in the middle of the day, but after a shower and some stretches, I set out with Bear to buy groceries, including the promised steak.

On our way back to the motel, we detoured past Eddie's Body Shop. It was late afternoon by now, but the work bay doors were still open.

The Mustang was parked outside the shop, along with a Honda SUV and a Chevy pickup that hadn't fared well in collisions. Inside, Eddie and another guy were working on a Ford Super Duty. If the Mustang was third on the runway, it would be awhile before I got it back.

When I looked into the car, I saw Eddie had at least cleaned out all the broken glass. The front left tire was flat. I squatted to look at the rim, which had come loose. There was a dent in the driver's door as well.

Bear let out a short bark: Eddie had emerged from the shop and was standing near us.

"Those windows didn't get broke from you ending in a ditch, did they? Someone shot at you."

I stood up. "True enough."

"Why'd you lie to me? I don't like that. Makes me think I shouldn't work on this car, if you've got some Chicago mobster chasing you."

"Yes, lying is almost always an unskillful decision. The trouble is, I'm a stranger here and I don't know who I can trust. I don't know who was shooting at me, and I don't know why. And as for telling you the truth—I have no way of knowing who you'd talk to if I did."

He nodded grudgingly. "If you've committed a violent crime, I'd tell the sheriff, for sure, but if you haven't, I'll keep it to myself. No reason for you to believe me, but that's a fact. Now try me. Why are you here in Ellsworth?"

Eddie squatted on a discarded fender; I sat on the Mustang's tailpiece, Bear in front of me, alert to stranger-danger.

"The shooting at the Tallgrass Meet-Up four years ago," I started.

"What do you have to do with that? You writing another book? We had about eight people in love with gory stories come through for local color on their books."

"No, I'm not writing a book. But this is about Lydia Zamir. Did you see the news stories about her, the recent ones? You know she's been living in Chicago, out on the streets?"

"Yeah, we all watched that story when it broke. Don't know why no one in a city that big had an extra bed for her."

"Her, well, mother-in-law I guess you could call her—her murdered lover's mother—put her up in an apartment, but she became less and less able to cope with daily life. The trauma, she stopped being able to connect to the bigger world. She stopped speaking. She moved out onto the streets. She ran away; I found her barely surviving in a hole in the ground. She disappeared and I wanted to find her, make sure she was okay. I also wanted to find out why a big Chicago law firm handled Artie Morton's defense.

"Someone told the Salina LEOs I was coming down here, and I'm pretty sure it was the law firm, but I can't believe they'd shoot me, or hire someone to shoot me. Someone thinks I know something, or have something, but I don't have any idea what it could be.

"And then—when I limped into Ellsworth, I thought

if I let the woman at Tales of a Traveler, and you, know I'd been shot at, you'd start talking and the word would fly back to whoever was after me. I'm out here alone and naked. My gun is in Chicago. And my only defense is this dog, who, to be fair, saved my life this morning, but he's not a match for a bullet."

Eddie mulled my story over in his mind. "Why'd you stick your neck out to begin with? You're not a cop, right?"

"I'm a private investigator. I'm looking for a killer who murdered two people a hundred yards from where Lydia Zamir was hiding. One of the dead men was dating one of my goddaughters. I don't expect Lydia to identify him, because she isn't talking to me or anyone. But if the killer thinks she saw him, she's at risk all over again.

"In the last two days, I've told three people why I'm here—Franklin Alsop over in Black Wolf, Clara Digby at the old rail hotel in Tarshish, and a lawyer named Gabriel Ramirez. Maybe one of that trio became angry enough to shoot me back to Chicago. Now you're the fourth, and you know I'm an easy mark."

Eddie grunted. "I know Clara. Least, I know her old man. He was in town this morning looking to buy some of Rufus McIlvie's chickens. I can't believe either of them would shoot you. Franklin—he keeps himself to himself, out on the Nicodemus Prairie he manages. He was in school with my older brother and he always went in for nonviolence. Martin Luther King, Gandhi, he was always talking about them. Must be the lawyer."

"Could be," I agreed politely.

"But if all these people know, they've told people. Not Franklin—he's clammed up since the massacre, but Clara likes to chat with people who stop at her hotel."

Eddie's coworker came out to give him an update on the Ford pickup, but stood watching me.

"'Night, Rick," Eddie said. "Good work on the tailgate. See you in the morning."

As Rick walked away, I could see him taking my picture and texting. Great.

"I know most people who live around here or grew up in the area," Eddie said. "I don't know this Coop, but I wonder if he used to work for Cassie on her Clarina Prairie. It's next to Franklin's Nicodemus Prairie— the two of them are hanging on to almost five hundred acres, and it isn't always easy."

"Because they don't have enough help?" I asked, thinking of Clara's story.

"Because someone wants to farm them."

"I thought all this land was the prairie." I gestured vaguely toward the world beyond the Ellsworth town limits.

"You have to ask Franklin or Cassie, or the brains over to K-State what makes something a prairie. Some of it has to do with letting the native plants have their way with the land. None of this tilling the soil, putting in herbicides, pesticides, the way we do to grow food for people in Chicago.

"Anyway, Cassie started restoring her family's farm to prairie, and early in the process, there was talk about a kid who showed up and helped her for a couple of summers. Wild kid, lot of anger, trying to beat up on guys twice his size if they looked at him sideways. No one knew where he came from, but he was good with animals and apparently took to plants, too. Cassie's a strange woman, not everyone's cup of tea, probably the right person for a confused angry kid to turn to."

"Was your brother in high school with her?" I asked.

He gave a reluctant grin. "My mother. Cassie's the kind of woman gets a reputation for being a little crazy, every year a little crazier, and people steer clear."

He took me into the office part of his shop and dug around in a filing cabinet for a county map. It was old, torn where the folds had been opened and shut, but easier to follow than a computer file.

The Clarina Prairie lay to the north of Alsop's Nicodemus Prairie. You could reach it from a different county road than the one I'd driven to Alsop's land. Of course, Alsop had probably already told Cassie about my visit, especially since it had ended in a hail of gunfire.

If Franklin or Cassie felt murderous about a Chicago detective on their land, I'd end my life in a Kansas cornfield. No, on a Kansas prairie, more ecologically valuable. They'd turn my body to compost and let the worms feed on me, which I guess would make a noble ending.

Eddie had a beater he rented to me. "You get it shot, you buy it, you pay to repair it."

45

Little House on the Prairie

Rain started to fall again as Bear and I drove back along Old U.S. 40, the road we'd taken this morning when we were fleeing the shooter. Eddie's beater was an old Chevy Impala, a boat of a car with a lot of give in the springs and not much tread on the tires: the car slid around on the gravel county road.

I saw the turnoff to the lane that led to Cassie's land a second after I passed it. I stupidly hit the brakes. The Impala bucked and fishtailed, but righted itself with the front left wheel dangling over the ditch. I managed to back it up, back it down the county road, and turn on to the lane without actually falling off the road.

A tractor might have made easy work of the muddy track, but the Impala hated it. We slithered across the mud. I went a cautious five miles an hour but had to gun the engine a few times to make the car leap over the biggest potholes.

Before setting out, I'd driven to the motel for a few supplies: my oilcloth coat, my boots, my work flash. In case we were stranded, I'd also taken Bear's food. Some snacks for me. My laptop, too. The locks at Tales of a Traveler didn't inspire me with confidence.

I undid the latch on the gate so Bear and I could slip through. As I was refastening it, he stood with his ears pricked, nostrils flaring. I shone my flashlight around, trying to pick out the trail through the prairie grasses, when Bear gave a short, urgent bark and tore off, almost at right angles to the path I was about to take.

I called to him. He stopped briefly to look over his shoulder at me, then ran again. The gray sky, the wet, the huge open land with its deceptive swales and rises, unnerved me. I abandoned the path I wanted to take and trudged after him. I couldn't run in the mud and in my boots, but he would stop periodically, let me get in sighting distance, carry on.

We'd gone on about twenty minutes, me with a stitch in my side, the dog loping ahead, when he disappeared into one of the hollows. He began a volley of barks. I picked up my pace and reached the top of the rise to see a door open in the hillside and a woman step out. Bear streaked past her through the open door. She started to follow him in when she caught sight of me, hustling down the path to her.

"Are you the person who trespassed on Franklin Alsop's prairie this morning? Just who are you and why have you come back?" She was old, with a lined face and thick white hair that stuck out wildly around her head, but she held herself erect and her voice was firm.

This was how my day had begun, with Franklin Alsop and his land. I was tired of being spun around, shot at, ignored, and basically stonewalled.

"I'm V.I. Warshawski. I'm looking for Coop and there's no point in your saying you don't know him, or where he is, because his dog, Bear, figured out he was here half a mile back."

"The Chicago detective," she said, shutting the door in case I was tempted to rush inside. "Coop isn't here, so you might as well leave."

"You're Cassie, right?" I moved over to sit on a short wood bench near her door. A dozen or so chickens scratched inside a coop just beyond the bench.

The rain pelted my raincoat and trickled down my neck. I longed to take off my boots and massage my feet, but my socks would get wet. I hadn't brought a second pair with me from the motel.

"Lies, secrets, and silence, that's what all detective work revolves around. The lies and secrets here are bigger than a lot that I encounter. Perhaps Coop isn't here in this literal moment, but he's been here recently enough to leave a scent along the ground."

Bear started barking from the other side of the door.

"Be quiet, you silly dog," Cassie said sharply.

Bear kept barking and scratching at the door. Cassie finally opened it, just a crack, to let him out and keep me from going in. He came to me, pawed at my leg, whined, trotted back to the door, barked at me to follow.

"Lydia," I said, my brain turning over. "Coop isn't here now, but he brought Lydia to you. Bear knows her and feels responsible for her so he went inside to find her. Now he's making a racket to let me know I should come in, too."

"You read dogs' minds?" Franklin Alsop materialized behind me, as mysteriously as he'd disappeared this morning. Perhaps there was another house in the ground nearby, or maybe he was like the Cheshire Cat, able to appear at will.

Cassie looked at him, and he nodded his head slightly. "We don't want you here," she said. "There's been too much shooting, too much murder around here, and I don't allow guns on my land."

"I'm not armed," I said.

"Shooters came after you this morning," she said, unarguably. "But here you are, and if they followed you again, we'll have to deal with them. However, Coop is safe, and anyway, he said that you could be trusted even though he's not crazy about you, so I suppose you can come inside and get Bear to quiet down."

As soon as she opened the door, Bear raced over to me. He scratched my pant leg and rushed back into the house, turning in the doorway to make sure I was coming. His expression seemed to say, *Why do they always give me the slowest kids to look after?*

Inside the door was a mudroom with a bluestone floor. I eased my feet out of my boots and put them on a board where Cassie had left her muddy clogs.

I followed Bear's toenails clattering on the floor and saw his stump of a tail disappear into a room at the end of a short hallway.

A skylight let in enough puny daylight to reveal Lydia Zamir. She was tucked into a narrow bed under a blue-and-white quilt. The walls around her were painted an eggshell blue. Bear was licking an arm that lay outside the quilt.

She lay so still that I had the macabre thought that she had died, that Cassie was keeping her body laid out as part of some hideous ritual. Then I saw a faint pulse in her neck, a throb that barely moved the skin around her carotid artery.

Cassie had managed to bathe her and to cut the wild

mass of hair. In repose, the anguish eased out of her face, Lydia looked younger. I felt a stab of anguish of my own. So much damage done to her.

I squatted next to Bear. I didn't try to touch Lydia. Cassie must have figured out a way to feed her because there was a little more substance to her face than when I'd last seen her, but the arm Bear was tending looked like a stick covered with flesh.

"Lydia, it's V.I. Warshawski. I'm glad you've found a safe resting place. I want you to stay safe. I won't tell anyone where you are, and I will do my best to find the people you're afraid of."

She flinched. She certainly understood me, even as she lay as still as death. I couldn't ask her anything. Whatever she knew about the Devlin & Wickham lawyers, or about Leo Prinz and Simon Lensky's killers, she was keeping shut in some deep basement of her mind.

I felt an unbearable grief, looking at her, and began to sing the songs of my childhood, my mother's Italian lullabies. I don't know if the music helped Lydia, but Bear stopped his compulsive licking and I myself felt calmer.

"Okay, now we know you can sing, it's time for talk." Franklin Alsop spoke from the doorway. Cassie was with him. The two led me into the heart of the house, a big common room buried in the hillside, lit by wall sconces. Bear stayed with Lydia.

Cassie clapped her hands, and an overhead light, mimicking sunshine, came on. I'd been expecting the kind of dirt home Laura Ingalls Wilder described in *Little House on the Prairie,* but Cassie's dugout was lined with wood and stone.

A series of beams presumably kept everything from falling in on her, but I still felt panicky at being shut in underground. I took some deep breaths, trying to slow my heartbeat. Lydia's room had smelled of lavender. The big room had a different scent, citrus-like.

Before I could ask about Lydia, Cassie demanded, "What do you want with Coop?"

"Information," I said. "Which I'd like about Lydia, as well. Did Coop bring her straight here? Has she seen a doctor?"

"She doesn't need a doctor. She needs safety," Cassie snapped. "You saw her yourself. She's recovering, and she can do it here, not in some noisy institution where they'd put her on drugs that would destroy her mind and her creative spirit."

"Her mind and her creative spirit have been pretty well depleted these last few years. She needs to eat, build up her physical strength."

"You think I don't know that? You saying Coop

didn't think that through? A hospital would take what's left of her poor little veins to analyze her blood. Besides, she doesn't have insurance. I feed her like an abandoned baby kitten: with an eyedropper. She gets broth, she gets herbs, you saw her: color is better and she's resting." She glared at me, defiant.

"Coop told us how she ran away every time the busybodies put her into care against her wishes. She knows she's safe with Cassie." That was Alsop. "She's better off here, as long as you don't bring shooters onto the land."

"Why were they shooting at you?" Cassie asked.

"I don't know. And I don't know who 'they' are—do you?"

They shook their heads, but Alsop said, "Why are you here, really? Why are you looking for Coop."

"Coop and Lydia have some kind of connection. He was the one person she would see in the weeks she spent at her mother's house after the shooting; he followed her from there to Chicago. He tried to look after her when she moved onto the streets."

"Coop told us that much," Cassie said grudgingly.

"Two men were murdered near where she was camping out. Did he talk about that?"

"He said the police wanted to frame him for the murders," Cassie said. "I won't let that happen."

"Coop had been going to community meetings where the two men were speaking. He'd gotten angry with them—he seems to lose his temper pretty easily and he started threatening them, or at least threatening the younger one."

"So you *are* here to locate him for the police," Alsop said, disgusted.

"It would be helpful if you let me finish, because you actually don't know what I'm going to say. This is a story with a lot of parts that don't hang together well, and information would be a lot more useful than a fight."

I waited a moment. Alsop's eyes glittered with anger, but he shut his lips, tightly, a gesture akin to a sneer.

I told them about Murray's story, which had driven Lydia into flight. Unlike everyone else I'd met in Kansas, Alsop and Cassie hadn't seen the online reports—they stayed off the grid as much as possible, I gathered. I described the hole in the ground where Lydia had hidden, and where I'd found the gavel that might have killed Leo.

"See? That's why she needs to be here, with me, not in some hospital!" Cassie cried.

I gave a tired smile. "You're probably right. Anyway, after Lydia disappeared, one of the biggest media companies in the country, maybe in the world, Global Entertainment, tried to hire me to find her. Even though I turned down the commission, they were pretty obsessed with locating her, so much that they offered a suitcase full of money to film me searching for her. I turned that down, too, but it made me concerned about her safety.

"She was so fragile that I didn't think she could survive long in the outdoors. I hoped Coop could talk her into getting care, but his reaction to me was always belligerent. And then came the night about a week ago when he left Bear outside my apartment building and disappeared. I don't know how he got here."

Cassie nodded slowly, weighing what I'd said. "This has always been Coop's safe place. He showed up here the summer he was seventeen, when I was first working to build the prairie. He was a runaway, a rural runaway. You don't hear much about kids like him, but they can be dreadfully isolated by the farm, especially if the parents lay too much work on them and don't let them hang out with kids their own age."

She frowned into her mug. "His story was a bit like that poor boy who did the shootings—"

"*Not.*" Alsop interrupted her. "Arthur Morton was not a 'poor boy.' He was a deranged redneck who hated people of color, Jews, immigrants, anyone outside his immediate white boy experience. He destroyed lives.

Coop lost his temper a thousand, maybe a hundred thousand times, but you can't see him climbing into a cave in Horsethief Canyon to open fire on a concert."

Cassie smiled sadly. "You know I don't disagree with any of that, Franklin, but it was the same rural poverty, the same inability to hold on to a piece of land, all the things that no one outside a few farm families ever cares about.

"Anyway, Coop knew something about how to work the land, but he was a rebel and he was happy to rebel against corporate farming. We learned about prairies together, and then he thought maybe he should take classes over at the Ag School, learn the science of land ecology. But he couldn't handle structure, and then he was ashamed for me to know he'd been thrown out, so he took off. He worked for a couple named Digby up near Tarshish, and then I don't know where, although he talked once about ranching in Mexico. He came back every now and then, when the world got too much for him. He was here when the Tallgrass happening was being planned. Franklin was involved, hoping it would stoke awareness of the importance of the prairies.

"Coop became, well, I suppose infatuated with Lydia—she came out here once and sang for us during the planning phase. He started helping Franklin out with the Tallgrass plans, hoping he could become part of her entourage or some such thing. Poor boy," she said softly. "Poor Coop."

"He was in the canyon when the shooting happened?"

She nodded. "He wasn't at the stage, though. He was in back, working in the sound truck. By the time he fought past the crowd and everything, Hector was dead and Lydia was being taken away in an ambulance.

"We were all in shock after that slaughter, so I wasn't paying close attention to anyone but Franklin, here. I think Coop followed Lydia when she moved back to her parents' place, but I couldn't tell you for sure. I didn't know she'd gone to Chicago, and him after her, until he brought her here this week. He said he tried to get her to stay in the apartment her lover's ma rented for her, but before she stopped talking, she told him she needed to be on the ground, because that's where Hector was."

She looked at me fiercely. "Just as well he kept an eye on her. Otherwise she would have died in that hole in the ground. So when he found her there, he brought her here. I know a thing or two about healing people, and she's been doing better since she got here."

"Now you know," Alsop said. "You can go back to Chicago."

46
No Herbal Remedies

Alsop put a hand under my arm, as if to yank me to my feet. I stood but didn't follow him to the door.

"I know you're protecting Lydia, and that's crucial, but that horrific set of murders four years ago—that story isn't done. If it was, someone wouldn't have been shooting at me this morning. And it troubles me that my wanting to get more information on the Horsethief Canyon murders has this big law firm that was involved in Morton's defense so roused that they alerted the Salina cops I was coming here.

"Besides that, these murders in Chicago that the cops want to pin on Coop—Lydia might have seen one of the murders. If she did, or if the killer suspects she did, then they're going to search hard for her. If she saw something—"

"You're not going to get any answers from Lydia," Alsop said with finality.

"Yes. I can see that. I just hope that I can figure out fast enough what my shooter wants, and who they are, before they put bullets in her as well as me."

"You are leaving Ellsworth, I trust?" Alsop said.

"Oh, yes," I agreed. "As soon as Eddie fixes my car. I also have a few people to talk to around Salina. And I want to look at Horsethief Canyon."

"You want to see if there's still blood on the rocks?" Alsop jeered. "I promise you there isn't."

"Franklin!" Cassie expostulated.

"Don't you know that's a tourist attraction?" Alsop cried. "Every year on the anniversary, buses full of the alt-righteous pull up to celebrate the massacre. They take back souvenirs from around where the stage was set up. You can go on their websites and buy stones covered in genuine brown or Jew blood."

"Oh, Franklin, don't bring that talk into this house."

Cassie's eyes filled with tears. She hurried to a wall hung with photographs of wildflowers and took out a handful of dried something from a chest standing there. She put it in a pot on top of the chest, chanting something under her breath, and set the contents on fire. The room filled with a scent that recalled my dope-smoking days in college, when incense blended with weed into a sweet, sickly smoke. Cassie chanted over it, waved her hands through the smoke, and then carried the pot around the room, making sure all the spirits troubled by Alsop's language could smell her concoction.

There was so much bloodshed everywhere on the planet that it didn't seem unreasonable to keep one small dugout in the Kansas hills safe from it. I don't know why the thought made me want to weep. Maybe my fatigue, or the strangeness of a house with no windows.

When Cassie finished, Alsop mumbled an apology. He turned to me. "What business do you have with Horsethief Canyon?"

"I have a photograph of the cave where Morton lay. I want to see what's on top of it."

I scrolled through my phone for the pictures I'd downloaded at the Salina library and showed them to Alsop.

"Four years of rain, blizzards, and disaster tourists, there won't be anything left up—" He stopped and held my phone up closer to his face, then enlarged the photo with his fingers. I knew which shot had caught his attention.

"You really think you'll find something?"

I shrugged. "Likely not, but one piece of hard evidence that would make the local LEOs take notice would be a good thing. Maybe a six-point-five-millimeter Creedmoor cartridge labeled 'shot from a Bergara by a left-handed miner wearing an Armani linen jacket,'" I said.

Alsop stared at me. "What does that mean?"

"It means Amelia Butterworth or Sherlock Holmes would have sorted this out weeks ago. It means I am clutching at straws. It means a beautifully dressed man keeps showing up, like a Shakespearean ghost—at the park meeting, at Morton's mother's house, at Morton's sentencing hearing. It means that the bullets fired at me this morning were six-point-five-millimeter Creedmoors."

I hadn't meant to blurt that last sentence—I was clearly more off-balance than I realized. I'd examined the shell casings I'd found in the Mustang as best I could under my flashlight, before setting out for Cassie's prairie. A lot of different rifles fire Creedmoors, but I was picturing the well-dressed stranger at Kelly Kay Morton's home, paying fifty dollars to look for Artie's computer. The well-dressed stranger showing up in court. Showing up (perhaps) at the SLICK meeting. He would own a high-end brand, not a Remington, but something that had to be imported, hand-finished.

I'd stuck the cartridges in my pocket when I left the

motel. I took them out now to show to Alsop, but Cassie flapped her hands in agitated shooing motions. No talk of murder, no guns, no bullets, in her home.

It was impossible to tell what the weather might be like outside, but it was after eight, past time I left. When Alsop said he'd guide me back to my car, I didn't hide my astonishment.

He gave a wry smile. "We can't have you tripping and falling out here on the land. Cassie's got her arms full looking after Lydia. She can't take on a clumsy city woman."

"Franklin!" Cassie cried again.

"More to the point, I want to make sure no one is lying doggo in the road," he added. "I don't want shooters finding their way to Cassie's house. If twenty percent of what the detective said is true, someone out there would kill Lydia as soon as look at her."

We all knew Bear was staying here with Lydia. I went back to her room to say goodbye. He was lying in the bed, his body stretched out next to hers. He looked at me, but didn't move. I knelt next to them.

"Lydia, I'd like to hold your hand." She didn't open her eyes, but a muscle in her jaw tightened. I leaned over Bear and took her hand. The palm and finger-tips were callused, but Cassie must have been rubbing some lotion into them because the rest of the skin felt soft.

"Lydia, it's V.I. Warshawski. We met in Chicago. I'm glad you're safe here with Cassie and Bear."

Her eyes twitched open and her breath came a little faster, but she didn't look at me.

"I wish I knew why you were trying to confront Jane Cardozo at Devlin & Wickham. It might help me keep the bad guys off your track."

At that she seemed to struggle to speak, but all that came out was a high-pitched mewling. Bear began washing her face.

Alsop hauled me to my feet and pulled me roughly from the bedside. "You're unbelievable, tormenting a sick woman with a police-style interrogation. Get your boots on. We're leaving."

Cassie came in, carrying a mug that smelled faintly like ginger. "You both go. Franklin, I'm counting on you to make sure the land is clear. Bear, move your big old head: I need to give Miss Lydia here her supper."

Alsop didn't speak while we walked back to the Impala. We moved quickly, more quickly than when I'd been trailing Bear: the dog had been following a straight line that led through thick ground cover, but Alsop knew a trail.

When we were about twenty feet from the road, Alsop put a hand on my shoulder to make sure I understood his signal to stay still and be quiet. An instant later, he disappeared into one of the prairie swales.

The moon was in its first quarter, but the clouds were heavy enough that the prairie was as dark as if it were the outer reaches of the galaxy. I wanted to be bold and decisive, to take action, move forward, but I felt unmoored, unhinged.

Alsop reappeared as silently as he'd gone. "You're clear, at least as far as the next intersection. Before you take off—who told you how to find Cassie?"

"Eddie, at the Ellsworth body shop."

"I guess that's okay. I know him, or his brother."

"Yes, you went to high school with his brother," I agreed.

"Eddie is still the kid brother, wanting attention. I hope he isn't that chatty with everyone," Alsop said.

I hoped so, too, but I only said, "Before I go, where is Coop?"

"Even if I knew, I wouldn't tell you, but I don't know. He brought Lydia into Cassie's place, made sure she was going to survive, at least for the near term, and disappeared. Three days ago, if you're wondering."

He stopped for a minute. "I believe you are not trying to bring harm to Cassie, or me, or the prairie, but you are so ignorant—about the land and about us—that you'll do damage without meaning to. That's almost worse than coming out here intending to do harm. I'm begging—imploring—you not to come back. Cassie's place is hard to find, but not impossible, and if someone is following you, they'll find her."

He melted once more into the darkness before I could respond.

47

Asleep in a Boat

The drive back to Ellsworth on the unlit country roads intensified my loneliness. It embarrassed me that I felt aggrieved with Bear for choosing Lydia over me.

I didn't know if Lydia was safe at Cassie's, because I didn't know what was keeping Devlin & Wickham interested in her whereabouts. The Salina cops might not know specifically where Cassie's prairie house was, but if Devlin & Wickham asked them to hunt for Lydia, they'd get on Cassie's trail easily enough.

I wasn't just lonely, but also frustrated to the point of tears that I didn't have the resources to keep Lydia safe. The Canadiens could help look after Bernie. Hopefully Angela would be safe in Shreveport, but this dark expanse of land made me feel puny, ineffectual.

I started singing to hold my tears at bay. I was trying to learn "Tradimento," by the Baroque prodigy Barbara Strozzi, and I was having trouble with the key shift at the end of the first stanza. Focusing on the music kept me going until I reached the lights of Ellsworth, such as they were.

The rain had stopped by the time I reached Tales of a Traveler. I parked at the edge of the lot and walked the few blocks to a restaurant with a full bar.

The restaurant menu ran heavily to steaks and burgers. The talk of the massacre and Cassie's revulsion made me squeamish about looking at meat. I ordered vegetable side dishes, all grown by local farmers, the menu promised, but the steaks made me remember the food I'd bought earlier. There was a steak for Bear still in my motel room refrigerator. Maybe I'd leave it there in the morning for the next guest. I also had his blanket and bowls, but he seemed fine at Cassie's without them. I'd take them back to Chicago and give them to Coop when we finally connected.

My whisky came and I sipped it, relishing the warm gold taste, while I checked my messages. I had forgotten Peter's WhatsApp message, letting me know he'd arrived in Ankara.

I tried to sound upbeat in my reply. Lively day on the Great Plains. I talked to people who knew Lydia and met people who are trying to preserve the ancient prairies. I hope you had fun, too.

It was almost five in the morning in Ankara. If he had jet lag he'd see my text and write me while I was sipping my Johnnie Walker.

I leaned against the banquette, but when I shut my eyes, women's faces spun through my mind—Lydia's in all its terror; Kelly Kay Morton's anger over her son's and her own fate buried under a thick skin of apathy; Lydia's mother, defiantly announcing that she'd shot at Coop; even Filomena, the Chilean disciple of Ayn Rand. They all belonged together, my brain was trying to tell me, but I couldn't figure out why.

"Do you want those vegetables cooked more, hon?" The waitress jolted me back to the room.

I assured her that I liked them crunchy. "Sorry. Long day."

"We're closing soon, hon. You want another Scotch?"

I wanted another Scotch, but a second whisky would make it hard for me to stay awake long enough to reach Tales of a Traveler. I settled the bill and walked back along empty streets to the motel. I thought of all the times I'd cursed the traffic and noise in Chicago, but being alone in a small town, knowing someone had tried to murder me this morning, made me long for a three-block traffic jam.

Franklin Alsop wanted to know why people were shooting at me, and I couldn't come up with a good reason. Maybe my downstairs neighbor had hired a hit man to save her the trouble of getting me evicted.

Alsop had said something else that made me cautious: he hoped Eddie hadn't been as chatty with everyone as he was with me. When I reached the motel, I didn't go inside but crept around to the back, trying to walk silently in my mud-crusted boots.

About a dozen other cars were parked in the lot. I hadn't paid as close attention as I should have, but I thought five had been there when I arrived back from Cassie's prairie. I wondered what brought people to Ellsworth late at night. They couldn't all be on a mission to attack Chicago detectives.

Homey lights shone through some of the curtains. My own room was black. I should have left a light on to welcome me home. And to see if someone turned it off in my absence.

I went around to the main entrance. No one was at the front desk. It was only 9:50; even if the motel didn't run to twenty-four-hour service it was still early to shut down for the day.

Two people were in the alcove with the vending machines, but they weren't buying anything. They looked at me furtively and one of them started texting.

I left, not running, but moving at a good clip. No one was behind me when I got into the Impala, but a light came on in my room. I kept the car lights off and took off as fast as possible without laying down rubber. Still keeping dark, I circled the downtown and followed signs leading to Great Bend. When I was in the open country, I turned on my headlights, looking for a place to pull off the road that wouldn't land me in a ditch.

I came on a big gate outside a field with a clearing in front just big enough for a tractor to pull off the road. I didn't want to take the time to open a gate, but a tangle of bushes and tall grasses covered the area on either side of the clearing. I got out to inspect the land, check where the drainage ditch ended, then backed the Impala carefully behind the sheltering plants. When I got out, I ran my hands through the grasses to make the ones I'd driven over stand upright. A car was coming; I ducked into the ditch, but it didn't slow.

I crossed the road and sat in the high plants along the shoulder opposite. In the next hour, nine cars drove by, six coming from Ellsworth, three heading to it. One slowed as it passed my hideout. It shone a police-style searchlight at the gate, but my work on the grasses had apparently been good enough—they didn't stop, and the Impala's metal trim didn't catch the light.

I waited another hour, but the car didn't return and no one else was searching. I crossed the road again and climbed into the backseat. I unlaced my boots but kept them on, just in case. I lay across the seat, knees drawn up, grateful Eddie's beater was such a big old boat, and fell heavily asleep.

48
Trouble Follows Me

It was six on another gray morning when I wrenched myself awake. I was stiff, with a painful knot in my neck. I massaged it and stretched it but I felt all the sticky-eyed discomfort you get sleeping on a surface about half your size.

I laced up my boots and drove back into town so that I could shower and perhaps even get a few hours of real sleep. When I reached the motel, travelers were starting to pull out for the day, and the woman behind the desk was busy handling checkouts.

"You ready to check out?" she said when my turn came, not really looking at me.

"I want to check in. My room key didn't work when I got in at nine-thirty last night, but there wasn't anyone working the desk. I had to spend the night in my car. Now I'd like your help in getting into my room so I can get a little benefit from the bed I paid for."

Her jaw dropped and her eyes widened. "You—I—they told me you'd be—that I shouldn't—"

"So you were on duty last night? And you're still at it this morning? Why—you wanted to stick around to see if they killed me?"

"No," she whispered. "I—they—we're short-staffed. I'm pulling two shifts."

"So some people came in last night, asked for a key to my room, you gave it to them because the hotel is short of rooms and everyone is doubling up?"

"I—no. Of course not. I—I don't know what you're trying to say, but let me get you a new key so you can use your room, of course."

She took a plastic blank from a drawer and programmed in a new key.

"And can you come down to the room with me? I'd hate to walk in on some kind of disaster, which I'm afraid might be why the door wouldn't open last night."

"I—Walter—he's the building engineer—I'll get him."

She picked up the front desk phone and asked Walter to come to the front to help a guest. Walter was a middle-aged man in jeans and a T-shirt that sported a photo of a motorcycle rally.

"No one on duty at nine-thirty last night? That's strange. Bethann comes on duty at eight. We're the only hotel for quite a distance, so we stay open twenty-four-seven just in case. Maybe one of her kids needed her; she'd have been gone only twenty minutes." He sounded reproachful, as if I should have waited for her to come back.

At my room, I tried the new key. The door opened onto chaos. My clothes were flung around the room, the big window shade had been slit, the lampshades were on the floor along with the mattress. I peered into the bathroom, which lay just to the right of the entrance. The shower rod had been dismantled.

"No one has ever wrecked a room like this. What went on in here last night?" Walter faced me with a motorcycle gang expression. "You dealing drugs? You a whore?"

"Don't be crude as well as stupid." My voice was cold with anger. "I wasn't here last night. Remember? My room key didn't work and Bethann was conveniently off the premises. I'm calling the police. They can fingerprint the room—the shower rod should hold some good prints so don't touch it. We'll phone from the front desk."

Walter was quiet as I put a DO NOT DISTURB sign on

the door and pulled it shut. When we got to the front desk, Bethann was handing a departing couple a copy of their bill. Her hands were shaking, I was pleased to notice.

"Bethann, this lady here wants to call the police on account of the damage in the room. Her clothes are every which way and somebody pulled apart the lamps, the bed, even the shower. You get any complaints about the noise? The cops are going to want to know."

Before she could speak, I said, "How much did they pay you to let them into the room and then disappear?"

"I—I'm sorry." Her voice was barely a whisper. "They said—they said they were old friends from college who wanted to surprise you."

"And then they said they'd take care of my room bill, because they'd whisk me away and I wouldn't be checking out?" I suggested.

She nodded, her face white. "They didn't say 'whisk.' Some other word, but pretty much that was it. And they told me to go home for half an hour. I—" She started to cry.

"Must have been a lot of money," Walter said. "You know that was wrong. This is gonna cost you your job, Bethann. I can't cover this up for you."

"It wasn't the money so much," she whispered, "but there was something about them—they were—it was like out of a movie. Gangsters or Mafia, something like that."

There'd been two, she said when I asked.

"What did they look like?"

She shook her head. "Like men who could break your arms if you didn't do what they wanted."

"Old? Young? Did either of them seem to have on expensive clothes?"

"They had on sports coats," she said. "That's why I thought they looked like Mafia. You know, in movies they're always going around in those heavy dark suits. These two, they had jeans on but still they wore heavy dark jackets. Of course I could tell they had guns underneath."

"How?" I wondered if that was an embellishment or if she'd really noticed the shape, but Bethann looked at me scornfully.

"I've been around guns my whole life. I can tell what a holster underneath a jacket looks like."

"Let's get the police over here. I'm dead on my feet and I need to get to bed, someplace."

"Do you have to call the police?" Bethann said. "If—if you want to stay another night we can put you in the bridal suite, free of charge. I can't lose my job."

"I don't want a bridal suite; I want a room no one is going to bust into."

Walter said, "If you want to take a nap right now, I'll make sure no one bothers you."

I actually didn't want the police, in case, like the Salina cops, someone in Chicago had been on to the Ellsworth department, alerting them to my presence in the town. I was pretending to waver, when Eddie from the body shop showed up, looking worried.

"Hey, Bethann, hey, Walt, that lady from Chicago—oh." He broke off when he saw me. "You okay?"

"Did you send some thugs over here last night?" I asked.

He shook his head. "That idiot Rick who works for me. At least, he didn't send anyone, but he posted a picture of the Mustang on his Instagram page. Some guy saw it and said he wanted to make sure it wasn't his car, said it had been stolen up in Chicago. Rick didn't think he needed to check with me, met him over to the shop. Guy looked all through the car, like he'd left something in it—Rick thought maybe you stole it with his phone in it or something."

"Did she steal the car?" Walter said. "Is this what that tore-up room is about? Someone coming after—"

"I didn't steal the car. It's mine, I have the title. Or I do if the guys who came by didn't take it."

"That's the point," Eddie said. "Rick offered to call the cops and they said they'd take care of it private, so Rick told the men the only place in town you could be staying was here at the Tales. When he told me all this, I came over to see what happened. But you're okay, so I guess it was a false alarm."

Walter said, "They did come here. Bethann let them spin her a story about them being this lady's old friends. They busted the place up pretty good, looking for something. We should call the cops, except Bethann doesn't want to lose her job."

If my would-be assailants had been pawing through the Mustang, and taking apart shower rods and window shades, I had a feeling they were looking for the Creedmoor casings. While Walter and Eddie debated whether to call the cops, I asked Bethann to check me into a room.

"And don't tell anyone, even Walter and Eddie, the number."

She nodded nervously, looked at her computer, cut a key. "I—can I bring you your stuff? If you're not going to get it fingerprinted?"

"Yes. But I want my clothes washed. I don't like the idea of putting on a bra that some vermin handled."

She agreed eagerly, and I moved into a room on the

second floor, wedged a chair under the door, took a long shower, and fell into a quiet sleep. When I woke up again, a little after twelve, I found a note from Bethann pushed under the door. My suitcase was all packed with my clean clothes and Walter had it; he would take care of checking me out so that the day clerk didn't make a fuss about the payment. She had signed the message with four large hearts followed by "Thank you, thank you, thank you."

I called down to the front desk, where the woman who'd checked me in yesterday was now on duty. She hunted up Walter for me. He brought me my suitcase and said he thought everything was okay, although Eddie had taken the Impala back to the shop to make sure no one tried to fiddle with the brakes or anything.

I dressed in clean jeans and my running shoes, a welcome change from my heavy boots. I wished I had a way of getting in touch with Cassie or Alsop, to find out how Lydia was doing, but I squared my shoulders and carried my suitcase up the street to Eddie's. I was afraid I might have to plead with him to let me borrow the Impala for another few days, but to my astonishment, he'd fixed the Mustang.

"My dad's sister's husband has a cousin with a Ford dealership over to Hutchinson. I told him to get me the windows and a new steering column; I'll send him the ones I ordered when they come in next week. Just charging you labor. Parts are on the house."

Labor in Ellsworth, Kansas, ran to about half of what it did in Chicago. Maybe I'd move here when I finished figuring out who killed Leo Prinz.

"Just thought it would be best for everyone if you got out of town quick, don't you know?" He grinned shyly, only half kidding and not sure whether I could take it.

"I'm on my way," I assured him. "Ellsworth's way too rough for me—I need a tame city, like Chicago."

49
CSI

"I'm not saying you did a sloppy job, doctor. The prosecution presented ammunition from thirteen people's bodies to the jury. I'd like to know if all the bullets were examined and if they were all Wolf seven-sixty-twos. And if there were any other calibers, what were they?"

I was in the pathology lab at Salina's Santa Fe Medical Center, trying to persuade Ida Markovsky to ask the police for a complete ballistics report from the Horsethief Canyon murders. Markovsky was the hospital pathologist; she also headed the county coroner's office. She'd performed the autopsies on the victims and had supervised the chain of evidence on bullets taken from the wounded.

The hospital and the lab were new buildings, and

Markovsky seemed to have access to all the newest, shiniest machines. A couple of technicians were doing something in a corner with slides and microscopes. A hospital path lab, after all, looks more at cells from living people than bullets from dead ones.

I knew from some preliminary research that Dr. Markovsky was only forty-two, but she had a brittle, stooped body that might have passed for seventy. Her hair looked as though she had dyed it black with shoe polish. She seemed to take offense easily, although perhaps as a woman coroner she'd been disrespected too many times, and so had an array of barrage balloons in position in case a strange PI came along asking questions.

I'd driven to Salina from Ellsworth the previous day and had spent the afternoon at the courthouse, reading the transcript of the Morton trial. The transcript ran to over a thousand pages, so I focused on what I most wanted in the moment: ballistics. Prosecutors like to present every scrap of evidence to juries, including each bullet used in a murder, even if everyone agreed all of them came from the same gun. When I was with the public defender, I thought they did it to intimidate me and my client—see, we have so much evidence we can bury you.

In big shootings, it's mind numbing for everyone to

go through each bullet. At the Morton trial, they'd entered into evidence "only" sixty-five of the total seven hundred–odd rounds fired.

When the courthouse shut down for the day, I'd found a big anonymous motel on the town perimeter where I rented a room as Halina Sestieri—my Warshawski grandmother's first name, my mother's birth name. I'd parked the Mustang on a town street about half a mile from the motel, where I'd managed six hours of uneasy sleep.

Before going to bed, I'd bought a new burner phone to call Mr. Contreras from an espresso bar. Come to think of it, anyone who knew my habits would know to lie in wait for me in an indie coffee shop. I hoped my adversaries weren't that insightful.

My neighbor had been worried sick when I hadn't phoned the day before. I did my best to skate over the shooting and the abortive attack at the motel, but he's known me a lot of years; he suspected I was in more trouble than I wanted to admit.

"Who done this, doll?" he demanded. "Who wants you dead?"

"I wish I knew. Nothing is coming together for me," I said.

I was reasonably sure the goons who'd come to the motel were looking for the shell casings, but that didn't explain who'd shot at me in the first place. Devlin & Wickham, acting for—whom? Surely no self-respecting law firm would shoot someone for even the most important and wealthy of clients. Then I thought of Michael Cohen and Paul Manafort and what they'd been willing to do for their clients. A full-service law firm might do anything for a powerful person with money.

When Mr. Contreras finally was willing to end the call, I phoned Donna Lutas. "It's V.I. Warshawski. Does Clarence Gorbeck know I'm still alive?"

"I—what are you talking about?" she stuttered.

"Could you let him know that I've sent the shell casings to a forensics lab? They'll test them for prints and DNA and whatnot, but the big point is, I don't have them, so he doesn't have to waste valuable resources trying to kill me to recover them."

I waited a moment for her to respond, but she didn't seem to have anything else to say.

In the morning, I went back to the county offices, wanting to see the complete ballistics report, not just the sixty-five entered into evidence. The DA's office told me to go to the police. I gritted my teeth, crossed to the other side of the building, and went in to talk to Chief Corbitt.

Vesna, the dispatcher I'd encountered last week, was behind the front desk. She'd taken my request in to the chief. This time, instead of telling her to send me into his office, he'd emerged to perform for an audience of Vesna, the charge sergeant, and a member of the public trying to weasel out of a speeding ticket.

"You're like a horsefly at a barbecue, Warshawski. No one wants you but no one can swat you hard enough to make you leave."

"That's an interesting image, chief," I said. "Would shooting up my car be an effort to swat me hard enough to make me leave?"

"Your car got shot up? You report it to the police?"

He knew that I hadn't: Ellsworth was the seat of the next county over, they surely shared regional crime reports.

"I figure if I let the attorneys at Devlin & Wickham know about it, cops down here would hear soon enough," I drawled. "Did Clarence Gorbeck think you were important enough to tell you in person, or did he give the job to Donna Lutas?"

That made him frown and change the conversation back to my wish to see the complete ballistics report created by the Kansas Bureau of Investigation's labs.

"I don't think you have any legal standing here, Warshawski. Unless you can give me a good reason to open up police evidence to a civilian from out of state, the answer is no."

It was clear I was never going to have a good reason unless I could find a judge who would issue a subpoena for me, and I could easily imagine how much time that might take.

"One other thing, chief, before I go. The nicotine patches that helped Arthur Morton end his life—I can tell you it's hard enough to get your hands behind your back to fasten a bra, but to put eight patches there—Morton must have moved like a circus performer."

"Maybe he was, maybe he was. Jail belongs to the county. You go over there and show them how to fasten a bra." The chief had chuckled and rubbed his hands together. "Vesna! You can wipe out Harold's ticket. We got him so many times already it's like he's paid for the new coffeemaker."

The member of the public smiled sheepishly and thanked the chief. I left with what dignity I could.

The trial transcript had included Dr. Markovsky's name. I tracked her down in the morgue at the Santa Fe Hospital.

"I took out all the bullets, all that I could find," Markovsky said. "I gave them to the police, who sent them to the state forensic lab. That's all in the trial transcript, which you say you read. Now you're trying to say I overlooked some bullets? I'd like to see you in a morgue full of dead babies and mothers, ripped apart by seven-sixty-twos, and see you respect those bodies and remove those bullets. Every bullet went into a bag labeled with the name of the person we took it from, okay? If you want to double-check, go to the police and look at the lab report."

"Doctor, I won't pretend to imagine how horrible it was to deal with all the dead and wounded. The trial transcript shows that you and your staff worked as hard as the first responders after 9/11. All I'm asking is that you go to the police with me to request the complete ballistics report, not just the report the DA submitted to the jury during the trial."

"You go—you like bothering people who are working hard at what they get paid to do," Markovsky said.

"I just came from the police," I said. "The chief doesn't want to share, so I'm begging you for help. Evidence suggests there was more than one shooter at the scene; the complete ballistics report could confirm or deny that."

"What evidence?" she demanded.

"You share the report, I'll share the evidence." I held my arms out wide, expansive; we were all pals who wanted to help each other.

She wouldn't budge. She knew and was sworn

to secrecy, she was afraid of the chief and the district attorney, she was protecting the sanctity of the chain of evidence. I squared my shoulders and smiled cheerfully—never let the winner see you care.

I was pretty much out of ideas for what to do next. Drive back to Chicago, I guess. Stop in the Kansas Bureau of Investigation office on my way to see if I could persuade them to share the Morton trial ballistics report.

It was a couple of miles from the hospital to where I'd left the Mustang, farther than I wanted to walk in the middle of a muggy day. I was standing in front of the building, opening my smartphone to use the Lyft app, when a man in scrubs approached me. He was thin, older, with lanky gray hair pulled back in a ponytail and a pronounced Adam's apple that bounced as he talked.

"Uh, Miss—uh—" he floundered.

I looked at him more closely. "Were you in the path lab when I was talking to Dr. Markovsky just now?"

He nodded and looked around nervously. "I was in the lab that day."

It took me a minute to untangle the syntax. "When the Horsethief Canyon victims were brought in, you mean?"

He nodded again and flinched as the entrance doors revolved and a couple of women in magenta scrubs came out. One of them called out, "Hey, Emilio," and waved; he bobbed his head.

I suggested we move around to the side of the building, and he followed me thankfully.

"It must have been a terrible experience," I said.

"It was, it was." The Adam's apple moved like a trombone slide. "Not when we were working flat out, you understand, but afterward. So many bodies, so much blood, it was in my sleep for months and even now sometimes—I worried I wouldn't be able to keep working, but the hospital, they got us counseling, and it seemed to help."

He chewed on the inside of his cheek, and then blurted out, "Here's the thing. Why no one wants you to see the report, I mean. Someone came and took three bullets. I—no one pays attention to me in the lab, I'm like a ghost to them, being just a tech, you know."

"Do you know who took them?" I asked.

"The chief came in, Chief Corbitt, he had a strange man with him. The chief talked to Dr. Markovsky, and she let this strange man have the bag we'd tagged with the bullets from one of the dead people. The man—I can't describe him except he was out of place. He—we were all covered with blood and feeling like crap, and there he was, all clean, his hair combed."

He fingered his ponytail, as if to make his point.

"He looked around to see if me or Patti were watching—Patti's the other tech. She was writing up labels and I pretended I needed to tie my shoes."

"Did you notice which body he took the bullets from?" I asked.

"Oh, yes. I was curious, see, so after everyone left—Dr. Markovsky, she went out with the chief and the strange man—I went to the gurney. It was the Mexican guy who'd been one of the speakers. They showed his face on TV when they were reporting the story."

"Hector Palurdo," I said.

"That's right. He was in the middle of a speech, about how billionaires are turning the rest of us into their slaves, farmworkers, miners, people in ware-houses. They showed the speech on television and then the bullet going into his neck. They kept showing it, you know, a thousand times, but I couldn't stop watch-ing."

He smiled tremulously. "It's been weighing me down all this time, me knowing and not being able to say. Dr. Markovsky, she's not a great pathologist but she's good enough, most of the time. Only she cares more about what the bosses think than maybe what's best for the patients."

My informant scuttled back into the hospital, but not until I promised never to tell a living soul that I'd learned about the bullets from him.

50
A Bad Day at Black Rock

The Smoky Hill River shimmered ice-blue near the mouth of the canyon. The day was hot, which made the water flowing through the grassy plain into the canyon look cool and inviting. Right below me the river had narrowed to a creek, stained yellow-brown by the rocks it had been carving for the last million years or so.

Horsethief was small, like a miniature Grand Canyon, but it was plenty big enough for me. It had taken me close to an hour to slip and cling my way to the ledge where I was taking a breather.

I'd driven down from Salina this morning, following Highway 140, which I'd been up and down so many times in the last three days that it seemed as familiar as the Ryan back home. In fact, since the road went straight through Ellsworth, I'd stopped at Eddie's body shop to see if he had a 4x4 I could borrow.

Eddie hadn't been actively hostile, but he hadn't hired a brass band, either. "Thought you'd made up your mind to go back to Chicago."

"There's one more thing I want to see, over at Horse-thief Canyon, and then, I swear by my mother's high C, that I will be covering I-70 faster than a NASCAR driver."

"Hi-C?" He stared. "Your mother made fruit juice?"

"My mother was a singer. That was the top of her performance range."

"You are about the weirdest person ever to come into my shop." He shook his head. "Rick has an old RAV4. I'll get him to lend it to you—he owes you for what he did, putting out those pics of your Mustang."

While Rick took me to his place on the edge of town for the RAV4, Eddie hid the Mustang inside the shop. He told me to text him when I got back, in case the shop was closed; he wanted to make sure I'd actually left town. "I don't want a car that people are shooting at in my garage."

I was hoping my message to Donna Lutas about sending the bullet casings off to my forensics lab would make my stalkers lose interest in me. There was a flaw in that logic, which occurred to me only when I was back on the road: I had the casings *because* someone had shot at me.

However, I was glad to have a beater with Kansas plates as a disguise—unless, of course, Rick had already told my shooters about it. A horse box would have been even better, I realized when I got to the canyon parking lot. The whole Kanopolis park was apparently a beloved destination for riders, and when I stopped at that first ridge to look back, I watched a line of horses wade across the river and up the trail facing me.

The path I was following was so narrow and rocky that a horse might not have been able to make it. It was hard enough for me, and I could grab onto shrub branches and rock outcroppings for purchase. I was glad I had my boots but wished I'd been smart enough to buy some hiking poles before leaving Salina. I hunted in the underbrush for a dried branch to use as a makeshift walking stick. It gave me a bit more confidence on a trail turned slick by all the recent rains.

Most of the rock faces were sandstone, colored a vivid ocher that stained my hands and jeans. Now and then I'd come across a smoother surface that looked like marble, pale white with gray and pink tones. Some rock formations rose up in layers, as if a giant had built a great orange wedding cake. Others formed caves that looked as though they'd been drilled into the rock face.

When I stopped for water, I realized I was on my own. The horses had disappeared, following wider trails, and I didn't encounter any hikers.

I watched the eagles and hawks circle and swoop down to the river. An eagle flew over the gorge close to me and landed in a nest built onto an outcropping on the other side. The fierceness of its glare, and the size of its claws, made my palms tingle.

Some caves I passed were barely big enough to hold one person. Others looked as though a whole family could camp out in them with room for their horses or wolves or other pets.

I worried that I wouldn't be able to identify the place where the Tallgrass happening took place, nor yet the spot where Morton had lain in wait, but at the 142-minute mark, the riverbed opened again. The river was higher now than it had been four years ago, the ranger at the park entrance had told me, but looking down, I could still see where a bowl of land formed a natural amphitheater.

People had hiked in, biked in, ridden horses in, to be part of the Meet-Up. The ranger explained the event had gotten permits to use big buses as well. Kansas had been in the midst of a severe drought at the time; the high grasses and scrub on the river's edge today had been dried-out river bottom four years ago.

From the photos I'd examined online, I could place where the stage had been set up, its back to the rock face facing me, with the sun setting behind it. Artie Morton's cave was almost directly above me. All I had to do was hoist myself up about fifty feet of rock face. My sweaty hands kept slipping as I fumbled for holds. I had not brought the right equipment—no hiking poles, no grip gloves. I ditched the stick so I could use both hands. Right hand up, grip hard, swing knee up, find foothold, left hand up, left foot follows. Ignore pain shooting through fingers and low back. Once, I put a hand up and an angry beak pecked me. I'd come close to a nest. Not an eagle, mercifully enough—I probably wouldn't have a hand left, but I was so startled I slid back about ten feet.

I pulled myself up the last few yards and sat panting in front of the cave, my arms trembling from overwork. My hands were blistered and bleeding, and the place where the bird had pecked me had swollen up.

Looking down on the bowl, I pictured Lydia Zamir standing there with her guitar, an electric smile flowing between her and Hector Palurdo, between her and the audience. The crowd would have gathered on both sides of the river, people standing on trails as well as in the floodplain. People linked arms, they felt good singing "Savage" with Lydia.

And then, a barrage of rifle fire. Shooting a gun from a distance turns death into something unreal, so I suppose Artie Morton hadn't felt any compunction or remorse. Perhaps even pleasure at watching the small figures below scream and run in terror.

The sun had started its descent to the western horizon. Back to work. I got to my feet and pulled my work flash from my day pack. The cave had a narrow entrance that curved like labia, pink stone folded back on itself and tilted slightly toward the sky.

Imagination is not a good quality for an investigator: I hesitated at the cave's entrance, skittish about eagles or mountain lions. Or snipers. I made myself step inside, shining the flash, keeping a hand on the labia so I could vault back to the outside.

Rock dust coated the floor and walls. Maybe blood tourists were too lazy to climb this high; they contented themselves with stones from where the murder victims had fallen. At the entrance, the roof of the cave was high enough for me to stand, but it narrowed about four feet back. The lip was exactly the right height to support a rifle stand. Artie would have stashed his ammunition sometime in advance of the slaughter. He'd have lain prone, rifle sight at eye level if he propped himself on his elbows. He pulled ammo from his stash and fed it in, firing seven hundred rounds.

The trial transcript told me that a SWAT team had arrived at the cave by helicopter, but Morton had seen their approach up the river. He'd rappelled down the back of the cliff to the mountain bike he'd hidden in the brush at the bottom.

I didn't see any shell casings, or any sign at all of his presence in the cave, except for a crumpled pack of Salems. Artie had been a smoker, but I had a feeling these had been left behind by a tourist, maybe even an ordinary person who didn't know the cave's horrific history.

I climbed back through the pink stone lips and looked up to the top of the cliff. It was about fifteen feet above me, but on the south side, the rocks had crumbled enough that scrubby plants were taking root. These were tough little desert grasses that cut into my fingers but made it easier to inch my way to the top.

The top fit the contours of the cave beneath, wider at the front, tapering to a narrow ridge. The back, like the south side, was filled with grasses and spiky shrubs, leading down to a different part of the canyon.

I got down on my hands and knees and began parting grasses, moving loose shale and pebbles that might have built up in the last few years. I started at the west-facing front of the ridge, where a second shooter had probably lain, firing his shells at Hector. Three hits, the three bullets he'd taken from the morgue. He'd collected the spent casings, slipped down before the choppers arrived, mingled with the hysterical crowd. At any rate, whether he'd collected the casings or not, I wasn't finding anything up here, not even an empty cigarette pack.

I stood and surveyed the canyon below. I needed to abandon my quest and get back to the trailhead before dark. I felt discouraged and foolish in equal parts. Why had I thought there'd be any evidence after all this time?

I took a last look down at the amphitheater-shaped land at the canyon bottom. And flung myself flat before my brain registered gunfire. I scuttled backward, behind a higher rock, and peered out. A figure across the gorge, on a pillar as high as mine. A black silhouette against the sun. Another burst of fire, bullets whining off the rocks.

I moved farther back, and the ground collapsed beneath me. Dirt, rocks, detective, hurtled down the back cliff face. I grabbed at shrubs as I fell and rocks pelted my head. I landed on a bush. Rocks and dirt crashed around me.

51
Rust in the Joints

I lay in the bush's branches with my eyes shut, ignoring the thorns poking through my jeans and T-shirt. When the rockslide ended, I opened my eyes long enough to see that I was on a ledge about halfway down the back of the cliff. I knew I needed to get up, make sure my legs and arms worked, find a way to the bottom, and hike out to the trailhead, but I was tired. My hands were horribly slashed; I didn't know how I'd drive, even if I made it to the RAV4.

A shooter who wanted to kill me so badly that he had stalked me through the canyon would make sure I was dead. He would cross the river and climb to the top of Morton's cave. He'd look over what was left of the edge and fire right into me.

I would die here, ignominious, flesh stripped from

my bones by eagles. Maybe that was a noble death, feeding a great bird. Who would write my epitaph? Here lies V.I. Warshawski, detective too stupid to stay in the city she knew, chasing the criminals she understood.

I touched my head and chest with bleeding fingers. You're lucky to be alive, V.I. Don't waste it on self-pity.

I struggled free of the bush. Stood. No broken legs or arms. Lots of raw skin on my arms and hands. My day pack was still with me. I took a long drink of water. Tried my phone, but there was no signal deep in the canyon.

I scraped dirt and rocks from the edge of the ledge with my feet, looking for handholds, checking for cracks that might give way when I started my descent. The south side looked to have the easiest angle and the most out-hanging bushes. I lowered myself cautiously. And stopped. In front of my nose, covered in dirt and nearly blending with the rocks, was a shell casing. I leaned against the rock face, stuck out a hand, picked it up by the edges, and managed to shove it down the front of my jeans.

Found a place to stick my right foot, left foot. Lowered myself to a squat, grabbed a bush, found a handhold, slid my right foot down and around until it caught in a crack. Repeated with left.

Birds darted around me, lizards, insects. Every time an animal made a noise the skin on my neck crawled, thinking of the shooter. Above me? Below me? Sliding back the bolt on the rifle.

My hands slipped and I slid to another outcropping, but I was nearly at the bottom. I looked down to see a figure standing almost directly below me. I took a breath and launched myself. Landed in yet more scrub.

"Crap, Chicago. You trying to kill us both?"

The face looking down at me was a black man's. I was dizzy, stunned with the fall, and thought for a moment it was an old lover, Conrad Rawlings.

"Franklin Alsop," I croaked. "The prairie preserver. What are you doing here?" My throat was so dry my voice was barely audible, even to me.

"Looking for you, you stupid city woman. What did you think you were doing?"

"Someone was shooting at me," I said.

"You think I'm deaf? Those shots echoed up and down the gorge."

"Where is he? If he thinks I'm not dead he'll be up on top of Morton's cave ready to shoot down."

"He might have done; he was on horseback, crossing the creek, when I came along. I told him park rangers were coming in ATVs—no shooting allowed in the park—and he took off for some other part of the canyon. Can you walk? We need to get going."

I could sort of walk, meaning one foot followed the other.

"What did he look like?" I asked Alsop as I hobbled in his wake.

"Like a cowboy from a dude ranch. Big hat, saddle with fancy silver or maybe platinum cut into it. Rope and rifle across the saddle handles."

"His face," I said.

"Can't tell you. He had on that big-brimmed hat, and he wasn't very close to me. He didn't speak, either, so don't ask me what he sounded like."

The setting sun turned the canyon walls a deeper orange-red. The raptors continued their relentless sweep of the riverbed, but other birds were starting to give their end-of-day calls.

"Where are the ATVs?" I asked. My legs and feet felt like large wood blocks, as if they were prostheses that I was having trouble manipulating.

"ATVs? Oh, that. Just something I told the guy so he wouldn't shoot me. Although it's true there's no hunting allowed in the park, and if the rangers had heard the shots they'd have been there."

"What made you show up when you did?"

"I went into Ellsworth for some supplies and ran into Eddie. He told me how you'd taken Rick's RAV4 and he didn't trust you to come back with the car or your own body in one piece. He mentioned the pair who took apart your motel room the other night. Neither of us thought you were smart enough to keep yourself from getting hurt here, although if I'd thought someone was going to shoot at you, I would have brought Eddie along. I don't own any guns, but Eddie has a couple of rifles and some handguns."

I forced my wooden legs to keep moving. I was having trouble with my joints. Rust in the screws. I had told the workshop to use titanium, but they'd put in plain old iron.

Alsop was slapping my face, pouring water over me. "No sleeping on the trail. You can do this, city girl. We're closer to the end than the beginning. Keep moving those legs. One after another."

I kept moving the legs, one after another, and finally made it to the parking lot at the trailhead. Alsop said he'd bring Rick over in the morning to collect his wheels; I was going back with him.

I slept most of the way to Black Wolf, didn't see where Alsop cut across the field in his Jeep. At one point, we stopped and Alsop got out of the car. He disappeared into the dark and was gone for what felt like a long time, but I was past a point of keeping track.

"Checking. I think we're clear."

He deposited me at Cassie's place. She had me strip and climb into a sunken tub, a kind of pool in a room farther back under the hill than I'd been before. It was filled with an herbal rinse that stung my flayed skin but then began to soothe it. I drifted off to sleep again, but when she shook my shoulders I managed to wake enough to hoist myself out, butt on steps, slithering up onto the edge, into a big towel, and then half-walking, half-crawling to a bed. Drinking something hot, nasty tasting. My last conscious image was of Bear, anxiously licking my face.

52

Meanwhile,
Back at the Ranch

Murray was lying between life and death at the University of Chicago hospital. Lotty had sent me text after text. Mr. Contreras had phoned a dozen times, and there were messages as well from Sergeant Pizzello. Cassie didn't have Wi-Fi or cell service. I saw the messages only after I was in the Mustang on my way east.

After a night and a day of Cassie's unguents and potions, I was not healed but I was well enough to leave, and everyone agreed it was high time I was gone.

Franklin Alsop put it baldly: "Warshawski, I believe you mean nothing but good, but your good creates burnt offerings in the world. I know you came down here hoping to sort out Lydia's and Coop's problems, but you brought ravening hyenas with you. And I'm not sure what you found out, except that someone doesn't like you and is going to a lot of trouble to prove it. If people think there's any chance you're hiding at Cassie's, they'll come looking and then it won't just be you with a bullet, but Cassie and Lydia, too."

Cassie didn't think my hands had healed enough to drive to Chicago, but she agreed with Alsop: if people were hunting me, they'd run me to earth sooner rather than later. Literally run me to earth at her dugout.

I didn't argue the point. Lydia was starting to walk around the house and to spend time on the flagstones outside Cassie's door, with Bear as her constant companion. It was hard to know, looking at the sky, whether hawks or drones were circling overhead. Nothing I'd learned in Salina or Horsethief Canyon explained why someone would work that hard to find Lydia, but best not tempt fate.

Lydia still wasn't speaking, but when she encountered me in the big room late in the afternoon, when I was drinking a last herbal brew, she knew—maybe not who I was, but the context where we'd met. She was agitated, making small chirping noises. Alsop thought she felt me as a threat and started to bustle me out the door, but Lydia shook her head, pointed at me, then at the ground.

I was bewildered, but I sat, and then she sat, cross-legged. Her eyes were shut and she began to produce a hoarse crooning sound. She made the swanlike gesture with her arms that I'd witnessed when I found her in her hole in the ground.

"I think she misses her music," I said. "I think she wants her piano. Can you find one for her in Salina?"

"We can't carry a piano out here," Alsop said.

"She played on a toy model, which disappeared when she ran away from the TV cameras in Chicago. Hopefully some store in Salina will have one."

Cassie clapped her hands with delight. "That's a splendid idea. Franklin, can you go over tomorrow to look for one?"

Alsop made a mock bow. "When three women all want the same thing, what can I do but say yes."

The atmosphere around me lightened for the rest of my short stay. Cassie urged me to take a nap. It was close to eleven when she roused me. The Clarina Prairie was shrouded in a darkness so complete it felt like a physical weight as I once again followed Alsop through the high grasses.

Alsop had moved my car into an abandoned barn

in the Black Wolf region. When he led me to it, he adjured me not to reconnect with my smartphone until I was on the far side of Salina: if someone was tracking my GPS, they'd be less likely to trace me to Cassie.

"I still need to talk to Coop," I said, before getting into the car. "He is the one person Lydia may have talked to, to explain what she had learned from Hector before he was killed."

"I told you before—"

"Yes, even if you knew how to reach him you wouldn't let me know. If he gets in touch, let him be the one to decide. If Lydia confided in anyone, it would be Coop. And despite what you think of me and my work, knowing what secrets she's harboring will make it possible for me to create a place of safety for her in the world."

He frowned; he didn't like it. I guess, even though he'd saved my life, he didn't like me. But he thought through what I'd said and let me give him a business card.

He'd put Kansas plates on my Mustang, taken from a car abandoned near the river for some months—it might keep local LEOs from pulling me over. And so I followed unlit side roads, using a route mapped out by Alsop until I'd worked my way far enough east to be off the radar of Ellsworth or Salina cops.

As I tried to avoid the animals that crisscrossed the road, tried to stay alert to dark, unmarked cars, I worried about who had been feeding information about me to the person who'd shot at me in the canyon.

Rick, the guy who worked in Eddie's body shop, had alerted my hunters when he posted pictures of my shot-up Mustang on social media. Maybe they'd seen him as an exploitable link. He could have told anyone that I'd taken his RAV4 to Horsethief Canyon. A man on horseback would have had no trouble finding me, the city woman slipping and sliding on the muddy trails.

Everyone out here knew one another. The woman at the lovely old railway hotel sent me to Franklin Alsop. She also knew about Coop—so did the women I'd met at the state university.

Someone gunning for me wouldn't even have had to suborn a witness. Except for Cassie and Alsop, everyone seemed happy to share anything they knew with a stranger, including the man at the path lab who'd told me about the bullets. I hoped he didn't have a crisis of confidence and start talking, because that could mean his own death warrant. And could increase pressure on me.

My brain thrashed round and round, keeping me company like some horrible talk show. The trash talk took me around Salina to the next big town going east.

I followed the signs to the interstate. At a gas station near the entrance I pulled off to fill up and to check in with my smartphone. And there were the messages about Murray, the calls from Mr. Contreras, the demands of Sergeant Pizzello.

I phoned Lotty at once.

"Victoria—thank God you're okay. I've been calling your neighbor, calling Sal at the bar, no one had heard from you."

"I'm still in Kansas; I've had to go dark—I'll explain when I see you. How is Murray? What happened?"

Birders had found him yesterday morning in the Burnham Wildlife Corridor. He'd been shot and left to die.

"They took him to the University of Chicago hospital. They have a good team in place and I'm getting regular updates, Victoria, but it's a serious injury. He's only alive by a miracle—the bullet went through his lungs but missed the main arteries. What was he doing there? They said it's the same park where Bernadine Fouchard's lover was killed. Was Murray hunting down the murderer?"

"I—I was rough on him." I was fighting back tears of self-recrimination. "He didn't tell me he had a lead; I think he was trying to prove to me he was still a good investigator."

Alsop's words rattled through my head: I created burnt offerings in the world around me.

"I'm two hours from the Kansas City airport," I said to Lotty. "Can you get Max's PA to book me on the first possible flight? I'm not taking time to call Mr. Contreras—can you let him know I'm safe, at least for the moment?"

I forgot everything my father had drilled into me about road safety and put the accelerator down hard. Kansas had a speed limit, but it seemed to be more a theoretical than practical number. Even with the limited lights lining the road, traffic carried me along at close to ninety. My hands sweated on the steering wheel; the gauze Cassie had wrapped them in came loose, but I didn't stop to rip it free.

I was on the outskirts of Kansas City when I had a text from Max's PA, Cynthia; she'd booked me on the 5:50 flight to O'Hare.

I put the Mustang into long-term parking and managed to rouse a shuttle to take me to the terminal, which didn't open for another hour. I lay on a stone bench near the entrance and called Sergeant Pizzello's cell. She answered on the ninth ring, in the mumbly voice of someone awakened from sleep. I was perverse enough to find that cheering.

"Talk to me about Murray Ryerson, Sergeant," I said.

A brief silence, the sound of bedclothes rustling, checking the screen for the caller name. "Where the fuck have you been, Warshawski, that it's taken this long to call—on a mountaintop contemplating your tan lines?"

"That's a clever line," I said, "but not even my tan lines are more important than Murray Ryerson. What happened to him?"

"We got the report just about twenty-four hours ago. He was found close to where the Prinz kid turned up, but they think he was shot on the bridge over Lake Shore Drive and carried into the underbrush to die. This was deliberate and premeditated. His phone was gone, his laptop, any backup drives are all missing. What was he working on?"

"The last time we talked he was trying to make sense of some architectural drawings that showed a major overhaul of the Burnham Wildlife Corridor. He couldn't tell who had done the drawings and he didn't know if they came from the Park District or if they were a proposal from a developer. What does Gifford Taggett say?"

A car pulled up to the curb by the terminal and a

man emerged from the passenger side. I put the phone down and braced myself, but a woman got out of the driver's seat, kissed the man, and drove off. The man moved to a bench facing mine and lit a cigarette.

I had to ask Pizzello to repeat her last few comments, which were mostly irritated sputtering about my suggestion that she talk to the parks super.

"If Murray thought he was looking at plans to repurpose the park, he would have made an appointment with Taggett," I said. "Or he submitted requests under FOIA. Can't you get his emails from his server, even without his phone?"

There was a long silence at her end before she muttered, "My chief has told me to treat this as a random mugging. They won't let me ask a judge for a warrant to search his computer files. Was Ryerson working on anything else, besides drawings I've never seen? And that I can't believe have anything to do with Taggett?"

"I don't know," I said. "Ask the *Herald-Star*'s assignment editor."

The cigarette smoke was making me sick to my stomach. I hadn't eaten anything for two days besides Cassie's prairie soups. My body also resented not having caffeine.

"They had me talk to the head of their cable division, guy named Norm Bolton," Pizzello said. "He told me Ryerson was involved in this series about what happened to formerly famous Chicagoans. He was working on a painter who used to have big museum sales but is in prison for running a meth ring out of his studio."

"Meth rings always attract a lot of criminals," I said. "Maybe Murray got too close to one of them. You'd have to ask Bolton what he'd reported back."

"Everyone at the *Star* says Murray was closer to you than to anyone," Pizzello said. "He must have confided something in you."

"Closer to me? That was in a different media era, Sergeant. I see Murray twice a year, once at Wrigley Field, and again at a Blackhawks game. Every now and then we have a drink at the Golden Glow. Get over your fear of your chief of detectives and have someone talk to Taggett."

A van pulled up and a couple of people in TSA vests got out and unlocked the terminal doors. It was still two hours before my flight, but I hung up on Pizzello and moved inside, away from the smoke and thick damp air.

53

Homecoming

I wasn't one of those clever investigators with a dozen driver's licenses and identities to slip in and out of: anyone tracking me would know that V.I. Warshawski had flown from Kansas City to O'Hare, landing at 7:23 A.M. No one fired at me as I walked from Terminal Two to the L, so perhaps I was a half step ahead of my Bergara-toting shooter.

The train was packed: airport workers leaving the graveyard shift for home and road warriors heading into the city for a day of meetings. I wedged myself into a corner at the end of the car and dozed until we reached the stop near my office.

In the coffee shop across from my building, while I greedily downed shots of espresso, I used my phone to look at my office's security footage for the past two days. A man had come around looking at the parking lot and checking the front door locks earlier this morning; he'd been there yesterday as well. Not someone in expensive clothes, just an ordinary street thug in a sports coat and blue jeans, with a bulge suggesting a gun.

I took my third espresso to the front of the coffee shop and scanned the street. It seemed clear; my stalkers must have lost track of me while I was at Cassie's and weren't sure whether I was home or away.

My shadowy companions had money to burn—they carried expensive rifles and ammo; they hired high-end hackers to break into Artie Morton's computer; they went into canyons and morgues and had thugs on call to shoot out car windows or take over motels. Maybe they were monitoring my home and my neighbors' phones, but I couldn't worry about every possible danger or I'd stop acting altogether.

I called Mr. Contreras to assure him I was safely back in Chicago. He needed a long conversation. I extricated myself as gently as possible, with a promise that we'd catch up before the end of the day.

Inside my office I didn't turn on lights: even on a bright August day they'd show through the skylights. I went straight to the shower in the back of Tessa's studio for a scrub down. I changed into the last pair of clean jeans and socks in my carryall.

I used two monitors to lay out all the documents and notes I'd kept since Bernie's panic-stricken call after finding Leo Prinz's dead body, an event that felt so remote it might have happened back when the Smoky Hill River started carving Horsethief Canyon.

I made notes by hand, using the Aurora fountain pen my mother had received on graduating from secondary school. I keep it in my office safe and use it only when I want to write carefully, in ink.

Murray, Leo Prinz, Simon Lensky

I wrote:

All connected to the mysterious plan to repurpose the Burnham Wildlife Corridor and adjacent lakefront. Larry Nieland, Nobel Prize–winning economist, had come to the SLICK meeting with a well-dressed man who had not been introduced.

Murray had said the mechanical engineer who drew the plans was named something like Mina Y. Punter. The letters on Leo's photo of the drawing had been as blurry as the photo itself. Maybe the name was Mona, not Mina. Perhaps SLICK's Mona Borsa was involved in the lakefront plan but pretended not to know about it. I had pegged her more as Taggett's cheerleader than as a major player, but I could be wrong.

I uploaded my copy of Leo's flash drive onto my desktop monitor and looked for the name of the mechanical engineer, printed by hand in a Gothic calligraphy. The script was hard to read, but I couldn't enlarge it too much without losing resolution. The first name was clearest: Minas, not Mona or even Mina. Minas y Puentes.

Spanish. Not the name of the mechanical engineer who'd drawn the plan. The name of one of the Chilean firms on Larry Nieland's website. I hadn't paid attention to it when I first looked him up, but now I went into the business press to find out everything I could on Minas y Puentes.

Their website mentioned projects in China, Brazil, India, one in Southern California. The company had been formed in the 1980s by a merger of Puentes y Torres with Minas Aguilar de Tocopilla.

One Guillermo Quintana was the president; Filomena Quintana Aguilar was the company secretary. I knew that name, as well: she was the woman who'd been on Global's *Digging up the Deep State* with Larry Nieland. Aguilar would have been her birth name,

Quintana her married name. She'd married Guillermo and her family's mining business married Guillermo Quintana's Bridge and Tower company.

I wrote all the names down carefully, in block letters, feeling as though a large explosion might occur if I made any sudden moves. The mines of Tocopilla. When Hector had come home from visiting them, he'd been furious about the conditions, furious with his mother—for what? Not telling him what she knew about the mines? Not telling him that his family was connected somehow to a Chilean mining heiress?

I tried to think it through. Did Palurdo have a sister with the same name as the mine owner's? Was the mine owner Jacobo Palurdo's sister? Maybe Jacobo had changed his name when his sister married the company boss? Then he thought she was dead to him and left Chile in disgust?

My stomach muscles were so tight that they were pushing my diaphragm up, making it hard to breathe, let alone think.

I searched for information about Guillermo and Filomena.

The oldest story was in *El Universal,* a Chilean paper. A story in 1974 covered the lavish wedding of Guillermo Quintana to Filomena Aguilar. The photos, digitized from microform, were grainy, but you could see Aguilar's satin gown, the two page boys in miniature soldiers' uniforms holding her long train, the floor-length veil pinned to her swept-up blond hair.

Guillermo was darkly handsome in a military dress uniform. The ceremony had been held at the cathedral of St. James in Valparaíso, with four bishops presiding. Besides the page boys, the bride was attended by eleven cousins and friends. The bride's father, Fernando Aguilar, beamed with pride. The bride's brother, also named Fernando, was not at the wedding: an acute stomach virus, the society editor said they'd been told.

I traced the couple through some dozens of stories in Spanish. Both had studied economics at the Pontificia Universidad in Santiago. Guillermo joined the army as an officer, he'd been part of the Pinochet government, developing an initiative to privatize health care and Chile's pension system, and when Fernando Aguilar died, he'd been made chief executive officer of Minas y Puentes. Filomena did hands-on work managing the Tocopilla mines before she discovered her gifts as a public speaker and television presenter.

A photo in the business presses showed Quintana shaking hands with various New York officials and with a couple of high-rolling developers when Minas y Puentes broke ground for a luxury complex in Brooklyn. I stared at the screen so long that my eyes began to hurt.

Guillermo was the man in the beautiful shirt at the SLICK meeting. Every person who'd seen him had remembered his clothes more than his face: his face was cold, indifferent—it didn't invite people in, and so they looked instead at his clothes.

I looked again at the blurry blueprint on my monitor. Minas y Puentes had drawn up plans for a luxury development on Chicago's South Side. Was Filomena Quintana's old pal Larry Nieland involved in the plan to repurpose the lakefront through his Capital Unleashed consulting firm? Or had he come to the SLICK meeting with Guillermo to support his friends?

I went back to Nieland's website, where his face, framed with unruly silver curls, beamed on the world like Santa Claus. Nieland was on the boards of nine companies, four in South America, five in the United States. Only one of the South American companies was publicly traded. Its principal shareholders included Minas y Puentes, and Capital Unleashed.

Capital Unleashed was Nieland's privately held company. Nieland had been Filomena Quintana's professor and mentor. And now here they all were together, happily divvying up Chicago's lakefront.

I imagined the amounts of money that Capital Unleashed dealt with—hundred-dollar bills filled large black cauldrons, the kind witches hover over in cartoons. Larry and his curated clients leaned over them, peering anxiously to see if the capital was cooked enough to be unleashed.

Had Nieland invited Minas to invest? Had Minas had the brainstorm and involved Nieland? It didn't really matter. However it came about, Park Super Taggett was easily persuaded to get on board with the project. Maybe Taggett had been thinking of a new beach at Forty-seventh Street, and Nieland saw this as a great opportunity to turn an underpopulated area into a billionaire's private preserve.

How had Simon Lensky ended up with a copy of this proposal? I couldn't imagine the SLICK trio as coconspirators. They were ordinary people who volunteered to help care for Chicago's parks. Taggett would have enlisted them to sell the Forty-seventh Street beach to the community; he wouldn't have involved them in a development project on the scale this blueprint suggested.

My best guess was that Taggett hadn't realized the drawing was in a packet he'd given Simon to help with the beach presentation. Simon fussed over it as he studied all his papers before that last fatal SLICK meeting.

I thought back to the dinner at the African Fusion café, right before the meeting, where the trio were nervous about my seeing any of their documents. I could imagine Mona, maybe even Curtis, worrying over what the drawing meant. Mona would perhaps have favored a direct question to Taggett, but none of them knew what to do. And then Leo had forced everyone's hand when he'd knocked all Simon's drawings to the floor.

Leo had snapped photos because he'd seen enough to be troubled. And when Simon revealed how troubled Leo was—to whom? To Mona Borsa? To Gifford Taggett himself?—someone had dealt expeditiously with the problem. They had killed Leo, gotten rid of his phone, his computer, scoured both his apartment and Bernie's to make sure there weren't any pesky little flash drives or printouts lying around.

And then they realized Simon must know they were behind Leo's murder, so he had to be eliminated as well.

"Oh, Murray, what did you do?" I whispered. "Did you submit a FOIA to the Park District for a copy of the plans? Or for correspondence between Taggett and Nieland or Taggett and Quintana? And so you, too, became a threat? Don't die, don't die, don't die."

I needed to see Lotty. I needed her and Max to use their influence to get a guard on Murray's room down at the university hospital.

I badly needed a car. I didn't want to rent one—the longer I could go without putting out an electronic signal that I was home and in action, the better. I ran through a list of the friends I could go to for help, but none of them owned more than one car. The Streeter brothers, who often helped me with surveillance projects, had an extra van they might lend me. It had bulletproof siding but didn't maneuver well. I'd give them a call if nothing else came to me.

It wasn't until I was closing my files that I remembered Angela Creedy's Subaru. She'd left her car keys with me so I could move the car on street-cleaning days. It had been ten days since she and Bernie had left Chicago; I hoped she hadn't already collected parking tickets—I'd have to pay them.

I took a taxi to Evanston. Angela's Subaru was a block away from the house where she and Bernie had been living. It was the perfect car for my needs: it was old and dirty, free of parking tickets, and it started on the first try. The only downside was that the seat adjustment was locked and Angela was five inches taller than me. Sitting bolt upright to drive would keep me awake.

I went first to Beth Israel, the hospital in Chicago's Uptown neighborhood where Lotty had her privileges. Max Loewenthal was the executive director, but was also a friend from Lotty's refugee childhood—and now that he was widowed, her lover as well. It was his PA who'd booked my flight this morning. If Lotty was at her clinic, a call from the hospital number would go unnoticed.

Cynthia was delighted to see me and happy to track down Lotty, who turned out to be in the hospital, making rounds. Cynthia put me in Max's conference room to wait, where I could entertain myself either with Beth Israel's annual report or journals from the American Hospital Association. Half an hour later, Lotty lifted my head from an article on a "Comprehensive curricular blueprint for resident education."

"I see you've found the perfect substitute for Ambien," she said dryly, but when she looked at me her expression turned to alarm. "Victoria! You didn't tell me you'd been injured. You need to be in bed yourself."

I blinked back tears: it had been a while since I'd been greeted with love and concern instead of being told I turned people into burnt offerings. Lotty examined my hands and arms, sent Cynthia to the pharmacy with an order for antibiotic liniment and bandages, and demanded an account of my week away.

I gave her the highlights and skirted lightly over my fall from the clifftop in Horsethief Canyon. "How is Murray?"

"A little good news this morning: he was able to

breathe for five minutes without the respirator. They'll keep upping that, but they're keeping him in a protective coma—too much blood loss, too big a shock to his system."

"Lotty, he was working on something that I pointed him to. It's—no matter what the police say, this wasn't a random mugging. He was shot to try to keep him from digging into a construction project, some scam between the Park District and a Chilean developer. I want to get a guard at his room, and I'd prefer no one knows he's improving, however minuscule the improvement is."

She kept her hands on my shoulders. "We don't have any authority in the university hospital, but I'll ask Max to make some calls. Do you think his company, the Global people, could they provide a guard?"

"I'd like to keep his Global people as far from him as is possible," I said. "It's even possible that they're the ones who attacked him to begin with." I told her about Norm Bolton and his efforts to monitor what I knew about Lydia Zamir.

"But that has nothing to do with the park," Lotty objected when I finished.

"I know. But Murray was trying to get permission to run the story and Bolton turned him down. Murray must have connected some dots, or asked too many questions—I don't know. And the police tell me his phone and laptop and so on are missing. The cops could get a search warrant for Murray's server, but they won't."

I didn't like that part of Pizzello's story one little bit. Taggett, the chief of detectives, Bolton—they were connected and not in a good way.

54

His Guy Friday

Peter Sansen had been trying to reach me. He missed me, he wanted to know I was safe.

I called him, but he was offline. I wrote a long message, trying not to sound whiny or scared. I wrote that I'd been shot at, then deleted it—he was six thousand miles away, and he'd be worried and feel impotent. Instead I wrote about the canyons and caves I'd seen in Kansas; I would never think the state was flat again. I'd met an herbal healer who lived in a dugout. She used solar panels to run her house. And I missed him. Missed having someone put his arms around me and give me comfort in the night. Missed someone who admired what I did and how I did it—*you do these things so well,* Peter often told me.

Three of my paying clients were demanding results. They were justified in complaining, but I felt like someone in a batting cage bombarded with balls I couldn't swing at fast enough. I called my clients to say I was making good progress on their problems and would have reports by the end of the week. If I lived that long.

It scared me when I thought about how my business was suffering while I wrestled with a giant octopus—one arm the Burnham Wildlife murders, another Lydia Zamir's problems, a third the mysterious stranger taking shells from the morgue where Hector Palurdo lay. Murray, SLICK, Larry Nieland, Guillermo and Filomena Quintana. It scared me when I thought of Murray lying close to death: someone wanted me dead, too.

Bernie and Angela, another arm. In the course of the morning, I heard from both mothers: Arlette called to say she was having trouble keeping Bernie caged up in the Laurentians; when did I think she could return to Chicago? Angela Creedy's mother had sent a similar message from Shreveport. I put the mothers in touch with each other—why didn't Arlette invite Angela to escape the muggy Louisiana summer in the mountains of Quebec?

I wished I could go, too. Way better than driving around in the muggy heat half asleep. My back was bugging me from leaning forward in the Subaru. I pulled into a strip mall where I picked up a cushion that would move me closer to the Subaru's steering wheel. I found eye drops in the pharmacy section—maybe lubricating my tired eyes could create the illusion of sleep. The sight of myself in the restroom mirror was unsettling. Despite my shower this morning, my T-shirt was already wilted and my hair had clumped into wads. I'd have to take the time to go home to change. Run the risk of being spotted. Talk to Mr. Contreras, try to avoid my bed.

Conversations with my neighbor are never short, but they can also be healing. Even though I had a list of people I needed to see, the hour we spent together in the garden helped me feel more like myself and less like a tsunami of hazardous waste. Mitch and Peppy greeted me with little whines of pleasure, we ate sandwiches with tomatoes picked from Mr. Contreras's plants, and we caught up on the trivia of daily life—his grandsons, his wins and losses at the track, my news from Peter Sansen, news from Bernie, a raccoon I'd seen on my way to collecting Angela's car. The hard thing about being on your own is no one is interested in those little things.

I took a second shower and changed into business casual clothes—summer-weight beige trousers, a white short-sleeved cotton top, and flat-soled shoes. I opened my bedroom safe and looked at my gun. People were shooting at me, after all. But if the man who'd tracked me into Horsethief Canyon was perched on a rooftop somewhere with his Bergara, my handgun wouldn't be much use. I locked the safe with the Smith & Wesson still inside.

It was mid-afternoon by the time I reached the *Herald-Star*'s offices. They were housed in an old warehouse along the Chicago River where they could see their rich parent's headquarters. Global One, where the streaming and cable and talk shows and so on took place, was up above, along Wacker Drive. Before I talked to Bolton, I thought I'd start with Murray's co-workers at the paper.

Despite the dingy building, the *Herald-Star* still had a security protocol. I showed my ID and asked to speak with Gavin Aikers, the regional news assignment editor. "Tell him I want an update on Murray Ryerson's projects."

Aikers came out to the front desk in person and ushered me inside, one hand on the small of my back, the power play. He was a short stocky man, muscled, not fat, with a shock of brown curls that made him look more cherubic than he probably was.

He clucked his tongue over Murray's fate. "The paper is offering a twenty-thousand-dollar reward for finding his attackers. Murray is one of our most valuable investigators."

The *Star* used the open floor plan so beloved of management, meaning a maximum of noise with a minimal possibility of concentration. Maybe this is why the paper didn't do much serious journalism anymore—too hard to follow the thread of a complicated story when the sound level was equivalent to an active runway at O'Hare.

As an assignment editor, Aikers rated a small office. It wasn't soundproofed, but when he closed the door, we could at least hear each other.

Aikers's face was solemn. "It's a shocking business. The city's become so dangerous—"

"Especially for a journalist. That wasn't a mugging, Mr. Aikers. Murray was looking at documents connected to the Park District's plans to expand the beach at Forty-seventh Street. A kid named Leo Prinz who was looking at plans for that beach was murdered there a month ago. Did Murray file any stories about the park or the murder?"

"What do you mean?" Aikers asked.

I smiled, more a sneer, that I hoped looked as ugly as I felt. "Since I'm not a journalist, maybe I don't have the jargon right. You know how it is in Chicago—you want to build something, you have to see that the right parties get their campaign funds bulked up. It's not what you do or who you know, but how much you can pay."

Aikers shifted uncomfortably, but no respectable journalist could deny the state's and city's infamous unwritten "pay to play" code.

"Had Murray written about any payers or players? Did he tell you about Norm Bolton's plan to film a joint search for Lydia Zamir? Did Murray find something Bolton or Global's lawyers want kept secret? You're his editor, so you must have seen what he was working on."

Aikers drummed his thick fingers on the desktop. "If he'd written anything, it was preliminary, not something he was ready to show me. I hoped—Norm hoped—he'd sent early drafts to you, since he trusted your judgment."

"I can't think of a single time in all the years I've known him where Murray shared a draft with me. He's like writers everywhere—he wants all the glory."

"We hoped he'd told you what he was working on. You were involved with the Zamir woman. You were involved with the Prinz kid's murder. You must know something!"

I shook my head. "If I knew anything I wouldn't be here trying to get information from you. Sergeant

Pizzello told me that Murray's phone and laptop are gone. Had he submitted FOIAs for information about the Forty-seventh Street beach expansion?"

"We don't know," Aikers said. "Murray's status— Pulitzer, decades of experience—he could follow a story where it took him until he was ready to share. Everyone says he was closer to you than anyone; we've all been sure you knew what he was doing."

"The police said the same thing in the same words, which makes me guess that's a line you fed them. I've known Murray Ryerson a long time and we covered some big stories together, but I'd say we were competitors more than BFFs. When he stopped being able to work on white-collar crime our paths stopped crossing, so I don't know what he was doing, besides that series on Chicagoans who used to be famous. Was he investigating the murders of the two men involved in the meeting where the plan was presented?"

"Murray mentioned their deaths, but the police had identified a suspect. A homeless guy who wanders the lakefront with his dog. I didn't think we should get involved in looking for him," Aikers said stiffly.

"But you still cut Murray a lot of slack and let him go where his nose led him?" I couldn't hide my contempt. "Anyway, now that he was left for dead in the same place as Prinz, you've assigned a reporter to trace a connection between their deaths and the attack on Murray, right?"

"The police are treating it like a copycat attack," Aikers said. "You know how it is with criminals— they want to be on TV, so they try to copy high-profile crimes and methods. Murray had a good rapport with the police and he said you did, too, being a cop's daughter. That's why I'm asking you to tell me what you know about the investigation—whether this sergeant you mentioned has said anything that suggests a suspect."

"Not how Hildy Johnson got results," I said.

"Hildy who?" Aikers repeated.

"Johnson. *His Gal Friday.* She would have been embarrassed to shift her reporting responsibilities onto the cops."

Maybe I should have taken a nap after all. I was having trouble keeping my temper under control.

"Norm Bolton talked to you, didn't he?" I changed the subject. "He had this idea about filming me trying to find Lydia Zamir after she disappeared. He was trying to get me to believe that Global felt guilty when she fled in terror, first from the TV cameras and then from the hospital."

"We did," Aikers protested. "Responsible, I'd say, not guilty. Murray had written the story, so it was a

Star issue more than a Global one. Norm and I talked it over together."

"So Murray could have been looking for Zamir and run afoul of whoever has her. Assuming she's even still alive, of course."

Aikers fiddled with a pen cup. "Everyone says that the man who killed the two guys in the park snatched the Zamir woman and has her hidden someplace. What do you know about that?"

"Nothing at all." I got to my feet. "When you next talk to Bolton, ask him if he's on the board of Minas y Puentes. He may not be grand enough, but he probably knows if your great-grand-boss belongs."

"Now what the fuck are you talking about?"

"Oscar Taney. He's Global's majority shareholder, in case you are really as ignorant as you're pretending to be."

55
Knitting the Raveled Sleeve of Care

I was outside, looking at the oily rainbows on the Chicago River, when someone tapped my arm. I whirled, braced for a blow, but it was Luana Giorgini, the *Herald-Star*'s entertainment and style editor. She was a youngish woman who wore the extremes of contemporary fashion without looking absurd. Today she was in a knee-length dress with a black-and-white photo of a Greek frieze on the bodice; the filmy skirt was printed with bold red flowers. She sported knee-high red boots and a glittery red clip in her thick hair that spelled TOUGH AND TOUGHER, yet she still looked like someone who could run the organization without help.

"Vic, did you learn anything from Gavin?"

I made a face. "He's a lying SOB who will jump through any hoop Norm Bolton holds out for him."

"Besides that. I'm worried sick about Murray. We all are, but we can't find out anything."

"I can't tell you more than whatever bulletins the hospital is putting out. He's still alive and is breathing off respirator for a part of each hour, but they don't know if—if there's long-term damage. Aikers was trying to get me to tell him what Murray was working on, but I don't know. Can you get into his files through your work network, see if he'd kicked open a hornet's nest?"

She shook her head, dark eyes full of fear. "I got our IT guy to do that when I heard about the attack. Vic, all his files had been wiped clean. It was done remotely, that was the only thing that Theo—our IT expert— could tell me. He said it was very skillful. Someone broke in, maybe using Murray's phone if they stole it, and took out, well, really, decades of work. Even files that are publicly available, like his work that got the Pulitzer. This is really frightening."

I rubbed my eyes. Despite the drops I'd bought, they were itchy with fatigue.

"Luana, I know a lot of what's going on, but not everything. If I called you, or texted you, and asked you to insert a paragraph into the online paper, could you? And do you have a personal email, not tied to the paper?"

She nodded, lips trembling. "Murray could be annoying, but he was just about the best journalist I ever met. He was great with women in the work setting. Mentoring in the important ways—he'd share sources, show you how to improve a pitch, all those things."

She gave me a convulsive hug and darted back into the building. A minute later my phone dinged—a text from Luana with her personal account.

The area around the *Herald-Star* offices was in transition from a central depot for food and beverage wholesalers to the town's hottest new residential neighborhood. Buildings were going up, warehouses were being repurposed to loft apartments, and chichi restaurants were springing up like nettles on a Kansas prairie.

I'd tried to park far enough from the paper that I could see if anyone was accompanying me, but streets and sidewalks were so crowded it was impossible to check. A block from the Subaru I ducked into a convenience store. I studied the faces that passed, but no one seemed to be slowing or paying attention to the store. I bought a *Herald-Star* and a bottle of Gatorade, lingered for a long moment in the doorway, and finally went to the car.

I decided I had to use my phone, that I couldn't operate if I worried about surveillance. Everyone who might want to find me must know by now that I was back in town, and it doubled the amount of time I spent in transit if I kept looking over my shoulder for tails. Besides, at least one of my assailants had a sniper rifle, which meant I'd have to huddle fearfully in a basement to keep safe.

I stayed in the car to make calls, despite the ugly remarks from other drivers who wanted me to move on so they could have my parking space. I first checked in with Max's PA, Cynthia, on whether they'd been able to set up security for Murray at the university hospital.

The hospital would let me post a guard if they had proper identification and received clearance from the head of university security, Cynthia reported.

I could see their point, but if I wanted to hire the Streeter brothers to look after him, it would take at least a day to work it out with the university. Unwelcome fingers of panic clawed at me again.

Before putting my phone away I scrolled through my message list. Five more from active clients. Junk calls. And one from area code 785, which covered the chunk of Kansas I'd been visiting.

Franklin Alsop had left a terse message; would I call him as soon as possible. I hoped that meant Coop had reappeared, but when I used one of my burn phones to call back, he had a demand.

He'd bought a piano for Lydia but it had only increased her agitation. However, it had also made her say the first words he or Cassie had heard from her: she wanted her own, old piano. She needed it; it was essential.

"Mr. Alsop, that's not possible. She lost it weeks ago and it is gone. I scoured the park where she was hiding—I was looking for murder weapons, but I would have seen that piano if it had still been around."

"I'm asking you to take one more look. You risked your life looking for one cartridge in Horsethief Canyon. And you found it. I thought you were out of your mind—still think so, actually—but you had luck on your side. Take another chance on your luck. No one will shoot you in a public park."

"One of my oldest friends was shot near that park three days ago and a kid I knew was killed there," I said.

"I can't save you in Chicago, but I did save you in Kansas," he said. "If you'd heard Lydia struggle to get out the word 'essential'—it made her sweat—you'd be in that park right now."

"This from the man who says I bring destruction wherever I go," I said bitterly.

"Unjust," he said. "I shouldn't have judged you when I don't know you well, but one thing that shines through about you is you are resolute in going after a goal, even if the goal looks crazy to an outsider. I'm asking—pleading—that you treat Lydia's piano with the same kind of resolution."

"Aw, gee, Mr. Alsop. Who could resist that kind of soap? I'll add it to the queue."

I had just enough energy to leave the Subaru a block from my office, to check the security footage on my phone before unlocking the door, and then I gave in to the summons from the daybed in my storeroom. I locked myself inside, turned off my phone, and slept.

In my dreams, Lydia Zamir was under the viaduct, wearing a black flowing concert gown, playing "Savage" on her little red piano. Murray was lying in a coffin next to her. Lydia looked at me with a ferocious grin and said, "Prove you do more good than harm."

Still, when I woke, my thinking became clearer. If Murray needed a bodyguard, I could be that person. It would keep me away from my apartment, in case the taunts I'd flung at Murray's boss prompted someone to come for me. This meant Mr. Contreras would be safe. Staying with Murray would bring me to the South Side. In the morning, I could go back to Forty-seventh Street to look for the piano.

I collected the industrial protective gear I keep in my storeroom: boots, waterproof coveralls, hard hat. I'd lost my work flash on the cliff top in Horsethief Canyon, so I swung by a hardware store for a new one. Also an industrial-quality protective mask. A trowel. If the piano still existed, I knew where it was.

56
The Luck Holds

The hospital made it disturbingly easy for me to stay with Murray. If I wanted to hire a bodyguard to protect him, I had to go through their security office, but saying I was his sister meant they let me spend the night in his room. They even brought in a giant recliner for me to sleep in.

The hospital had shaved Murray's beard, I guess to make it easier to stick tubes into him. He looked naked, defenseless with his face bare. I got in bed next to him, cradled him, arms carefully tucked underneath all the drips and lines, and sang the same lullabies I'd done for Lydia.

"I'm on the trail, Murray. Don't die. You need your name on the byline. Wish you could tell me whose cage you rattled."

I dozed for the rest of the night in the big recliner, never getting into the deepest sleep, but resting in between visits from staff to check his status. No one tried to kill him, but it did make me nervous, knowing how easy it was to gain access to the room. I left at seven when the day shift came on duty, but I gave the floor head my details.

"If he wakes up, or if—anything changes—"

I couldn't finish the sentence, but she smiled reassuringly and promised that everything would be fine, but they would call me if needed.

I was still wearing the business casual clothes I'd had on when I left home yesterday. When I drove up to Forty-seventh Street, only the drugstore was open. I bought four pint water bottles as well as a Sox T-shirt. At least I could leave my blazer and silk shirt in the car.

When I walked up the stairs to the Forty-seventh Street train platform, a handful of commuters was waiting for their train. They were attached to their devices and didn't pay any attention to me as I pulled on my gear. Even this early in the day, the August sun was merciless. Inside my rubber clothes I felt as though I'd sealed myself into a turkey roaster. I drank most of one of my pints. Slid to the ground. Crawled underneath the platform.

The mound of garbage was sickening. The things

people discard—bottles, rotting food, plastic bags, used train tickets, shoes, T-shirts, part of a cooktop, house keys, tire rims. Everything was coated in a slimy film from the disintegrating leaves and plants that the wind swept in.

The garbage under the platform had a life of its own; each time a train roared past, the layers shifted. Each time a train stopped, another shower of paper and food fell down. Despite the heat, I was glad to be covered in rubber.

I began digging the mound apart. My trowel was so small it felt as though I were emptying Lake Michigan with an eyedropper. My raw palms started bleeding inside my work gloves. But Alsop had been right on both counts: this was an insane undertaking, and my luck came through. I found one of the red plastic legs. And two yards or so beyond that, the case and keyboard, miraculously intact.

I edged out, clutching the instrument to my body with one hand, bracing myself against the platform joists, until I reached the safety of the stairwell. A young couple climbing the stairs looked at me sideways but forbore any comments until they thought they were out of earshot.

"Isn't that the homeless woman who's been on the news?" the youth said.

"God, she smells terrible!" his companion replied.

I did smell terrible, but I felt worse. I put the piano down to take off my outer layer, but then I had to carry the filthy gear in one arm while I lugged the piano in the other. I shuffled along Forty-seventh Street, my gait the same as the other homeless roaming the street looking for cigarette ends or dropped change.

There was a UPS store in the strip mall where I could express the piano to Alsop. I took the time to drink another pint of water and to sponge off some of my worst stench with a third bottle.

When I lifted the piano, the top came off in my hands. Toy pianos aren't designed to come apart—they don't have soundboards or strings that need tuning. As I fitted the cover back onto the case, I saw an eight-by-ten envelope taped to the cover's underside.

Lydia had taken the piano apart. She had tucked an envelope into it. My piano is essential, she'd said to Cassie and Alsop, sweating to produce the word. Essential, because she had packed a secret inside it.

My fingers were trembling as I pried the envelope free. I drove home, hoping my luck would still hold and no one would attack me there. Maybe Donna Lutas's presence would keep her boss or his pals from siccing their hellhounds on me. I came in through the alley, through the back gate and up the stairs to my kitchen entrance. I could hear Mitch and Peppy yearning to be with me as I passed Mr. Contreras's back door, but I didn't stop.

I put all my clothes, the protective gear, my good trousers, the Sox T, into a big garbage bag. I'd sort it out later. I showered and shampooed and wrapped myself in a towel. I put on a pair of light cotton gloves, the kind you use for handling photographs, and gently pried the envelope lip from the body.

57

The Affectionate Aunt

The top two documents were written in Spanish by
someone with a firm hand, black ink on gilt-edged
cream stock. A gilt monogram on both was grimy and
chipped with age. Both held dirty fingerprints and
thumbprints, showing where someone with dirty hands
had clutched them.

The one phrase I was sure I knew was "*Querido
hermano,*" my dear brother. Elisa Palurdo said that
Jacobo's only sibling had been his sister, Filomena,
who'd been murdered.

Despite the similarities between Italian and Spanish,
there was too much I couldn't understand. A friend from
childhood had died; he was (I thought) a Communist,
union organizer, not a patriot, but that was about it.

The third paper was in English, the same gilt-edged

stationery, the same firm hand, but with fresher ink; it had been written more recently, and was addressed to "My dear Lydia."

I hope you will excuse my addressing you in a personal manner, but you are essentially my niece. My nephew's death is a terrible tragedy and I am myself deeply grieved. I met Hector only once but his ardent spirit and sensitive intelligence made a deep impression. He was the son of my only brother, and so his loss is painful not just for you but for me as well.

Dear Lydia, I would ask you to be more temperate in what you say on paper. You cannot say, for example, that I have no understanding of what bloodshed means. This shows only that you do not understand the melancholy history of bloodshed in Hector's father's homeland. Hector's father chose to abdicate responsibility for his people but I have stayed here to be consumed by responsibility.

I know that there were disagreements in the family about Hector's actions at the mine. I put his behavior to his inexperience. At no time was his life threatened by any of his cousins. Dear Lydia, you must not let your mind be unsettled by your grief. Do not descend into the conspiracy theories so beloved throughout the Americas. If an economist makes a dramatic assessment of a financial situation, such an opinion does not make him a murderer. And you should not believe everything you see in the Rettig Report. It was created to pacify people who would rather re-create bloodshed than learn to live in a global economy.

If you travel to Tocopilla it will be my pleasure to show you the scenes of Hector's father's childhood, as I showed them to Hector. But even if Hector left a will, naming you as his heir, the lawyers assure me that he did not take steps to prove his identity in Chile and so his claim to be a first-order heir has no standing in Chilean courts.

Believe me, *querida sobrina, tu tía cariñosa*

The signature was a set of bold curlicues, which I finally deciphered as a capital *F* with a lot of other letters superimposed.

The final document was handwritten on the letterhead of Samantha Watkins, JD, with an office in the Board of Trade Building.

I have not been able to persuade the Chilean courts to reconsider their decision. Call me if you wish to discuss. SW

I placed the papers gingerly onto my dining room table, as if they were magical and might vanish in a cloud of smoke.

Lydia had written to the woman with the dear brother after Hector's murder. The letter was signed, *tu tía cariñosa*—your affectionate aunt. Lydia had accused the aunt of—what? She'd been intemperate in her language—she had accused the aunt, or an economist of something heinous.

I used a toothbrush to remove some of the crusted dirt from the monograms on the three documents. Looking at them side by side, I reconstructed the letters: *Q* in the middle with *F* and maybe *A* on either side.

A lot of Spanish women's names start with *F.* Flor, Fernanda, Felisa. And many surnames start with *A* or *Q.* But the probability was that these documents had been written by Filomena Quintana Aguilar.

Filomena's brother, Fernando, had skipped her wedding to Guillermo Quintana. On the death of her father, Filomena's husband took over the senior leadership position at Minas y Puentes. None of the news stories I'd found made any further mention of the brother, either in the society or the business news. No death had been reported. He had evaporated, as if never born.

The idea dangling at the back of my mind seemed

absurd, but somehow the only possible explanation. Using a burner phone, I called Stu Shiffman, the Latin American scholar who'd been Hector Palurdo's college roommate.

"I've found some documents in Spanish," I told him, brushing aside the usual social niceties. "I think they're important—essential—to knowing what happened to Hector. I don't read Spanish well. If I email them to you, would you have time to look at them soon? Such as—as soon as you get them?"

I'd been so abrupt he had trouble figuring out what I was saying. I calmed down enough to explain that I thought there were some strange aspects to Hector's life story, or more accurately to his father's.

"I'm beginning to think—it's hard to put into words—but I don't think his father was born Jacobo Palurdo. Or maybe he was, but he was connected to an important Chilean mining family. These letters— they'll help reveal his history."

Shiffman was interested, but cautious. He wouldn't do anything that would damage Hector's memory. He also wanted to know how I'd found them.

"Lydia had hidden them. I came on them by a complete fluke. I can't promise they won't damage Hector's memory, but I don't think so."

I hung up and photographed the letters. I sent them

to Shiffman, from an email address I don't often use, hoping my encryption was strong enough to protect me from outside eyes. I included the letter from Lydia's "affectionate aunt" and added, "Do you know what Hector did at the mines? I'm assuming these were the Aguilar mines in Tocopilla."

I sent copies as well to my lawyer, with a note saying I would express the originals to him.

I needed to get in touch with Alsop. With him, since I didn't have an email address for him, I decided to play it safe, writing, sending it by overnight mail.

Please tell Lydia that I have not yet found her piano but that I am putting my best person onto the search.

And then I had to wait. I got dressed. I did my exercises. I checked on Murray. I went downstairs to talk to Mr. Contreras. I took the dogs on a long walk to the lake.

When we got back, Donna Lutas was opening the outer door to the building.

"Hey, Donna," I greeted her cheerily. "I just got home from Kansas but so far no luck with Lydia Zamir. However, I had a really interesting day in Salina with the Saline County coroner. Did you know that there was a second shooter involved in the Horsethief Canyon massacre?"

She stared at me. "What are you talking about?"

"The Horsethief Canyon murders. Your boss defended the one shooter who was arrested. I hope you remember, since you and Rikki Samundar were on the scene fetching water and nicotine patches and so on.

"Anyway, it turns out there was a second shooter who used a different weapon and everything. The shell casings have turned up, so I foresee some exciting legal battles. The casings are at a forensics lab, but defending the second shooter could be your chance for a promotion. And despite our differences, I'd be right there in court cheering you on."

She fumbled for words, but I'd dumped too much information on her too quickly. She finally said that she was still planning on taking me to the condo board for eviction proceedings.

"That's a good idea, Donna," I said earnestly. "Because I have an ugly feeling that the next time someone tries to shoot me here in my home it may be a thug hired by Clarence Gorbeck and it would damage your career if I managed to kill the thugs first."

When I'd sauntered back up to my apartment, Stu Shiffman had sent me back the translations in an email:

My dear brother

I know you are bitter about the death of your childhood friend, but that was a friendship that should never have survived into adulthood. You say you cannot forgive me for reporting him to the Army but Tilo was a Communist, a Union organizer, and he was not a Patriot.

If we are to make accusations and talk of blame, I myself cannot forgive you for letting Tilo stay on the estate. Mama and Papa might have been arrested as subversives. So do not write me these melodramas from America, where you live a life of safety and comfort and abjure all responsibilities for the lives of the thousands of people entrusted to our family's care.

My dear brother

The firm's managing director informed me of your letter giving up all claim to the Aguilar estate. You see yourself as some hero in a Greek tragedy, but you are merely lazy and irresponsible, cruel as well to your own child, cutting him off from his patrimony because you never learned to grow up and to accept adult responsibilities. You also seem not to understand Chilean law: your son is in fact a first-degree heir of our father. You cannot by your own fiat remove him from the family's trusts.

Please note, Shiffman's email added,

In Pinochet's Chile, saying someone was not a Patriot was a code phrase for "traitor to the regime." They were then susceptible to summary arrest by the army and, certainly in the early years of the regime, subject to torture and death. As to which economist is being referred to in the letter to Lydia, or what dramatic assessment he made, the Pinochet cabinet was full of economists making dramatic assessments of Chile's financial position. I couldn't begin to guess who the letter-writer means.

My own guess began and ended with Larry Nieland.

58

Where the Rain Never Falls/ The Sun Never Shines

I read Shiffman's message and his translation over and over.

How had Lydia ended up with those letters to "the dear brother"? Had Hector found them in his father's toolbox, along with the photo of Jacobo Palurdo with his boyhood friend?

I pulled up the copy I'd made of the photo and looked at the two teenagers, happy in their youth and camaraderie.

The darker teen's teeth were crooked and chipped; the fair man's, Jacobo's, were even and white. How could I have imagined that a wealthy patron had taken care of Jacobo's teeth? Not even a woman who treated a poor boy like her pet monkey would invest in expensive orthodontia.

Jacobo and Filomena had worn beautiful clothes to their first communion. These had been stitched by hand, not by their mother but by someone on their estate, perhaps even Tilo's mother.

Jacobo Palurdo's work friend, Jesse, said they called Jacobo "professor," poking fun at his upper-class Spanish. Which he had learned because his own family was wealthy.

I went back to the letters. Hector and Lydia's *cariñosa tía* had mentioned something called the Rettig Report, but I'd glossed over it. When I searched for it now, I saw it had been published in 1991 by the Chilean government, which had set up a truth and reconciliation commission after Pinochet was voted from office. The commission was given a short timeline to discover what had happened to the forty-some thousand disappeared, and so they had focused only on the executions and murders where evidence was easily come by. The commission's efforts were further hampered because Pinochet was still head of the army, with a lot of supporters in other government posts—including Guillermo Quintana, listed as a "senior economic advisor" to the government.

The Rettig Report ran to thousands of pages, but

fortunately an English translation was available online. When I skimmed through it, looking for references to Chicago and economists, I found a brief paragraph stating that Chile had been a pawn in the old cold war between the United States and the Soviet union: the report said that the United States tried "to prevent Salvador Allende from coming into power" because a South American country electing a socialist meant the USSR had scored big points in the cold war. However, Allende was elected, and so, the report continued, the United States tried "to destabilize the new government economically." U.S. efforts "are directly related to the devastating economic crisis Chile underwent starting in 1972."

The paragraph sickened me. The country that had given my own mother refuge in the harsh years of Italian fascism had undermined a foreign government because of our global battle with the Russians? I felt a childish anger—why can't they leave people alone to live in peace?

I looked for "Filomena" and "Palurdo" but didn't find anything. However, a search for Tilo, the person Hector's aunt mentioned, brought up a few sentences. Jacobo Tilo had been a union organizer at the Aguilar mines before the 1973 coup. Early in 1974, an army platoon found him hiding in a cottage on the Aguilar estate. He and six unnamed other men were marched to the Tocopilla mine and shot in the back of the head, their bodies dumped into the mine. The army claimed Tilo was leading a group that wanted to sabotage the mine.

I sank back in my chair, as if the words on the screen had been a physical blow. Hector had gone to Chile with the photograph of his father and his father's best friend. He'd met someone in Tocopilla who recognized both youths. Maybe someone told him what had happened to Tilo, or maybe Hector had read the Rettig Report. However he'd learned about Tilo's fate, he'd been distraught and had done something at the mine— not reported in the press. He'd probably told Lydia, but until—unless—she started speaking again, I would never know what he'd done.

Mr. Contreras came to the door, eager to make me dinner. I told him I had one last errand to run today but that I'd be back in an hour.

I drove to the Palurdo home on the Northwest Side, not bothering with my usual tap dance: texting Elisa Palurdo, waiting in a parking lot for a response, setting up a discreet meeting at the library. I rang the bell, listened to the Akita growl behind the front door, waited two minutes, and then spoke to her security camera.

"V.I. Warshawski, Ms. Palurdo. I'm back from Kansas with fresh information about your son's murder and his heritage. I want to know how much you already knew about the Aguilar and Quintana families before Hector went to Chile."

After another minute, she undid the locks but didn't invite me in. The dog stood next to her, keeping up a rumbling commentary on my appearance and my manners. Purple shadows were smeared under her eyes like makeup applied by a child.

"I thought you were coming into my life to help me cope with Lydia's disintegration, not to fling accusations at me."

"Hector took two letters to Chile with him that were written by your husband's sister. Did you know about them?"

"You really are a madwoman. I told you my husband's sister was murdered. I believe what he said to me about his family. If my husband cherished letters from his sister, that was his private affair, and now it's my business alone. I don't owe you any explanations."

"Don't you owe something to your son's memory?"

She bit her lips and turned away.

"Were those letters in your husband's toolbox, along with that photo of him with his boyhood friend?"

"My husband's sister was murdered. Those letters in the toolbox—they had nothing to do with Jacobo." Her voice crackled. Anger or grief? A mix, maybe.

"Listen." I kept my voice calm with an effort. "Your husband's sister Filomena isn't dead. She's married to the head of her family's mining company. Your husband inherited half of it, but he repudiated the bequest. However, Hector was still your husband's heir: he stood to inherit perhaps half an interest in a copper mine. And he bequeathed that interest to Lydia.

"After Hector died, Lydia wrote to Filomena. I don't know what she said, but she did lay claim to Hector's share of the business because he had made her his heir.

"In the letter Filomena sent back, she made it clear that Hector's father was part of an important family and that he had 'turned his back' on his responsibilities. Did Lydia ever show you that letter from Filomena?"

Palurdo's mouth moved convulsively. "Lydia believed—Lydia said—conspiracy theories, all these theories—I didn't want to hear them. Hector is dead. My only child. I can't bear for his death to turn into a drama of conspiracies."

I felt anguished at continuing to push her, but I said, "Ms. Palurdo, didn't Hector tell you about your hus-

band, that he was part of a wealthy, politically powerful family?"

"Hector pounded on me the way you're doing.
Hammer, hammer, hammer, as if my life—Jacobo's
life—had been a lie, but it wasn't. His father came
from a poor mining family. How could he own a copper
mine?

"I told Hector that he was suffering from the family romance syndrome, you know, where you think
you were adopted and your real parents were important people. It was always that way with him: Hector
needed to go to a big-name school, even though his
father wanted him to stay away from the University of
Chicago. Jacobo despised their theories about money
and the state. When Hector won his scholarship, Jacobo
was beside himself."

My adrenaline high was collapsing and I was having
trouble keeping the conversation on a useful track.

"Ms. Palurdo, five days ago I was in Kansas, looking at the place where your son was murdered. Someone shot at me, deliberately, trying to kill me and put
an end to my investigation." I held out my arms, showing the gauze wrappings Lotty had put around the torn
skin on my palms and forearms.

"I'm short on sleep and long on bruises and I'm not

as coherent as I'd like to be, but let me put a different scenario to you: Hector couldn't find anyone in Chile named Palurdo because there is no such name. Your husband reinvented himself when he came to Chicago and he took as his last name a word meaning a 'hick' or a 'yokel.' He couldn't overcome the upper-class Spanish that Jesse and his other coworkers teased him about, so he made up a story to explain it, a story about his mother working for a wealthy woman.

"I'm guessing your husband took his friend Tilo's story and made it his own. The two were close companions, growing up side by side, miner's son and mine owner's son. One with straight white teeth, the other with the crooked broken teeth of someone whose family can't afford a dentist.

"But then Tilo was murdered. At the Aguilar mine. Shot there with six other men. It's in the Rettig Report. I'm betting that your husband witnessed their execution. His own father, or perhaps the man whom his sister married a short time later, oversaw the execution of seven miners. Bullets in the back of the head and thrown into the lower depths of Tocopilla."

"Don't!" Elisa cried.

The Akita growled more loudly. I saw its shoulder muscles tense, braced to jump. I took a few steps back and spoke quickly.

"Okay. You can send the dog to tear out my throat, but it won't change the past. Your husband took his dead friend's first name when he moved here. He never talked about his family because the pain of their actions ran too deep. When he said his sister had been murdered, I think he meant something metaphoric: the regime had murdered his relationship to her. She married his friend's killer. Your husband didn't go to his sister's wedding at the Valparaíso cathedral. He fled the country. And he hated Hector going to the University of Chicago, because he associated the economic theory there with the economists who created the Chilean policies that he believed led to Tilo's death."

"No!" Elisa cried. "No, no, no!"

She swayed in the doorway and collapsed against the frame. The dog and I exchanged malevolent looks, but I put my arms around Elisa and half-carried, half-walked her into the house, down to the room where we'd spoken when she'd shown me the photo of her husband with Tilo. The dog paced next to us. When I'd deposited her on the chaise longue where she'd sat before, the Akita put himself between Elisa and me.

"Can I call a friend—Jesse, maybe? Get you water?"

"You can leave," she said in the thread of a voice. "Don't come back. I can't survive another conversation with you. I thought you wanted justice for Hector and Lydia, but all you want is destruction."

My own mouth worked with the pain I felt. She was saying the same thing as Franklin Alsop about the harm I caused.

I walked to the front door on leaden feet. As I left the house, a late-model Honda Pilot pulled up in front. Jesse got out and marched up the sidewalk to me. "Elisa told me you were here. Why can't you leave her alone?"

I suppose she called him while I was waiting for her to answer the door. "She needs you," I said. "She's in the lounge with the dog."

He watched me, arms akimbo, until I got into the Subaru. He had his own key to the front door. I wondered how Hector would have felt about Jesse as a stepfather. I wondered what Jesse knew about his dead friend. Had Jacobo Palurdo/Fernando Aguilar felt the need to confide in someone, or was his revulsion against his family so thorough that he never thought about them? Still, he'd kept those letters.

I turned on the engine but lay back in the broken seat, eyes shut. Maybe I needed a new career, caring for lepers, perhaps—something where the value of my work was widely recognized.

"Get away from the house now, or I'm calling the

police." Jesse had pulled open the Subaru door and was shaking my shoulder.

I blinked at him muzzily, trying to clear my head. I'd been in a closed car on a hot evening. I'd fallen asleep. I was not operating at peak levels.

"Did Jacobo confide in you?" I asked. "Did he tell you about the Aguilar mines?"

His face turned blank. After a long moment, he said, "Jacobo *Palurdo* was a good friend to me, always. I respect his memory."

59

The Boy Reporter Wakes Up

I again spent the night in Murray's room at the hospital. He'd been weaned completely from the respirator; the ICU nurse said they were starting to bring him out of his coma. As soon as they could assess the level of brain impairment, they might be able to move him to a regular ward.

I knelt next to him, massaging his hand. "Murray, it's V.I. You're in the hospital. You're going to recover, okay? Repeat after me: 'I am recovering. I am the king of reporters and no one can shut me up.' Lotty is watching over you and so am I. All you have to do is get well. And tell me who shot you so I can make them sorry they ever got out of bed in the morning."

"He's lucky to have such a devoted sister."

I started. The charge nurse had come in behind me on silent feet.

I asked if anyone but me, Lotty, and Max had been asking for updates on Murray. She said his editor at the newspaper, who was distressed to know Murray was still in a coma, called several times a day.

"Don't let them get their hopes up too fast," I said. "They will want him to get back to work too soon if they think he's on the mend."

"We won't lie to anyone, even for worker's comp claims," the nurse said frostily.

"Not for insurance reasons—they'll pressure him and he'll feel unable to say no. Not just his passion for the job, but you know how it is—older guy with lots of experience, they'd love to get rid of him for someone young and cheap."

"It's too early to know if he'll ever be able to return to work, actually." The nurse unbent. "We need to see how much memory he recovers."

When she left, I turned back to Murray. He was probably safe as long as the larger world thought he was still in a coma. If his editor passed word up the chain to Norm Bolton that Murray was recovering consciousness, then whoever had ordered the hit would worry that he'd start talking about the plans for the Burnham Wildlife Corridor.

Once again, I lay next to him, singing to him, talking through for him everything I'd been finding out, and how I was trying to piece it together. The shadow looming over the whole story—that the Quintanas might have conspired to murder their own nephew, along with sixteen other people—was so enormous, so monstrous, that I couldn't get near to it. Besides, I was so tired that my brain had frozen, like a set of pistons deprived of oil.

I moved to the recliner and fell into an uneasy sleep. Murray's groans woke me a little after seven. He was thrashing in the narrow bed and two nurses on the day shift were fiddling with his IVs. A fine bodyguard I'd turned out to be—the staff had come in and wedged themselves between the recliner and the bed without my stirring.

I staggered to my feet, shoved the recliner out of the way, and checked that the two women were in fact nurses attached to the hospital. I went to the far side of the bed, where I squatted and rubbed Murray's shoulder. "It's V.I., Murray, I'm here with you."

His eyes fluttered briefly open, so bloodshot you couldn't tell their color. "Vic?" His throat was swollen from intubation, but my heart lifted; he knew me right off the bat. His memory was good.

I squeezed his hand. "Yes, it's me, Murray. You're

going to be fine. Someone shot you but I'm going to track them to the ends of the earth."

The nurses looked at me in alarm. "Don't get him agitated."

"I'm trying to reassure him," I protested. "He knows I do what I promise."

"It would be better if you didn't promise violence," the woman said.

I was getting really tired of being criticized for everything I did. I bent back over Murray. "No worries, Murray. You're safe here. Lotty's looking out for you. Even Mr. Contreras."

I thought I saw his mouth twitch, as if he were trying to smile at the thought that Mr. Contreras might be rooting for him.

"Vic. Dunce." He tried to sit up, his fingers scrabbling on the sheet, trying to find mine.

I took his hand. "Not a dunce, Murray. The boy reporter following a lead. Can you tell me what it was?"

"Dunce. Dunce."

The nurses, with an exasperated glare at me, squirted something into his IV line and he fell back into sleep.

60
The Dunce

I'd brought a go-bag with me, a change of clothes, a toothbrush. I showered in an empty patient room, brushed my teeth, gave myself a pep talk. *Warshawski is in the forward line, she's moving the ball, she's scoring!* Right.

The one document in Lydia's piano I still wanted to explore was the cryptic message from Samantha Watkins, JD: *I have not been able to persuade the Chilean courts to reconsider their decision. Call me if you wish to discuss.*

According to Watkins's website, she practiced general family law, with a specialty in wills and trusts. She was trilingual in English, Spanish, and Portuguese and had experience in handling estates in South America. Her photo showed a woman in her forties, dark hair, with a somber expression that seemed to say she was tough enough to fight the big boys. Or girls.

An assistant answered the phone when I called. Ms. Watkins was on her way to court, but the assistant would take a message and see whether Ms. Watkins wanted to schedule an appointment with me.

I spelled my name. "I'm working for Lydia Zamir. Does Ms. Watkins know she's been living on the streets and now is recovering in a private clinic? She has entrusted me with some documents, including a note Ms. Watkins sent her with a message about the Chilean courts. It will help me protect Ms. Zamir if I know the details."

I was on hold for five minutes and then the assistant told me that Ms. Watkins would see me at eleven for fifteen minutes.

I went to a coffee bar and tried to organize my case notes. The more I learned, the more helpless I felt. I didn't know why the Quintanas and Nieland needed to eliminate Hector. I didn't know who had killed Leo Prinz and Simon Lensky—thugs hired by the Quintanas? The men from Taggett's entourage who had threatened me? All I knew was that I couldn't figure out any way to act, any way to remove a threat from Murray's life, Bernie's life, Lydia's—not to mention my own.

I put the problem to one side while I went to meet Samantha Watkins. In person, she was as serious as her web photo. She shook hands perfunctorily, announcing she could give me only fifteen minutes for a consultation. Since she'd kept me waiting for over twenty minutes, that was annoying, but I needed her more than she needed me.

"What is your involvement with Ms. Zamir? I've had detectives in here before who were trying to get access to Ms. Zamir in the hopes of cashing in on Hector Palurdo's book royalties. It is not a confidential matter to tell you that Hector was my client; I wrote his will, which has been through probate; he left the bulk of his estate to Lydia Zamir."

"If you want to check on my reputation, I have clients who are willing to talk to outsiders about my work."

"When we're done, you can give a few names to Inesa"—her assistant, who was in the room with us taking notes. "But let me hear what you think I will tell you."

"I stumbled onto Lydia's problems like Alice falling down the rabbit hole, by complete accident, but I ended up looking at a horrific crime—the deliberate use of an emotionally disturbed man to carry out a mass shooting. While that slaughter was taking place, the person behind this vile manipulation lay on a cliff above the mass shooter to make sure his real target was killed. That target was Hector Palurdo."

That startled Watkins: of course she knew about the massacre, she said, and she'd followed Arthur Morton's trial and death. There had never been any mention of a second shooter.

"This is one of the facts I uncovered when I went to Kansas a week ago to meet the people involved in Hector's death. Another fact: while the coroner was conducting autopsies on the massacre victims, someone helped himself to the bullets from Hector's body; they were a different caliber, and came from a different weapon, than the one Arthur Morton used.

"Another fact: the firm of Devlin & Wickham came in from nowhere to muscle away the public defender assigned to Morton's defense. They wouldn't use any of the material the PD had come up with—including the websites on Morton's computer that seemed to herd him toward Horsethief Canyon, and Morton's own belief that he heard another rifle near him. Interesting, don't you think?"

Watkins took time to digest this, drawing a series of boxes on her yellow pad. "And?"

"I got involved in Lydia Zamir's life, as I said, by accident." I told her about SLICK and Bernie, the deaths of Leo and Simon, the attempt on Murray's life, and the secret drawings showing the rebuilding of Lake Shore Drive and the park to create a luxury beachfront resort.

"The firm that drew up the plan is Minas y Puentes."

"What? No! That's not possible. That's the firm—" She broke off in confusion.

"That's the firm that Hector Palurdo hired you to do battle with," I said quietly. "On a trip to Chile, he discovered that his father fled the country after witnessing his own brother-in-law, or perhaps his own father, oversee the murder of Jacobo's closest friend. Their dead bodies were thrown into the family mine. Hector caused some kind of disturbance at the mine, but when he came back, I'm guessing he hired you to help him with a legal battle in Chile. And you weren't successful; you wrote that note to Lydia, after Hector died."

I showed her the photo I'd made of the documents in the piano.

"Where did you find these?" Watkins demanded.

"Where Lydia had hidden them." When she pushed harder for an answer, I said, "You want to make sure I'm reliable but I have no idea whether you are. The

Aguilar and Quintana families and their lawyers are prepared to put a lot of effort and money into finding Lydia and killing her. They've tried to kill me. You're a solo practitioner—maybe the Devlin & Wickham lawyers have come around bribing you, or threatening you. Maybe you'll be on the phone to them as soon as I leave."

Inesa, her assistant, started to sputter denials.

"It doesn't matter," I said. "That is, I hope you aren't under their thumb, but it doesn't matter if you tell them what I've told you because they are already gunning for me. I don't know why I'm not dead, except that perhaps they want these documents. I will figure out my next steps without your help. But if you told me what you were trying to accomplish with the Chilean courts, it might make my next steps easier."

Watkins shut her eyes, communing with herself. At length she gave a tiny nod, and said, "Okay, you've taken a chance with me. I'll take one with you. It's true what you said about the discoveries Hector made in Tocopilla. As you can imagine, they shook him to the depths of his being. And he behaved in a way very uncharacteristic of him—he says he created a scene, at the mine. He wouldn't tell me what happened, just that he lost his aunt and uncle's support. And the Chilean government deported him. I could only assume he had tried to harm his aunt, but that had no bearing on proving his status as an heir.

"Then began a legal battle. The aunt and uncle stated that there was no proof that Hector was the son of Fernando Aguilar and not the child of a welder—the photograph he was waving about proved nothing. And, of course, they were right to do that—anyone can claim to be the heir to a great fortune.

"Hector had his DNA tested. And he demanded that Filomena Quintana Aguilar do the same, to see whether they were in fact related."

"So he signed his death warrant," I said sadly. "No way were the Quintanas going to allow Hector access to his inheritance. And that's what you tried to do, after Hector's death?"

"Yes. It mattered greatly to Lydia. We tried to get a Chilean judge to force Filomena to undergo a DNA test, but the Devlin & Wickham lawyers in Santiago were too powerful for me.

"That note I sent her—it was the last straw for Lydia. She tried to attack the lawyers from Devlin & Wickham, she wanted me to force the woman in their transcription unit to turn over all the correspondence between the lawyers, the Aguilars, and an economist who is on the board of Minas y Puentes."

"Larry Nieland."

"Yes, Nieland. Anyway, after they took out restraining orders on her she retreated, and I lost touch with her. I—" She flushed painfully. "I couldn't do this work pro bono, and she had no money to pay my bill. I didn't realize she was living on the streets. I'm sorry about that."

"What happened to Hector's DNA test? Do you know the company that performed it?"

"Oh, I kept a copy of the results in his file, in case we succeeded in forcing the aunt to provide a DNA sample."

"What about Hector's mother? Was she in the will?"

Watkins smiled sadly. "He left her his love, and the first editions of his books. He'd published three, and I'm not sure they were valuable."

She had spent almost two hours with me, not fifteen minutes, and she and Inesa both exclaimed in horror when they looked at the time: she was late for a meeting elsewhere in the Loop.

Inesa raced to her desk and grabbed a folder for her boss, who snatched it on her way out the door.

I walked the mile from Watkins's office to the lake, blind to Kate Buckingham's fountain, oblivious to the crowds pushing against me. Anyone could have shot me, or injected me with ricin, while I stumbled dumbly along. I knew almost everything, but I couldn't prove it. At least—I couldn't prove it in a way that would discredit the Quintanas or Nieland or Gifford Taggett.

I stared at the horizon, where boats looked like shadows, the sails a wispy white, shape barely visible. They might have been paper cutouts in a puppet theater.

When I'd been cooling off in the lake at Forty-seventh Street a few weeks ago, an outsize sailboat had been cruising near the shore. I'd idly wondered if it might be Nieland's antique yacht, the *Abundance*. I pictured Larry Nieland anchoring there and having a powerboat ferry him to shore when it was time for his lectures at the university. The water there was shallow. An outboard motor would get caught in the rocks or sand. A good reason to put in landfill, move the shoreline out so that bigger boats had access.

Dunce, Murray had repeated the word urgently. He wasn't calling himself names, he was trying to say "abundance." He was too savvy to go to the Burnham Wildlife Corridor alone, but if Larry Nieland promised him an exclusive aboard the *Abundance*, he'd have leapt at the chance.

61
Recording Artist

"No, absolutely not." I was in Mr. Contreras's doorway.

I had to speak loudly for him to hear me over planes on their final approach to O'Hare, people laughing in a neighboring garden, and other sounds of a summer night.

"But, doll, you can't go there, either," my neighbor said. "If that gal has come back and is playing her piano again, you know that guy, the one with the dog, he'll be there. She don't need you. Look who's been killed there—that boy Bernie was dating, Murray close to being dead. You stay up here."

Behind me, something hit the ground with a thud. I whirled to see Donna Lutas opening her own front door. She'd dropped a bag of groceries and was trying to pick them up while clutching her briefcase to her side.

"Hey, Donna," I said without enthusiasm, and headed for the stairs.

My neighbor pushed past me to help her pick up the peaches that had rolled free. I stopped on the landing when Mr. Contreras said, "She's so gol-darned pig-headed. Someone told her that singer gal has been back playing her rinky-dink piano in the park—"

"Lydia Zamir?" Donna said, eagerness flooding her voice.

"That's the one. Vic, she thinks she always knows best, she thinks it's her job to go down and hunt out this gal, who's hiding in the park somewhere, and I say let nature take its course, why put yourself in front of the kind of people who beat your brains out—oh, there's another peach over there, no, I got it—oh, dang, now I dropped the others."

Donna assured him she could manage. "Why does, uh, Vic care so much about Lydia?"

"I don't know. Some tangled story about how Ryerson—now there's a guy I don't have a lot of use for. It's always about him, well, he got himself shot and now Cookie—Vic—she wants to get her own self shot? After people been shooting at her all over Kansas? This Lydia's hiding something, and Vic aims to be the first person to find it. Who's got an ego as big as the Sears Tower now, I asked her—you in competition with Ryerson? With her it's, oh, no, she's noble, she's doing it for justice, and there's something about DNA, some aunt has DNA. Don't we all have DNA? I expect your aunt has—"

Donna shut him off with more speed than grace. When I heard the door to her apartment bang shut, I went on up to my own place, while I worked out what to do.

I'd dated a musician for several years, an accomplished bass player. When he moved to Switzerland the relationship foundered, but I'd remained on good terms with his friends, including a man named Cousins. Cousins had a recording studio in his house—Jake and his friends used to try out their performances there.

Cousins helped me create a playlist: the accompaniment for "Dido's Lament," Lydia's "Savage," and a song I created, using the music and lyrics from the Impressions's "For Your Precious Love" as a template. I didn't need the tinkling sound of a toy piano—Cousins created that with a synthesizer—but I still spent the rest of the day hunting for a red piano like Lydia's, and investing in a bunch of remote speakers.

The other task that consumed me that day was trying to set up protection for the people I cared about.

I was worrying about everyone close to me, especially Murray, but also Lotty, Max, and Mr. Contreras.

Max, who lived alone in a house next to Lake Michigan, moved into Lotty's high-rise, which at least had a doorman. Beth Israel's security team agreed to send him and Lotty an escort to and from work for the next few days. I hoped that would be good enough.

With Max's assistance, I got the university's security department to approve my request for the Streeter brothers to guard Murray. That took the best part of three hours. As I sat on hold for thirty minutes at a time—transferred from university security to hospital security, putting both on a conference call with the Streeters—my anxiety level kept growing. I wanted to scream at them all, but had just enough self-control to know that would end the process in its tracks.

By the time I had it all settled, it was near the end of the evening rush hour. I left the Subaru in a downtown garage and boarded a Metra electric train, holding a big box with the piano inside. I had switched out the colorful carton it came in for plain cardboard.

The electric train ran parallel to the Burnham Wildlife Corridor. I rode it to Eighty-third Street, where I got off and took a northbound train halfway back to the Loop. I made the maneuver three times, until I was sure I didn't have company.

On my last circuit, I left the train at Forty-seventh Street, where I waited until night had truly fallen. In the dark, I walked up the tracks to the hideout Lydia had used three weeks ago. I shone my flash around inside it, and a small gray animal scurried to the back.

I suppressed a shriek. Tough detectives are not afraid of possums, raccoons, rats, or voles. We're a little scared of skunks and porcupines, but I was pretty sure this was a vole.

I wished I had worn my hard hat and my heavy protective gear, but I unpacked the piano and climbed down with it into the hole. I knew I ought to be quiet, but I sang "Men of Harlech" in a loud deep voice so that the voles would keep their distance. When I had the piano hidden, I backed out of the hole as quickly as I could and jogged back to the Forty-seventh Street platform.

I was covered in dirt. I looked like that most disgraceful member of American society, a homeless woman. When a train stopped, the conductor insisted I ride in the vestibule, even though I proved I had a valid ticket.

All the way downtown, where I'd parked the Subaru, all the way north to my building, my mind was focused on a shower, but when I reached my front door, I realized that looking homeless was not just a disgrace, but a badge of invisibility. I couldn't disguise myself any more thoroughly than this. I hated getting into bed covered in dirt, but I spread a sheet across the cover and removed only my shoes and socks before lying down.

I could have used help, but I was unwilling to put the life of anyone I knew at risk. Mr. Contreras was furious that I'd turned him down. Hadn't he saved my life back when I was fighting off the Sturlese cement company? And down at Dead Stick Pond, and—

"And you're the best. That's why I'm not going to let you risk your life jumping in and out of trees on the South Side."

Early the next morning, when the sky was turning from black to gray, I slipped out of my building, so quietly that the dogs didn't hear me. I left Angela's Subaru in a parking garage a mile north of my apartment. On my way south, I stopped at my office to stick my smartphone in the big safe there.

I rode the L to Thirty-fifth Street and walked the mile to the lakefront. I had a burner phone for emergencies, a driver's license, and a hundred dollars in small bills in the heel of my left shoe, a handful of singles in my jeans pocket.

I was carrying my big backpack, packed with speakers, a remote, a groundsheet, some snacks, a toothbrush, but no clothes. I'd had a shower right before meeting with Cousins yesterday morning, but moving around in the heat with a heavily laden backpack was rapidly giving me and my clothes a sour smell.

By the time I reached the north end of the Burnham corridor, the sun had streaked the morning sky a wild orange-pink. Early commuters were backed up at the entrance to Lake Shore Drive. They were all focused on their own issues; no one paid me any attention. I skidded down the hill into the park, my pack banging against my kidneys.

I left a speaker under a wicker sculpture near the north end of the Wildlife Corridor and a second one under the stairs at the south end of the Forty-seventh Street train platform. Hiking several miles through the scrubby plants in the heat was exhausting, but before I joined my sister and brother homeless on the park benches, I rode the L back to the Loop to use a pay phone.

Luana Giorgini and I had worked out a simple code: hanging up after two calls meant no action. Hanging up after three meant she should put some text that we'd worked on into the *Star*'s online edition.

After that, I drifted into a coffee bar. To their credit, the young staff behind the counter took my order for two cortados. They gave me a plastic cup filled with ice water, only let me pay for one drink, and threw in a croissant. Customer reaction ranged from determined obliviousness through mimed disgust. One woman with a baby in an outsize stroller told me I shouldn't be allowed in a facility with children in it.

"God bless you, miss," I said. "And God's blessing on your little one. May she grow up to have a compassionate heart."

I took my drinks outside. When I finished them, I rode back to the South Side, to the rocky place at Forty-seventh Street where I'd swum earlier in the summer. Late on a weekday morning, it was deserted, and I took a chance on my belongings to strip and rinse off in the water. Even though I had to put my stinking clothes back on, I felt better.

After that, I waited out the hours until sundown. You don't know how dependent you are on your device until you've gotten rid of it. I rested under the shade of an old oak but finally wandered to the ultimate refuge of the homeless, the public library, where I looked up the *Herald-Star*'s online paper.

Luana's little squib made the home page.

A little bird tells us that singer-songwriter Lydia Zamir may be back in Chicago. The musician, who'd been living homeless on Forty-seventh Street, vanished in the middle of a dramatic chase along the Metra tracks almost a month ago and hasn't been seen since. A little bird heard the musician cheeping the last few nights and dropped a note in our ear. Is this the start of one of music's great comebacks?

Perfect. I blew Luana a kiss across the airwaves.

At six, the library closed. At ten, I crossed the bicycle bridge over the drive at Thirty-fifth Street and used my remote to switch on the speaker under the nearby wicker sculpture. I let it go through my playlist three times, but no one seemed interested, so I turned it off and walked south. I stayed out of the park, keeping to the Lake Shore Drive shoulder. Even so, I felt exposed, open to attack. I imagined the hand with the gavel smashing in Leo Prinz's head. I felt the heat of a Creedmoor 6.5 just before it went into my chest.

The summertime crowd using the pedestrian bridge at Forty-seventh Street was lighter than it had been earlier in the season. Still, there were enough people out that I had to find a darkened space in the park to pull my remote from my backpack. I turned on the speaker under the train platform, and Lydia's voice singing "Savage" floated into the night.

"That's Lydia!" a voice cried out from the overpass.

"Zamir? Is she back?" "Where is she?" "She sounds good, like nothing ever happened to her." "She must have gotten treatment."

People started clambering around the station stairs and in the parking lot, looking for her. I moved the playlist up to the song I'd recorded.

Your precious love means more to me,
Than DNA could ever be
For when I wanted DNA
I was so lonely and blue
But cariña Tía Filomena
You took me by surprise
Oh, when I first realized
That Hector found your DNA
When Hector brought it home,
Oh, darling auntie, you told the courts
Your DNA won't grow
But I just want to tell those courts they don't know
For your hands touched some paper
And your DNA came through
Your DNA grew wider
Deeper than any sea
Your DNA brings Hector,
Yes, to you, and brings him back to me.

I saw Luana Giorgini, hand in hand with another woman, in the middle of a group scrambling up the stairs to the platform. I switched off the speaker before anyone pinpointed it.

After that, the crowd murmur became louder. New music. Lydia must be well, she hadn't written anything new since *Continental Requiem.*

"Lydia, we love you." "Come out and speak to us." "When can we get the new album?" "What's the story about the DNA?" "Who's your aunt?"

I walked the mile down to the university campus and spread my groundsheet near the chapel walls. I didn't know if it was really safer to lie out there than along the lake, but at least the turf was smooth and thick and I managed a kind of sleep.

62

A Little Bird Cheeps

Larry Nieland's administrative assistant was absolutely not letting me talk to him.

"That's okay," I assured her. "Give him a message, please: Lydia Zamir may be back in town. People say she gave a brief performance last night that included a new song, all about her darling aunt Filomena's DNA. That would be Mr. Nieland's pal Filomena Quintana, from Minas y Puentes, wouldn't it?"

The assistant demanded that I identify myself.

"No, ma'am. I'm a principal negotiator for Zamir. I only identify myself to the other principals involved."

I hung up on her request for my phone number. I was once again using a pay phone in the Loop, but I didn't want to linger at the spot. I bypassed the coffee bar near the phone for one where I had to pay for both shots. They also didn't hand free food to smelly people. However, when you're undercover, or avoiding death, you cannot create a routine.

I was stiff and punch-drunk after a day and a night outside. A university security officer had pushed me to my feet a little after five. I wasn't exactly asleep at the time, but I wasn't awake, either. The cop wasn't mean, just matter-of-fact: private property, get going.

None of the campus buildings had been open that early, but I brushed my teeth at a drinking fountain in the park. Hygiene keeps you sane.

Even though I was only going as far as Forty-seventh, a scant mile, I boarded the Metra train at Fifty-seventh Street. I was already tired. I wasn't going to deplete myself further with long walks. The conductor again told me to stay in the vestibule. I didn't argue—I couldn't afford to raise my profile. I did wonder, though, if I were really homeless, would I acquiesce so quietly? I had paid full fare, after all.

At Forty-seventh, I went into the Wildlife Corridor to place more speakers. Joggers don't use this overgrown park, but early birders were out. I kept a wary eye on them but managed to get speakers where I wanted them. I finally rode to the Loop for my phone call and my coffee. Caffeine is not a substitute for sleep: it just makes being awake more bearable.

At a convenience store I picked up some cheese sandwiches and three bottles of water to get me through the day. It costs a lot of money to eat when you don't have access to a kitchen. I was getting a crash course in the humiliations and burdens of the homeless.

Since I was already downtown, I went to the main library, where Luana's little bird once again made the home page.

> A little bird heard Lydia Zamir sing last night. She's come back fresh from her time away with a new variation on her fusion formula. Last night she dug deep into the history of soul and gave us a new impression of the Impressions's "For Your Precious Love." Who is Lydia's dear aunt Filomena? What is it about her DNA that makes Lydia nostalgic for her beloved Hector, gunned down in a savage massacre four years ago? And will she be back tonight?

As the sun was setting I climbed up onto the footbridge over Lake Shore Drive at Forty-seventh Street and studied the park. A crowd of Lydia worshippers had gathered in the Burnham Wildlife Corridor, holding candles and playing cuts from *Continental Requiem*. Every now and then, they set up a chant for Lydia to appear and sing to them. She was withholding herself tonight; no sound came from the trees or the platform.

A dozen or so people were on the overpass with me, but none of them wanted to stand too close. That meant that I could choose the best vantage for seeing into the Wilderness Corridor.

A couple of squad cars were in the parking lot next to the viaduct where Lydia used to live, but the cops seemed easy; they were laughing with some of the group, keeping an eye on the perimeter, but apparently not anticipating trouble. Luana was there, with her same friend from the previous night. They seemed engrossed in each other, but they were staying on the edge of the crowd, where they could see if anything newsworthy happened.

Around nine-thirty, as the disappointed Lydia fans were starting to drift away, blue strobes flashed in the southbound lanes—a cop car at high speed, a black SUV behind it, another squad car flashing blue to bring up the rear. They turned off at Forty-seventh and drove into the parking lot.

The officers from the two squads already there instantly stiffened and started looking sternly at the remnant of the crowd, pushing people out of the way, bringing a sawhorse over from near the fence to block the entrance to the lot.

The SUV parked between its two escorts. A couple of heavy-set men got out, one from the driver's seat, one from the rear passenger side. While the driver faced the back of the car, his hand on a gun, the other heavy opened the front passenger door. Superintendent Taggett emerged.

Taggett tried glad-handing some of the crowd, but this wasn't his base; no one knew who he was. He shrugged with seeming good humor and gave directions to the cops already in the lot.

They switched on their flashlights and started to work their way into the park itself. I could see their lights bobbing as they covered the wilderness from side to side and then headed up the embankment to the tracks.

Everyone still on the overpass was focused on the action below. I took out my remote and switched on a speaker at the south end of the train platform. The remaining spectators let out a cheer. They chanted "Lydia! Lydia" as they surged toward the platform. I again shut off the music before anyone found the speaker.

As soon as most of the bobbing police flashes converged on the platform, I turned on a speaker I'd placed in a tree on the east edge of the corridor, next to Lake Shore Drive. Cousins had recorded the accompaniment to "Dido's Lament" in a tinny sound, close to the resonance of the toy piano. Cops and crowd began circling in bewilderment, looking for the speakers, but also searching for Lydia herself.

I glanced at Taggett, who was focused on his device. His bodyguard had joined the cops in searching the park, but the driver got one of the cops who'd remained in the parking lot to open the iron gates partway. He and Taggett crossed Forty-seventh Street to join me on the overpass.

For a heart-thudding moment, I thought they had used some kind of fancy sonar to pick up the signals from my handheld, but Taggett ignored me, moving to the far end of the footbridge, which led down to the lake. I followed, to see what had drawn him.

Night had turned the water into a vast swath of black that merged with the sky. If not for the running lights of late-night boaters, I'd have thought I was look-ing at the end of the world. As my eyes adjusted to the darker view, away from the lights in the parking lot, I saw a shape outlined in the foreground: a two-masted boat, sails down, no running lights. Above the sound of cars roaring below me, I could just hear a motor on the water: a launch bringing the yacht's passengers onto shore.

Luana and her friend had come up behind me.

Luana didn't seem to know me, but I put a hand briefly on her arm. She flinched and drew away from the importuning smelly woman, but I kept a hand on her long enough to say, "A little bird should take some pictures of whoever is getting out of that launch. If it's a woman with silver blond hair, see if you can get her to touch something that will hold a fingerprint."

Luana gasped, started to cry out my name, but recovered quickly. "Got it. Now go beg somewhere else. Or take a bath. You smell like the lion house at the zoo."

Taggett's driver was busy with a lapel phone. Suddenly the overpass was swarming with cops. We were pinned against the iron fence in the middle of the overpass. The cops shoved us together so tightly it was hard to breathe. People were screaming, elbowing for space.

I could just make out Luana through the press of bodies. She had her press pass on a lanyard and was arguing with a cop as the yacht's entourage arrived, surrounded by another of police in riot helmets.

Luana was holding up her cell phone, light shining into the middle of the group, onto the face of a handsome woman in her sixties, hair pulled back from her face. Somehow, Luana talked her way into the center of the group, had her arm around Filomena, was getting Filomena to hold the phone while they took a selfie.

Nieland was behind Filomena, chatting with Guillermo. Taggett hovered next to them, anxious to be close to the power trio. The entourage moved slowly past us, oblivious to the crowd behind the wall of police. When they finally left the overpass, the police herded us to the ground, chivvied us to the viaduct, and ordered us to disperse.

They barred entrance to the train, telling people to take buses or taxis.

Many of the group got out their phones, texting or ordering Lyft and Uber. I slipped around the cordon, moving away from the park, walking on the shoulder to Lake Shore Drive until I was north of the parking lot.

I drifted into the underbrush, moving slowly, keeping my head down, watching for snakes and raccoons and drunks. The action was all at the south end of the park, where cops were escorting their VIPs up to the train platform. I climbed up the embankment and risked my flash to locate Lydia's hole.

I shone my own flash into the hole, disturbing the voles who were setting up housekeeping there.

"Sorry, guys," I murmured. "I just need the piano and then the place is all yours."

I pulled the piano out of hiding and up onto the boulder that hid the hole's opening. I'd hung another speaker in a nearby tree and I turned that on, let "Precious DNA" play into the night until the swarm of power flashlights began to draw near. My heart was pounding, my fingers were shaking, but I switched the speaker from my playlist to a connection with the piano and began to pick out the melody to "Savage" on the keyboard, singing my own version of her song.

"*Filomena, queen and chief,*
Are you a savage?
Yes, a savage
Did your nephew threaten you?
What did he really plan to do?
Take from you your mine and gold
It's covered with the miners' blood
But you're a savage,
Yes, a savage!
Hector's death was just one more
After thousands you stopped keeping score
The mine and gold you need to keep
Because you're savage."

The flashlights shone in my eyes. I held up a hand as a shield, trying to see past the glare. Larry Nieland was there, in white shorts and a rumpled white shirt, while Guillermo Quintana was in something dark. Filomena was between them.

"Lydia? You're alive and singing your lies, still?" she screamed. "You are the savages, you and Hector. What silly game are you playing? I never touched Hector's papers, but if I had, no court will believe your lies. You think you can come down from the north and waltz into our lives? You think that running a mine is something that uneducated savages like Tilo can do? You are an idiot. Hector was an idiot. He thought he could prove he was of my blood, and that he could turn that mine over to Tilo's friends and their lazy, useless offspring. You *earn* the right to property, you don't grab property."

"*Cariña tía*," I said, "is that what happened in Tocopilla? Hector wanted to share ownership with people who actually work for a living? And that freaked you out so much you had your husband organize his murder? We know Guillermo went into the Saline County Morgue and made off with the bullets from Hector's body. We know Guillermo rode his horse onto a cliff in Horsethief Canyon two weeks ago to try to shoot me."

I saw light glint on metal and flung the piano at them, but I slipped and fell backward and disappeared into darkness.

63

Lavender Fields Forever

I was in a field of lavender, listening to my mother sing Grieg's "Swan." Did this mean I was dead? If I opened my eyes would I see my mother's face?

"Victoria, you must wake up."

I opened my eyes with an effort. Lotty, not Gabriella. Lotty, bathing my forehead with lavender water. I started to cry, weak invalid tears. I so wanted to see my mother again.

My chest was sore; when I moved my arms, to lift a cup of water to my mouth, pain stabbed through me. I shut my eyes again.

Later, Lotty explained that Guillermo Quintana had tried to shoot me, but when I threw the piano, the bullet shattered it. Plastic shards had been driven into my pecs. I'd fallen backward onto a jagged rock on the edge of Lydia's hole and knocked myself out.

Lotty barred all visitors for the first two days after my injury. A horde wanted to talk to me—cops, reporters, lawyers, and friends, including, of course, Mr. Contreras. He showed up with the dogs, despite efforts by hospital security to keep them out. When Peppy and Mitch burrowed into the bed next to me, squeaking because they thought they'd never see me again, the nursing staff pretended they didn't see it happen.

Sal came by from the Golden Glow. Arlette and Pierre sent the world's largest bouquet, festooned with Blackhawk and Canadien memorabilia. Darraugh Graham delivered a basket of fruit with a note urging me to rest and recover fully before getting back to work. *Don't push yourself as hard as you like to. You will always be a valued member of my team.* That was a relief. I hoped my other clients would be as understanding.

Luana Giorgini and Sergeant Pizzello arrived together on the third day. At first, all they did was annoy each other, since both felt they had priority in talking to me. Finally they decided to work together.

"Quintana was surrounded by cops. And weren't you still hovering there?" I said to Luana. "Why did he shoot me? He doesn't seem like the kind of person to lose his head."

Luana grinned. "My guess is that he carried out so many successful murders it didn't occur to him that he couldn't shoot anyone he pleased whenever he wanted. And even though Taggett was there and ordered the cops not to charge Guillermo, there were just way too many witnesses."

Pizzello eyed her coldly. "No one in my district shoots someone in cold blood. Quintana has been booked, and is currently waiting for a bond hearing."

"And the diplomats and lawyers and whatnot will send him back to Chile." Luana said.

"I don't have any control over that part of the justice system. Just don't write in your paper that the cops in my district don't know the law and don't enforce it. We do, without regard to who's breaking it."

"Okay, okay, I get it, crime doesn't pay in Chicago's Second District." Luana spoke with a kind of impudent friendliness that robbed her words of their sting.

"What about Taggett?" I asked. "Is your chief still blocking any inquiries into his involvement in the lakefront redesign?"

Pizzello scowled—I was putting the lie to her claim of operating without fear or favor, but Luana picked up the ball for her.

"Murray has made a super recovery," Luana said. "He says he had found evidence that Taggett was squirreling away money in an offshore account and he submitted FOIAs that triggered Taggett's attention. The police think it was one of Taggett's bodyguards who killed Leo and Simon, but—get this—it was Guillermo Quintana himself who probably shot Murray!"

Her eyes sparkled. "Murray told me he got a message from Larry Nieland inviting him to come to the *Abundance* to talk about the benefits to Chicago of turning the south lakefront over to a private firm. But Guillermo, or whoever, shot him from the yacht while Murray was still up on that overpass over the Drive."

Pizzello revived. "Larry Nieland, the hotshot economist, has been backing away from the Quintanas like a crab from a campfire. He *says* he invited Ryerson to his boat to try to talk over the pros and cons of the lakefront project, but that Quintana shot Ryerson before they spoke. Can you believe that? Then someone—probably Nieland's crew—carried Ryerson to the Wildlife Corridor, hoping he'd bleed out there and it would be treated like a random mugging. I ask you!"

"Has Nieland been charged?" I asked.

Pizzello made a face. "The state's attorney says that there's no way to prove Nieland knew Quintana was going to shoot Ryerson. There might be an accessory or obstruction charge, but probably not. He's famous, the university is about the biggest employer on the South Side, he brings in cash-paying foreign students. And so on."

"So there is one law for the rich and another for the rest of us," I said bitterly.

"Not in my book," Pizzello snapped. "I can't control the S.A., but we had cuffs on Nieland and Señora Quintana, at least long enough to get them to the station. Put them in that cell your kid—goddaughter?—occupied."

"What about Taggett?" I asked. "If Murray found out about an offshore account, and learned he was taking money in exchange for giving Nieland and the Quintanas carte blanche on the lakefront?—"

"Also out of my hands," Pizzello said. "The White Collar division is subpoenaing all Taggett's bank accounts. But we did match prints on the gavel that killed Leo Prinz to Taggett's driver, and he and the bodyguard apparently lured Simon Lensky to that apartment and bludgeoned him to death."

Luana shuddered and changed the subject. "Guess what? I did get Filomena's DNA. She held on to my phone while I took a selfie with her. You know, the way I dress and all, no one takes me seriously as a journalist, so I get stuff no one else can. The phone's a perfect surface, all shiny, took prints like a charm. They had enough sweat in them for a good DNA sample. I sent the phone to that private lab you use, and they're running the test for us. Palurdo's lawyer is salivating at the thought she can go back to court with proof that Hector is Filomena's first-degree relative."

I was still weak enough that Luana and Pizzello didn't linger longer. When they left, they were exchanging phone numbers and promising to get together for a drink to sort out the myriad loose ends that remained. I wondered if it would ever be possible to implicate the Quintanas in Hector's murder, or in Artie Morton's prison death.

Hector's lawyer, Samantha Watkins, came to thank me for my support of her clients, dead and alive. After Filomena's outburst about Hector's visit to Tocopilla, Watkins found a miner willing to speak out about what had happened when Hector was there.

"No one wanted to speak when I went to them because they didn't think I could stand up to the Quintanas, but now they are more hopeful. It's a pipe dream, to hope Lydia can recover, that I can prove Hector's right to a share in the mine and prove Lydia has a right to inherit his share. But now—because of your work—people are at least willing to speak.

"When Hector went to Tocopilla, he was shocked by the conditions the miners worked under. After figuring out that his father was really a member of the Aguilar family, he announced his intention of turning the mine into a workers' cooperative—exactly what Filomena was spitting out at you that night by the train tracks. And so she and her husband put together this extraordinary plot to murder their nephew. I don't think we can ever prove that, but if the DNA on Luana's phone proves a match with Hector's, I can go back to the Chilean courts."

I didn't tell her I wasn't optimistic. Maybe she would prevail. Every now and then, you do have luck on your side. I'd had more than my share this time. Even though I didn't think the charges against Guillermo Quintana would stick, it had been luck that saved me in the canyon, luck that brought Filomena to the Wildlife Corridor, luck that saved Murray and Lydia.

The most infuriating reaction came from Larry Nieland. He actually came to the hospital to lecture me on the importance of turning public lands over to private developers.

"Giff Taggett made a few bad decisions about using offshore banking, but his head was in the right place. How many people use that lakefront every day, and how much do they contribute to keeping the paths in good shape and the garbage picked up? People like me are subsidizing people like them, and yet I can't use the lake for what I most want, namely a place to keep my boat close to where I live. Taxes are always an unfair burden on people with the most money. The rest of the city, or state, or country, suck on us like leeches.

"Chile showed how you could make true monetary policy work for the good of the whole economy. If you hadn't been so officious and, really, so totally ignorant, I could have prepared a blueprint for showing how monetarism could work in America. It's disappointing to think that this university awarded you your degrees. We need to set higher standards."

I looked at him in disbelief. "You know, there's a ward in this hospital where you could build cities out of blocks and knock them over for fun. They'd probably also let you have a little tub and a toy boat to splash around. You'd be happy and the rest of us would be safer."

I pressed the call button and told the nurse who answered that my visitor had been pushing on my wounds and wouldn't leave me alone.

"That's a goddamn—"

"Truth," I said. "I have a lot of wounds from the general mayhem you and your pals inflicted on people like Lydia Zamir and Elisa Palurdo. You go home and play with your toys and don't talk to me again until you know how to think straight."

If Nieland's was the worst reaction, the best came from Murray. He came to see me the day he himself was being sent home. He had lost twenty pounds and some of his swagger, but his beard was reappearing.

He sat on the edge of my bed, playing with the call button cord. "I was grandstanding, you know."

I shook my head. "You were shot. You know the mantra: don't blame the victim."

"I was grandstanding. Go down to Forty-seventh Street at night for an exclusive, don't tell anyone, especially not the damned righteous Warshawski. I was going to show her that I could dig up a story with one computer tied behind my back."

"Luana told me—you found Taggett's offshore account. That took some serious doing."

"Oh, you know—I know a guy at the SEC. He knows a guy who knows a gal. The big story was about Global. Big to me, anyway. Global is a principal investor in Globo Giratorio in Santiago. That's the cable-TV outfit that airs Filomena Quintana's show. Minas y Puentes owns the maximum permissible share in Global Entertainment by a foreign entity; Global owns a chunk of Minas y Puentes. That's why Bolton wanted to keep an eye on the Lydia investigation. It would have broken

all their hearts to have Lydia alive and well and liti-
gating."

"Bolton will never let that story see the light of day,"
I said.

"You're right about that, Warshawski. It's why I'm
quitting—as soon as I make sure I've got my hospital bills paid by their insurance plan. This is between
you and me, but I have a contract with Gaudy Press
for a book on the story—how these global media giants
withhold news from us and make us live in a world of
conspiracy and innuendo."

"Start wearing body armor, Ryerson. You getting
shot—that was very hard. Don't make me go through
it twice."

"Says the lady who took a chestful of shrapnel. Vic—
you singing those Italian songs to me—I heard you, it
was a lifeline." He leaned forward to kiss me. "Sansen's
one lucky SOB. Hope he knows it."

He left without looking back at me, which was just
as well. I cried easily these days.

Peter flew in from Turkey the day I was released.
He came directly to the hospital from the airport and
helped me dress, helped me into the wheelchair that
you're required to use when you're leaving.

"I told you not to go hanging out of windows without me standing by," he murmured into my hair. "I

didn't know I needed to beg you to stay away from toy pianos."

I got stronger. We took a trip to the Laurentians, where Arlette and Pierre welcomed us almost too enthusiastically. Pierre had the Canadiens' trainer on tap, and I started each day with a round of physical therapy. In the afternoons we hiked or canoed. Bernie practiced on the rink her father and Boom-Boom had installed in the village hall when they first bought their mountain property, while Arlette drove Angela Creedy to use the village's gym courts. Angela's mother was still there, but Angela and Bernie were getting ready to go back to school.

The Canadiens were making their plane available again to take the young women to Chicago. We all flew down together. Peter had to return to Turkey; it was time for me to show my clients I could still do a job. Bernie's and Angela's mothers wanted to oversee their daughters' choice of housing—no more ramshackle Victorians with doors that thugs could break down.

"It was so dangerous for weeks, and now, all at once, it isn't. Why is that?" Angela asked on the plane.

"It's the nature of vermin," I said. "You have to shine a lot of light on them to get other people to pay attention, but once they've been well and truly exposed, they end up like the Wizard of Oz, just tiny people using lights and mirrors to prop themselves up."

"Do you think Lydia will get the mine and turn it over to the workers, the way Hector wanted?"

"I think it's very unlikely," I said soberly. "Guillermo Quintana has already been released and sent back to Chile under diplomatic cover, and he and his wife have so much power in that country I can't believe the courts will find in Lydia's favor."

When we landed, Peter came back to my place with me. Before he returned to his dig, he wanted to make sure Donna Lutas didn't go ahead with eviction proceedings. If she did, he hoped I would move into his own condo.

Lutas was feeling more bitter toward me than ever, Mr. Contreras reported: after she overheard Mr. Contreras's and my staged conversation announcing that Lydia had been seen in the park, Lutas rushed to her managing partner with the news. The disastrous way events had unraveled for two of their most important clients caused Devlin & Wickham to make Lutas a scapegoat: Gorbeck fired her.

When Lutas went to the condo board, she couldn't muster any support from the other people in my building. My neighbors were sorry for me because I'd been injured. They were grateful to me for drawing gunfire in a park, not in our home, I was down to two dogs. Mrs. Sung even apologized to me for adding to my worries when I was working so hard to protect my god-daughter.

I accepted the apology with appropriate solemnity, but it seemed a strange takeaway. I thought of all the gritty sleepless nights in Kansas and Chicago, of dodging bullets, of the murder victims in Chile, Horsethief Canyon, and Chicago.

"You did protect Bernie," Peter said when I told him about the interchange. "You couldn't stop people so thoroughly evil—so full of their own entitlement—from murder. Protecting the Bernies in your life is worth something. You saved Lydia's life, too. You kept the cops from arresting Coop. And for me, most important, you saved your own life."

He pulled me to him; the wounds in my chest protested a little, but I told them to shut up and let me enjoy the moment.

The day after Peter flew out, I went back to Forty-seventh Street. The beaches were officially closed for the year, but the days were still hot and the water was warm. I floated under a cerulean sky, did a few lazy strokes to test my pecs. They had nearly recovered but weren't ready yet for a strenuous workout.

I climbed out and sat on one of the rocks, letting the air dry me. A wet nose shoved itself into my leg. A jolt of fear went through me, but then I felt the head and shoulders rub against me.

"Hey, Bear." I nuzzled the snout next to me.

"Hey, yourself, Warshawski," Coop said. "Quite a ruckus you created. You got them to shut down any talk of turning the park into a resort. You got them to stop wanting me to be that poor kid Leo's killer. You saved Lydia, and I couldn't do none of those things."

"You did save Lydia. You got her to Cassie, got her the help she needed."

"Yeah, maybe." He lapsed into silence.

"Where did you go when you dropped her off?" I asked. "Franklin Alsop and Cassie protected you, you know."

"Yeah. Cassie, she's like—well, the mother you always hope you'll wake up and find out replaced the one who was whacking you with a hot frying pan." He gave a laugh that turned into a coughing fit.

"But, yeah, I dropped off Lydia at Cassie's and hightailed it for northern Minnesota. I was hanging out near the border, just in case, you know. When I saw the news reports about Taggett and those Chilean dudes, I hitched back to the prairie and then headed over to here. I went to try to find you but you was out of town.

Your neighbor, the old guy, I thought he was going to push my brains through my ears with that pipe wrench of his when I tried to find out where you were and what you were doing. Anger management—we all need a dose from time to time."

I grunted noncommittally. "You staying around long?"

"Nah. City life isn't for me. I'm heading back to the prairie. Just wanted to say thanks in person, that's all."

64
Still Living in Love

The prairie in fall seemed to my untrained eye more beautiful than it had been in high summer. The plants had turned different shades of brown, ranging from chestnut to sienna, with touches of gold and purple. Grasses swished against Peter Sansen's and my legs as we walked along a nearly invisible trail from the lane to Cassie's house. Franklin Alsop had taken Mr. Contreras there in an electric wagon that he kept for heavy hauling.

In the months since my shooting, I'd gone back to regular work, the kind you mostly do with the aid of the Internet, not with climbing up and down cliff faces. I was doing serious rehab work; I wanted to climb again, although hopefully not with someone using me for target practice.

Murray had made a strong recovery himself, and was enthusiastically working on his book. Some of what he knew he put out in a podcast, just enough to whet appetites for the book when it came out.

Taggett was facing embezzlement charges, but no one was ready to indict him as an accessory in Leo's or Simon's murders—the roots of his favor tree in Cook County's patronage jungle grew too deep. I was less happy when my alma mater defended Larry Nieland's role. I was trying not to pay attention to the dreary side of the justice system, the side where people with billions of dollars and millions of lawyers skated away from the charges against them.

The best ending came when Lotty Herschel persuaded Cassie to send Lydia to a rehab center that used music to help victims of violence recover their mental poise. To my surprise, Coop had sided with me on urging Lydia to go.

She'd been there for three months and had come back to Cassie's for a weekend visit. Franklin Alsop invited Peter and me; we'd brought Bernie and Angela, along with Mr. Contreras and the dogs. Lotty and Max; Gabe Ramirez, the public defender; Sam Watkins, Lydia and Hector's estate lawyer. Elisa Palurdo showed up with Jesse.

We sat on blankets in the prairie plants, far enough from the dugout patio that we wouldn't seem threatening. Lydia came out the front door, one hand on Coop's arm, the other holding a guitar. She'd gained weight, her hair had recovered its gloss. She sat on a chair that Alsop placed for her. Bear planted himself in front of her.

She played to herself for a time, letting the guitar follow the sound of the wind. We all listened quietly. No applause, the rehab center had stressed. No making moves or sounds that might be seen as boundary violations.

After half an hour or so, she eased into song. Her voice was still rusty, and she couldn't find a true pitch, but the broken sound made the music more deeply moving.

> "The art of loving
> is the art of death
> love's opposite isn't hate, not hate
> love's opposite is lonesome
> one lone swan.
>
> "Love gets us through those lonely times
> Hate keeps us up all night.

A swan whose lover dies
Is one lone swan
A swan whose lover dies
Still lives in love
That gets her through the night."

Thanks

This is the first book I've written without my husband. Through twenty-three books and many short stories, he was the lodestar of my life and work. He buoyed my spirits, kept me from drowning in self-doubt. He used to call himself "Tailgun Charlie," the man who covered my back.

Many people stepped forward to help me through this hard loss. Barb Wieser, more sister than cousin, made frequent trips to Chicago, often at a moment's notice. Jo Anne Willis's friendship was a gift. Dan and Jonathan, Carol and Rachel, my beloved nieces Eve and Heather, were often here. Jeremy's insightful letters stepped me back from the ledge more than once.

Timothy and Philip, while grieving their father, were rocks.

I'm grateful to many friends: Lorraine Brochu, Barbara Bogosian, Terry Evans, Ann Christophersen, Dave Donnersberger, Jean Fishbeck, Fred Reeves, Randy Nixon, Sally Neely, Noah Cruickshank, Matea Varvodic, Judy Popovich, Gail and Jerry Sadock, Kathy Lyndes, Louis Arata, Ruth O'Brien, Stuart Rice. Eddie Chez and Dan Gurian helped keep legal issues from swamping me. I am grateful to many for many acts of kindness; forgive me if I have not listed you here. Many readers sent me heartfelt love and insights: thank you all.

My agent, Dominick Abel, was a constant presence. My editors, Emily Krump and Carolyn Mays, were also steadfast in their support.

I relied on Drs. Manuel Alejandro Barrios and Guillerno Villegas for help with Spanish in the text. They generously translated documents for me. They suggested given names for the South American characters in the novel, and helped me view Miguel Littín's *Acta General de Chile,* his clandestine film of the Pinochet era.

José Antonio Velasco advised me on Chilean courts and inheritance laws. Adi Altshuler generously made that connection for me. The Rettig Report, which

I mention in this novel, is a real report on what happened to some of the forty-thousand-odd disappeared Chileans during the Pinochet regime. Jacobo Tilo is fictional and so of course is not in it, but the quotations about the use of Chile's elections as proving grounds between the United States and the USSR during the cold war come directly from the online English translation of the report.

My brother Nicholas helped me understand neoliberalism; my brother Jonathan provided legal advice on the trial of a murder suspect in Kansas.

Terry Evans, whose passion for prairies has infected me, introduced me to Kelly Kindscher and Jake Vail, who gave me insight and tours of Kansas prairies. Terry and her husband, Sam Evans, pointed me to Horsethief Canyon.

I have taken a few liberties with the canyon, and more liberties with the life of a Chicago police sergeant. Lenora Pizzello is a fictional character who seems to work all three shifts at the Second District. In real life, the union would protest this. I also restructured the footbridge over Lake Shore Drive at Forty-seventh Street so that a pedestrian could see the parks on both sides of the drive.

In a hardboiled novel, the private investigator is almost always at odds with the actual police. I have therefore set the Salina, Kansas, police department and the Saline County coroner in opposition to V.I. Warshawski. All the characters in this book and their actions are complete works of my imagination. I beg forgiveness for taking liberties with my home state's hardworking law enforcement teams.

Chicago real estate code allows people five animals in their homes, unless they live in an animal-free building. V.I.'s condo board got an exception to limit residents to one animal each.

Questions about whether to monetize Chicago parks are proving divisive these days, but the behavior of my fictitious superintendent is completely imaginary and bears no resemblance to our actual hardworking parks super. Chicago is a town with a long history of citizen activism in many arenas, including care for our parks and for our jewel, the Lake Michigan coastline. There are many citizen groups working to protect and preserve the parks—including keeping garbage out of them. SLICK is an imaginary organization, unconnected to any actual civic group in Chicago.

Although it is true that the University of Chicago established an economics department at the Pontificia Universidad Católica de Chile in the 1950s with CIA support, none of those erudite thinkers bear any resemblance to the characters in my novel.

Lorraine Brochu read this manuscript carefully many times. She tried to help me make chronology and other events consistent. All errors are my own failure to follow her excellent advice.

Another sad loss this year was Andi Schechter. With her permission, I named Hector Palurdo's friend Stu Shiffman for her own late husband.

About the Author

Hailed by P. D. James as "the most remarkable" of modern crime writers, **SARA PARETSKY** is the *New York Times* bestselling author of twenty-two novels, including the renowned V.I. Warshawski series. She is one of only four living writers to have received both the Grand Master Award from the Mystery Writers of America and the Cartier Diamond Dagger from the Crime Writers Association of Great Britain. She lives in Chicago.

HARPER LARGE PRINT

We hope you enjoyed reading
our new, comfortable print size and found it
an experience you would like to repeat.

Well – you're in luck!

Harper Large Print offers the finest in
fiction and nonfiction books in this same larger
print size and paperback format. Light and easy to read,
Harper Large Print paperbacks are for the book lovers
who want to see what they are reading without strain.

For a full listing of titles and
new releases to come, please visit our website:
www.hc.com

HARPER LARGE PRINT